## Praise for *The Sound of Light*

"*The Sound of Light* is an awe-inspiring story set within the beauty, language, and culture of Denmark. Sundin's craft is inimitable, and her literary finesse radiates from every page."

**Booklist** starred review

"Sundin's prose reveals the deepest emotions of the human heart. Full of gorgeous imagery and metaphor, this novel demonstrates that one person doing the right thing might just save a nation. Each Sundin novel tops the last."

**Library Journal** starred review

"Sundin grounds this suspenseful tale in rich historical detail, weaving throughout probing questions of faith as characters struggle to behave in moral, godly ways, especially when it entails risking one's life for a stranger."

**Publishers Weekly**

"This is one of the most thoughtful, yet dramatic, novels set in WWII-occupied territory. A unique and engaging read."

**Historical Novel Society**

## Praise for *Until Leaves Fall in Paris*

"Sundin is a master at her craft. With meticulous historical research and an eye for both mystery and romance, Sundin rises to the top of WWII fiction."

**Library Journal** starred review

"Fast-paced and rich with historical detail, Sundin's narrative captivates by leaning in to the complexity of what it means to live by Christian principles in a morally compromised world. This potent synthesis of history, love, and faith will delight romance readers, religious and nonreligious alike."

"Sarah Sundin delivers another epic tale filled with danger, romance, and all the good feels! If you love WWII books, intrigue, danger, and romance—this book has it all."

## Praise for *When Twilight Breaks*

"Sundin's novels set the gold standard for historical war romance, and *When Twilight Breaks* is arguably her most brilliant and important work to date."

"Entertaining, pulse-pounding, with space to ponder some deep questions, *When Twilight Breaks* is Sarah Sundin at her best."

"This richly detailed historical adventure romance will be sure to thrill fans of Sundin's work and be a hit with any fan of inspirational WWII novels."

# EMBERS
*in the*
# LONDON
# SKY

# Books by Sarah Sundin

*When Twilight Breaks*
*Until Leaves Fall in Paris*
*The Sound of Light*
*Embers in the London Sky*

### Sunrise at Normandy Series

*The Sea Before Us*
*The Sky Above Us*
*The Land Beneath Us*

### Wings of Glory Series

*A Distant Melody*
*A Memory Between Us*
*Blue Skies Tomorrow*

### Wings of the Nightingale Series

*With Every Letter*
*On Distant Shores*
*In Perfect Time*

### Waves of Freedom Series

*Through Waters Deep*
*Anchor in the Storm*
*When Tides Turn*

# EMBERS
## *in the*
# LONDON
# SKY

*a novel*

## SARAH SUNDIN

Revell
a division of Baker Publishing Group
Grand Rapids, Michigan

Published by Revell
a division of Baker Publishing Group
Grand Rapids, Michigan
RevellBooks.com

Library of Congress Cataloging-in-Publication Data
Names: Sundin, Sarah, author.
Title: Embers in the London sky : a novel / Sarah Sundin.
Description: Grand Rapids, Michigan : Revell, a division of Baker Publishing Group, [2024]
Identifiers: LCCN 2023022174 | ISBN 9780800741853 (paperback) | ISBN 9780800745738 (casebound) | ISBN 9781493444878 (ebook)
Subjects: LCGFT: Christian fiction. | Novels.
Classification: LCC PS3619.U5626 E43 2024 | DDC 813/.6—dc23/eng/20230518
LC record available at https://lccn.loc.gov/2023022174

Scripture quotations are from the King James Version of the Bible.

Published in association with Books & Such Literary Management, www.BooksAndSuch .com.

24  25  26  27  28  29  30      7  6  5  4  3  2  1

*to* Arden
Our first grandson
Our very heart

1

A s soon as she escaped to England, Aleida van der Zee Martens would cut her hair and have her son photographed for the first time.

Sebastiaan approached from behind. Why couldn't her husband ever wait until she finished brushing her hair? Sometimes he interrupted at seventeen strokes, sometimes at thirty-one, today at forty-three.

He wove his fingers into her hair halfway down her back, and she tensed.

In the bureau mirror, Aleida met his gaze. Warm gray today, not chilled steel.

Regardless, every muscle stayed taut.

He kissed her cheek. "Breakfast in ten minutes, Lay-Lay."

"Yes, Bas." A smile rose. She and little Theodoor would never breakfast with Bas again.

After he headed downstairs to listen to the morning news, Aleida finished brushing her hair. Only seven strokes remained to remove the feel of him. Not enough, but today of all days she couldn't go above her customary fifty strokes.

9

She set her brush on the silver tray, centered between her comb and her perfume atomizer. At the base of her brush lay her rings. First she put on her grandmother's sapphire ring. Then her engagement ring, which she would sell in London.

Her fingers trembled, and she drew back lest she knock something askew, knock her plan further askew.

With rumors of German troops massing on the Dutch border, she'd decided to move up her plan an entire week.

But it was a good plan.

For the last time, she coiled her hair the way Bas liked.

After Bas left for work, while the cook cleaned up after breakfast and the housekeeper scrubbed the downstairs floors, Aleida would sneak out a suitcase. She'd already hidden her essentials and Theo's in bureau drawers, ready to pack.

When the housekeeper went upstairs to scrub the guest rooms, Aleida would announce she was leaving for her hair appointment, timed for when her mother-in-law across the street was away for her own hair appointment and wouldn't see Aleida and Theo leave with luggage.

Tonight, she and her three-year-old boy would be safe with Tante Margriet and Uncle James in the English countryside.

Yet her fingers still trembled.

A voice climbed the stairs—Sebastiaan's. Shouting orders, closer and closer.

Her chest seized, bile rose up her throat, and she gripped the bureau top. "Not today. Please."

The bedroom door banged open, and Bas wrestled three suitcases inside. "We're leaving in fifteen minutes. Start packing. Only necessities and valuables. Hurry."

"What?" The word poured out in a breathy haze. She did plan to pack—but not with Bas.

He heaved the suitcases onto the bed and flung open his wardrobe. "You have family in England, ja? A cousin? An uncle?"

She'd hoped he'd forgotten. "I—I don't understand."

"Don't get hysterical." Bas folded business suits into the largest suitcase. "The Germans invaded at dawn. Parachutists landed at airfields and bridges. Tanks crossed the border. I can't possibly run a profitable business under the Nazis, but I can in England."

Acid burned her throat, coated the inside of her mouth, corroded her hopes.

Bas flicked up his gaze to her. "Pack or don't pack, but we're leaving in fifteen minutes. Cook is preparing a hamper of food, the chauffeur is warming up the automobile, and I already have visas in our passports. I planned everything."

So had Aleida. Her plan covered every contingency.

Except this.

Sebastiaan cursed and stomped on the brake.

Aleida braced herself on the dashboard. They'd managed to cross from the Netherlands into Belgium, but refugees and soldiers clogged the roads.

Bas ran his hand through thick blond hair. "I have enough petrol to reach Boulogne, but not if I have to stop for these idiots."

A stoop-shouldered woman with a shawl over her head pushed a heaping handcart. She glowered at Aleida.

Aleida ducked her chin. Only three people occupied their large vehicle.

If only she could join those on foot, hide in peasant's garb, and blend into the masses.

Her plan lay in shards on the floor of her mind, and she tiptoed through and poked at the splinters. Could nothing be salvaged? With Bas at Tante Margriet's, where could Aleida and Theo go to flee from him?

A whimper rose from the backseat.

Bas scowled at Aleida.

She offered an apologetic smile. "If I could sit in the back-seat—"

"No." He slapped the seat between them. "A wife belongs with her husband."

Theo slumped against the door with his white-blond hair mussed and his perfect little mouth warped by fatigue. He held his stuffed elephant, cupping the floppy trunk against his cheek. More whimpers bubbled out.

"Tay-Oh," Aleida sang out with a sunny smile. "Tay-Oh. Would Oli like to play a game?"

Theo blinked, sat up, and handed Aleida his best friend.

She held the elephant down in her lap. "Oli, where's Theo? You've forgotten? Please say you haven't forgotten, Oli."

Theo shook his head, and his eyes shone. "Oli not forget."

"That's right, *Schatje*. Elephants never forget."

Bas snorted. "Who made up that nonsense?"

Aleida's mouth tightened. "It's an English saying. If you want to go to England, you'd better get used to it."

His gaze knifed into her. She'd pay for that flippancy later.

But now her son needed her. She dangled Oli's trunk over the seatback and pointed it at Theo. "That's right, Oli. There's Theo."

Giggles poured out, and Theo slid off the seat and scooted behind Aleida. "Where am I now, Oli?"

Aleida swung Oli's trunk in a loop, then pointed it at her son. "See? Oli will always find you. Oli will never forget—"

"What's this?" Bas spoke with an air of gleaming anticipation.

On the road, people scattered to each side, cars pulled over, people spilled out, ran.

"Oh no." Aleida leaned forward, craned her neck up.

Two dark green shapes winged down from the sky, spitting sparks, dragons scorching the earth.

German aircraft!

"Theo!" Aleida sprang to her knees and groped over the seat for her son. She had to get him out to safety. "Come to *Moeder*! Come—"

The car leapt forward.

Aleida almost toppled over the seatback. "What on—"

Bas sped down the road, unimpeded.

"Bas!" She ducked to see out the windscreen. "The planes!"

"They don't care about refugees, only soldiers. Now's my chance." His jaw set in that hard way of his.

The dragons swooped lower, foul breath spinning in silver discs.

"Theo, stay down! Cover your head." Aleida folded herself low. Her hands formed the flimsiest of helmets. "Stay down!"

The roar of the auto's engine merged with the whine of the planes. Pops rang out, and Aleida screamed.

The whining and pops veered away.

"Told you we were fine," Bas said. "I'm the only person on this road smart enough to see it."

Aleida stayed low, breathing hard, burying her fingers in the hair she'd coiled so neatly.

He expected her to praise him for his insight and courage.

She dug her fingers deeper into the hated hairstyle. Why should she have to praise foolishness? Why should she have to lie to a man who endangered his wife and child? Why couldn't she get away from him?

Why couldn't he die?

Aleida choked on that dark thought.

Bas groaned, and the car slowed. "At least I gained a mile."

She peeked over the dashboard. Refugees dragged carts onto the road, herded animals around . . .

Around a horse and a man sprawled on the road.

Red. So much red.

Aleida gasped and clapped both hands over her face. The Germans did kill refugees. It could have been them.

The car lurched down to the right, and Bas cursed. "Must have blown a tire."

What did he expect racing at such speeds? But Aleida kept that thought to herself.

Bas eased the car into a line of trees, where dozens of refugees were setting up camp. "You prepare dinner while I change the tire."

"All right." Her voice and her legs quivered as she climbed out of the car.

She opened the back door and gathered Theo into her arms. He clung to her. "It's all right, Schatje. You were so brave."

Bas shrugged off his suit jacket. "Hold this."

She shifted Theo so she could take the jacket.

Bas opened the boot of the car and hauled out the spare tire. "Don't let the jacket out of your sight. Our passports are in there."

Aleida took a step back. Another.

While Bas changed the tire, she and Theo could walk away. Simply walk away. She could exchange her couture hat and coat for a peasant's shawl. And keep walking.

With her passport, she could cross the Channel. With Sebastiaan's, she could block him from following.

"Here's the food hamper." Bas set it under a tree.

Aleida jolted out of her dream. What was she thinking? Hasty decisions led to disaster. Like marrying Bas.

She knelt beside the hamper. "Let's see what Cook packed for dinner, Theo."

He twisted to see, and she set him down.

Aleida spread a cloth under the tree and arranged bread, sausage, gouda, and mustard.

Bas's tools still clanked, so she leaned back against the tree trunk. Theo crawled onto her lap, and she kissed his silky hair. Before them, golden barley waved in the fading sunlight.

If only she could tune out the trudging feet and honking

horns behind her and pretend the Germans hadn't invaded the Low Countries and Bas hadn't invaded her plan.

"Green!" Theo pointed up to the leaves with his right hand, the one with no fingers, only five darling little bumps, as if his digits had been sleeping when the order to grow was issued.

"You're so smart, Theo."

"Blue." He plopped his hand close to Aleida's eye.

She laughed and gazed into her son's sparkling greenish-blue eyes. "Just like yours." Thank goodness her son had inherited the van der Zee eyes, not Bas's cold gray.

"Red." Theo tugged down her lips, and he giggled.

She kissed his hand, each darling bump, leaving lipstick behind. "Now your hand is red."

A click.

"That's swell," a man said in American-accented English. He crouched in front of them, holding a camera and grinning. "A swell bunch of photos."

He'd taken pictures of them? Aleida's heart pounded in hope—photos of her son at last?—and in dread.

"I beg your pardon," Bas said in English. He marched over, his face a cool mask. "Did I give you permission to photograph my wife?"

Aleida curled inward and gathered Theo closer.

"Good evening, sir." The dark-haired man tipped his fedora. "I'm with the United Press."

Bas's gaze bored into Aleida. "Was that *thing* showing?"

"I—I don't know." She tugged down her son's sleeve. "I didn't see him until it was too late."

"Give me that camera." Bas held out his hand.

The photographer let out a scoffing sound. "I don't need to do that."

"*Vader* angry." Theo burrowed in Aleida's arms.

He was indeed. The poor American didn't know he'd entered a bear's lair.

"I will tell you what you need to do." Bas's fingers clenched and unclenched. "I am a powerful man with powerful friends. If you print those photographs, I will destroy your career."

The photographer's lips twisted in disbelief, and he turned to Aleida.

A sob burst from Theo's mouth, and Aleida begged with her eyes. "Please don't cross him, sir. Please. You don't know what you've done."

Dark eyes widened, and the man's jaw fell slack. "I beg your pardon, ma'am. I promise I won't print the pictures."

"If you do." Bas's tone rose in a clap of thunder.

"Hey! You have my word." He raised a hand in surrender and hurried away, shaking his head. "Crazy."

The thunder rolled Aleida's way, and Theo wailed and wound his arms around her neck.

"Make it shut up. Now!"

"Hush, Schatje." Aleida rocked her boy with her gaze locked on the bear. "Hush."

"I'm sick of the crying." Bas flung his hand toward the car. "Go to bed. No dinner."

"Yes, Bas." Hunger was the least of the punishments she could have received.

She struggled to her feet, climbed into the backseat, and lay down with her sobbing son in her arms.

"Make it shut up." Bas thumped his hands on the car roof. "Or I will."

"Hush, Schatje." Her tears dampened her son's hair. His welfare—his life—depended on his silence.

Salt-crusted eyes resisted opening. Aleida rubbed them, and faint daylight emerged. Then came the memory of what caused that salt, and she tightened her arms.

Around nothing.

Theo? Had he fallen?

On the floor of the car, Oli lay upside down. His thick gray legs jiggled in the air.

The car was moving.

"Theo?" She sat up.

Bas was at the wheel. He'd put Theo up front with him? How unusual.

But no one sat with Bas in the front seat.

Her mind emptied. Her lungs emptied. Her heart emptied. "Where—where's Theo?"

"Don't get hysterical." Bas honked the horn. "Hurry, you idiots."

Aleida's fingers coiled into the seatback. "Where is our *son*? What did you do with him?"

Bas shook his head. "Why do you always get hysterical?"

Of all times, now she had every right to hysterics. "Where is our *son*? Our *son*?"

"I told you to shut him up, but you never do. Is peace and quiet too much to ask?"

"What did you do?" Aleida's voice ground out.

"Last night, a couple agreed to take him to London for us."

"You—you gave our son to total strangers?"

Bas shrugged. "You saw it yesterday, mothers shoving their children through car windows."

Desperate mothers, certain their children stood a better chance in a car than on foot. "But we already have a car. What on earth? Where—how—what were you thinking?"

A horse-drawn cart stopped in front of them, and Bas stomped the brakes.

Aleida scrambled out of the car, her chest heaving. She had to find her son.

"Aleida! Get back here."

"No!" She ran down the road and wove through the crowd. "Theo! Theo!"

She peered into the open window of a black sedan. No Theo. "Have you seen a little blond boy, three years old, with an English couple?"

"No. No, I haven't." A middle-aged woman looked at Aleida with alarm.

A hand clamped onto her arm, and she cried out.

"Get in the car." Bas jerked her around to face him.

"I will not." She yanked her arm in vain. Why could she never break free of this man?

Something hardened in her, hardened so brittle it snapped, and she glared into Bas's thundercloud eyes. "I will not go with you. I'm looking for my son, and I never want to see you again."

His lips curved up. "Now, why would you want to leave me? I'm the only one who knows the couple's address in London."

Air and hope and strength leaked from her chest. She was trapped. The only way to find her son was to stay with the man who'd given him away.

"If you ever leave me . . ." Bas's grip drilled into her arm, dug grooves between muscles. "Or if you *ever* talk that way to me again, you'll never again see that monstrosity you call a son."

A cry spilled out, all her grief for Theo mingling with the burning pain in her arm.

More cries rang out, as if the whole world wept with her.

Someone bumped Aleida.

All around, people scurried off the road.

She gasped. Three aircraft dove down.

"Get in the car." Bas dragged her down the road. "Your hysterics have cost me too much time."

He didn't care about her, didn't care about his child, only about himself.

At the car, Bas reached for the door handle.

A coiled spring burst inside her. She planted one foot and

spun backward, toward Bas, slammed her shoulders into his arm, broke his grip.

She bolted for the trees.

"Get in the car!" Bas yelled. "One!"

When he reached three, he'd beat her senseless.

Aleida flung herself flat under the trees and covered her head.

The airplanes roared closer, screaming, spitting.

"Two!"

Aleida hunkered low among strangers crying and praying and pleading to live.

Shots clattered along the pavement, a giant chain saw ripping the road in two.

"Thr—" Bas's voice spiraled up into a squeal, almost girlish.

The aircraft noise died down, but everyone still cried and prayed and pleaded to live.

Bas never finished the word *three*.

Aleida forced herself to stand, to walk. Numb.

Sebastiaan Martens, a powerful man with powerful friends, lay by his expensive car, his limbs at grotesque angles, his eyes dull as ancient pewter.

So much red.

Aleida had wanted him dead. Now it had happened.

But now, how could she find her son?

2

## DUNKIRK, FRANCE
## WEDNESDAY, MAY 29, 1940

The sun shall soon set over the beaches of Dunkirk, but the day is not done." BBC correspondent Hugh Collingwood stood outside the mobile recording van on the sand of those beaches. "Through my microphone you may hear the deep retort of artillery as the brave men of the British Expeditionary Force and the French First Army hold back the Nazi forces. You may hear the hollow boom of our antiaircraft guns. You may hear the growling engines of dozens of ships and boats. But you will not hear the sound of panic. Of despair. Of dismay."

Inside the open back door of the van, Hugh's recording engineer, Tom Young, gave Hugh a thumbs-up and adjusted a knob. Young had wanted to make the recording in the van with its better acoustics, but Hugh craved the realism and immediacy of recording outside.

"The men of the BEF may be tired," Hugh said. A gray sky hung low over the gray sea, and hundreds of soldiers stood in long, snaking queues over the battered beach. "They may be bloodied. But they are not defeated. Some have described this force as having their backs to the sea. On the contrary, they face the sea. They face England. Thanks to the gallant men of the Royal Navy, thanks to the rugged fishermen and intrepid yachtsmen who have piloted their craft across the Channel to Dunkirk—thanks to them, the men of the BEF face a future fighting once more for the land they love.

"The day is not done. The day is just beginning. This is Hugh Collingwood reporting from Dunkirk for the BBC."

"That's all, Collie," Young said. "The battery died, and that's the last of our petrol."

Across the sand, François Jouveau approached wearing a buttoned-up gray overcoat and a British tin pan helmet like the one Hugh wore.

"Say, Young," Hugh said. "Pretend we're still recording. That's a good chap."

Then Hugh spoke into his dead microphone. "I would like to introduce Monsieur François Jouveau of Radio-Paris. Monsieur Jouveau, would you please join me?"

Jouveau's small dark eyes widened, and he shook his head, not in refusal but in disbelief.

Hugh beckoned him closer. "Monsieur Jouveau and I followed the Allied forces into Belgium. Please tell the listeners in Britain what you see here at Dunkirk."

Jouveau lifted his narrow chin, and one corner of his mouth rose. "The BBC will not allow my words."

"I should like to hear them."

Jouveau swept his gaze over the beach. "What I see here at Dunkerque is the British army fleeing the battlefield as the French army defends their perimeter. I see British ships refusing to evacuate French soldiers, only British. I see the English leaving the French to defend France alone, despite every assurance that we are Allies."

Jouveau's charges would raise a furor in England, with good cause. If Young were actually recording, the BBC would snip every word out of the metal disc. But Hugh gave a sympathetic nod. "Do go on."

"For what purpose?" Jouveau shrugged. "Young isn't recording."

A smile twitched on Hugh's dry lips. "Just having some sport."

"As usual."

"Say, Young." Hugh leaned into the van. "I'd like to slip as many recorded discs into our knapsacks as possible." Days had passed since he'd been able to telephone a story to London.

"Good. This last disc will be ready soon."

"Any items on the smaller side we could rescue?"

"I'm afraid not." Young removed his headphones and smoothed his ring of graying hair. The BBC would be furious at the loss of their expensive equipment, but if the BEF couldn't transport tanks and artillery, they certainly wouldn't evacuate a recording van.

"She has served well, the valiant maiden." Hugh patted the van's door. "Now, shall we find some grub?"

The three men worked their way along the back of the beach behind the queues. As civilians, they belonged at the end of the queue.

Booms rose from the sea and the land.

"Ack-ack." Young cursed the Germans and their Stuka dive-bombers. Three Luftwaffe air raids had struck Dunkirk since dawn.

Once again, Stukas screamed, diving close to shore, targeting ships.

"Watch out!" Jouveau pointed to the west.

Four Messerschmitts zipped down the beach, directly toward them.

Hugh threw himself down and clamped his helmet over the back of his head and neck. Grains of sand dug into his cheeks and nose.

The fighter planes' engines built to a fever pitch, machine-gun bullets thumped into the sand, and a rush of wind buffeted Hugh's overcoat and trousers.

Then the fighters roared down the beach.

Hugh's breath spilled onto the sand. But no blood.

Behind him, Jouveau groaned. "I—I've been shot."

"Oh no." Hugh rushed to his friend. Red bloomed on Jouveau's trouser leg above the knee. "Orderly! Orderly!"

"No use." In the queue, a Tommy pushed himself back to his feet. "They're all at the field dressing station. Too many wounded."

Hugh's mind raced. He needed to stop the bleeding, but with what?

"Pardon me, old chap." He worked his fingers into the bloody hole in Jouveau's trousers and ripped the fabric. "Young, remove his shoe."

While Young did so, Hugh tore the trouser leg all the way around. Then he slipped it off and tied it around the wound. "This isn't the best of bandages, but it must suffice."

Grimacing, Jouveau nodded his approval.

Young squatted beside him and wrapped Jouveau's right arm around his shoulders. "Can you stand?"

"I must."

Hugh ducked under Jouveau's left arm, and he and Young helped the Frenchman up.

Jouveau groaned, and his face twisted. "I saw an aid station by the pier."

The pier—more properly, the mole—where poisonous black smoke spewed from the hulks of ships bombed earlier in the day.

Hugh fought back a shudder and forged ahead, as fast as he could bearing half Jouveau's weight and with sand miring each step.

The queue of soldiers parted at their approach, and concerned Tommies pointed toward the field dressing station.

Hugh's breath came harder, but was he approaching his

limit? He readjusted his grip on Jouveau's wrist and waist. He refused to let his weakness bring harm to his friend.

"Almost . . . there." Close to fifty years of age, Young huffed even harder than Hugh.

The acrid smell of burning oil and hot metal snaked into Hugh's nostrils and lungs. His chest tightened a notch. "Not now," he muttered.

Ambulances parked by the mole, and orderlies carried stretchers onto a paddle steamer while the queue of soldiers waited their turn.

Near the base of the mole stood tents marked with the red cross.

Hugh shouldered his way into a tent. "My friend has been shot."

"Right this way." An orderly ushered them inside. "You're civilians?"

"Correspondents." A wheeze entered Hugh's voice. He winced as he and Young lowered Jouveau to the designated cot.

A medical officer strode over. "Patient's name?"

"François Jouveau," Hugh said.

The medical officer's eyebrows rose. "He's French?"

"Yes, sir." Hugh stretched tall and drilled his gaze into the doctor. "He's a correspondent. You *will* be able to treat him."

"Of course."

The medical officer untied Hugh's bandage and examined Jouveau's leg. "It looks like the bullet went through. Orderly, clean and bandage the wound, then take him to X-ray."

"Yes, sir."

The medical officer smiled down at Jouveau. "You're a lucky man. This wound qualifies you for evacuation. You should be ready to leave tomorrow morning."

Hugh and Young exchanged a relieved look. But the tightening in Hugh's chest increased, and each breath fought its way in, fought its way out.

Young tipped Jouveau a salute. "See you on the other side of the Channel."

"Thank you, my friends." Jouveau raised a shaky hand. "Au revoir."

Young turned to Hugh. "Let's scrounge up some supper."

Hugh's breath threatened a revealing whistle. He needed medicine and he needed privacy. He pulled the notepad from his overcoat pocket. "I'll stay and get another story. I'll meet you at the van later."

Young chuckled and departed.

As soon as the tent flap closed behind Young, Hugh spun to the medical officer. "Excuse me, sir. I'm having an asthmatic attack. May I please have some epinephrine?"

"You have asthma?" The medical officer practically pushed Hugh down to a cot. "What in heaven's name are you doing on a battlefield?"

"I'm a correspondent." Hugh opened his overcoat.

The medical officer burrowed his stethoscope under Hugh's suit jacket. "I hear the wheeze. With your condition, you should know better. You don't belong here."

Hugh stiffened. If he let his condition dictate his life, he'd never go anywhere.

The medical officer straightened up. "Orderly, administer epinephrine, then put this man directly onto the next ship."

"No, sir." Hugh fought to keep his voice strong. "Correspondents have lowest priority. I won't take the place—"

"You're as lucky as your French friend. Luckier, in fact. Next ship." He marched away.

Hugh groaned, shrugged off his jacket, and rolled up his shirtsleeve for the injection. How could he board that ship while soldiers remained on the beach? While stories remained on the beach?

Soon the blessed medicine warmed his veins and relaxed his airways, and air flowed freely once again.

"Do you feel better now?" The orderly spoke to Hugh as if he were a child. Or an invalid.

This was why Hugh concealed his asthma. As his tutor, George Baldwin, had said, "If you don't want to be treated as an invalid, don't allow anyone to see you as one."

Hugh pulled on his jacket. "I feel quite all right. Simply smashing. Thank you." He stood, tossed his coat over his shoulder, and headed for the exit.

"Excuse me, sir. I'll take you to the boat now."

Hugh sent the orderly a smile. "Right after I retrieve my kit."

"No kit allowed, sir." The orderly took Hugh's arm in his beefy grip. "Right this way."

He couldn't let this happen. If captured by the Germans, Hugh would be interned in a posh hotel and probably repatriated to England. But if the soldiers were captured, they'd be imprisoned for the duration of the war. And Britain needed them. Hugh intended to be the last man off the beach—and when he left, he'd carry a knapsack full of recording discs and notes.

The orderly marched Hugh to the base of the mole, where soldiers inched onto the rocky pier beside a large paddle steamer bearing the name of *Crested Eagle* on the prow.

The orderly parked Hugh in a gap in the queue and addressed a burly soldier. "Don't let this man leave. Make sure he gets on the boat. Medical orders." He gave Hugh a warning look and headed back toward the field dressing station.

"Medical orders?" The soldier wrinkled his dirty nose. "You don't look wounded. You look like a lazy dodger."

Grumbles rolled down the line.

Hugh let a mischievous grin rise, and he whipped out his notepad. "What I am is a BBC correspondent using a ruse to get a story—and a correspondent determined *not* to board this ship."

"BBC?" The burly soldier frowned. "Your voice sounds familiar."

"Hollingsworth?" his buddy said.

"Collingwood!" The burly soldier thrust a thick finger in the air. "Hugh Collingwood."

"Right you are." Hugh slipped out of the queue on the far side of the field dressing station. "What is your regiment? What is the first thing you plan to do back in Old Blighty?"

The soldiers' faces lit up, and stories flew. Hugh transcribed their answers, thanked them, and edged down the queue, asking questions, fielding answers, and increasing his distance from the large gray ship threatening to haul him away.

"Hughie?" A voice rose from farther back in the queue.

Hugh tensed. Only one person in the world used that horrific nickname. Even his parents had been persuaded to abandon it.

With a forced smile, he turned to face his brother. "Captain Cecil Collingwood. Fancy seeing you here."

Cecil marched toward him, sand pluming behind his boots. He wore battle dress, dirt and smoke smudged his face, and his muscular frame looked thinner than usual. "What on earth are you doing here?"

Hugh gestured with his notepad. "Reporting from the front."

Cecil glowered down at him, reminding Hugh how illness had stunted his growth, at least by Collingwood standards. "But your health. You'll have an attack. You shouldn't be here."

"I'm fine." Hugh softened his mouth and his thoughts. "But how are you? How's your unit? The fighting has been beastly."

"It has." Something dark washed through Cecil's hazel eyes, the same shade as Hugh's. "We boarded a destroyer this morning, but it was sunk in an air raid. Everyone survived, thank goodness, and now we're boarding yet another ship."

Hugh's pen moved to the pad as if magnetized, but he restrained himself.

"You haven't answered my question." Cecil had inherited

Mother's doggedness. "Whatever possessed you to come to a battlefield?"

"To inform the people of England of the brave exploits of your unit and—"

"Stop it." Cecil's lip twitched. "This isn't a game, a lark for bored gentry. This is war."

"And I'm reporting on it."

"You're thirty years old now. Isn't it time you found a more fitting position? Perhaps take Uncle Elliott's seat in Parliament."

"Take it?" Hugh arched an eyebrow. "Only death could pry him from his seat. Even then, even if I convinced his constituency to elect me, I wouldn't want it. Besides, isn't it the job of the second son to be irresponsible and a trifle scandalous?"

A smile flickered under Cecil's quite responsible mustache. "Of all the jobs for you to take seriously."

Hugh pressed his notepad over his heart. "Anything to elevate my dear brother's star in the family constellation."

"It'll take more than a rakish brother if Joan and I don't produce an heir."

Hugh managed not to roll his eyes at the antiquated notion—because a sad wistfulness emanated from his brother. Cecil and Joan had been married eight years.

"Then what are you waiting for, old chap?" Hugh knifed his hand toward the *Crested Eagle*. "Board that ship and fulfill your familial duty."

Cecil's smile hinted at the shy little boy he'd once been. Then his face turned serious. "Get on the first ship you can. Understood?"

With a flourish and a click of his heels, Hugh saluted. "Yes, sir!"

Cecil marched off after his unit, and Hugh ambled along the shore, where the receding tide had left the sand flat and dark and firm.

His brother's tall form headed down the mole and up the

gangplank. He stopped, silhouetted against the gray sky, and waved.

After Hugh waved back, Cecil stepped onto the ship, and men swung away the gangplank.

Hugh's heart stuttered. If he'd followed medical orders and boarded that steamer, Cecil would have been left behind.

He sat on the sand, in no mood to find dinner or return to the van.

A lark for bored gentry, Cecil had said.

His shoulders bowed, and his heart bent low.

He flipped open his notepad. Scattered notes told of soldiers plucking cheer and courage from the cauldron of defeat. Hugh would write the story and record it in London, exactly the sort of broadcast that the BBC desired most, that the British people desired most.

Their approval would have to do.

With a sigh, Hugh stood and brushed damp sand from his coat. The *Crested Eagle* had already sailed partway across the harbor.

He trudged over the beach, nudging detritus with his toe. Dozens of shoes from men who had waded out to fishing boats and yachts and barges. Kit bags. Rifles. Tins of bully beef. All spoke of an army escaping with naught but their lives.

Booms rose in the distance, and the racket built, closer and closer. Yellow flashed on the ships in the harbor as their guns opened up.

For the fifth time that day, Hugh threw himself to the sand and covered his head.

A terrific explosion at sea.

Hugh twisted his head toward the water. A fireball roiled over a large ship.

*Please, not Cecil's.*

Hugh sucked in a breath and pushed up to his knees. "Not Cecil's ship. Please no."

But it was.

A starburst of metal and flame and black, black smoke.

"No!" Hugh staggered to his feet and plowed down to the water, into the water. Frigid. Up to his waist. "Cecil! Cecil!"

Icy water tugged at Hugh's trousers, his coat, his heart, and he suddenly felt very alone.

*3*

## Haddenham, Buckinghamshire, England
## Sunday, June 2, 1940

While yesterday's honesty about her marriage had given Aleida a mad sense of elation, today the resulting pity drained her.

She walked with James and Margriet Sinclair up the lane to their country house after church. Her first church service since her wedding day, another fact of her life that had shocked her aunt and uncle and added to the pile of pity.

"We're so glad you're here." Faint wrinkles fanned from Tante Margriet's eyes—eyes of bright van der Zee blue. Like Theo's.

Aleida managed to smile. "I am glad too."

After Sebastiaan was killed, Aleida had loaded the car with refugees and had driven to Boulogne. Days had passed until she'd found passage to England.

But in London, her search for Theo had proven futile.

Where could she even begin?

Uncle James raised his face to the fair sky. "Quite an uplifting service, was it not?"

It was, full of thanksgiving for the British soldiers snatched from Dunkirk, out of Hitler's grasp.

Tante Margriet glanced at her husband from under the brim of her hat. "You'll understand if we Dutch don't celebrate."

The Netherlands had fallen to the Germans in five days and Belgium in seventeen. Did France stand a chance? Did Britain?

Aleida gripped her left hand in her right, and she tapped one finger back and forth across her knuckles as if playing scales on a piano. One, two, three, four. Four, three, two, one.

"Regardless, my dear," Uncle James said. "If one wishes not to live in a state of despair, one must train one's mind toward the good, like the miracle at Dunkirk."

"Like our Aleida's safe escape." Tante Margriet gave her a fond smile.

Aleida stopped tapping and breathed the fragrance of the garden surrounding the house of ancient gray stone. "Like this home."

The van der Zee cousins had gathered at Bentley Hall each summer. They'd roamed the countryside, frolicked in the gardens, and learned to ride. Aleida and some of her cousins had been educated in England and had spent many a holiday with the Sinclairs.

Sadness marred the memories. From what she could tell, the rest of her family remained in the Netherlands under Nazi rule.

Her aunt had been stunned by how little news Aleida brought with her. Aleida had seen her family rarely since her wedding and not at all since Theo's birth. Sebastiaan wouldn't allow it.

But Aleida hadn't come to Bentley Hall to grieve. She'd come for advice.

A breeze played with her hat, pinned over the coil at the nape of her neck. Now she couldn't cut her hair or Theo might not recognize her. "Tomorrow I'll return to London to—"

"London?" Uncle James turned wide brown eyes to her. "My dear, you mustn't. It simply isn't safe. Hitler is certain to attack."

"I need to find Theo." Her voice choked. Her son had to be terrified and confused. What must he have felt when he awakened in a stranger's car? Or had he awakened to hear his father give him away?

Tante Margriet's brow knit together. "Where will you look?"

"I was hoping you'd have some ideas. All I know is Theo is with a British couple bound for London. If they have a car, they have money. They must have been in the Netherlands or Belgium on business or with the government."

"I suppose that helps." Doubt stretched out Uncle James's words.

Aleida strolled up the flagstone path bounded by lilac bushes. "Theo has no papers, he doesn't know my full name, I doubt he can say his own full name, and he doesn't speak English." She'd been careful not to teach him English for fear Sebastiaan would discern her escape plan.

Tante Margriet sighed. "If you must return to London, please stay in our flat in Knightsbridge. We won't return with the war on, and we haven't been able to sell it."

"We'll provide any necessary funds," her uncle said.

"That's very generous." A hotel didn't feel like home. "I'd appreciate the use of your flat, but I have plenty of funds."

After Bas's death, she'd tossed his suitcase by the roadside. But she'd found another suitcase in the boot of the car, small but extraordinarily heavy.

Full of gold.

Aleida didn't need funds, but she did need advice. "I placed adverts in the newspapers, and I'll keep doing so. Do you know which government ministries are concerned with refugees?"

"I'll make a list," Uncle James said.

Tante Margriet paused at the front door. "If you give us a photo of Theo, we could show it to—"

"I have no photos of him."

Her aunt pressed a hand to her lips. "You poor dear, fleeing in such a hurry."

"I have never had a photo of him. Sebastiaan wouldn't allow it."

Uncle James's upper lip curled. "Wouldn't allow? Why ever not?"

Aleida's cheeks warmed. "He didn't want anyone to know about Theo's deformity."

"Deformity?" Tante Margriet said. "We never heard—"

"I wasn't allowed to tell anyone. Theo was born without fingers on his right hand."

"The poor little thing." Tante Margriet's face crumpled. "And to have a father . . ."

Uncle James jutted out his chin. "If I'd known, I would have wrung that scoundrel's neck."

"And no photos." Tante Margriet gripped Aleida's arm, and fresh pity swam in her watery eyes.

All Aleida had to remember her son was a suitcase full of tiny clothes. And Oli.

## LONDON
## WEDNESDAY, JUNE 12, 1940

The curved façade of Broadcasting House rose in Art Deco splendor, its sleek lines broken by heaps of sandbags, its gleaming white walls painted drab gray for camouflage.

At the door, Hugh showed his pass to a guard wearing the khaki-and-black brassard of the new Local Defence Volunteers.

"Mr. Collingwood, sir." The man's wide face brightened. "I listened to your broadcasts from Dunkirk. My grandson was there."

"I'm so sorry. I do hope—"

"He's back, safe and sound."

"I'm glad to hear it." Hugh smiled at the man and entered the semicircular lobby.

Over three hundred thousand troops had been rescued at Dunkirk, but thousands had been captured, and thousands would never come home.

Like Cecil.

The black armband around Hugh's suit jacket cinched tight as he crossed the lobby to the staff lifts, set in walls of pinkish-gray limestone.

On the fourth floor, he made his way down the curving corridor, stopping to shake hands with friends along the way.

He entered the office of Norman Fletcher, his editor.

Fletcher's secretary, Miss Peters, smiled at Hugh. "Collie! What did you bring me from France? Perfume? Chocolate?"

Hugh placed his fedora over his heart and smiled at the redhead. "I'm afraid my many gifts for you had to be discarded on the beach beside the recording van."

"The story of my life." She heaved a fake sigh. "Mr. Fletcher is waiting for you."

How late was he? Hugh glanced at his watch. Only ten minutes.

Inside the office, Fletcher stood facing the window with the telephone cord stretched to his ear. He looked over his shoulder at Hugh, motioned to the chair in front of his desk, then returned to the window. "I understand, but I don't—"

Hugh sat in a rounded chair of leather and steel, and he placed his hat in his lap.

Fletcher raised one hand, his fingers coiling. "I understand how important this is to the Honorable Mr. Hastings, but the BBC doesn't serve as a mouthpiece for every MP and his pet project."

Hugh winced. Uncle Elliott Hastings had no end to pet projects. At least Fletcher didn't know that Hugh was his nephew.

Muffled words, quite annoyed, emitted from the phone.

"Tell—tell—please tell—please tell Mr. Hastings I will take that into consideration. Good day." Fletcher thumped the receiver into its cradle and glared at Hugh. "You're late again."

"I do apologize." Hugh put on his most contrite face.

Fletcher ran his hand into graying fair hair and sank into his chair. His expression softened. "I was sorry to hear about your brother."

"Thank you, sir. I'm ready to go back to work. I have an idea."

With a circle of his hand in the air, Fletcher told Hugh to proceed.

Hugh leaned forward. "Since Italy declared war on Britain on Monday, rioters in London have attacked Italian restaurants and businesses."

Fletcher was already shaking his head.

So Hugh injected more passion into his voice. "Yesterday our government ordered the internment of all Italian men who have been in England less than twenty years, and—"

"Stop." Fletcher kept shaking his head. "You're not telling that story."

"I'll interview the government ministers who gave the orders, those who favor internment, as well as families of the interned—"

"Too controversial."

"I'll tell both sides. It's imperative—"

"It's imperative that you not tell that story."

Hugh mashed his lips together. "Britain is a democracy. How can we say we're better than the totalitarian nations if we lock up civilians, including those who fled from Hitler and Mussolini, those who oppose them?"

"I didn't say I disagreed with you." Fletcher's long face set like flint. "I said you're not telling that story."

"The BBC isn't censored."

"Because we censor ourselves. Do you know how much of

your material from Belgium I had to cut? You didn't spill military secrets, but you interviewed too many who criticized our generals."

Hugh had also reported on the fortitude of the British soldier and the stunning beauty of the evacuation. He sank back in the chair. Telling only one side defied everything he'd learned reporting for the *Times* and in his first year at the BBC. "Sir, I—"

Fletcher flipped up one hand. "You're in the posh set, Collingwood. If the BBC fires you, you'll flit to the next thing that amuses you. But me? I had to work my fingers to the bone to come this far. There are no other broadcasting companies in Britain. Those toffs at the Ministry of Information—like that twit Albert Ridley—they're waiting for this scholarship boy to make a mistake. If I let you broadcast a story like that, my career is over."

A framed photograph on Fletcher's desk showed his pretty, much-younger wife and his two tiny girls, now evacuated to the country. What would happen to them if Fletcher lost his position?

Hugh sighed. "Very well, then."

Fletcher laced long fingers on top of his desk. "Try to be more like Gil."

"Gil . . . is a fine chap." But Guy Gilbert's reporting managed to be both ingratiating and dull.

"You be a fine chap too. Find a story to make the public want to do their bit. We're at war, and things are grim. The Ministry of Information wants us to boost morale."

"To educate, inform, and entertain," Hugh said in a soft voice, repeating the BBC's purpose.

"Yes." Fletcher poked one finger toward Hugh. "To educate, inform, and entertain so we have a fighting chance of not becoming another Nazi vassal state. Understood?"

"Yes, sir. I'll find something exceptionally inspirational."

"Quite right, you will." Fletcher waved his hand to the door.

Hugh stood, bowed his head to his boss, and left Broadcasting House.

He strolled down Regent Street toward the family townhouse, past boarded-up windows and sandbags piled high. After the fall of Poland in September 1939, eight months of the "Bore War"—a practical hush on the western front—had lulled Britain into complacency. Everything had changed with Hitler's blitzkrieg through the Low Countries and now to the very gates of Paris.

He passed a woman carrying a bolt of black fabric, for blackout curtains, no doubt. Yes, he needed to encourage people to do their bit and remember the nation's ideals. But he also had a duty to reveal when the nation violated those ideals.

At Oxford Circus, Hugh turned right on Oxford Street, too quiet with petrol rationing in place. How much of his reporting from Belgium and Dunkirk had been cut? Perhaps he'd spent too much time listening to François Jouveau.

Jouveau was recovering nicely in a London hospital, and Hugh had secured him a position with the BBC European Services. The French Service was thrilled to hire an experienced and popular radio correspondent for their shortwave broadcasts to France.

A young man strode down the street carrying a sack far from his body. A squirming, growling, hissing sack.

"Pardon me." Hugh tipped his hat to the man. "May I ask—"

"Throwing me master's cat in the Thames. He's a devil cat, he is."

"In the Thames!" After England had declared war in September, far too many people had destroyed their pets. And regretted it.

The young man gestured over his shoulder with his thumb. "You know what they say, guv, what with food rationing and the Nasties coming. It's more merciful-like to put them out of their misery now than let 'em starve later. And this one—a right devil cat he is."

"I'll take him." What was he saying? He couldn't take a cat.

"No, me master said—"

"Your master wants to be rid of the cat. You can walk over a mile to the Thames, or you can give him to me and be done with it."

The man puffed his cheeks full of air, then blew it out. "All right, guv."

The bag jerked, curved claws pierced the fabric, and "Mrrow!"

Hugh gritted his teeth and wrapped his hand around the knot in the sack. Holding the snarling bag far from his body, Hugh hurried down Oxford Street.

What had he done?

Passersby parted before him with alarmed expressions, and Hugh merely tipped his hat at them. How could he explain to them when he couldn't explain to himself?

With his asthma, he'd never been allowed near dogs or cats. He knew nothing of cats. He'd have to find this poor creature a home. Somehow.

The graceful brick façade of the townhouse greeted him, and Hugh climbed steps framed by curved wrought-iron banisters.

He flung open the front door. "Simmons, I brought a guest for dinner."

That guest let out a terrific run of snarls and hisses.

Simmons, the butler, trotted down the stairs. "What in heaven's name?"

Hugh lifted the bag. "It is a cat. A rather angry cat, I'm afraid. But if someone tied me in a sack and threatened to toss me in the Thames, I'd be rather angry too."

"I say, sir. I do say." Simmons met Hugh's gaze, his pale eyes wide. "Whatever shall we do with it?"

"I need to find him a home. In the meantime, we'll have a

rather angry houseguest." Hugh could only pray an asthmatic attack wouldn't be the reward for his hospitality.

Simmons gazed around the entryway. "If you release him here, he'll tear up the drapes and upholstery. Best to place him in a confined space until he calms down."

"The loo." Hugh marched down the hall to the lavatory with Simmons behind him.

In the tiled bathroom, Hugh stared at the sack. "How do we release him without being eviscerated?"

"I'll get the shears."

While Simmons ran his errand, the sack jolted, and the cat cussed at Hugh.

"Watch your language, young man."

When Simmons returned, Hugh held the sack at a distance, close to the floor, and Simmons snipped at the sack below the knot.

Soon the sack dropped to the floor. It gyrated and screeched, and a streak of gray and white shot out, leapt, ricocheted off the wall by Hugh's head.

The men cried out and ducked.

With a great skittering of claws, the cat disappeared beneath the bathtub.

Simmons stared, his jaw dangling. "Perhaps we should leave him alone, sir. I'll fetch food and water, a blanket, and fill a bin with earth from the garden."

"Earth? Oh yes. Quite right." A cat couldn't use the loo. "I'll stay with him."

After Simmons left, Hugh squatted to look under the tub from a safe distance. Or was any distance safe from a creature who could leap off walls?

Said creature crouched low with his gray fur puffed up along his spine. He had a white belly and white paws, and a triangle of white rose from his jaw up between his eyes. Two green eyes glared at Hugh.

"Good day, sir. My name is Hugh. And yours?"

The cat hissed.

"How do you spell that?"

The cat growled, long and deep in his throat.

Hugh settled onto his backside and draped his arms over his knees. "Gratitude is the proper response when someone saves your life, but I understand you've had a most trying day."

Then Hugh frowned. His eyes and nose didn't itch. His breath flowed freely. Perhaps he wouldn't have to find the creature a new home after all.

The cat never broke his acidic green glare. His tail thumped in a demanding sort of way.

Sour, indignant, and demanding. Rather like the heroine of *The Secret Garden*, the novel that had altered the course of Hugh's life. "I shall call you Mary Lennox."

The cat hissed.

"I do apologize. You're a tomcat and a handsome one. How about you and I come to a gentleman's agreement? You agree not to make me wheeze, and I—I shall call you Lennox."

For the first time, the cat blinked.

Agreed.

4

Aleida stroked Oli's trunk twelve times. A perfect number. She could still see little Theo cradling the elephant's trunk around his cheek, and her eyes filled. What horrors had he endured? What fears?

With a strengthening breath, she positioned Oli precisely on her bureau. She hadn't seen her son for forty-seven days.

Elephants might never forget, but little boys could.

Aleida pinned on the dove-gray hat that matched her suit, applied lipstick in a subtle shade of rose, and left for the Ministry of Health in Whitehall.

On the Piccadilly Line, she opened her notebook. On each page, she'd listed places Theo might be or places to inquire. She'd listed the worst possibilities in the back.

The worst—Bas had lied and abandoned Theo by the road. The English couple had abandoned him. The couple had been stranded on the continent.

Holding her pen in her right hand, she tapped her knuckles with her left index finger. One, two, three, four. Four, three, two, one.

She could do nothing about those possibilities. Besides, a couple wealthy enough to own a car had the means to return home, and anyone with half a heart wouldn't abandon a child.

Her vision blurred. She glanced out the window and blinked until the circular red signs for Piccadilly cleared before her.

Aleida disembarked, switched to the Bakerloo Line, and took a seat.

She had to assume the couple had brought Theo to London. They could have left him at a refugee center or an orphanage or a hospital. She listed each institution she found in her notebook and checked them off with notes after she visited.

The Dutch Embassy had its own page. They'd promised to do what they could.

What if the couple had sent Theo to the country as many parents had done? The Ministry of Health oversaw the evacuation process.

Only sixteen more items to put on her list until she reached forty, the biblical number of trial and fulfillment. Forty years in the desert, then the Promised Land. Forty items on the list, then she'd find Theo.

At Trafalgar Square, she stepped outside to a blue sky streaked by plumes of clouds. Using Nelson's Column to get her bearings, she headed down Whitehall past government buildings of cool gray stone.

Aleida entered the Ministry of Health and consulted a directory to find the correct department. Up stone steps smoothed by time, down a hallway, and Aleida entered an office.

At a desk behind the counter sat a young woman with rich brown skin and shiny black hair curling below her chin in a fashionable style.

"Good morning," Aleida said. "Is this the department that oversees the evacuation of children?"

"Yes, ma'am. May I help you?"

Aleida took a deep breath. "My name is Mrs. Martens, and I fled from the Netherlands. On the road when I was sleeping, my husband—without my consent—gave our three-year-old son to an English couple who promised to bring him to London. My husband was killed the next morning before he could tell me their name or address."

"Oh no." Distress shivered in the woman's large dark eyes. "Do you think your son arrived in London and was evacuated?"

Aleida gripped the edge of the counter. "I must believe the best."

"Evacuation *is* the right thing to do." The woman tipped her head to a poster on the wall stating, "Children are safer in the country . . . leave them there."

Safer, yes. But "the country" meant many different places. "Do you have records of where the children are?"

The woman came to the counter. "Children are evacuated in three ways. Schoolchildren are sent with their school. Younger children are sent with their mothers—this department oversees those arrangements. And certain families, especially those with means, make private arrangements."

Filing cabinets lined the wall behind the desk. "You have records for each child?"

The woman frowned. "We know which schools went to which towns. The other children are gathered at the train station. When they receive their billets in the country, they send a postcard home with their address. And we have no records of private arrangements."

A bleak void opened inside her. The couple who had Theo had means.

"Miss Sharma?" a woman called from an office in the back. "Where's the report?"

"Soon, Miss Granville." Miss Sharma gave Aleida an apologetic look. "I wish I could help. We're extremely short-staffed. Now that France has fallen, the government has ordered another round of evacuations—for the children who returned home during the Bore War."

"Oh." If only she could peek in those filing cabinets.

"Perhaps you could work here." Miss Sharma tipped a smile.

"Work here?" Aleida already had a job—finding her son—and the Ministry of Health was only twenty-fourth on her list. But learning how the system worked might create leads.

"Would you like to?"

She could still search in the evenings and on Saturdays. "Why, yes, I would."

Miss Sharma bolted to the office door. "Miss Granville, a lady would like to work here."

"Oh?" A woman in her thirties came out, tall and big-boned, with dark red hair and a friendly smile. She extended her hand to Aleida. "I'm Miss Granville."

"How do you do? My name is Mrs. Martens."

Miss Granville snatched her hand from Aleida's. "You're German?"

"No, ma'am. I'm Dutch. I fled from the Germans."

"Yes," Miss Sharma said, "and she was tragically separated from her young son. As a mother, she'll have compassion on the evacuees and rapport with the mothers."

Miss Granville looked as if she'd swallowed bad mustard. "Mothers belong at home."

"I'm a widow," Aleida said, "and I have no other children. What better way to fill my time than helping other women's children?"

The mustard remained. "This position requires a certain knowledge of the special needs of English children and an understanding of English ways."

"I am not deficient in that area." Aleida would need to appeal to the woman's snobbery, and she named the elite boarding school she'd attended.

Sugar replaced mustard. "That's my school too."

45

In British society, school ties were everything, and yet the woman's eyes narrowed again.

Miss Sharma's eyebrows rose, then she turned to Aleida. "Do you do your bit for Britain? I volunteer at an Air Raid Precautions post with Miss Granville." She inclined her head toward her boss in a deliberate way.

Was that how Miss Sharma had overcome Miss Granville's dislike of foreigners? "I'd planned to volunteer after I became more settled," Aleida said.

Miss Sharma pressed one finger to her chin. "After you found a job, perhaps?"

"Perhaps." She gave Miss Granville her most innocent look. "Do you need more volunteers at your ARP post?"

She did. Aleida received the job.

Twenty-four was a good number indeed.

### Tuesday, July 9, 1940

"On this day, our illustrious government banned the spreading of rumors. Are we to fight censorship in occupied lands by practicing it here?" Hugh fastened his necktie in a Windsor knot. "My dear Lennox, you are the only creature who shall hear that speech."

Across the room, Lennox sat on an armchair, unimpressed.

Although the cat acted annoyed by Hugh and the household staff, he never escaped through open doors, possibly due to the bounty of mice in the attic. Since he hadn't aggravated Hugh's asthma, Lennox remained, as sour as his namesake, but no devil cat.

After Hugh buttoned his suit jacket, he donned his gray fedora. "And now, Lennox, you are about to witness broadcasting history, in which Hugh Collingwood actually pleases his editor. Wish me the best."

With one lazy blink, Lennox did so.

In fifteen minutes, Hugh arrived at an Air Raid Precautions post near Green Park Station. A BBC mobile recording van was parked outside, and Hugh greeted Tom Young and his crew.

"We're already hooked into the telephone line." Young leveled his gaze at Hugh. "Remember, this is a live broadcast."

Fletcher had put faith in Hugh to allow an outside broadcast. Misguided faith on Fletcher's part, but Hugh intended not to break it. "Someday gold shall aspire to be as good as Collingwood."

A smile twitched in the corner of Young's mouth. Then he tapped his wristwatch. "You'll have three minutes. I'll give you signals at thirty seconds, ten, and five. I'll bring the microphone when it's ready."

"Thank you. I'll go inside and arrange my interviews." Hugh entered the building, housed in a school that had evacuated to the country.

A petite middle-aged woman crossed his path, wearing the ill-fitting blue mackintosh coat used by female wardens.

"Excuse me, ma'am. I'm Hugh Collingwood with the BBC, and I'm—"

"Hugh Collingwood!" She clapped her hand over her mouth. "That voice—it's as handsome in person—that is—I mean—"

"Mrs. Byrne, why don't you see to your duties?" Beatrice Granville approached. "Ah, Hugh, it's good to see you. It's been too long."

"It has." Hugh shook the hand of the tall redhead who had once been good friends with Cecil. "I'm afraid I have little time before our broadcast. Would you please introduce me around? I'd like to interview three volunteers. I've already met Mrs. Byrne."

Mrs. Byrne giggled like a schoolgirl.

With not much work, Hugh could put her at ease and have a charming interview.

"You'll interview me only," Beatrice said. "No one else is capable or willing. And two are foreigners. They have accents."

He'd judge capability, willingness, and accents for himself. "Please introduce me."

Beatrice dipped her chin and introduced half a dozen men and women, none beyond hope. In Hugh's experience, keen interest and stimulating questions never failed.

Last, Beatrice introduced him to Nilima Sharma and Aleida Martens. Each had a confident carriage and a light accent. This was exactly what Hugh wanted, to show all of London rising above differences and pulling together. "Would you ladies be interested—"

"Miss Sharma, you're late for your duties," Beatrice said. "Please take Mrs. Martens with you, as she is still training." She clapped her hands twice, a woman accustomed to dismissing the help.

"Yes, ma'am." The two ladies hurried off.

And . . . the other volunteers had disappeared too.

If Hugh weren't careful, he would have the dullest of interviews as Beatrice pontificated for three minutes.

He had Beatrice describe the volunteers' duties so he knew which questions to ask, and he planned the order for his interview.

Soon Young brought in Hugh's microphone and headphones, trailing yards of cord back to the recording van. Young also wore headphones. They could each hear the BBC broadcast, and Young studied his wristwatch, synchronized with the clocks at Broadcasting House.

After Hugh heard his introduction on the air, he smiled at Young as if he were every man, woman, and child seated around a wireless set tuned to the Home Service. "This is Hugh Collingwood reporting live from an Air Raid Precautions post somewhere in London. The volunteers at this post have left for their rounds, armed only with helmet and torch. And on those meager tools and on those watchful eyes rest the safety of a nation."

Hugh lowered his voice a grim notch. "Whilst we are loath to imagine German bombers over our fair isle, we must prepare ourselves for that possibility. Taking proper air raid precautions applies not only in London but in every village and town. Although Hitler might not wish to bomb your village green, the lights in your cottage could lead his pilots to the airfields and ports he does indeed wish to destroy."

Hugh faced Beatrice and let light back into his voice. "I'm standing here with Miss Beatrice Granville. Miss Granville, would you please describe the duties your volunteers will perform tonight as the city sleeps?"

Beatrice pontificated, but in an articulate way and with a refreshing touch of self-effacing humor. Hugh guided her with questions and comments as she discussed blackout regulations.

When Young signaled thirty seconds remaining, Hugh helped Beatrice complete her final thought. And when he signaled ten seconds, Hugh spun to face his engineer.

"So tonight, if your air raid warden should chide you for the sliver of light peeking from your kitchen window, please be understanding and leap to close the curtain. The wardens are seeking the safety of your family, your town, and your nation. This is Hugh Collingwood reporting from somewhere in London."

He finished just as Young made a fist to say his time was up.

Hugh thanked Beatrice warmly, then helped Young roll up cord on the way back to the van. "Wasn't I indeed as good as gold?" Hugh asked Young with a grin.

"Blindingly so."

Out on the dusky street, Hugh passed the microphone and

headphones to Gerald MacTavish in the back of the van. Not a gripping broadcast but full of information for the public good. No one at the Ministry of Information would complain, not even his old family friend, Albert Ridley.

"Excellent work, men," Hugh said to the crew. "Thank you."

"Good night." Young shut the door and drove away.

"Excuse me, Mr. Collingwood." A woman stood behind him—the attractive blonde with the light accent. She wore a blue mackintosh and a blue helmet printed with *W* for warden.

"Yes. Mrs. Martens, was it?"

"Yes, sir." She glanced around him toward the door of the post, then across the street where Miss Sharma stood, then back to Hugh. "Would you please tell my story on the BBC?"

"Your story?" The lady would earn Beatrice's ire if she were seen talking to Hugh, so he angled his body to block the view from the door. "What would that story be?"

Her hands twisted around her darkened torch. "When I was fleeing the Netherlands in May, I was separated from my three-year-old son. He is probably in London. If you were to broadcast about him, someone might recognize him."

Hugh's chest collapsed at the anguish in the young mother's eyes, dim though they were in the twilight. "I'm sorry, Mrs. Martens. What an ordeal this must be for your family."

"His name is Theodoor—Theo for short. He has light blond hair and bright blue eyes, and on his right hand he has no fingers."

Hugh's breath lodged in his throat. "You talk about it so—openly."

She glanced down at her torch, twisting and twisting. "In Dutch, we have a word—*rechtdoorzee*. It translates as 'right through the sea'—direct and straightforward. I must be rechtdoorzee to find my son. There are many little blond boys in England, but very few with a hand like his. If you tell about him on the BBC, I may find him."

The BBC had a policy not to broadcast about missing persons. But ideas swarmed in Hugh's head, buzzing, and all the bees lined up. During the exodus from France and the Low Countries, millions had fled in great chaos. How many families had become separated? He could broadcast that story—and include the story of Theo Martens.

Mrs. Martens lifted a jaw too sharp to be beautiful but with dignity that was beauty itself. "Besides, I am not ashamed of my son. Far from it. His hand is . . . sweet." Her voice trembled.

She was a brave woman, Mrs. Martens, and a loving mother.

Hugh pulled out his notepad and found a bit of space. "I would like to tell your story, but I must receive approval from my editor. May I please have your address and telephone number, if you have one? If I receive approval, I'll ring."

A smile transformed her face from attractive to lovely. "Thank you. I'd be forever grateful." She gave her address and telephone number, and he bid her goodbye.

"Rechtdoorzee," Hugh whispered as he walked home on the blacked-out streets. The English prized circumspection above directness, propriety above openness.

Hugh's infirmity was invisible, one he could hide most days.

What if he were rechtdoorzee about it?

He knew full well what would happen. He'd be told he couldn't do this and shouldn't do that and was he feeling quite well? Would he like to sit down? Take a rest?

No, he wouldn't.

The good stories and exciting stories would no longer come his way.

If he plunged right into the sea, he'd drown.

5

Twenty-seven wasn't a good number after all.

Aleida had such high hopes when she'd written it in her notebook with "BBC" at the top of the page.

"Please, sir," she said to the guard at the entrance to Broadcasting House. "If I could—"

"I'm sorry, ma'am." Compassion turned down the corners of his full gray mustache. "You can't enter without a pass, and you can't get a pass unless you have business with the BBC."

Aleida edged aside to let people exit. "But Mr. Collingwood promised to broadcast my story, and it's been a week, and he hasn't contacted me."

"You could write a letter."

A scoffing sound came from behind Aleida. A matronly woman—one of the people who had just left—wore her wiry pewter hair swept high on her head, crowned by a tiny flat red hat. "With that golden voice, Collingwood must receive great heaps of mail. She won't get through."

The guard sighed. "I know, but—"

"I understand," Aleida said. "No pass, no entry."

The matron beckoned to Aleida with brisk motions of gloved fingers. "You want to speak to Collingwood. Why?"

Something about the woman prompted Aleida's usual speech to tumble out, this time with an addition about her pressing need to find the BBC reporter.

"He promised to broadcast your story?" The woman tipped a red-lipped smirk. "Collie is a great many wonderful things, but organized isn't one of them. I'm Louisa Jones, *Chicago Tribune.*"

A bit dazed, Aleida shook the American's hand. "Aleida Martens. You know Mr. Collingwood?"

"Come with me, child." Mrs. Jones strode down Portland Place with short, quick steps.

Aleida rushed to fall in beside her.

Mrs. Jones gestured ahead with one plump hand. "As we speak, Collie is holding court at the Hart and Swan, I'm sure of it. British reporters, Americans, French, everyone stops by. Collie is there most evenings. Poor child's still single. Keeps turning down my marriage proposals, which, granted, is a sign of intelligence. Or character. Take your pick."

Had Aleida ever met anyone like Mrs.—Miss Jones? "Are all Americans so . . ."

"Heavens, no. Most are quite tame." She gave Aleida an appraising look with close-set green eyes. "Your English is good. Well educated?"

"My aunt married an Englishman. I went to boarding school here."

"Pff. Boarding schools. Just enough education to make you sound cultured, but not enough to challenge a man. All posture and place settings and curtsying to the king."

And not nearly enough mathematics. "I always wanted more."

"Good girl." Miss Jones grasped a fistful of air before her. "I grabbed hold of every morsel of learning. Oh, here we are."

Miss Jones led Aleida through a dark green door, through

the wood-paneled pub to a room in the back, where four men sat at a table, including Mr. Collingwood.

A man with slicked-back blond hair sat across from Mr. Collingwood. "You simply must do something about that uncle of yours. In times of peace, he's merely an opinionated eccentric, but now he recklessly endangers our nation."

Mr. Collingwood shook his head of wavy golden-brown hair and laughed with that golden voice. "Not one creature in God's little green earth can sway the mind of Elliott Hastings."

"Good evening, boys," Miss Jones said.

All four men stood with cries of "Lou!"

Miss Jones guided Aleida to the table. "Collie, I believe you've met my new friend."

Mr. Collingwood searched her face with a faint smile.

How could she expect him to remember her? "I'm Mrs.—"

"Mrs. Martens from the ARP." He bounded forward with a radiant smile and grasped her hand. Then his smile dove deep into concern. "How are you? Any news on your little boy?"

"Little boy?" Miss Jones plopped her purse on the table. "The missing little boy you promised to broadcast about? And haven't?"

Mr. Collingwood released Aleida's hand and bowed his head. "My apologies for the misunderstanding. I promised to ring if the story was approved. It wasn't."

Her dream of Theo's story humming from every wireless set in Britain leaked away with the air in her lungs, and she tapped her knuckles.

"You promised a story?" The blond man curled his upper lip. "The BBC doesn't broadcast about missing persons."

Mr. Collingwood pulled out two chairs. "Please do join us, Mrs. Martens."

Aleida hesitated.

Miss Jones sat and looked up at her. "Got anyplace better to be?"

Her silent flat where she'd fret about Theo, all alone. She sat.

"Gil's correct. The BBC doesn't broadcast such stories." Mr. Collingwood directed hazel eyes at the man across from him, then at Aleida beside him. "But you aren't the only refugee searching for family. I was in Belgium and France with the BEF—so was my friend François Jouveau." He nodded to the dark-haired man on his other side.

Then pain flickered across Mr. Collingwood's face.

Aleida stopped tapping. He'd seen. He knew. He understood.

"I planned to tell about refugees searching for family, including you, Mrs. Martens." Faded freckles crossed Mr. Collingwood's cheeks and nose. "However, my editor did not approve the story. The BBC has limited airtime, and every minute must prepare us for the German onslaught. Maybe in the newspapers? You have more space, right, MacLeod?"

An older gentleman sitting across the table harrumphed. "Haven't you heard? With paper rationing, we're now limited to eight pages. Besides, that's old news. As Churchill said, 'The Battle of France is over . . . the Battle of Britain is about to begin.'"

"Has already begun," Gil said. "For the past week, the Germans have been bombing our ports and our ships in the Channel."

Aleida's throat swelled. The Nazis would invade soon. She had to find Theo before the chaos of clashing armies and fleeing civilians.

Miss Jones made a sweeping motion as if brushing away the men's words. "Sounds like censorship to me."

"Censorship?" Gil all but spluttered.

Miss Jones whapped Gil's arm with the back of her hand. "Being told what you can and can't write—that's censorship. Why, I'd write Mrs. Martens's story myself, but a fat lot of good it would do to tell Chicago about her little boy."

Aleida rolled her fingers around her purse strap. If only Miss Jones wrote for a London paper.

"Not censorship," Gil said. "Priorities."

Mr. Collingwood's eyes lit up, and he poked one finger at the table. "We do have priorities, and we mustn't broadcast anything that might benefit the enemy. But my reports from Dunkirk were edited to eliminate any hint of criticism of British military strategy."

Gil's narrow nostrils almost closed. "Criticism is bad for morale."

"But the free exchange of ideas is vital for democracy," Jouveau said.

Something stirred in Aleida's chest, fed the intellect starved during her marriage.

Mr. Collingwood scooted forward in his seat, and his shoulders rippled with energy. "As a nation, we must examine our actions and our government."

"You reporters." A middle-aged man stood by Mr. Collingwood's chair with a towel draped over his arm. "You need to watch your tongues."

"Ah, Irwin." Mr. Collingwood lifted an arm to him. "Dearest of old chaps. Would you be so kind as to take the ladies' orders? Tea? Coffee?"

"A pint for me," Miss Jones said.

"I'll have tea," Aleida said. "No milk."

Irwin nodded to the ladies, then frowned at Mr. Collingwood. "You mustn't speak ill of Mr. Churchill."

"I think the world of Mr. Churchill. He's the right man to run our country. But calling attention to failures is the duty of the press. Lou—you're an American. You agree."

A smile dug into Miss Jones's plump cheeks. "My country can afford the luxury of squabbling with each other. We aren't at war."

"Oui," Jouveau said. "Which is another topic we must address."

"No arguments from me." Miss Jones flipped up her hand. "But try to convince the average Midwesterner why he should care a fig about yet another European war."

Aleida's heart burned. "Then you *should* tell my story. Make them care."

Murmurs of approval swept the table.

Miss Jones gave her a slow, narrow-eyed smile. "A solid point. You've got a deal."

"Thank you." The story wouldn't help her find Theo, but it might encourage sympathy for human beings on the other side of the world—and a willingness to fight for them.

Aleida pulled her notepad from her purse, opened to number twenty-seven, and made notes.

"What's this?" Mr. Collingwood smiled at her notepad.

"My notes on my search for my son—where I've looked and where I might inquire. Orphanages, the Dutch Embassy—"

"And the BBC." His eyebrows bunched together. "I truly am sorry. This ordeal must be difficult for you and your husband."

Aleida's mouth set. "My husband is responsible for this ordeal. And now he's dead."

Silence thudded like a millstone in the middle of the table.

She smoothed a page hard, trying to remove a crease. "You'll think me callous. But Sebastiaan ripped my son from my arms as I slept, sent him away with strangers without my knowledge or consent, and refused to give me the couple's name or address. Then a fighter plane strafed him because he was too arrogant to take cover." She glanced at Mr. Collingwood's sleeve. "I wear no black armband."

Her violation of every rule of British decorum pulsed in the silence.

"Rechtdoorzee," Mr. Collingwood said in a low voice, ragged around the edges. The corners of his eyes turned down, but in that sadness shone a tiny light of admiration.

"Good for you, Aleida," Miss Jones said. "We can call you Aleida, can't we? After you spilled your guts like that?"

"Ye—yes." Her eyes stretched wide. "What do you mean—good for me?"

"Call me Louisa." She leaned close, her green eyes kindling. "He was a cruel man, your husband. Wasn't he?"

"Yes." Honesty cleansed like a flame.

"Most women blame themselves for a man's cruelty, but not you. Not me. My first husband beat me when he was angry. He beat me when he was sad. He beat me just for the fun of it. His fault. Not mine. I dumped him. Good for me."

"Very well, Lou." MacLeod adjusted his glasses. "What's your excuse for husbands two, three, and four?"

Louisa ticked off points on her fingers. "Bored me, cheated on me, died. So who wants to be number five? Come on, fellas. The ride may be short, but it's a whole lot of fun."

As one, the men held up their hands, shook their heads, and laughed.

Aleida laughed too. It had been so long.

6

Even the windows of Collingwood Manor wept for the lost heir.

Hugh sat on the window seat with one leg up on the cushion, sipping tea. Jagged light brightened the leaden sky, and a rumble rolled over the damp lawns and gardens.

Someday the estate would be his. He'd never expected it. Never embraced it as his. Told himself he'd never wanted it.

Father's sigh emerged as the thunder ebbed. He sat at his desk, surrounded by piles of dusty tomes. If Nigel Collingwood had been born in a different social class, he would have enjoyed a brilliant career in academia.

"How goes the book, Father?"

"Hmm?" Father lifted his head, adjusted his reading glasses, and found Hugh. "The book. Yes. It goes. And yet . . ."

Yet he'd lost his oldest son only two months ago. Hugh raised a gentle smile. "It's such a fascinating topic and of great importance."

"Yes." A semblance of light passed through his gaze. "It is."

"I have an idea." Hugh swung his feet to the floor. "You're

writing for a scholarly audience. What if I were to help you write for a broader audience—a translation, if you will—for the common man?"

Sitting by the fireside, Mother clucked her tongue.

"Yes, Mother. A significant portion of the population might read Father's work—it's a brilliant topic—if only the language had a simpler touch, a journalistic touch."

Father shook his graying head. "It isn't that sort of work."

Mother topped off her tea. "You've spent far too much time with . . ."

"With those beneath my station?" Hugh tipped up a mischievous smile. "I find them vastly interesting and far more intelligent than we give them credit."

"But you're becoming quite coarse. That will have to change now that—" Mother's voice clamped off, and she gave her head a tiny shake and took a sip of tea.

Now that he was the heir. Hugh wrestled back a wince.

The front door opened and shut, and male voices mingled as the butler greeted their guest and took wet coat and hat and umbrella.

Hugh stood as Elliott Hastings swept into the room.

"Mary, darling." Uncle Elliott took his sister's hands and kissed her on the cheek. "How are you?"

"I'm fine, thank you." Mother's black dress spoke the truth her words denied.

Uncle Elliott shook Father's hand, then Hugh's. "How's my favorite neph—" His face froze.

Now he was the only nephew. Hugh had once relished that greeting. His fellow square peg, Uncle Elliott had always called him. To Mother's dismay, he'd done his best to sharpen the corners of Hugh's peg.

Mother poured tea for her brother, and everyone sat on the sofas flanking the fireplace.

Uncle Elliott smoothed the meager hairs crowning his head.

"So, Hugh, what sort of trouble have you been getting into lately?"

"Sadly, none." Hugh stirred milk into his tea. "I'm rather jealous of Charles Gardner in Dover reporting live on the dogfights over the Channel for the BBC."

"Smashing good reporting."

"Indeed." The Luftwaffe continued its attacks in the Channel, sinking dozens of British ships. "But I'm assigned to London now, so I tell safe little stories telling folks to do their bit."

"Quite safe. Quite respectable." Uncle Elliott's tone withered with sarcasm.

Mother sniffed. "There is nothing respectable about radio reporting."

A lecture would come, as sure as thunder followed lightning, so Hugh turned to his uncle. "I hear you're causing trouble with Norman Fletcher."

"Oh yes." Smug wrinkles fanned around his eyes. "He quite loathes me. But I am determined to call attention to the plight of the refugees, and he is the man I must persuade."

"I wish you luck." Hugh raised his teacup to his uncle. "Even if Fletcher agreed with you, he couldn't put the story on the air. It isn't considered relevant."

"Poppycock. He's worried I'll criticize the government. As I should. Some of our illustrious ministers fear improving conditions for the refugees would attract more of them—and horrors!—more Jews."

Hugh had heard the same, although in politer terms.

That pugnacious Hastings chin pushed its way forward. "At its heart, this isn't about the refugees. It's about censorship. It's about shutting up all who might criticize. It's about men like young Albert Ridley making himself king and executioner."

"Elliott." Father frowned into his teacup. "The Ridleys have been friends of our families for generations."

"Young Ridley would do well to remember that the next

time he sees fit to berate me publicly as if I were an errant child."

A stiff English silence filled the room, and Hugh searched for a change in conversation within his teacup.

Refugees . . . Aleida . . . Perhaps Uncle Elliott might lend insight into her dilemma. After Hugh refreshed his tea, he related the story of Aleida and Theo.

His uncle listened with fervent compassion. When Hugh finished, Uncle Elliott gave a single firm nod. "Ask her to visit my office. We might be able to assist her."

"Thank you." Hugh scribbled a reminder in his notepad and grinned at the thought of Aleida starting a new page in her own notepad with her pretty handwriting. She came to the Hart and Swan several times a week, adding her refreshing, nonjournalistic viewpoints to the banter.

Mother's eyebrows lifted in feigned innocence. "May I ask about your interest in this young lady?"

Hugh raised one hand to stop her. "Mrs. Martens lost her husband not three months ago, and she's searching for her son. I have no designs on her."

"Yes. Well." Father sent Mother a look as if begging for a reprieve.

Mother gave him none.

Father gazed at his folded hands. "Your situation has changed now. Now that . . . you have duties."

Hugh huffed. "To marry well and produce an heir to carry on the Collingwood name."

Mother's eyes turned watery, and she pressed her hand to her mouth. "You mustn't speak so flippantly."

His shoulders squirmed, and he released a sigh. Even in times of peace, such archaic notions deserved a measure of flippancy. But now a Nazi invasion loomed. How could his parents be preoccupied with an heir?

Father cleared his throat. "It's time you set aside this—this—"

"This youthful nonsense," Mother said. "You need to find a more fitting position."

"More fitting?" Uncle Elliott's voice rose. "Hugh is an excellent correspondent. Have you heard him?"

Father's nose twitched. "We don't listen to the wireless."

Why would they? Hugh's hands curled around the delicate porcelain cup. His former tutor, George Baldwin, had always told him he only needed approval from the Lord, not from any human being, not even his parents.

But it would have been nice.

"What would you have him do?" Uncle Elliott asked.

The eternal question Hugh had never been able to answer. A portrait of Cecil in dress uniform stood guard on the mantelpiece. But the military had rejected Hugh.

Father sat up straighter. "There are positions appropriate for a man of your constitution. The law, of course."

He'd be dreadful in law, and his lips folded in.

"Or the government." Mother raised a smile. "Elliott, you could find him a position."

Uncle Elliott tapped his chin with one finger. "Perhaps the Ministry of Information, given his experience with the press."

The danger to the porcelain grew too great, and Hugh set down his cup.

"Yes," Mother said. "That would do."

"That would most definitely *not* do." Uncle Elliott brandished that finger at Hugh. "Stuffing a vibrant young man like Hugh in a stodgy desk job would kill him."

"That's quite enough." Hugh bolted from his seat and marched to the window. "I have no intention of leaving the BBC."

"You must." A pleading tone drew out Mother's voice. "Parading the Collingwood name on the airwaves alongside those of crass entertainers."

"Crass entertainers?" Uncle Elliott said. "Like the BBC Symphony Orchestra?"

Hugh pressed his forehead to the window. A soaking and the risk of a lightning strike appealed far more than this conversation.

"You, Elliott." Mother's voice trembled. "You, of all people, should know the dangers of radio broadcasts. Receiving death threats."

"Death threats?" Hugh spun back to his family.

Uncle Elliott glanced over his shoulder with a chagrined expression. "You haven't heard?"

"Heard?"

"You introduced me to François Jouveau." Uncle Elliott draped his arm along the back of the sofa. "He interviewed me in a broadcast to France. We discussed the French refugees in Britain and the repatriation of French soldiers to Vichy France."

Hugh nodded. The French soldiers who had been rescued from Dunkirk in the last days of the evacuation.

Uncle Elliott cringed. "I'm afraid I mentioned the date a repatriation ship was leaving. It was sunk by a German torpedo boat."

Hugh's breath caught. The *Meknes* had been lost with over four hundred French soldiers. The number had been censored in the press, but Hugh knew.

Uncle Elliott's pained expression said he knew too.

"Oh dear." Hugh sank down to the window seat. "But it might not be related to your interview."

"Not to hear young Ridley talk."

"As I told your uncle, this wouldn't have happened in a proper newspaper interview." Mother gave Hugh a pointed look. "He and Albert Ridley almost came to blows."

Hugh's jaw dangled. "He threatened you?"

"The death threat was an anonymous letter." Uncle Elliott shrugged. "The police think it was an angry Frenchman."

"And you . . . ?"

"I think it was someone who wants to shut me up."

"I could investigate," Hugh said.

"Hugh, please." Mother patted her chest. "Haven't you caused us enough embarrassment?"

Hugh turned to the window. To the relative peace of the rain. The lightning. The thunder.

## 7

**LONDON**
**THURSDAY, AUGUST 15, 1940**

At the school in Stepney, thirty-seven women jeered at poor Edith Fuller. Aleida sat beside her on the stage, lending silent authority as a mother, according to Miss Granville.

"I did what your lot said last year, took your train into the country with my little ones." A woman shook her fist at the lectern. "That farmer woman treated me like a servant. 'Fetch this, scrub this, don't steal anything.' Never gave me a night off neither."

Miss Fuller fussed with her gray curls. "I—well, it's still vital—"

A mother in a shapeless brown dress swatted Miss Fuller's words away. "I won't send my Nellie off again. They made her sleep on the floor after she wet the bed. Called her names, they did."

Aleida's hands tensed in her lap. How was Theo being treated, wherever he was?

"Please listen, ladies." Miss Fuller's spindly fingers shook as she made a patting motion.

The jeering intensified.

Miss Fuller was supposed to be persuading the mothers of the East End to evacuate their children yet again, Miss Granville's usual job, but Miss Granville wasn't available. Just as well, because her upper-crust condescension would have grated even more than Miss Fuller's middle-class condescension.

Miss Granville had ordered Aleida not to open her mouth, lest her foreign accent lead to open hostility.

"My Bobby liked the country life." A woman shook back scraggly blond hair.

Miss Fuller stretched taller and smiled.

"Liked it too much." The blonde crossed her arms. "Why can't I have a pony, he says. Why don't we have grass and roses? Why don't we have milk and pudding every day? Your lot ruined him. He'll never have things like that. He won't."

The evacuees and their mothers faced problems Aleida had never considered. She'd taken the job to search for Theo, but maybe she was there for another reason too.

Behind the strident voices beat hurting hearts. Hearts that loved their children, that missed their children when they were apart.

"You don't understand how dangerous the situation is," Miss Fuller said.

Aleida's mouth went taut. The woman couldn't have chosen a worse set of words.

The mother in the brown dress swatted even harder. "And you don't understand us at all."

Miss Fuller's narrow face buckled. If she burst into tears, all was lost.

She was correct about the danger though. In the past few days, the Germans had switched from bombing ships to bombing airfields. The invasion would come soon, and when it did, London would be a horrific place for children. As Rotterdam had been in May.

If only they knew.

Something stirred in Aleida's veins and down to her legs. She approached the lectern. "May I speak?" she whispered to Miss Fuller.

"Miss Granville said—"

"I can't make it worse, can I?"

Miss Fuller's thin shoulders settled down a notch. "No, you can't." She backed away.

In silence, Aleida studied the thirty-five women. Two were storming out the door. Silence did its work and quieted the women into curiosity.

Without smiling, Aleida gave a nod of greeting. "My name is Aleida Martens, and I came from the Netherlands in May. I didn't stay long enough to see bombs fall on my country, but they did fall. Hundreds of men, women, and children were killed. While we were fleeing, my husband was killed by a German plane. That pilot didn't care that my husband wasn't a soldier. And I—I was separated from my son. My three-year-old boy. I don't know where he is."

Her throat clogged, and she took a moment to compose herself.

In the audience, women covered their mouths. Eyes widened.

Aleida hauled in a rough breath. "Before the Germans came, if I'd had the chance to send Theo into the English country-side, I would have. Even if he were lonely, at least he'd be safe. I'd know where he was. You ladies—you've been given that chance. I beg you to send your children to safety before the bombs start falling."

Silence returned, heavy and momentous, and Aleida let it weigh on them. Then she stepped to the table with the registration sheet, where Miss Fuller joined her.

Not all the women signed up, but some did.

Afterward, Aleida and Miss Fuller took the District Line from Stepney Green to Charing Cross Station, where they parted.

Aleida transferred to the Bakerloo Line, and she held on to a leather strap overhead as the train swayed down the tracks deep beneath the city.

On a seat near her, a woman in a dark green hat held a little girl on her lap. So many photos showed smiling evacuees playing games in flowery meadows. But how many mothers and children had struggled as the families in Stepney had?

If only Aleida could find out.

At Oxford Circus, she emerged into the sunshine and headed up Regent Street.

Everyone always welcomed her at the Hart and Swan, even though she wasn't a reporter. The conversations reminded her of living with her parents, who had encouraged her to read the papers, to know what was happening in the world.

Sebastiaan had said such knowledge was beneath a woman's comprehension and only stoked hysteria.

Aleida squared her shoulders, bought a copy of the *Times* from a newsstand, and entered the Hart and Swan. Without a hint of hysteria.

In the back room, Collie sat with a middle-aged man Aleida hadn't met.

Only the two of them, and Aleida paused.

If it were only Guy Gilbert, she'd turn and leave.

Gil flirted. Despite her cool rebuffs, he flirted. Despite Louisa chiding him for pursuing a widow of only three months, he flirted.

Collie didn't flirt, but he *was* charming. And charm made her leery.

He laughed with the voice Louisa had called golden. Caramel fit better—not just golden, but thick and rich. And sweet. Charmingly so.

He sat turned in profile to her, with caramel-colored hair rippling back from his forehead. "Every morning, Lennox leaves a gift at the foot of the bed. I must take care. It is most unpleasant, in my early-morning fogginess, to tread upon a dead mouse."

His companion chuckled. "That cat has taken a shine to you."

"In his own disturbed way, he—" Collie spotted Aleida, and he grinned and rose. "I hoped you'd come today. I brought my uncle, Elliott Hastings."

His uncle—the Member of Parliament who had offered to help. She dashed over and shook the man's hand. "It's an honor to meet you, sir."

"Ah, no, Mrs. Martens. The honor is mine in meeting you." Hazel eyes sparkled, much like Collie's. Charm apparently ran hard in the family.

Collie held out a chair for her. "Uncle Elliott said you haven't come to his office yet. I realized your hours must coincide with his, so I brought him here."

Aleida sat, set down her purse and newspaper, and studied Collie as he returned to his chair. He'd done that for her. "Thank you."

Mr. Hastings sipped amber liquid from a tumbler. "Hugh already told me your story."

Aleida raised an eyebrow at Collie. "Hugh?"

"It *is* my name." He leaned closer and cupped his hand beside his mouth. "Don't tell the others, but I much prefer it to Collie. I'm always afraid they'll toss a stick and ask me to fetch."

Aleida smiled at his joke. Humor and cheer formed the pillars of charm. Along with feigned interest in others.

But Collie's—Hugh's—interest seemed genuine.

Mr. Hastings pressed his hands together and pointed them at Aleida. "Before my nephew runs off to herd sheep and before we discuss the search for your son, I wanted to ask about your situation. Do you have a safe place to live? Does your job pay enough to cover your needs? Have you been treated well?"

"Forgive my uncle's impertinence," Hugh said. "He's quite concerned with the plight of the refugees."

"Oh." Aleida's gaze shifted from uncle to nephew, from charm to charm, from kindness to kindness. "I've been treated very well. And I have family in England, a flat in town, and plenty of money."

"Good." Mr. Hastings's mouth bent down. "Too many refugees don't, and far too few people care."

"You do." Hugh's eyes shone with pride. "If refugees could vote in your constituency, you'd win in a landslide."

"Not if the French voted." Mr. Hastings winced. "I don't blame them."

"He's received a death threat," Hugh said to Aleida.

She gasped. "A death threat?"

Mr. Hastings related how he'd broadcast the departure date of a ship repatriating French soldiers—which had been sunk by the Germans. His face twisted with regret. "The police think the death threat came from a Frenchman, but I think it's from the MoI."

"M-O-I?" Aleida hadn't heard that term.

"Ministry of Information," Hugh said. "However, if it came from someone there, Jouveau would have been threatened too. Ridley blames him even more than he blames my uncle." Hugh inclined his head toward Aleida. "Albert Ridley is a ministry advisor to the BBC."

"I see." Aleida's mind spun with questions. "Who else would threaten you?"

Hugh's mouth curved without parting, a most pleasant smile. "I'm afraid my dear uncle has more enemies than friends."

A huff came from behind her, from Mr. Irwin, the owner of the Hart and Swan. "I'm not surprised." He glared at Mr. Hastings and stomped away.

"This is why my tea is out." Hugh lowered a pout to his cup. "Irwin thinks my uncle shouldn't speak disparagingly of anyone in government. It isn't patriotic."

Aleida glanced behind her to make sure Irwin was gone, then she flicked a smile to the men. "Is Irwin a suspect?"

Mr. Hastings chuckled and raised his tumbler to Aleida. "Ah, she likes a mystery."

"I do. It's rather English of me, don't you think?"

"Quite so," the men said in unison.

Aleida did like a mystery, and she liked the company, and she liked how Hugh Collingwood looked at her with enjoyment and appreciation, as if she were unforgettable.

Her breath stopped. Charm. She knew better.

## 8

**Saturday, August 24, 1940**

A live broadcast. Even more astounding, a roundup of eight live broadcasts from throughout London.

Tamping down his excitement, Hugh squatted at the rim of the circular antiaircraft gun emplacement and aimed a torch to help Tom Young and Gerald MacTavish feed down cable so Hugh could interview the crew on duty.

If only the British public could hear the half-hour *London after Dark* program, but it would be crossing the ocean to America on the Columbia Broadcasting System. Edward R. Murrow of CBS had invited Hugh, along with correspondents from the BBC, CBS, and Canada's CBC to participate.

"Leave this area clear, men." The GPO—the Gun Position Officer—indicated an area to the rear of the gun.

"Yes, sir." Hugh shifted his torchlight for Young. He'd arrived not long after sunset to learn how the battery and the crew worked so he could report knowledgeably and clearly.

*London after Dark* was meant to give a slice of nighttime life in blacked-out London. Men were reporting from locations including the Hammersmith Palais dance hall, Euston Station, an Air Raid Precautions post, and Piccadilly Circus, to close with Big Ben tolling at midnight.

Young returned to the van and brought Hugh his headphones. "You go live at 11:40 p.m., and you'll have exactly three minutes."

"Thank you." Hugh slipped down into the gun pit, turned off the torch to spare the precious battery, and put on his headphones. He'd be able to hear the other correspondents, plus the announcer back at Broadcasting House, where the live feeds would come together and be sent by shortwave to America.

A technological feat.

"Good evening, Hugh." Albert Ridley's large form stood silhouetted by moonlight low on the horizon.

Hugh wrestled back the grimace that might tighten his voice. Instead he propped up a smile for one of his brother's oldest friends. "Bert—what a surprise to see you here."

"Surprise? Surely not as great as my surprise upon seeing your name on Murrow's list. After the censorship issues you had in Belgium." Only six years of age separated them, but he managed to sound more disapproving than Hugh's own parents.

However, Hugh had thirty years' experience with disapproval. He pulled off the headphones and climbed out of the pit so he could look Ridley eye to eye. Well, almost. Ridley stood half a foot taller than he, with a rugby player's build.

Hugh offered a rueful smile. "I'm dreadfully sorry you didn't enjoy my reports, but Murrow did. The BBC and the MoI approved my participation."

Ridley jutted out his shovel of a jaw. "Live broadcasts are dangerous, as your uncle and that blasted Frenchman proved."

If Hugh told Aleida about this conversation, she'd add Ridley to her list of suspects, writing neat notes in neat rows.

With a huff, Ridley stepped closer. "Need I remind you what's at stake? There are Nazi sympathizers in America who communicate with Germany. Watch your words."

Like a slap, but Hugh couldn't step back, away, without falling into the pit. Ridley was right. Reckless, uncensored words could bring harm.

He pulled in a ragged breath. "I promise to be careful. Now, if you'll excuse me, the broadcast is set to begin in a few minutes."

"I'll be here." Ridley tipped his bowler hat to Hugh.

Of course he would.

Hugh dropped into the gun pit and pulled on his headphones. He worked his hand beneath his coat, and the letter from George Baldwin crinkled inside his suit jacket. If only he had Lennox's night vision so he could read it again.

His former tutor reminded him to seek approval from the Lord alone, then he'd be free to do his best in the world, unfettered by the expectations of man.

Hugh sagged back against the concrete wall. What would the Lord want? Surely his heart broke at the suffering and destruction Hitler caused.

Did Hugh's work help the Allied cause or hinder it, as Ridley implied?

"Collie—your microphone."

Hugh opened his eyes. His engineer held the tool of Hugh's trade, the instrument that would carry his voice across an ocean to thousands, even millions of ears.

His hand dragged through the night air as through tar. His words could indeed cause harm. Or they could help people see and feel and think and act.

The microphone felt weighty in his hand. But right.

"It's half past eleven." Young also wore headphones so he could keep time.

Hugh's headphones crackled. The announcer stated "London after Dark" in his American accent, and he described what the listener would hear in the next half hour.

From the command post, an alarm sounded, and the battery

came alive. Men rushed out of huts and toward the four gun pits, dozens of dark figures against the purple sky.

The GPO ran over to Hugh. "I'm frightfully sorry, sir, but an air raid alarm is about to sound. We'll need—I do apologize, but—"

"But I can't be here." Hugh scrambled out of the gun emplacement, coiling cable as he moved.

Men thumped down into the pit, their steel helmets in place, gas masks slung to their sides.

"Collie!" The whites of Young's eyes shone eerily gray. "We must broadcast."

"I know." They couldn't leave three minutes of silence in the middle of the program, and it was too late to ring the BBC and ask them to fill in with something, anything.

A wail arose, the air raid siren warning civilians to take shelter. Few would, since it was the fourth alarm of the day. No bombs had fallen on London, but the airfields had been devastated over the past week and a half. Rumors were, the men of the RAF were at their breaking point.

"Sir." Hugh leveled his gaze at the GPO, even though the man had more important things to do than help a correspondent. "Where could I broadcast without being underfoot?"

His gaze darted around. "The command post. Please continue. The chaps have talked of nothing else but being on the wireless."

Hugh smiled. He understood. "Thank you."

He and Young dashed to the command post standing in the midst of the four guns.

In Hugh's headphones, the BBC's Sandy MacPherson played on the great organ at St. George's Hall.

Searchlights snapped on, dueling swords of light clashing in the dark.

The siren kept wailing, and the men at the command post called out positions to the guns, which swung as one to the southeast.

Ed Murrow's sonorous voice came live with the air raid siren in the background. "This . . . is Trafalgar Square."

"Surely you're not proceeding." Ridley stepped in front of Hugh.

Hugh held up his microphone with one hand, pressed the headphones over his ear with the other, and averted his gaze, trying to listen to Murrow describe the searchlights, a red double-decker bus.

"Hugh!"

"Not now." Hugh ground out his words, and the drone of aircraft rose in the distance.

"You can't broadcast in the middle of an air raid."

"Ed Murrow is doing so, even as we speak. Please excuse me." Hugh stepped to the side.

To his relief, Ridley backed away. Just in time for Hugh to hear Murrow set his microphone close to the ground to pick up the sound of footsteps, calm but purposeful, heading to the shelter beneath St. Martin-in-the-Fields.

"Masterful," Hugh whispered. In the simplest of words, Murrow had described the scene, and every American sitting by their wireless would see and hear London at war.

The announcer at Broadcasting House switched to the Savoy Hotel, where the band played a lively tune and Robert Bowman of the Canadian Broadcasting Company interviewed the French chef.

Bob's cheerful voice and the happy sounds of dining and dancing—Americans would love it, and Hugh smiled.

Overhead, the sirens died away, the drone faded, and searchlights winked out.

The men at the command post remained vigilant, tracking the skies with the spotter identification telescope. They wouldn't return to their huts until the all clear sounded.

The announcer cut in, interrupting the chef with his colorful accent. "Somewhere in London at this very moment, Hugh

Collingwood of the BBC is stationed at an antiaircraft gun post, and we'll hear from him now."

Hugh had a more serious story than Bob, and he set his face to match. "I'm standing by the command post of an antiaircraft battery, and I would like to give you a picture of Britain at war, Britain in action."

He described how the crew had rushed to their stations when the alarm sounded, and how the spotters prepared to call out bearings if the searchlights trapped an aircraft in their beams.

The GPO shouted a command, and searchlights popped on again.

They'd seen something. For a moment, Hugh continued his prepared talk as his mind flew over the necessary deviation—the chance for some thrilling reporting.

His time was almost up, and his voice rose in excitement. Machinery cranked beside him, enemy aircraft rumbled overhead, and the GPO called out bearings. All those sounds would be picked up in his microphone.

Young held up his hand—five, four, three, two, one, and the announcer cut off Hugh midsentence.

He didn't care. It was exhilarating.

He almost wanted to thank Hermann Göring for sending his Luftwaffe across London's skies for this moment.

But not at the cost to the airfields ringing the city, to the beleaguered fighter pilots risking their lives, shedding their blood.

Not if bombs should fall on London and her citizens.

Off to the side, Ridley walked away into the night.

Hugh saluted his defeated back. Murrow and his team were showing America the dangers England faced, her fortitude, and her cheer.

For thirty minutes, those listeners weren't in Boston or Wichita or Hollywood. They were *in* London.

That was the power of live broadcasting, and Hugh raised a grim smile.

9

With a railway map before her and a list of towns beside her, Aleida planned her survey.

When Aleida had proposed recording the problems faced by evacuees, Miss Granville had shown no interest. Until Aleida suggested a positive report might persuade mothers to send their children to the country.

Miss Granville did have concerns about a foreigner inquiring about the children, but no one else in the department was free for the venture.

Aleida marked locations where children had been received, places where she could also ask about Theo.

So many towns, and her heart dove low. But each town offered a sliver of hope.

Motion and noise, and Aleida lifted her gaze from the map.

A tall, dark-haired man in his thirties marched out of Miss Granville's private office and out of the department.

Miss Sharma scurried to Aleida's desk with a light in her big eyes. "Granny had a fit."

"Shh." Aleida couldn't allow herself to laugh at the disrespectful nickname, no matter how appropriate. "Were you listening at her door?"

"Always." Miss Sharma rested her hands on Aleida's desk and leaned closer. "I don't know who he was, but Miss Granville was not pleased at his visit. Did you notice how quickly he left?"

"You don't know who he was?" Aleida frowned at the front door. Miss Sharma had worked for the ministry for five years—two years longer than Miss Granville—and she seemed to know everyone.

And the man had entered as if he owned the place. "Doesn't he work here?" Aleida asked.

"No, I've never—"

"Ladies." Miss Fuller stood nearby, glaring at them. "We mustn't gossip, especially about our superiors."

Miss Sharma rolled her eyes for Aleida alone, then gave Miss Fuller an innocent smile. "I only wish to guard Miss Granville's schedule. That gentleman didn't have an appointment, and her time is valuable."

Aleida ducked her head to hide a smile.

"Oh! It's time for lunch. How time flies." Miss Sharma grabbed her purse.

Aleida wanted to become better acquainted with her. "Would you like to get lunch?"

"Thank you, but I'm meeting friends." She waved and departed.

"Why do you keep asking her?" Miss Fuller cast a dark gaze at the shutting door. "Those Indians eat strange foods, and they keep to themselves."

Did they keep to themselves out of choice? Or due to a lack of welcome? Aleida hardly blamed Miss Sharma, but she also disliked eating alone. "How about you, Miss Fuller? Would you like to get lunch?"

"I'm eating at home, but thank you."

Aleida stifled a sigh and set on her hat.

"Want some fish and chips?" Louisa Jones stood at the counter with two newspaper-wrapped bundles.

"Louisa!" Aleida sprang to the counter. "We've missed you this past week."

Louisa raised an eyebrow at the door shutting behind Miss Fuller. "Real friendly sorts."

"They're fine in the office. But—"

"But if you're more than one step above or below their class, most won't associate with you. Come—we foreigners can stick together."

Aleida picked up her purse and smoothed the skirt of her short-sleeved summer dress, sprigged with blue flowers like Delft china. "Still warm outside?"

"For London, yes." Louisa wore a lightweight suit of medium gray with a plum-colored blouse and matching hat. "Come, child. Chips only taste good hot."

Aleida and Louisa headed out of the Ministry of Health and toward St. James's Park. Silver barrage balloons hovered above the government buildings to force enemy aircraft to higher altitudes and decrease bombing accuracy.

"I've always found it interesting," Aleida said, "about the differences between English and Dutch society. The English have horizontal layers of class. We Dutch have vertical layers— *verzuiling*, we call it—pillarization."

"Pillarization?" Louisa's close-set green eyes brightened. "I haven't heard about that. Tell me."

Aleida passed the Treasury Building, hemmed by sandbags and armed guards. "There's a Catholic pillar, a Protestant pillar, and a nonreligious pillar. Each has its own political parties and schools and newspapers. They even have their own unions and shops and clubs. Most people never meet people outside their pillar."

"Fascinating." Louisa forged across Horse Guards Road, stopping a black taxi with the power of her gaze. "Awful, but fascinating. The human race is bound and determined to sort ourselves into categories and exclude people outside our own category."

"What do you have in America?"

"Race and nationality, of course. In Chicago, everyone has separate neighborhoods—the Irish, the Poles, the Negroes, the Chinese." Louisa picked up her pace as she entered the park. "But come, we're not here to mourn the pettiness of our fellow human beings, but to celebrate."

A bounce entered Aleida's step. "What are we celebrating?"

Louisa headed down a tree-lined path. "President Roosevelt announced he's trading destroyers to England in exchange for military bases in the Western Hemisphere. That'll keep those convoys afloat, bring more food to this island."

"That *is* good news." Shortages had arisen, even though food rationing regulated necessities from meat and butter to sugar and tea. "Will the United States enter the war?"

"Not until after the election in November." Louisa winked at her. "Roosevelt may favor the Allies, but he's a canny politician."

Weren't they all? A yellow-and-black sign stating "To the Trenches" pointed to the trench shelters dug in the park, a place to hide if caught outside during an air raid.

Aleida settled onto a bench overlooking the meandering lake, and she took a packet of fish and chips from Louisa. "Tell me about your assignment this past week."

Louisa snorted and unwrapped her meal. "The Battle of Britain is raging. The RAF fighter pilots are heroes. And all my paper wants from me is the woman's angle. Talk to the ladies in the towns near the airfields. See what they think about the raids and the pilots. At least one of those flyboys was home recovering from combat wounds when I was interviewing mother dear, so I sneaked his story into my article."

Blue skies arched above the trees, empty but for the barrage balloons. "Other than the alarms, it's hard to believe a fierce battle rages all around us."

"Fierce, yes. And deadly." Louisa's voice sank to a murmur. "And we're losing."

"Losing?" Aleida whispered. "But the papers—"

"The papers say what the people need to hear so they keep their spirits up." Louisa gnawed on a chip. "Yes, more German planes are falling than British, and the factories are churning out plenty of fighter planes. But the men are exhausted. And they're dying."

Aleida shuddered. If the RAF were defeated, the German army would cross the Channel. She had to find Theo before they did. Searching for him now was hard enough. How could she do so in the turmoil of invasion? In the oppression of occupation?

"But we're here to celebrate." Louisa slapped the park bench. "Tell me something good, something funny. I'll even settle for gossip."

Settle? She lived for it. Aleida took a bite of tender, flaky fish and searched her thoughts for something light. "The other day, Jouveau and MacLeod were teasing Hugh about his jumbled notes, and—"

"Hugh? You mean, Collie?"

Aleida shrugged. Was she betraying a secret? "He told me to call him Hugh."

"Did he now?" A smile exploded on Louisa's face. "I knew it. He's sweet on you."

"Sweet on me?" She hadn't heard that term, but she could figure it out. "I don't think so."

"Open your eyes, child. He looks at you as if no one else was in the room."

"That's his way. That's how he talks to everyone."

Louisa chewed and swallowed. "When you aren't there, his

attention bounces between us and the door. As soon as you arrive, the bouncing stops. I've never seen him do that before."

The way he looked at her, as if riveted to every word—it was heady. Disconcertingly so. "He's too charming."

"Hmm." Louisa frowned at the sky. "Let me guess, Sebastiaan was charming."

A chip turned mealy in Aleida's mouth, and she swallowed. "Quite."

"Why was he charming? For what purpose?"

"To make people like him. So he could control them. So he could win."

Nodding joined the frowning. "Why do you think Collie is charming?"

Aleida opened her mouth to say, "The same," but it didn't seem right.

"Stumped you?" Louisa gestured to her with a limp chip. "Collie's charm comes from his utter fascination in people, in their stories, what makes them tick. And he likes them. When someone finds you interesting, you find them interesting too. That is true charm. That's what people like Sebastiaan fake for their own purposes."

How could one determine the purpose behind someone's charm? How could one avoid getting ensnared by a person with cruel motives?

Louisa stared at Aleida's lap.

She was tapping a chip, tapping it so hard, she'd mashed a hole in it.

"Don't worry about Collie." Louisa raised one eyebrow. "He's seen how you act when Gil asks you out."

Aleida groaned. "Gil."

"He isn't as bad as you think. Decent fellow, just desperate. You've seen how he limps, how he never uses his right hand."

Had she? Aleida hadn't noticed.

"Cerebral palsy," Louisa said. "He's a brilliant young man,

works hard, and he's built a solid career. But he underestimates himself and comes on too strong."

"I had no idea." Poor Gil simply faded in Hugh's bright light.

"He resents Collie's easy life—high class, money, any job he wants, and everyone likes him. Because he likes everyone, even Gil. Even though Gil can't stand him. And Gil wants what Collie has. Now Collie is sweet on you, so Gil wants to win you first."

Aleida's eyes were drying, and she reminded herself to blink. "You know all this?"

Louisa flipped her hand over her shoulder and raised a beatific smile. "Child, I'm a writer. I know all things. Some say I guess all things. Some say I fabricate. I prefer 'know.'"

"I . . . I know nothing."

"That, my child." Louisa thrust a chip rather too close to Aleida's face. "That humility is part of your charm. That and your directness are why all the golden goodness of Hugh Collingwood focuses squarely on you."

If only it didn't.

10

**Friday, September 6, 1940**

In Hugh's study at the townhouse, Lennox batted at the type bars stamping the page.

Hugh untangled the *M* and the *N*. "Whatever did I do before you became my editor?"

Since Uncle Elliott's handwriting was as atrocious as Hugh's, he was typing up his uncle's list of institutions that worked with children and adding addresses.

Lennox sat on the open telephone book and wrapped his gray tail around his white-tipped feet.

Right below that fuzzy gray, Hugh read the address for the Waifs and Strays Society in Kennington. The tail whapped twice on the page.

Hugh leaned back in his chair. "Do you doubt my motives, good sir? Doubt, you should. Am I doing this for the lady's benefit or my own?"

Lennox's green eyes gave him no quarter.

"Ah, Lennox. If you heard her laugh. It's like a carillon. Is it wrong to want to elicit that laugh, to bring beauty into this drab world?"

One slow feline blink challenged him.

Hugh sighed. "I know she's a recent widow, and she's anxious about her son. Yet here I come." He put on a smarmy voice. "I brought you a list, my dear. Prepare to fall in love."

Lennox stood, stretched his back, and sauntered across the typewriter keys.

Now the address read, "Kennington, S.E. 11 x:u."

Hugh hit the carriage return and typed the next item on the list. "The honorable course of action would be to bring her the list at the Hart and Swan and not ask her to dinner."

With his elbows on the desk, he stretched up his hands, his fingers splayed, and he groaned. "Or am I being ridiculous? 'Faint heart never won fair lady,' and all."

Lennox sniffed Hugh's ring finger.

He'd never come this close, and Hugh froze.

The cat ducked his gray head and brought it up under Hugh's hand.

Before he could think, his fingers curved down into warm softness. He'd seen people scratching cats and dogs behind the ears. Was Lennox asking for that?

Holding his breath, he slowly, reverently gave a tentative scratch.

Lennox nudged his hand higher, a bit to the side.

"I'm sorry. Did I scratch the wrong spot?" Hugh scratched where indicated, and the cat leaned into it.

Warmth and softness and awe flowed into Hugh's smile. A gift as precious as Aleida's laughter.

Perhaps Hugh could stretch out his hand to Aleida. She could turn up her pretty nose and walk away. Or she could lean in.

Only one way to find out.

Down the length of the light oak table in the Programme Conference Room on the fourth floor of Broadcasting House, Norman Fletcher and Albert Ridley stared each other down.

Hugh sat back to avoid the electric current between the men, entertaining though it was.

Ridley sat straight with his massive hands clasped before him on the table. "The BBC simply must do better. First, that dreadful mess caused by François Jouveau and Elliott Hastings, and now—"

"I beg your pardon." Fletcher spoke in measured tones, but the taut muscles below his chin gave away his anger. "Jouveau works for the BBC European Services, not the Home Service and not in Programming. I have no authority over him."

"Regardless." Ridley snapped up one hand. "It speaks of a general recklessness. Now I've heard from our men in the United States. On a recent broadcast to America, one of your correspondents allowed his microphone to pick up the shouting of coordinates. Any Nazi sympathizers in the States could send that information to Germany, information that would allow the German Air Force to improve their navigation."

Only if Hugh had broadcast his own position, which he hadn't.

Ridley avoided Hugh's gaze. Whether out of deference for his old friend Cecil or for the Collingwood family, it wasn't fair to the other men in the room, who would have been called out by name in similar circumstances.

"That was my report," Hugh said. "On Columbia's *London after Dark*. Since I never revealed my location, the coordinates were meaningless and the enemy would have received no comfort. However, I promise to be more careful in the future."

With a lift to his broad nose, Ridley strengthened his glare at Fletcher. "This wouldn't happen if all reports were read from scripts, recorded in the studio, and edited before broadcast."

The man didn't understand how radio worked.

Hugh sat forward. "I do understand your position, Mr. Ridley, but reporting live and on the scene lends power and immediacy. Look how Ed Murrow and Eric Sevareid and Larry

LeSueur are swaying the hearts of the American people by conveying the sounds and voices of our fair city. That's the future of broadcasting."

Ridley's dark eyes narrowed. "I expected better from you, Hugh."

"Better?" And why the overly familiar use of his given name?

"What's more important? The future of broadcasting or the future of England?"

Hugh's breath caught.

Across the table from Hugh, Guy Gilbert bunched his pale eyebrows together. "If England falls, there will be no BBC, no true news, only vapid readings of German propaganda."

"Right you are." Ridley nodded. "Hugh, you should listen to . . . to your colleague."

Gil's moment of victory disappeared, as did the glint in his eyes. What did Gil gain in earning Ridley's favor if Ridley didn't know his name?

He knew Hugh's. Because Hugh came from the same circle. Gil didn't, nor did Fletcher. But Gil worked hard, and his heart was in the right place.

Hugh gave Gil a soft frown. "Thank you, Mr. Gilbert. That is a sobering thought."

It was. But also sobering was the thought of adopting fascism in order to fight it. Surely a better way could be found.

## 11

Aleida tore off coupons for her weekly ration of two ounces of tea and eight ounces of sugar, and she handed them to Mr. Byrne, the grocer.

"It isn't right," a woman behind her muttered to her friend. "Foreigners stealing our food."

Aleida's cheeks burned. Since she didn't take sugar in her tea, she only took her ration every few weeks.

"Foreigners, Mrs. Winslow?" A frown crossed Mr. Byrne's wide face and deepened the wrinkles around his mouth. "Like the Polish fighter pilots shooting down Huns faster than even our boys do? Like Mrs. Martens here who volunteers with my wife at the ARP? I think you meant to say Allies, not foreigners."

Mrs. Winslow spluttered out embarrassed apologies, probably worried about losing favor with the grocer who controlled the supply of rationed goods.

Aleida gave Mr. Byrne a grateful smile and headed outside into a warm and sunny afternoon. Thank goodness, far more Londoners shared Mr. Byrne's attitude than Mrs. Winslow's.

Aleida had spent her day off visiting orphanages, giving each her address in case a boy matching Theo's description arrived.

The man at the last orphanage she'd visited had suggested that Aleida give up her search. If Theo was in England and hadn't been sent to an orphanage, that meant the couple was caring for him. And as long as Theo was safe, what else mattered?

The audacity! Aleida would sooner give up her life than give up her son.

Her hand tightened on her string bag. One hundred twenty days since she'd seen Theo. Twelve times ten—and yet no success.

She sighed, forced her hand to relax, and turned onto Montpelier Square.

A man strolled toward her—Hugh Collingwood, suave in a light gray pin-striped suit. He raised a confident smile and tipped his fedora to her. "Good afternoon, Aleida."

Her heart lurched in an unnerving mix of joy and apprehension. "Good afternoon."

He gestured toward her building. "I see why you weren't at home. May I help with your package?"

Such a small bag, but she passed it his way. "Thank you. What . . ." How could she word it without sounding rude?

"Why am I here?" His smile never faltered. "I brought the list my uncle promised."

A gasp flew out, and she restrained herself from snatching the portfolio from his hand.

"Hold on," he said with a laugh. "Shall we take in your groceries first?"

"Yes, yes." She trained her eyes to her path so she wouldn't trip over the doorstep. Hugh held open the door for her, and she trotted up to her second-floor flat, plunged the key into the lock, and swept inside.

Hugh paused inside the door, and his smile collapsed.

On the coatrack hung Theo's little gray cap and blue coat.

"When I find him," she said, "I'll be ready."

With his lips pressed tight, Hugh handed her the portfolio. "I'll put your bag in the kitchen."

At the round card table with its top of inlaid wood, Aleida tugged her notebook out of her purse and opened Hugh's portfolio.

A full typewritten page lay before her. She pressed both hands to her chest, and her eyes watered. So many homes and institutions and societies. Some already graced her list, but many didn't.

"Thank you, Hugh. Please thank Mr. Hastings for me."

He returned from the kitchen, sat across from her, and set his hat on the table. "I will."

Something was wrong though. "In what order is the list? It isn't alphabetical. Is it by borough?"

Hugh raised one eyebrow. "The order my uncle thought of them, I suppose."

How could Aleida write down information until she put it in order?

"My apologies for the typographical errors." Hugh crossed his arms on the table and leaned forward. "I take full credit for some, but some I can honestly blame on my cat."

She smiled. "Lennox."

"No matter what I'm reading or writing, he simply must sit upon it, and he plays with the typewriter as I work. He is no ordinary cat." His eyes shone with almost-paternal pride.

Happy memories of her family's many cats filled her mind. "There are no ordinary cats."

His smile flashed, edging up his faded freckles. "I shouldn't be surprised. For the first time, I'm learning what fascinating creatures they are."

"You've never had a cat? Do the Collingwoods prefer dogs?"

His gaze dimmed. "No dogs either."

"Oh?" She rested her chin in her palm. "I thought all Englishmen kept a pack of hounds."

The sparkle returned to his eyes. "There are no ordinary Englishmen."

Aleida laughed and ducked her gaze. Hugh Collingwood, for one, was anything but ordinary. She found the next page in her notebook. She ought to list them by borough, but she wasn't familiar enough with London.

Hugh leaned back in the chair. "I wish I were as organized as you. I'm forever misplacing things, and I have a dickens of a time finding my notes."

Having seen the inside of his notebook, she wasn't surprised. "I could teach you."

His eyebrows sprang toward the wavy lock of caramel hair he should have smoothed after removing his hat. But she was glad he hadn't.

"Could you?" he said. "I'm rather a hopeless case."

"I could help at least a little." Her cheeks warmed. Was it wise to offer to spend more time with him? She waved at the blank page before her. "If anything, I'm too orderly. Look—I can't write a word until I decide how to organize the list."

His gaze circled her flat, and his toe tapped on the wooden floor. "Your notebook is orderly, your flat neat, and you even perform your mannerisms with precision."

"My mannerisms?"

He grinned at her notebook. "Every time you turn a page, you smooth it three times. To the top corner, to the bottom corner, then straight across."

She did, didn't she? But once wasn't enough. Neither was twice. Thrice was perfect.

Hugh walked to the fireplace and rested his hand on the mantel. "If you'd like, I could teach you to be less organized."

What an idea! "That would allow me to work faster."

Hugh's smile grew in strength and mischief, and with one finger, he nudged a candlestick on the mantel an inch to the side.

It looked wrong. She should ignore it. After he left, she could fix it.

He moved it another inch.

Aleida darted to the fireplace and slid the candlestick back in place. "Let's not be hasty."

Hugh's laugh rolled out, rich and melodious. "I won't do that again, at least not on purpose."

"Maybe I don't want to learn after all."

"I can see why." He stood several inches taller than she, tall enough, but not overwhelming. "You can find things."

She ran one finger along the polished oak mantel. "And routines keep my life in control."

"They do?" His voice pitched higher. "Your life?"

Her mouth slipped open, and she gazed into the browns and greens and golds in Hugh's eyes. Did routines keep her life in control? Impossible. They controlled her minutes and days, yes. But not her life.

"Perhaps," he said, "they make you feel controlled. That could be comforting."

Aleida wobbled, and she gripped the mantel for support. "That would be a false comfort. I can control only my words and actions, not those of others. I know that. I do."

"Then you're human. What we know and what we believe can be two separate matters. We know what we know, but we don't always know what we believe."

"I don't understand." Her hand rested only a few inches from his, but she didn't move it.

"Forgive me for speculating." His eyebrows drew together over softened eyes. "Perhaps deep inside, deep beneath your knowing, you believe if you do certain things just so, you'll find Theo."

Worse. If she neglected to do them, she'd never find him.

Her eyes shut. "I must. I simply must find him."

"I can't begin to imagine how overwhelming this must be

for you." His voice dipped low and rough. "If you don't mind, I'll pray for you. The Lord knows where Theo is."

"He does." She knew that. But did she believe it? Considering how little she'd prayed in the past four months, maybe she didn't. "Thank you. I—I need to pray too."

His mouth curved in a gentle smile.

What were his motives?

Kindness, genuine interest, concern for her and for little Theo.

She knew and she believed.

Hugh drew in a breath. "I should go. I didn't mean to stay, only to deliver the list."

"Oh." Disappointment sagged in her chest. Surprisingly so. "Oh yes."

She walked him to the door, and he picked up his hat on the way.

In the open doorway, he paused and faced her. "I admit I did come for another reason—to ask if you'd like to accompany me to dinner tonight."

"At the Hart and Swan?"

"I'd like to take you to the Savoy."

He was asking her on a date, and her heart and her face froze.

"Oh dear." Hugh grimaced. "It does sound as if I brought the list for the sole purpose of enticing you on a date. I promise, I didn't. The list—I would have brought it anyway. To the Hart and Swan. I should have done that after all. I didn't want to wait until Monday, but—"

"It's all right." The poor man—she'd never seen him undone.

"No, it isn't all right. You've been widowed only . . . four months and—"

"Not quite four."

"Not quite four," he said with definition. "And you're searching for your son. The last thing you need is a correspondent bumbling into your life."

Nothing suave or confident about him now, and her heart went out to him. "That wasn't charming at all."

He squeezed his eyes shut and jerked his chin to the side. "My apologies. I'll leave now."

"No, that's what I liked. I'll go."

Hugh turned back to her and gave his head a little shake. "Pardon?"

With her hands gripped together, she took one step closer. "You're right. It is too early, and I need to find my son, but I would like to go to dinner with you."

Incomprehension raced in furrows across his forehead. Then comprehension dawned, and a smile stretched wide. "Very well, then."

He bounded down the hallway.

Aleida leaned out the door. "Hugh? What time?"

He spun back with a laugh. "Six o'clock?"

Her wristwatch read 4:43. "I'll see you then."

Hugh waved and raced down the stairs. He was rather darling when he bumbled.

A wail rose outside. The air raid siren. Again. They had to sound it whenever German planes came near London, but false alarms interfered with sleep and routines.

Hugh raced back up the stairs. "Do you have a shelter?"

"We have Anderson shelters in the garden. I'll show you the way."

He shook his head. "I meant for you. But would you please show me to the roof beforehand?"

Of course, the reporter wanted to watch for action. "This way."

She led him upstairs and onto the roof. The sun blazed warm to the west, an hour and a half from setting.

To the southeast, silver sparkled in the sky, streaming closer and closer, bigger and bigger.

"Hundreds," Hugh mumbled. "There must be hundreds of aircraft."

A sickening feeling churned in Aleida's belly. "They're over London, aren't they?"

"I'm sure they're passing over to bomb an airfield." Hugh shielded his eyes with his hand. "And yet . . ."

"And yet?"

His face darkened. "They never bomb airfields en masse, always in small groups."

Hollow booms rose from the east. Shafts of fire and smoke.

"They're hitting the East End." Hugh pointed toward the Thames. "I should be there."

"Be where?" Where bombs were falling?

He slapped on his hat. "The bombers will be gone by the time I arrive."

But the stories wouldn't. Something strange stirred within her. "May I come with you?"

Hugh met her gaze for the first time since the raid started. "You should go to the shelter."

How could she explain it? "For four years I was isolated. I—I want to be in the middle of things."

His expression shifted. It was faint, but it was a smile. "Let's go."

They hurried downstairs and down the street to Knightsbridge Station.

A Home Guardsman stopped them at the entrance. "I'm sorry. No sheltering in the Tube."

Hugh pulled out his wallet and flashed a card. "I'm with the BBC. I need to report on the air raid. She's with me."

Aleida offered a feeble smile.

"Hugh Collingwood?" The Guardsman's mouth dangled open. "Me and the wife love your stories."

"Thank you, sir." Hugh gestured to the entrance. "May I? Are the trains running?"

"Yes. Yes, they are." He stepped back and let them through.

Hugh and Aleida paid their fare and trotted down staircase

after staircase to the almost-deserted platform and onto an almost-deserted train.

She sat beside him. "Why won't they let people shelter down here? This seems safer than the layer of tin in an Anderson shelter."

Hugh rested his hands in his lap. "I interviewed a man from the London City Council. They're afraid we'll become a city of cave dwellers. If they let us in, we'll never come out. It's rather absurd, in my opinion."

That didn't make sense. "What about neighborhoods without gardens for Anderson shelters? I didn't see any gardens when I visited the East End with the Ministry of Health."

"That's where the bombs are falling." Hugh frowned out the window as concrete walls swished by.

Aleida tapped her knuckles. Of all the places in London, the East End would tempt the Germans most, with docks and shipyards. And of all the places in London, the East End would be the most vulnerable, with working-class citizens crammed into poorly constructed tenements.

In half an hour, they arrived at Stepney Green Station.

With his hand to the small of Aleida's back, Hugh guided her up the stairs. "Stay close. Let's not get separated."

His protectiveness felt chivalrous, not controlling, so she nodded.

On the ground floor, they headed outside.

Aleida stopped short. A few streets ahead, flames roared, orange and angry and devouring. Buildings lay crumpled. Jagged spires of masonry pierced the twilit sky. Red embers floated on the wind, winking, taunting, eluding. Menacing.

Beside her, Hugh stood motionless. While stories whirled around him.

Time for his first lesson in organization, and she tucked her hand in the crook of his arm. "Your notebook, Hugh." Her voice sounded small. "Open to a fresh page. Date it at the top.

Start interviewing, and don't change pages until you fill the first one."

Hugh shook himself and charged ahead.

At the first collapsed building, he found a blue-helmeted ARP incident officer directing a rescue party, and he fired questions without getting in their way.

Piles of rubble lay before Aleida, and moans and cries issued from the ruins. Her hands itched to help, but with a rescue party on the scene, it was best to stand back unless directed to assist. Removing debris without proper care could cause rubble to fall onto victims below.

A man stumbled down a pile of wreckage, aided by a rescue party worker with an *R* on his helmet. Bright red streaked the gray dust coating the victim's clothing.

"Jack!" a woman cried.

"I'm all right, Betty." Jack raised a shaky hand to her and sank to the pavement. A man from a stretcher party, his helmet marked by *SP*, wrapped Jack's bleeding head with a bandage.

Betty rushed to her husband, towing a small boy. She wore a shapeless brown dress. "Nellie! Where's Nellie?"

Aleida gasped. One of the women from the meeting. Nellie was the little girl whose foster family had mistreated her for wetting the bed.

"She—she was in the kitchen." Jack pointed out the direction to the rescue party.

"My little girl! Someone, help!" Betty's gaze swung around and landed on Aleida. "You were at that meeting. From the government."

"I was." Aleida dropped Hugh's arm and went to Betty. "See, they're searching for your daughter now."

Betty raked her free hand deep into her brown hair. "Why— why didn't I send her away?"

Aleida patted Betty's shoulder. "Please don't doubt yourself. I know you love your daughter."

"Here! Over here!" A man from the rescue party dug through the ruins.

A small, limp arm lay on the rubble.

"Nellie! Nellie!" Betty's voice shattered.

The party shoved aside broken masonry. Then they hovered over the place they'd excavated, quiet and still.

"Oh no." Aleida wound her arm around Betty's thin shoulders. If the child were alive, they'd be hurrying.

"Nellie! Nellie? She's all right, isn't she? She's just asleep, isn't she?"

One of the men turned toward Betty, and his face warped with devastation.

"No . . ." Betty sagged.

Aleida embraced her, stumbling under the weight of her body and her grief.

Strong arms wrapped around both Aleida and Betty—Hugh, supporting, comforting.

Betty moaned and sobbed.

The poor woman. Aleida murmured to her, but her throat clogged. She knew what it was like to lose a child—and yet she didn't.

Aleida still had hope.

12

A stiff westerly wind toyed with Hugh's fedora and the hem of his trench coat while he waited for the bombers.

They would come. They had come every day and every night for almost a fortnight.

The deflating balloon of a moon overhead guaranteed their arrival.

Standing on the roof of Broadcasting House, Hugh interviewed Edward R. Murrow of CBS, who was preparing to broadcast live to the United States.

Murrow's serious dark eyes and serious dark voice drove his point home. "The people of America have heard the courage of the people of London, that calm strength. You've shown the world how a free people can live in the most trying of circumstances."

"Thank you, Mr. Murrow," Hugh said. "And tonight, my dear listeners, if an air raid should come, if the bombs should fall, we will not be alone, for the citizens of America shall be listening alongside us. This is Hugh Collingwood reporting from somewhere in London."

Tom Young gave the signal, and the recording ended.

"Excellent, Ed. Thank you." Hugh handed his microphone to Murrow. Young's team would aid Murrow as well, but Murrow's report would air live in America. Hugh's recording would air tomorrow.

Hugh had behaved himself. In his interview, he hadn't asked Murrow about his struggle with the Ministry of Information to be allowed to broadcast live from the rooftop. He hadn't even hinted at how Murrow had appealed to Winston Churchill himself to obtain that permission.

Hugh had respected his editor while meeting the needs of his audience.

He joined François Jouveau at the railing around the roof and nudged his friend with his elbow. "Norman Fletcher is visiting his wife and children in the country." Not far from the Collingwood estate, as it turned out.

Under his black homburg, Jouveau gazed hard at Hugh. "Fletcher's no friend of mine."

"He took Gil with him." Hugh leaned his elbows on the railing. Fletcher had scowled at Hugh when he announced this, adding, "Not all of us have an ancestral country estate to escape to on the weekends." Then Fletcher proceeded to deride Elliott Hastings for throwing a lavish country house party with guests staying for days—while London burned.

Jouveau raised one eyebrow.

Why indeed had he told Jouveau about Fletcher and Gil? He grinned. "With Fletcher away, perhaps I could sneak a live broadcast into the programming."

"Is that possible?"

Hugh shrugged. "I won't, tempting though it may be." Not only would it end his career, but it would end Fletcher's, which wasn't fair or right.

Besides, his work had never been so vital. Now that London was the front line of the war, he was reporting hard news again.

Jouveau sniffed and pointed his chin to the side. "Another reason to resist temptation."

Albert Ridley approached in his black bowler hat and Savile Row overcoat. He frowned at Hugh and glared at Jouveau.

But Hugh offered a smile. "Good to see you, Bert. I came by your office today, but your secretary said you were out."

"I was here in London. I was in meetings all day." His voice sharpened as if Hugh had accused him of idleness.

"Ah, but your secretary answered my question, so all is well."

Jouveau tilted his head in Murrow's direction. "Did you come to see the Yankee make history?"

"A circus is more like it."

Hugh gave a nonchalant shrug. "I know live, on-the-scene reporting of air raids isn't possible here in Britain—American broadcasting *is* rather more advanced . . ." He waited for his statement—though quite untrue—to awaken Ridley's patriotic fervor.

Awaken it did. Ridley inhaled sharply. "Surely you don't mean that. Why, the BBC is the premier—"

The air raid siren released its howl, rising and falling in lament for the hundreds of lives to be lost in the coming hours. Already several thousand civilians had perished in the Blitz.

Searchlights slashed across the partly cloudy sky.

After Ridley left to talk to Young, Hugh turned to the southeast, the usual route of attack. He would take notes on the raid, but he wouldn't use most of them. BBC news reports typically stated, "Damage is slight and casualties are few."

Hugh had to find other angles. Tonight, to enhance his interview of Murrow, he'd report on the reporters reporting. The British people were fascinated by Murrow and treated his team like royalty.

Hugh flipped open his notebook to a page with a bit of remaining space.

No, he needed to follow Aleida's advice.

Under the shifting bluish searchlight beams, Hugh found an empty page, wrote the date at the top, and even underlined it as Aleida would do.

Hollow booms of antiaircraft fire sounded by the Thames in the ravaged East End.

After their first aborted date that tragic evening, Hugh hadn't asked Aleida out again. It seemed wrong with bombers coming nightly. Besides, he now worked every night, and she had ARP duty one evening in eight.

However, he saw her at the Hart and Swan more often than ever, in the early evenings before the raids. The last two days, service at the pub had been atrocious. Mr. Irwin hadn't come in, nor had he informed his staff of his absence.

Hugh frowned. It wasn't like Irwin.

The bombers droned closer, and Hugh searched the skies for where searchlights "coned" enemy aircraft, trapping them in their beams and illuminating them for antiaircraft gun crews.

From his eighth-story perch, Hugh traced the streets to Aleida's neighborhood. Had she gone to the shelter, or had she surrendered to the strange thrill felt by so many Londoners—by Hugh? Watching bombs fall like a child standing in the rain heedless of lightning.

Murrow went on the air, and a glowing cigarette jiggled in his free hand.

The Luftwaffe contributed to the punch of the broadcast, flying nearer as if homing in on Murrow's signal, as if aiming for the American.

Hugh's heart raced as he scratched down notes. Antiaircraft fire thumped, aircraft roared, bombs pounded a few streets away, the floor rumbled beneath him, and Murrow continued his slow, methodical report.

The raid seemed lighter than usual, maybe only a hundred aircraft, but what did that matter to those who would lose homes or loved ones?

When Murrow finished, the men on the rooftop began to depart. The raid continued, but one building was as dangerous as another. Hugh might as well take his chances in his own Anderson shelter, where he might be able to sleep.

He and Jouveau headed downstairs, then Jouveau headed east into the Soho district favored by European immigrants, and Hugh west to Mayfair.

By the filtered light of his shielded torch, he made his way through Oxford Circle past the Tube entrance. The authorities had quickly decided to let Londoners shelter in the Underground—after East Enders "invaded" stations.

Hugh turned down Oxford Street, which had been devastated in a raid only three nights earlier. At Hugh's townhouse, the raid had knocked down artwork and plaster and sent Lennox skittering under Hugh's bed.

Crews had cleared most of the rubble and broken glass on Oxford Street. A gaping black hole was all that remained of the John Lewis shop, but D.H. Evans and Bourne & Hollingworth were already close to reopening.

A yawn contorted his face. Like everyone in town, he received precious little sleep with air raids day and night.

Through a gap in the buildings, fiery red glowed to the south, silhouetting a handful of bombers. Now that the Luftwaffe had shifted their attacks from fighter airfields to London, RAF Fighter Command was rebuilding strength. Fields were being repaired, aircraft were no longer destroyed on the ground, and the pilots could sleep.

If only they could attack the bombers at night, but they simply hadn't the means to locate the raiders in the dark. Only four German night bombers had fallen in September, and all to antiaircraft guns.

However, the Germans had made a critical strategic mistake. If Hitler had known how close he'd come to wiping out the RAF, he wouldn't have switched to bombing London.

Hugh blew out a long breath and a grateful prayer, and he climbed the steps to the blacked-out townhouse.

A light shined from the sitting room, so Hugh quickly shut the door behind him.

"Mowrp." Lennox trotted up to Hugh and rubbed against his leg.

"Good evening, sir." Hugh let the cat sniff his fingers. As soon as he received approval, Hugh rubbed Lennox's soft head, then down to his neck, over his arched back, then up the fuzzy gray pinnacle of his tail.

Perhaps the daily brush with death made Lennox more appreciative. Regardless, the affection made Hugh's heart hum.

"Good evening, Mr. Collingwood." Simmons stood in the doorway to the sitting room.

Hugh tilted his head at the butler. "You didn't go to the shelter?"

"I was waiting for you." Simmons's face stretched long. "Your father rang. He wants you to ring him back, no matter the hour."

No matter the hour? A hole as black and gaping as a bombed-out lot opened beneath him, tugging at his ankles and coattails. Had something happened to Mother?

Hugh dashed to the sitting room, to the phone, and he forced his wooden fingers to dial the operator. The connection took long, too long, but in time his father answered.

Father never rang or answered—Mother did the ringing and the staff the answering. "Hugh?" Father's voice faltered. "Thank goodness. I'm afraid your mother is too distraught to come to the phone. Your Uncle Elliott—he's dead."

Hugh sank into a chair. "Dead?"

A hiccup filled the pause. "Murdered."

Hugh gripped the arm of his chair, and that gaping black hole whirled.

# 13

**HERTFORDSHIRE**
**FRIDAY, SEPTEMBER 27, 1940**

Instead of writing your appointments on scraps of paper, write them straightaway into your diary. It takes no more time." Aleida sorted bits of paper tucked in Hugh's diary. Dates without times, times without places . . . how did he manage to get where he needed to be?

He hadn't responded.

As the train chugged down the Buntingford Branch Line, Hugh stared out the window, atypically listless.

"Hugh?" she said in a soft voice.

"Hmm?" His gaze swam around before finding her, then he frowned at his diary. "I apologize. I'm a dreadful pupil and frightfully poor company."

"Another time." She hadn't come to be entertained. In the week since Elliott Hastings's death, Hugh had been distracted and restless, insisting that he wouldn't attend the funeral, which made no sense. But grief often made no sense.

Then Aleida had mentioned that Buntingford was on her survey list. Could Hugh introduce her around? As a foreigner, she could use the help of a local. Hugh had invited her to stay at his parents' home . . . and realized she'd convinced him to attend the funeral.

"Here we are," Hugh said. "Welcome to Buntingford."

The train pulled into a red brick station with a steeped roof. As in all railway stations, the signs had been removed to confuse any invaders—but outsiders suffered as well.

Hugh retrieved their suitcases from the overhead rack and led Aleida to the platform. Along with a half dozen other passengers, they passed through the station building and turned left onto the main road into town, hemmed by greenery.

"I do thank you for coming." Hugh frowned at the cloudy sky. "It *is* only proper that I attend the funeral, but I dread it, dread what people will say, especially my parents. Perhaps with a guest present, they will be kinder."

A cool breeze played with the rim of her hat. "Why would they not be kind?"

"They blame me for my uncle's death. Well, not directly, but they blame the press." His mouth twisted to one side. "And I—I blame myself."

"Nonsense." She studied his expression, shadowed by his fedora. "How could you possibly be to blame?"

He jerked his head to the side. "Everything's a lark to me. Even a death threat is nothing but a bit of sport. If I had taken it seriously, I would have investigated, asked more questions."

Aleida stopped to force him to turn to her. When he did, she leveled a sober gaze at him. "Don't do this. The police took it seriously. They investigated and asked questions. And they couldn't prevent it. Neither could you."

Hugh mashed his lips together. "I have to find out who did this."

"Very well." Aleida resumed walking. "What do we know? He was shot on his estate grounds whilst hosting a house party."

Hugh's oxfords slapped the pavement. "At daybreak, Uncle

Elliott went to survey the hunting grounds. They found him later that morning in the woods, shot with his own gun straight in the chest at close range."

"They know it wasn't an accident?"

"There were signs of a struggle, two sets of footprints, and there were no fingerprints on the gun, even though Uncle Elliott wasn't wearing gloves."

"So the killer wiped it clean."

"He did." Hugh's jaw edged forward. "This was no accident."

"Who are the suspects?"

"His guests were friends and colleagues, but many had motive." Hugh crossed a lane running beside a gray stone church. "Uncle Elliott made political enemies and professional enemies—he had several rows with my editor, for example. And he was known for his . . . romantic entanglements. My aunt divorced him several years ago. A lot of people didn't like him even if they pretended to."

Aleida sighed. "I liked him."

"As did I." He raised a melancholy smile.

Even sad, Hugh radiated charm. But a safe charm.

Aleida walked beside him past buildings of white and gray. He hadn't asked her out to dinner since the first night of the Blitz. Completely understandable. Everyone was exhausted by endless days and nights of bombs, and Hugh was busier than ever on the job and now mourning his uncle.

She'd been forgotten, and for the better. She had no business starting a romance when she had a son to find.

They passed a red brick church, and a market square opened up. "Market Hill, St. Peter's Church, the Crown." Hugh nodded toward a red brick pub with cobalt blue trim.

He led her into the next building of creamy stone. Upstairs, they entered an office.

An attractive brunette in the smart bottle-green uniform of the Women's Voluntary Service rose from behind the desk.

"Hugh." She stretched out his name with fondness. "How good to see you."

"Cathy." He set down the suitcases, took both her hands, and appraised her. "You look marvelous. I see John is taking excellent care of you."

"Yes. Yes, he is." A tilt of her head, and she released Hugh's hands.

"Cathy, may I introduce Mrs. Martens with the Ministry of Health? Mrs. Martens, this is Mrs. John Fielding."

"How do you do?" Aleida shook the woman's hand. "Thank you for meeting with me."

"I don't see why this is necessary." Mrs. Fielding's smile cooled, and she waved Hugh and Aleida toward two chairs before her desk and settled into her own chair. "As the billeting officer in Buntingford, I ensure our evacuees are happy and healthy."

"We are most thankful." Aleida crossed her hands on top of her purse. "By interviewing evacuees and foster families, we hope to convince the mothers of London of that fact. Far too many are reluctant to send their children away, even with bombs falling. Even with children . . . dying." Aleida's throat clamped at the thought of little Nellie lying in the rubble.

Cathy's eyelashes fluttered. "In that case, I can help. I'll ring some families and make appointments for you. Tomorrow?"

"Tomorrow afternoon, please," Hugh said.

After the funeral. Aleida gave him a soft smile.

"Very well." Cathy stood and offered her hand. "I assure you, you'll find nothing amiss in Buntingford."

"Indeed." Aleida stood too. "One more thing—have you seen a little boy among the evacuees, three and a half years old, with blond hair and blue eyes? He may have a Dutch accent. He's missing all the fingers on his right hand."

"Oh dear." Cathy's perfectly shaped eyebrows rose high. "The poor little chap. No, I haven't seen such a child."

"Thank you anyway." Aleida's smile wobbled. She looped her purse over her shoulder, shook Cathy's hand, and left the office with Hugh.

"I'm sorry," he said.

"Thank you, but at least I can check one more town off my list." Her hands found each other.

Aleida ripped them apart and clutched her purse strap, her fingers coiling and flexing, coiling and flexing, aching to tap, tap, tap her into false comfort.

"Here." Hugh set down the suitcases, took her free hand, and tapped her knuckles.

In the wrong order.

His eyes twinkled between warm brown and mischievous green. "Does that help?"

No. And yet it did. Not the tapping, but the understanding, the humor, and the friendship.

# 14

Ancestral earth scattered across the top of Uncle Elliott's coffin in the ancestral plot on the ancestral estate.

Hugh clenched his hat in his hands by the graveside. Dust to dust. All that was left of a life brilliant and bold, selfish and generous, reckless and caring.

William Hastings brushed the dirt from his hands. An officer in the Royal Navy, Uncle Elliott's oldest son had been at sea when his father was killed.

Hugh bowed his head as the vicar pronounced the benediction.

After the amen, the mourners turned to talk amongst themselves under a sky streaked with shrouds of cloud.

Joan Collingwood, Cecil's widow, had a comforting arm around Mother's shoulders, and Hugh stood beside Father, silent and still.

Joan shook her head, making the black veil on her hat shiver. "If only Uncle Elliott hadn't spoken so rashly to that French reporter."

"Elliott was always rash, even as a child." Mother dabbed her eyes with a handkerchief. "In a proper newspaper report, editors would have removed his rash statements. But live on the wireless? Why, the BBC is as much to blame for Elliott's death as the man who pulled the trigger."

Hugh winced and edged away. This was why he'd resisted coming home for the funeral. His profession had been put on trial at Collingwood Manor, convicted, and sentenced.

At least Aleida's presence kept a cap on the malignant comments.

Where was she? She'd been right behind him.

There, near a copse of ash trees with leaves of bright autumnal yellow, Aleida stood talking with Beatrice Granville. Beatrice and William and Cecil and Ridley had been inseparable friends.

Wearing a black coat and a wide-brimmed black hat, Beatrice extended her hand to Hugh. "I do admit, I was surprised to see Mrs. Martens here. She tells me she's your guest." The way she said *guest*, she might as well have said *fiancée* or *paramour*.

Aleida's wide eyes appeared dark blue against the dark blue of her hat and coat. "I told Miss Granville we're friends, and I came to meet with the WVS in Buntingford."

Beatrice's smile tipped closer and closer to *paramour*. Aleida's straightforward ways were misinterpreted in high society.

Hugh offered a rueful smile. "I admit I brought her for my dear mother. Knowing Mrs. Martens is a widow searching for her little boy—well, Mother's filled Aleida with tea and biscuits. Having someone to comfort can serve as the best comfort of all."

Aleida smiled as if he were actually rather wise. "She's been most kind."

"I offer my condolences on the loss of your uncle." Beatrice shuddered and pressed her hand to her chest. "So soon after the loss of dear Cecil. Such a nasty business."

"Thank you," Hugh said. "It's been quite hard on my mother."

"Mr. Hastings could be a wrongheaded fool, and yet I was rather fond of him." Beatrice frowned toward the grave. "If only I'd come to the party. I was invited. Perhaps . . ."

"You couldn't have prevented it," Hugh said.

"Thank you." Beatrice patted his arm and excused herself.

Hugh gave Aleida his most contrite expression. "I apologize for making you the object of gossip."

Aleida shrugged one narrow shoulder. "I'm to blame. I all but invited myself."

"I'm glad you did. Think of the gossip if I'd stayed away." Hugh affected a dowager voice. "How odd that Hugh didn't attend his uncle's funeral. You don't suppose he might possibly be guilty of . . . *murder*?"

He winced. Once again, making sport, and at a most inappropriate time.

But Aleida chuckled. "I wouldn't worry. No one would suspect a jolly sort like you."

"You'd be surprised." Hugh tilted his head toward the house. "Shall we go in for more tea, biscuits, and condolences?"

Aleida walked beside him up the slope. "Will you interview the suspects?"

"I wish I could, but it would be unforgivably crass." Hugh nodded to the men and women ambling toward the stately gray stone manor. "That man in the bowler wanted Uncle Elliott's seat in Parliament but could never win the by-election. Wrong party for this constituency, poor chap. That tall fellow *will* be elected and looks rather too pleased about it. Those three argued with him in the Commons, and I'm afraid he had liaisons with far too many of their wives. Most of them were at the house party."

A breeze twirled a loose strand of Aleida's hair, and she tucked it into the coil at the nape of her pretty neck. "The police interviewed them all?"

"Yes, but they're convinced the murderer was a Frenchman.

Jouveau disagrees. He says if the leak about the repatriation ship were the motive, he would have received a death threat as well. After all, Ridley places equal blame on Jouveau and Uncle Elliott."

"Ridley—he's with the Ministry of Information?" Aleida brushed one hand along the rim of the stone fountain. "Is he here?"

"No, he isn't." Frowning, Hugh climbed the steps to the terrace. "Rather odd, considering our family ties."

"Is he a suspect?"

Hugh shrugged. "That would be most convenient. Murder solved, justice served, and the BBC would have one fewer impediment on the road to truth. But alas, he has an alibi. Besides, he's a rather decent old chap, and I'd hate to see him sent to the gallows."

"Very well, then. Who else?" Aleida stopped on the terrace. "Any suspects who aren't here today?"

Hugh waved a hand to the south. "I don't suspect them, but Fletcher and Gil were staying in Braughing, about two miles away. Both rather disliked my uncle."

Aleida tapped the toe of her black pump on the stone terrace. "With Gil's hand, could he fire a shotgun? My son can do many things with only one hand, but not all."

Hugh's eyebrows rose. Gil never talked about his condition, and Hugh had never seen him use his affected hand. "I don't know."

"And Fletcher? He had problems with your uncle?"

"They had many a row. Fletcher has quite a temper."

"I hate to even suggest such a thing, but do you think Gil and Fletcher could have worked together?" Her blond eyebrows pinched together with the horror of it all.

Hugh pressed his lips tight. "That would take planning. Nothing about this murder feels premeditated."

"He used your uncle's gun."

"Precisely." Hugh gazed toward the woods where his uncle had died, and his chest clenched. "It's as if they were arguing and started shoving, and in the heat of the moment . . ."

"Hugh?" Aleida's voice fell low. "You don't suspect Gil or Fletcher, do you?"

"I don't." He met her gaze and searched for the reason for his quick answer. "Gil's a good sort, a man of principle. And Fletcher may have argued with Uncle Elliott, but only because my uncle wanted to use the BBC as his bully pulpit. But in his heart, I think Fletcher likes what my uncle is—was striving for."

"Whilst we're discussing improbable suspects, what about Irwin?" Mischief flickered in the corner of her mouth. "He didn't like your uncle, and he was absent from the Hart and Swan that day without excuse."

"Ah, Irwin." Hugh almost laughed at the thought. "He was ill. He couldn't ring, because his telephone line was out due to the Blitz. He may be a curmudgeon, but he's a loveable one."

"Dear Hugh. You think too well of people to be a detective." Aleida's eyes crinkled with amusement, with . . . fondness? "It's good that you are a correspondent."

He had to guard his heart against false hope, but he returned her smile. If only Mother and Father agreed with her.

## 15

**LONDON**
**SATURDAY, OCTOBER 5, 1940**

Outside Charing Cross Station, workmen removed rubble and carted building materials.

Aleida stepped around a wheelbarrow and crossed the pavement to an ornate monument topped by a cross.

Under a cloudy sky, Hugh stood by the monument in his tailored black overcoat, a gray homburg, and a big smile.

Her heart made a little hop in her chest, and she met him halfway.

Hugh nodded over her shoulder. "Jouveau's right behind you."

Aleida turned and greeted François Jouveau. "Thank you for taking me to the hotel. If there's any chance someone's seen my son—"

"Think nothing of it." Jouveau waved one hand. "It was Collie's idea."

"But you have the connections in the refugee community," Hugh said. "Come. It's only a few streets away."

They headed along the Strand, past stately buildings of cool gray stone. Aleida counted her steps. Stopped herself. Counting would neither bring Theo to her, nor would failing to count keep him from her.

But her steps lengthened and quickened.

"Most of the refugees at the Strand Palace Hotel are French." Jouveau took a drag on a cigarette. "But Dutch refugees stay there too. Belgian, Czech, Polish. I visit when I can. The refugees are often overlooked now that tens of thousands of British subjects have lost their homes in the Blitz."

"Nationality shouldn't matter. British, foreigners—they've all lost their homes due to the Nazis." Hugh's mouth shifted to one side. "If only I could tell the story of the refugees, but it isn't the story for the time."

Aleida passed the remains of a building. Three walls reached high, jagged along the tops, but the insides poured out toward the street, a heap of stone and glass and twisted bits of furniture.

The Blitz was the story for the time, the only story, the only part of life for most.

Every night the bombers came. Every night, hundreds of buildings were destroyed. Every night, hundreds of people died.

Aleida had become accustomed to snatching sleep in the damp Anderson shelter in the garden, to changing Underground routes due to bomb damage, to making do with interrupted electricity and gas.

The Germans bombed in the hopes of demolishing morale so the people would rise up and force the government to sue for peace.

Hitler didn't know these people, who passed Aleida with purposeful strides, their chins high, their clothes neat.

"Fletcher would never let you tell the refugees' stories," Jouveau said with a sniff. "He's become Ridley's pet dog."

"Fletcher?" Hugh gaped at his friend. "He rather dislikes Ridley."

"And Ridley rather dislikes me." Jouveau leaned closer to Aleida. "That means he despises me."

Aleida gave him an understanding nod. "These English never say what they mean."

They crossed a street, and Jouveau led the way. "Ridley despises me, because I criticize the British government."

"You do on occasion," Hugh said. "But overall, you've been most appreciative, and your broadcasts to France promote the Allied cause. You encourage resistance and support de Gaulle and the Free French."

Jouveau brandished his cigarette. "All of which Ridley forgets the instant I breathe a critical word. Then he yells at Fletcher."

"Fletcher?" Hugh frowned. "He isn't your editor."

"Ah, but my actual editor ignores Ridley, so Ridley yells at Fletcher and Fletcher yells at me. Not only is Fletcher angry at my transgressions, but he's angry that Ridley unjustly blames him for my actions and causes trouble for him at the Ministry of Information."

Aleida hitched her purse strap higher on her shoulder. "That isn't fair."

"I care not." Smoke plumed alongside Jouveau's cheek. "My editor is pleased with my stories, de Gaulle is pleased, the French people are pleased, and the Germans hate me. So I am pleased."

"Perhaps I could speak to Ridley." Hugh gave his head a sharp shake. "No, he wouldn't listen. He has no respect for me."

"And I have no respect for him," Jouveau said. "Did I tell you Ridley accused me of flirting with his wife at a reception, because I made her smile? Meanwhile, he was making eyes with the daughter of an MP."

A group of businessmen approached, and Hugh motioned for Aleida to precede him. "If we Englishmen learned how to make ladies smile, we'd be less suspicious of you Frenchmen."

Aleida smiled to herself. Hugh had already learned that lesson well.

"Do you know what I dream at night?" Delight glistened in Jouveau's brown eyes. "I dream of the police arresting Ridley for your uncle's murder. Ridley hated Hastings, called him 'quite indiscreet.'"

"So sorry to disappoint you." Hugh flashed half a smile. "Ridley has an alibi."

"Hugh says the police suspect a Frenchman," Aleida said.

"The police are wrong." Dark eyebrows drew together. "We French know Hastings's mistake was an honest one. Hastings was our champion in Parliament. He worked with aid societies, and he was about to introduce a bill to increase funding for refugees. Sadly, that bill has died with him. He is much mourned by my countrymen."

"Thank you." Hugh's voice sounded rough. "Ah, here we are."

The entrance to the Strand Palace Hotel was an Art Deco wonder of glass and mirrors and polished steel. Inside the lobby, glass-and-steel columns and balustrades glowed with light from inside.

Jouveau led them through a mirrored revolving door and to a large restaurant, full of long tables to feed the hundreds of refugees at the hotel. The smell of potato soup filled the air.

Families huddled at the tables, their clothes drab, and muted voices in a dozen languages bounced off the mirrored walls.

Aleida's chest seized. These people had neither money nor family in England. Without Sebastiaan's gold or her aunt and uncle in Britain, this would have been her.

A woman passed, holding the hand of a brown-haired girl.

Aleida swept her gaze around the teeming dining hall, searching for little blond boys. How much had Theo grown in the last five months? No matter how he'd changed, she'd recognize him instantly.

"Come along," Hugh said with a soft look in his eyes.

Aleida sucked in a breath and followed the men.

Speaking French, Jouveau greeted a middle-aged man,

someone he obviously knew, and he asked where the Dutch refugees were. His friend led them across the dining hall.

The familiar sound of Dutch filled her ears, and a sweet pain flooded her chest.

A ruddy-cheeked man in his forties rose and shook Jouveau's hand, and Jouveau introduced Aleida in French.

Aleida switched to Dutch, and her story poured out, her description of Theo. Her sorrow.

The gentleman introduced her to dozens of other Dutch men and women. Over and over, she told her story. Over and over, eyes widened at the horror of Aleida's plight. Over and over, heads shook. They hadn't seen Theo.

No one had.

At Hugh's suggestion, she asked about other locations where Dutch refugees were billeted, and she wrote them in her notebook.

Her hand trembled. Her breath became erratic.

She smoothed the page once, twice, three times. She grimaced and added a fourth, but that only made her breath choppier.

"Is there anyone else she can talk to?" Hugh asked the Dutch gentleman in French.

"No, that is all of us."

Aleida managed to slip her notebook into her purse, and she extended her hand to the Dutchman. *"Heel erd bedankt."*

*"Graag gedaan,"* he said. "I hope you find your son."

Aleida's throat constricted, and she could only nod in reply.

"I'm sorry." Hugh led Aleida and Jouveau out of the dining hall. "At least you have a few more places to search."

She didn't want more places to search. She wanted her son, and her breath wrapped around her vocal cords and strangled them.

In the lobby, Jouveau gave her a sympathetic frown. "I'll keep asking. Collie—will I see you tonight at the Hart and Swan?"

"Indeed."

Aleida plunged one hand into her coat pocket to prevent tapping. "Thank you, gentlemen. I'll see you later."

Jouveau departed, but Hugh stayed, a slight frown on his face. "Do you have further appointments today?"

"I need to ring these other hotels." Her voice wavered.

"Not yet." He set his hand in the small of her back. "Let's walk."

Did she want to walk? She had appointments to make. Yet she was in no state to do so, and the gentle pressure of his touch slowed her breathing. "All right, then."

After Hugh guided her outside, he lowered his hand.

Aleida clenched her purse strap with one hand and her pocket lining with the other, trying to keep the two magnets from colliding and tapping and luring her with false hope of control.

"Let's go to the river." Hugh led her across the street toward the Savoy Hotel, down a lane, and to the Thames.

Trees lined the embankment, and Aleida and Hugh headed to the walkway alongside the gray waters.

The Waterloo Bridge stretched incomplete across the Thames, its reconstruction slowed due to the wartime shortage of labor.

Beyond it, black clouds billowed from fires from the previous nights' air raids.

Hugh led her west, away from the worst of the bomb damage. "I have a suggestion. I'd like you to list all your fears about your son."

Aleida's step faltered. "List them?"

"You like lists. List your fears. Name those monsters, so you can fight them." A fierce light burned in Hugh's eyes.

Her pocketed hand stretched toward her purse-clenching hand, straining her coat.

Hugh slipped to her left side. "Hold my arm, walk, and list."

She stared up at him, breathing hard. She didn't want to

name those monsters. Yet their names howled inside her mind, all day and all night. Named or unnamed, they howled.

With a sudden inhalation, she wrenched her hand from her pocket and gripped Hugh's arm.

"Name them." Hugh proceeded down the concrete embankment. "What's your worst fear? That Theo is dead."

Aleida slammed her eyes shut. "Yes." So many ways he could have died—strafing, starvation, accident, illness.

"What else?" His voice managed to be both strident and calming.

"That he—he's abandoned. Alone. Wandering." Her fingers dug into fine wool, into Hugh's solid arm. "That he's still on the continent, in an orphanage, living under the Nazis. That the British couple brought him here but left him in an orphanage or a refugee camp. Or they're beating him. Or neglecting him. Or they sent him to an even worse home in the country. Or they didn't send him away, and he's living through the bombings."

"Mm-hmm." Hugh covered her digging hand with his. "What can you do about those?"

Her eyes burned, and her breath snagged on her airways. What indeed could she do?

"You can do what you're already doing." Hugh squeezed her hand. "Keep searching in your diligent way. What else?"

Clouds filled the sky, but on the horizon . . . a band of pale blue. "I can pray."

"Yes. What does the Bible say? 'Casting all your care upon him; for he careth for you.'"

So many cares, and her chin quivered. She put all her effort into firming it. The Lord was strong enough to carry her burdens. Certainly stronger than she was. So why did she cling to her cares as if the clinging connected her to her son?

"And you can hope." Hugh's voice drew out in golden strands. "Hope Theo's in a good home with people who care for him."

Her stomach contracted, her eyes squeezed shut, and she stopped and covered her mouth.

"Aleida?" Hugh said. "I thought that might bring a feeble smile of sorts."

She shook her head. Why was that thought almost worse? She wanted Theo to be happy, didn't she? So why was she trying to burn away the image of Theo in a happy home, looking on the English couple with love . . .

A sob burst between her fingers. "What if he forgets me?"

"Forgets you?" Hugh set his hand on her shoulder. "How is that even possible? You're an extraordinary woman."

"He's only three. How much do you remember from that age?" Her throat clamped shut.

Hugh rubbed her shoulder. "I know he's young. Over time, he may forget your face. But he'll never forget your love."

The emotion in his voice pried open her eyes, and the compassion and hurt on his face pried open her heart.

"I . . ." He coughed and cleared his throat. "I'll never forget my sister's love."

"You have a sister?"

"She died when she was six. An asthmatic attack." His gaze darted to the side, then back to her. "I was three and a half, about Theo's age. We do have photographs, but we don't talk about her. Caroline. Her name was Caroline."

"Caroline. I can see you loved her."

The sound of his sister's name cleared some of the pain from his hazel eyes. "I loved her very much. Caroline played with me and fussed over me like a little mother. I will never forget."

Memories flashed through her mind, of playing with Theo and reading to him and singing with him and holding him when he cried and scolding him when he was naughty. Of *loving* him with all her heart.

"He won't forget?" Hope threaded through her words.

Hugh's gaze settled on her, soft but firm. "Never."

124

**16**

D rops splattered on the pavement as Hugh shook off his
foot. In the blackout, he hadn't seen the puddle. If only
the rain clouds had remained over London. Clear skies
and an almost-full "bomber's moon" promised a heavy raid.

If the Germans kept to their usual schedule, Hugh had
about an hour to enjoy the company of friends before being
waylaid by the company of enemies.

Hugh opened the door of the Hart and Swan and shoved
past the blackout curtain.

In the back room, Aleida sat with Lou, Gil, Jouveau, and
MacLeod, and Hugh greeted everyone.

Gil and Louisa flanked Aleida, so he contented himself with
the chair across from her as she resumed her conversation
with Lou.

The two women couldn't possibly have been more different,
which only strengthened their friendship. Aleida needed a
no-nonsense friend like Lou, and Lou needed Aleida's moral
compass.

Hugh asked MacLeod about the latest dealings in Parliament, but although he always found the older reporter insightful, he couldn't concentrate as usual.

Aleida's gentle voice rolled across the table to him, enticing his attention. Lamplight glowed on her golden hair and pink cheeks, and her laughter sang to him.

As if she knew he was watching, she met his gaze. A fond smile rose.

Hugh jerked his attention back to MacLeod and nodded at something about bills and votes.

He didn't deserve Aleida's fond smiles. He felt closer to her than ever after she'd shared her fears, and she apparently thought he'd opened the vault by sharing about Caroline.

He'd opened it only a sliver. As soon as he'd considered telling her about his own asthma, he'd slammed it shut.

This was why he'd never had a romance of any depth or length. He could be honest about everything except his infirmity, and women always sensed he held something back.

Across the table, Gil said something to Aleida, and she responded in a short but polite manner.

Gil was a good sort, far more deserving of the affections of a fair maiden than Hugh. Poor old sod.

MacLeod came to a natural lull in the conversation.

Hugh swung a grin to his colleague. "I say, Gil. Smashing story the other day about the black market."

Gil's blond eyebrows rose, and pleasure sparked in his blue eyes. Then a monologue commenced about how he'd researched and written that story.

Aleida listened, but that smile didn't shift to Gil. It remained on Hugh and shone fonder than before.

It would fade when she realized he was concealing something.

MacLeod rose and pushed in his chair. "Good night, ladies and gentlemen."

Hugh bid him farewell, then caught Aleida's gaze. "When are you going home? It's half past seven."

"A few more minutes. I do want to go home before the bombers come."

Gil ducked into her line of sight. "I'd be honored to walk you home."

"Thank you, but I'll decline." As always, Aleida used a cool tone and made no excuse. But that never stopped Gil.

Stomping footsteps approached, and Norman Fletcher barged into the room.

Fletcher never came to the Hart and Swan, and Hugh rose to greet him.

"Do you know where I spent the last two hours?" Fletcher marched to Hugh, his face livid. "The police. They questioned me about your uncle's murder."

Hugh took half a step back, and his jaw drifted low. Although he'd pondered Fletcher as a suspect, he never thought the police would.

Fletcher flung his hand wide. "A posh house full of toffs, all of whom wanted Hastings dead—straight out of an Agatha Christie novel—and who do the police come after? The scholarship boy." The more he talked, the more his northern accent asserted itself.

Hugh held up one soothing hand. "I'm sure the police don't truly suspect you. After—"

"Is that so?" Fletcher closed the gap Hugh had created, and his grayish eyes burned like coal in the grate. "I was staying nearby. Gil went out for a stroll and my wife and daughters spent the morning in the garden, all so I could enjoy an extra four hours of sleep uninterrupted by the Nazis. And what is the price for those four hours? I have no alibi. But I do have motive, they say. And how—how is it they came to suspect me?"

"I can't imagine . . ." A sickening feeling churned in Hugh's belly. "You don't think I—"

Fletcher jabbed Hugh in the chest with a long finger. "Who else knew I was in the country, knew of my arguments with Hastings, knew that Hastings pressed the BBC to fire me?"

"Fire you? Sir, I never knew." Hugh drew back his chin. "And I would never have accused you."

Seated at the table, Jouveau let out a scoffing noise. "Everyone knew of your rows with Hastings."

Fletcher shot Jouveau an acidic glare.

"And, sir," Hugh said, "your trip to the country was no secret. As for what Uncle Elliott did . . ."

Fletcher cussed under his breath and clapped his hand to the back of his neck. "Of course. A lot of people knew."

Hugh assumed his calmest voice. "I'm sure the police will realize your innocence. You might have clashed with my uncle, but it was never about his policies. Other news simply had higher priority, and no MP has the power to dictate broadcasting priorities—or to dictate firing a highly esteemed editor."

With a grunt, Fletcher tore off his homburg.

"I fail to see any motive on your part," Hugh said. "Why would you kill someone who wants to help the common man and take the toffs down a notch? Especially when he's certain to be replaced by Algernon Bradshaw."

"Bradshaw." Fletcher spat out the name. "Simpering fool."

Jouveau smirked. "Bradshaw was at the house party."

"I interviewed him last week." Gil rested his forearms on the table. "He's far too pleased about his prospects in the coming by-election."

Hugh pulled out the chair MacLeod had vacated. "Would you care to join us?"

Fletcher glanced around the table, scowled at Jouveau, relaxed looking at Gil and Louisa, then paused at Aleida.

Hugh nodded toward her. "Aleida, may I introduce my editor, Norman Fletcher. Mr. Fletcher, this is Aleida Martens with the Dutch Service of the BBC."

Aleida's gaze flew to Hugh, part incredulous, part amused, part chastising him for the naughty boy he was.

He liked each part, and he winked.

Amusement won, and she nodded to Fletcher. "I'm afraid I'm not with the Dutch Service, but I am pleased to meet you."

"Pleased to meet you too." Fletcher sank into the empty chair.

Hugh sat and faced his editor. "Bradshaw."

"Motive, means, and opportunity," Fletcher said through gritted teeth. "Hastings was strong and healthy, and he'd never resign. How else could Bradshaw get his seat?"

Louisa shrugged. "Bradshaw's a milquetoast. I can't see the man getting in a scuffle. He might dirty his shoes."

"How about Sutherland?" Gil said. "He wants the same seat."

"Wrong party," Hugh said. "He doesn't stand a chance in that constituency."

Fletcher pointed a finger at Hugh, and his eyes brightened. "Not against Hastings, but he might stand a chance against Bradshaw."

"Good point, and if the war goes poorly and the people turn on the men in charge—"

"Sutherland's a suspect in my book." Fletcher slapped the table.

"The former Mrs. Hastings was at the party too, was she not?" Jouveau said.

"She divorced him years ago," Hugh said. "The time to have murdered him would have been when they were still married."

"Their children?" Fletcher said.

"They preferred my uncle to my aunt. Uncle Elliott had little virtue but much compassion. Aunt Rosamund has much virtue and no compassion. My cousins loved their father dearly, and William—the heir—was at sea, so—"

The air raid siren wailed its alert.

Hugh grinned at his friends and quoted a popular line from the BBC's broadcasts for workers. "Good night and go to it."

"Work at war speed." Gil continued the quote in a sardonic tone as he donned his hat.

Mr. Irwin leaned into the room. "Hurry! Down to the shelter."

Hugh pulled on his overcoat. "Your basement is the safest and most hospitable in London, but the news calls."

The reporters spilled out of the room, but Aleida sipped her tea and glanced at Hugh over the rim of her cup. "Where are you going tonight?"

"I haven't decided." He buttoned his coat. "I'll go to the roof of Broadcasting House to observe. Will you go to Irwin's shelter?"

She set down her cup and frowned at it. "I don't mind Anderson shelters, but I don't like basement shelters. I've seen too many rescue parties at work. May I come with you?"

He opened his mouth to tell her she'd be safer anywhere but with him, but she raised eyes filled with a strange mix of fear and bravery. He also had seen buildings collapse into their basements. He also preferred to be on top of buildings.

And she'd never reach her garden shelter before the bombers came.

"How can I argue with courage?" Hugh pulled her dark blue overcoat from a hook on the wall and held it out for her.

She slipped her slender arms through the sleeves, he settled the coat on her shoulders, and she faced him with all fear erased. Only courage remained and a spot of anticipation.

Hugh set his fedora on at an angle. "Come along, my intrepid friend."

They dashed outside and up Regent Street. The siren had stopped wailing, and only footfalls broke the hush.

In the moonlight, Hugh didn't need his torch to find his way, not when Broadcasting House towered before him.

At the entrance, Hugh tucked Aleida's hand around his arm and flashed his card to the guard. "She's with me."

"Yes, Mr. Collingwood." The older man let him in.

Hugh led Aleida across the Art Deco lobby to the lifts, past people coming and going to work.

In the basement, the news readers would be preparing for the nine o'clock news broadcast. Throughout the building, engineers and telephone operators and others worked around the clock. Although most BBC departments had evacuated from London at the outbreak of war, others remained, including the news department.

"It's a beautiful building." Aleida admired the sculpture of The Sower next to the lifts.

"It is," Hugh said. "Sleek and modern and specially designed for broadcasting."

The lift doors opened, and Hugh pressed the button for the eighth floor.

By the time the doors opened again and they'd climbed a flight of stairs to the roof, all had changed.

German engines grumbled above, steady and unrelenting. Bright beams sliced the night sky. Bombs thudded in the distance. Antiaircraft guns barked their reply.

Hugh went to the railing near the southern point of the building with Aleida beside him.

If this raid mimicked the others, waves of bombers would arrive throughout the night, dropping loads of death. At least the Luftwaffe had abandoned daylight raids for the past fortnight, granting Londoners a slight reprieve.

After six weeks in a row of nightly raids, Hugh was running out of fresh angles for stories. And how could he concentrate on the news with Aleida standing close to his side, the warmth of her radiating to him?

He squinted into the night. Fires arose to the south along the Thames.

"What was it like growing up here?" Aleida said. "Were you mostly in the country or in the city?"

Hugh stuffed his hands into his coat pockets and chewed on his lips. He'd spent his childhood watching through windows while Cecil played outside, healthy and hale. He'd squandered the early years of his education since no one expected him to live, including Hugh himself.

But Aleida's eyes shone in the moonlight, and her coat sleeve brushed against his.

Hugh gave a vague response, then inquired about Aleida's childhood.

To his relief, her stories spilled out with the slightest prompts. She loved and missed her parents, and she told of her cousins coming to England each summer and exploring her aunt and uncle's estate, having out-of-doors adventures as children ought to do.

Hugh loved the cadence of her Dutch accent, the music of her laughter, and how her hands relaxed as she talked about family.

But the bombs fell closer. To the south near Victoria Station. To the northeast near St. Pancras Station. Closer, toward Oxford Street.

Aleida fell silent. Hugh gripped the railing.

Faintly through the rumbling bombers and thumping guns, Big Ben's gong resounded. Once, twice, nine times.

A whistling overhead.

"Get down!" Aleida flung herself flat to the roof.

Hugh strained his gaze upward. Where were the bombs falling?

"Hugh!" Aleida tugged on the hem of his coat. "Get down!"

He blinked hard, then dropped to his knees.

A crash of metal and cement to the north, and the roof trembled, bucked beneath him.

Hugh threw himself down between Aleida and the crash.

Had Broadcasting House been hit?

Whistles rent the air, but softer, fading, the stick of bombs working its way west.

Aleida pushed up on her elbows, her hat askew. "Were we hit?"

Hugh had hugged her to his belly, and he released her. "So sorry. I—let me see." He rose to his feet, and his knees wobbled.

Halfway up the length of the building, a cloud of dust rose from along Portland Place.

Hugh leaned over the railing for a better view. A jagged hole pierced the side of Broadcasting House around the seventh floor, and bits of masonry littered the ground.

"I heard the bomb hit." Aleida stood back from the railing. "But I didn't hear an explosion. Do you think it's a UXB?"

Unexploded bombs created deadly work for the men who removed and detonated them. "Some bombs have time delays."

"Oh no."

Hugh backed up and groped for Aleida's hand. "We—we should leave."

He spun her around and ran for the stairs. He didn't want to be trapped in a lift, have the cable severed.

Their feet pounded down the steps, they bumped sides as they whirled around landings, and her hand gripped his like a vise.

At each landing, more people joined them, but Aleida never released his hand.

Rumors floated down the stairs with them. The bomb had come to rest on the sixth floor, someone said. No, the fifth. Near the music library—a woman said she'd seen it with her own eyes.

Hugh guided Aleida through the lobby and out the main entrance. The guard stood aside and stared as dozens of people passed him.

Still, the Luftwaffe droned overhead. Beams searched in vain and antiaircraft fired in vain.

If the public knew how few bombers had been shot down by those guns, how even fewer bombers had been shot down by RAF night fighters . . . but that was a story he couldn't tell. Wouldn't tell.

Hugh and Aleida crossed Portland Place. Her hand felt small and taut and right in his, and he gave it the slightest squeeze. "May I interest you in sheltering in the Tube?"

"Yes, please." Her voice came out thready.

He headed up Portland Place toward Regent's Park Station. Oxford Circus Station was closer, but also lay closer to the bomb falls.

Noise ripped the air before them.

Glass and masonry spewed from the side of Broadcasting House, about five floors up.

"The bomb," Aleida whispered.

If they'd remained in the building . . .

Without thinking, Hugh pulled Aleida to him.

She let him.

**17**

MONDAY, OCTOBER 28, 1940

Miss Granville set her blue tin pan helmet on top of her perfectly coiffed copper hair. "I'm so sorry you wasted time on those interviews, but the ministry simply can't use such a report."

At the ARP post, Aleida turned her own helmet in her hands. Over the past two months, she'd interviewed dozens of evacuees, foster families, billeting officers, and teachers. While Miss Granville appreciated Aleida's registry of children in each town, she didn't want the children's stories.

Miss Granville set a hand on her hip. "If we were to tell the mothers of London that even one child was unhappy, it'd be the end of the entire evacuation scheme."

"Most of the children are in splendid situations, but some are not. The families should know the truth."

"The truth?" Miss Granville lifted her hand like a shield. "The truth is, a child in even the most unfeeling country home is far better off than in city squalor. A city is a most unnatural place for English children. They need greenery and fresh air and wholesome living."

"But we should do something for the children who—"

"Chin up." Miss Granville nudged up a fist and a smile. "Assembling your registry will be smoother without the burden of interviews. Now, shouldn't you prepare for your duties?"

"Yes, ma'am." Aleida suppressed a sigh and headed to meet Tommy Thorne, her messenger.

Nilima Sharma intercepted her, took her arm, and looked her hard in the eye. "Write that report, Mrs. Martens. I don't care what Granny says, write it. People need to know."

Aleida's heart warmed at the urgency in Nilima's big brown eyes. Those stories had been entrusted to her and shouldn't be wasted. "I will."

The front door opened with a puff of cold air, and Hugh entered in his black overcoat. His gaze fell on her, and he raised his gorgeous grin.

Her heart tumbled in her chest. What was he doing here?

He doffed his hat, strode to Miss Granville, and shook her hand. "Good evening, Beatrice. As I mentioned on the telephone, I'd like to record another broadcast here in a few days. Tonight I'd like to observe your volunteers in action."

Miss Granville slid a sly look toward Aleida. "Since you're *friends* with Mrs. Martens, perhaps she could show you around."

"That would be lovely, thank you."

Aleida felt every eye in the post. If only she could fade into the racks of equipment. She'd been widowed less than six months ago. Was it too early to be linked romantically?

Did she want to be linked? Sometimes she wanted it dearly, like on the night the bomb blast at Broadcasting House killed seven people, and Hugh had protected her and held her. Other times, something inside her balked when he was near.

And he came nearer, smile lines radiating through his cheeks, and he bowed. "Good evening, Mrs. Martens. May I have the honor of accompanying you on your rounds?"

With her winter coat bundled beneath the thin and shapeless ARP coat, she cut no picture of elegance, but Hugh always put her at ease. She dropped a curtsy. "The honor is mine."

"Shall we?" He held out his elbow to her.

"Not yet." She fastened her helmet, found one for Hugh, and made sure she had her torch and gas mask.

Aleida took Hugh's elbow and led him outside into the dark night with Tommy behind them. She flicked on her torch, its beam dulled by blue paper. "The bombers don't usually arrive until eight, so we use the hours after sunset to check blackout conditions and make sure routes to shelters are clear."

"The moon won't rise until after three in the morning. Might be a lighter raid tonight."

She passed a quartet of men on their way home after work. "We can hope."

Hugh patted her hand. "I must confess. I do plan to broadcast from your post, but I came tonight to ask about your weekend in the country. How could I wait?"

Aleida peered at a home and checked for slivers of light. "You're very naughty."

"So I've been told all my life." He didn't sound sorry.

"I didn't find Theo, but I enjoyed seeing Tante Margriet and Uncle James, and I visited several villages."

"How go the interviews?"

Aleida skirted a pile of rubble on the pavement. "I met the dearest woman yesterday. She loves her evacuees so much, she wants to adopt them. Since their mother was killed in the Blitz and their father is absent, it's possible."

"What a lovely lady."

"She is. I've spoken to dozens of families who weren't eager to take evacuees but have grown fond of them. But then the others." She shined her torch around the entrance to the Green Park Tube station.

"What have you heard?" A growl rippled the caramel voice.

Aleida waited for a dozen people to pass as they exited the

station, then she turned the corner onto Piccadilly. If only she could banish the image of that hard-hearted woman. "I talked to a woman who sent back the first two children she was assigned. The third child she kept. Unlike with the first two, she was able to paddle the girl into submission."

Hugh's arm tensed in her grip. "Dreadful."

Aleida nodded, and her stomach twisted. Across Piccadilly, Green Park lay dark and foreboding under the moonless sky. "I met a wealthy couple who wanted praise for billeting seven children. But they don't even know the children's names. They let them run wild around the estate and make their staff care for them in odd bits of spare time."

Hugh grunted. "Good on you for interviewing them. Now something can be done."

"No, it can't." Aleida's sigh flowed into the frosty air. "Miss Granville doesn't want my report. She's afraid parents will bring their children back to London or refuse to send them away."

"The truth needs to be told."

Aleida faced him. Pale blue light illuminated the frustration on Hugh's face. "Do you see my dilemma? If I fail to speak out, children will continue to be neglected or worse. But if I do speak out, children will be brought back to London, where they could die. As a mother, I want my son to be safe from the bombing, but I also want to know if he faces abuse or neglect. Is one danger truly greater than the other?"

"Will you speak out or keep silent?"

Aleida's eyes slipped shut. "I will write my report in its full, uncensored truth, and I'll give it to Miss Granville. But it'll end there."

"I could talk to her."

She skewered him with her gaze. "You will do no such thing."

He chuckled, and puffs of his breath warmed her cheeks. "I admire a woman who fights her own battles."

SARAH SUNDIN

"Thank you." Her cheeks warmed even more, and she resumed her patrol.

"Your dilemma is similar to the one we reporters face. The uncensored truth could leak information to the enemy, which would cost lives. Or it could cause morale to plummet, which would cause production to plummet and could cost us the war."

Aleida frowned and turned onto Bolton Street. "So you must conceal some of the truth."

"Yet I firmly believe people are intelligent and resilient. I believe the truth helps the public make wise decisions."

A chink of light shined from a second-floor window, then disappeared behind a swish of curtain. "There's no easy way."

"No, there isn't." He gave her a sad smile. "Now, let me pretend to do my job. Please tell me more about your duties."

"Each warden has assigned streets within our sector. When the alert sounds, we guide people to the nearest shelters. If I spot an incident, I send a report with Tommy back to the sector post." She nodded to the bored youth pushing a bicycle behind them.

Hugh tipped his helmet to Tommy, who raised a shy grin.

Aleida swung her beam around a gaping site where a house had once stood. "Our post rings the Report Center, which compiles the information and notifies the Control Center. They send out the necessary rescue parties, stretcher parties, and fire pumps. I remain at the site until the incident officer arrives, and I guide the various parties and assist where needed."

"Important work. I'll want to meet some of the other volunteers too."

Keeping him to herself would be selfish, but she didn't want him to leave yet. "Any news from the police about your uncle? You haven't mentioned anything lately."

Hugh huffed. "I haven't heard anything lately. No arrests and no good suspects."

"No one you *want* to suspect."

"Hmm?"

Aleida squeezed his arm. "A fortnight ago, you mentioned Mr. Fletcher had motive and opportunity. Then he marched into the Hart and Swan, enraged. Within two minutes, you'd calmed him down, eliminated him as a suspect, and would he please join you for a nice spot of tea?"

Hugh stopped and stared at her, agape.

She clucked her tongue at him. "You're entirely too amiable to be a detective. All those pleasant traits make you an excellent reporter, but not a detective."

"Is that so?" Amusement drew out his words.

"You always think the best of people, and when you think the best of someone, it's impossible to think them capable of murder, yes?"

He laughed. "Yes, it is."

Someone so amiable, who saw the best in people and brought out the best in people, who used his considerable charm for the good of others—why couldn't she yet trust him with her heart?

18

L ike all good pub tables, the reporters' table at the Hart and Swan was a thick slab of oak, stained and polished and scratched and rubbed rich with color and age.

At the head of that table, Hugh set down his notebook and grinned at Jouveau. "Wait until you hear the story I'm working on."

Jouveau wagged a finger at him. "No, my friend. Wait until you hear *my* story." Then he flagged down Irwin and ordered a drink.

On Hugh's other side, Aleida bent her pretty head over her little black diary and made tick marks. Yesterday's page had eight entries, from appointments to train schedules.

"The precision of it all." Hugh set his finger on the page. "It's stunning."

She gave him a sidelong look and capped her pen. "If you were willing to learn . . ."

"I do try." He slid her diary closer and flipped a page. "I see you're visiting two orphanages tomorrow morning. You're not needed at the ministry?"

141

"On Saturday I worked in the country on the registry of evacuees, so I have a day off."

Louisa Jones entered, bringing the scent of rain, and Aleida rose to greet her.

The ladies stood chatting. And stood. And chatted.

Hugh still had Aleida's diary. He uncapped his pen and did his mischief.

"Well, look who's still in town." Barnaby Hillman filled the height and width of the doorway.

"Barn!" Hugh sprang up and shook the hand of the American reporter. "I heard you made the leap from the papers to the wireless. Mutual Broadcasting System?"

"Guilty as charged. And back in Old Blighty, as you fellows call it." Barn opened his attaché case and dumped the contents onto the table. "Gifts from your rebellious former colonies."

Packs of cigarettes littered the table, and most of the reporters exclaimed.

Hugh fought a grimace and settled back into his seat. In his opinion, the cigarette shortage was one of the few benefits of the war. How often had he cut evenings short when smoke aggravated his lungs?

Jouveau took a long drag from a cigarette. "Magnifique. Almost as magnifique as my story." He gave Hugh a satisfied smile. "I believe I shall soon solve your uncle's murder."

"You shall?" Hugh's heart hitched, and he sat forward. "Who is it?"

Jouveau blew out a leisurely lungful of smoke, adding to the growing haze. "Since our discussion the day we visited the Strand Palace Hotel, I've pursued a lead. Tonight I have an appointment that should answer my last questions."

"Who did it?"

"No, my friend. This is *my* scoop." Jouveau caressed his notebook on the table. "Today I told Fletcher how big this story will be. After the murderer is arrested, I want to broadcast on the BBC Home Service."

"The Home Service?" MacLeod gave him an approving smile. "Big break for you."

Jouveau scoffed. "It would be if Fletcher weren't a fool."

"I say." Gil glared at him. "Is that quite necessary?"

"Quite." Jouveau blew smoke through his nostrils. "He said the story would deserve no more than a line in the nine o'clock news."

Hugh slumped back in his seat. With a war on, the murder of an MP was minor news, even if that murder greatly affected those who loved him.

Barn added more smoke to the haze. "I've never met this Fletcher fellow, but you give him a big enough story, and he'll pounce on it."

"Au contraire," Jouveau said. "He ordered me to drop the story. Since I now know the murderer was not French, Fletcher says the case has nothing to do with me."

What an odd thing to say, and Hugh frowned.

Jouveau poked a finger up into the sickly gray cloud. "The man is a fool!"

Gil yanked a cigarette from his mouth. "How dare you speak about him like that?"

"Because it's true. I told him I'd come back tomorrow with the proof, and he said he'd refuse to see me. Fool!"

Gil's face reddened. "He's doing his job. You think you can dictate what the BBC broadcasts? Typical French arrogance."

Jouveau cried out. "French arrogance? You English drip arrogance."

Gil shoved back his chair and started to rise.

The men had never liked each other, but heat filled the room, as toxic as the tobacco smoke ringing their heads.

A diversion was needed.

Hugh grabbed Jouveau's notebook and bolted from his seat.

"What do we have here?" He opened the notebook with a flourish.

"Collie!" Jouveau stood, scraping chair legs over ancient floorboards, and he lunged after Hugh.

Laughing, Hugh circled behind his friends, keeping the table between him and Jouveau. A diary entry for 3 November at nine o'clock in the evening read, "JI-GB."

Standing behind Aleida's chair, Hugh squinted at the letters. "JI? GB? Great Britain?"

With a chuckle and a theatrical spread of his arms, Jouveau plunked back into his chair. "Do you think I'd give away my scoop so easily?"

Hugh's heart and his smile sank. "I don't want a scoop. I want to know who killed my uncle."

Aleida glanced up over her shoulder at Hugh with a sympathetic frown.

Jouveau's smug smile drifted down. "I understand, my friend. Soon I shall know. Then you will know. Come. Sit."

The smoke was thicker up high, and it tickled his throat. He returned to his seat and set Jouveau's notebook beside his own.

Lou lit a second cigarette. "Gil and Jouveau raise an interesting question. Who gets to decide what is worthy of news? The reporter? The editor? The paper or radio network? The government? Or the public? And if we agree it's the public, who speaks for the public?"

"The government speaks for the public." Gil's complexion had returned to its usual pale tone. "And the BBC speaks for the government."

Disgusted grunts circled the table, and Hugh shook his head. "The BBC Charter clearly states we are independent of the government."

"In times of war, they have the right to take over the BBC," Gil said. "They haven't, but they could. They should."

Hugh kept shaking his head, and his chest tightened. The

smoke was too thick. He had to leave before he had an attack, but he couldn't let words like that go unchallenged. Recently, the director-general of the Ministry of Information had proposed taking control of the BBC, but Duff Cooper, the Minister of Information, had refused, thank goodness.

Gil slapped the table. "The government should control the news for the good of the nation."

With a cough, Hugh cleared smoke from his shriveling lungs. "For the good of the nation?"

Louisa lifted a sardonic smile. "What *is* the good of the nation?"

"To defeat Germany," Gil said.

"We all agree on that." Louisa raised one eyebrow.

Hugh followed her train of thought. "How does the news affect the war effort? We spread necessary information about blackouts and sheltering, about doing our bit by volunteering and taking factory work, yes?"

Everyone nodded and murmured agreement.

His airways clenched, and he coughed to loosen them. "What about war news? When Britain prevails, we all agree on truthful, detailed reporting."

More nods, more murmurs of agreement.

"But when Britain suffers defeat, what then?" A whistle entered his voice. He needed to leave. But how? The conversation promised no lull.

Jouveau smashed the stub of his cigarette in an ashtray. "We should hold to the same standards in defeat as in victory."

Hugh agreed, and the BBC agreed in principle. But on not too rare an occasion, the War Office, Admiralty, or Ministry of Information had interfered.

However, speaking would elicit an unmistakable wheeze.

"We cannot report defeats in such a way." Gil made a slashing motion with his good hand. "People will lose heart and lose the will to fight."

"Will they?" Aleida inclined her head. "London has been pummeled by bombs for fifty-seven nights in a row. Over ten thousand have died. Even more have lost their homes. But the will to fight is as strong as ever. Stronger, I believe."

"Smart girl." Lou nudged her friend with an elbow. "I, for one, want to know what's really happening, even the hard stuff. No matter what, don't lie to me."

"Yes," Aleida said. "When does glossing over the truth become lying?"

With each breath, Hugh's lungs tightened more. But he needed an opening, an excuse. Why hadn't he left as soon as Barn unloaded his stinking treasure?

MacLeod waved his cigarette in a circle. "Exactly. Sometimes being vague is necessary. For example, reporting where bombs fall would help the Luftwaffe improve navigation. But from what I've seen, the public is hungry for the truth."

"I disagree." Gil's face blurred in the haze. "We must keep up morale."

"Morale?" Jouveau wrinkled his nose. "Is that the sole purpose of our work? To create a happy and deluded populace? Or an educated populace, braced for action?"

Hugh couldn't breathe. He needed his medication. By waiting too long, he'd forfeited the opportunity to leave without making a scene.

He shoved back his chair, grabbed his notebook, and fled into the night.

19

Hugh?" Aleida stared after him.

"What got into Collie?" the man called Barn said in his American accent.

"I don't know," Aleida whispered. Over the past few minutes, he'd grown paler, with distress wrinkling his brow. But lively debates usually made him even more animated and excited.

He'd left his coat and hat, and it was raining. Something was amiss.

Louisa nudged her. "Go find out, Aleida."

"Yes," Jouveau said. "You're his girl."

Aleida whirled to face him. "I'm not his—"

"Go." Louisa's eyes flashed green fire. "He hasn't come back for his coat."

Something was very amiss. Aleida sprang to her feet, tugged on her coat, and grabbed her belongings and Hugh's.

Outside, she raised her umbrella and peered into the black, rainy night. Had he gone home? She wasn't sure where he lived. Somewhere in Mayfair close to Hyde Park.

She broke into a jog so she had some chance of catching him.

Rain pattered her umbrella, and she wrestled her torch out

of her coat pocket, not easy with Hugh's hat in her umbrella-holding hand and his coat draped over that arm.

A door opened across the street, releasing an illegal shaft of golden light, which silhouetted a hatless man.

After Aleida swung her torchlight both ways down the darkened street, she ran across, her shoes slapping the wet pavement.

The man turned right at Oxford Circus, and Aleida followed. "Hugh!"

The man startled and glanced back. His shoulders hunched, and he forged ahead.

Why would he ignore her? She ran up to him. "What's wrong?"

He shook his head and plowed forward. Rain droplets dotted his face. "Go . . . home." No meanness tinged his words, only . . . resignation?

"You forgot your hat and coat." She extended her burdened arm toward him.

He jerked his gaze to her and took his things with only a minor hitch in his step. "Thanks." But he put on neither hat nor coat.

She'd never seen him like this, avoiding her gaze, breathing hard. "What's wrong?"

"Leave . . . me be." His voice wasn't caramel, but thin and crackling. He gripped his chest.

Like an air raid survivor with smoke in his lungs. "Are you having trouble breathing?"

"Please . . . go home." He picked up his pace, but his course wobbled.

With torch in hand, Aleida wound her arm around his to steady him. He tried to shrug her off, but she had no intention of leaving him. Who would call for help if he collapsed?

The fight went out of him, but he kept up his pace, even as wheezes shredded each breath.

As they charged on, Aleida held her umbrella over his head

and watched for a first aid post. The cigarette smoke had been bothersome at the pub. Had he inhaled too much? Or did he have asthma?

Like his sister who died. Aleida's own breath caught.

He turned down a narrower street and mounted the steps of a Regency home. He rang the doorbell over and over, then flung open the door.

Why ring the bell knowing it was unlocked?

Aleida slipped inside behind him.

A middle-aged man with thin dark hair raced down the stairs. "Mr. Collingwood?"

"Pneumostat." Then Hugh shot Aleida an anguished look. "Go."

Aleida caught the eye of the other man. "I'm his friend. I think he needs a doctor."

Hugh waved her off and marched to the back of the house.

The older man nodded toward a sitting room. "Please have a seat, miss. I need to assist him."

Aleida stood in the entryway. Her umbrella dribbled on the marble floor, and her heart strained toward Hugh. Was he having an asthmatic attack? Did this man—the butler?—know how to treat it?

Should she leave as asked?

How could she, not knowing whether he was all right? She set her umbrella in the stand and hung up her coat and hat.

In an ornate mirror, she smoothed her hair and tucked loose strands into the coils.

From the back of the house, metal clanged on wood and a soft but urgent voice rose.

She should wait in the sitting room as told, but she followed the sounds to the back stairs and down to the basement.

Light arose from the kitchen. An electric motor whirred and liquid bubbled.

Hugh sat at a table before a black metal apparatus, and he

held a rubber mask over his nose and mouth. Wet hair curled over his forehead. He spotted her, and he squeezed his eyes shut.

"Breathe slowly and deeply." The butler helped Hugh remove his soaked suit jacket.

A pit opened in Aleida's stomach. "I shouldn't have intruded. How rude of me."

"It's never rude to help an ailing friend." The butler hung Hugh's jacket over a chairback. "I'm Simmons. Whilst you wait, why don't you make a pot of tea? It helps. Kettle's on the stove, and tea's in a tin on the shelf above."

Aleida took the kettle to the sink and turned on the water. "Tea is the British cure for everything, yes? Even an unwelcome intruder?"

Simmons toweled off Hugh's hair. "In this case, tea is truly a cure. It opens the airways."

"Asthma." Aleida set the kettle on the stove and lit the fire. Her vision blurred, and her heart ached for Hugh, not just because of the disease but because of his embarrassment. Embarrassment she'd caused.

She spooned tea into the teapot. "I'm sorry, Hugh. You didn't want me to know, and now I do. You told me to go home, and I didn't. I was worried about you, but that's no excuse to violate your privacy."

Aleida blinked her vision clear, raised her chin, and faced him. "The kettle's on, and the tea's in the pot. I'll leave now."

Hugh lowered the mask. "Simmons, please show Mrs. Martens to my study. I'll join her shortly with the tea."

Aleida cringed. "I should—"

"Please come with me, ma'am." Simmons gestured to the stairs.

Wearing the mask again, Hugh nodded without meeting her gaze.

Aleida followed Simmons upstairs.

He pointed toward the rear of the house. "If the bombers come, the shelter is in the garden through that door."

"Thank you."

"His treatment lasts a quarter of an hour." Simmons led her into the study, and he turned on a lamp. "Thank you for seeing him home. He could use a genuine friend."

Aleida offered a weak smile, and when he left, she settled into a brown leather armchair. What a curious thing to say. Hugh had dozens of friends. Everywhere he went, he made friends.

The room smelled of leather and tea and ink. Papers and notebooks lay scattered over the surface of a rolltop desk, and three teacups sat on top, divorced from their saucers. A low cabinet rested by her chair, supporting two saucers and more papers. Two bookcases boasted a riot of books, most lying on their sides.

A single saucer sat on the floor beside the desk chair. Dear, disorganized Hugh.

A small sob spilled out, and she clapped her hand over her mouth. Had she destroyed their friendship? How she would miss his humor and cheer and compassion and brilliance.

After fifteen painful minutes, Hugh entered with a tray. He'd put on a brown wool jumper and had combed his damp hair. She'd never seen him so subdued. Depleted.

Words stuck in Aleida's throat. Asking how he felt would be polite, but calling attention to an ailment he'd concealed seemed most impolite.

He set the tray on the cabinet and poured two cups of tea. "Would you care for a biscuit?" His voice still sounded thin but no longer crackled.

"No, thank you."

Hugh handed her a cup, poured a stream of milk into his own cup, and sat in his chair. He stirred, not meeting her eye. "When I told you about my sister, I wanted to tell you about my asthma. I chose not to."

"You're ashamed of it." She kept her tone soft.

His face agitated, and he said nothing.

Aleida took a sip of warm comfort. "Sebastiaan was ashamed of Theo's hand. Were your parents ashamed of your asthma?"

Hugh swung his head back and forth. "Not ashamed. Terrified, especially after losing Caroline. They coddled me, kept me inside. No exertion, no cats or dogs, no school. They let me do whatever I wanted. I became a holy terror."

Yet he was now a vigorous and kindhearted man. "What changed?"

"George Baldwin came as my tutor when I was ten." Hugh reached across his desk and stroked a book leaning against the back in a place of honor. "After a week enduring my nonsense, he made me read *The Secret Garden*."

Aleida swallowed a sip of tea. "I read that one summer at Tante Margriet's. I loved it."

"I thought it was a girls' book, but Mr. Baldwin insisted." Hugh pulled the book into his lap. "I quickly saw myself in Colin, the spoiled, bedridden boy. But Colin changed. He grew strong and caring. I wanted to change too. I wanted to go to school with Cecil and the other boys."

Aleida's chest caved in. If Sebastiaan had lived, he would have sentenced Theo to an isolated life like that.

One corner of Hugh's mouth lifted in a slight smile. "Mr. Baldwin had to sneak me outside. We trekked through the country, and he taught me to ride and box and play cricket. He pushed me in my studies, and I worked hard. After two years, I was ready. Then Mr. Baldwin stood up to my parents and convinced them to send me away to school. He put himself out of a job for my sake, and I'll forever be grateful."

"He sounds like a good man."

"The best. We still write, and we see each other on occasion." Hugh set the book back in place. "He also taught me to hide my asthma."

"Why?"

Hugh shoved back his chair and went to the bookshelves, keeping his back to her. "When people know, they no longer see me, only the asthma. They treat me like an invalid and set limits for me. But I know my limits. Tonight I failed, which I rarely do. If I'd left five minutes earlier, you wouldn't have followed me and no one would have been the wiser. Now I'll have to fabricate an excuse for my hasty departure."

"I don't understand." Aleida frowned at his knit-clad back. "They're your friends."

"Friends, yes." He shot a rueful smile over his shoulder. "But also competitors. If Fletcher found out, he wouldn't allow me to report on air raids or anything requiring exertion. And Gil—fine chap though he is—would be more than happy to inform Fletcher of my weakness. That would end my career."

Earlier in the evening, Hugh had argued fervently for the sharp-edged truth, but in his own life rounded off the edges.

"You think less of me now." Hugh's eye twitched. "I see it in your face."

She traced the rim of her teacup with one finger. "I don't think less of you for having asthma."

"For hiding it, then."

Round and round her finger smoothed over porcelain. It did bother her, because of how Sebastiaan hid Theo's condition and how his shame affected Theo.

Hugh watched her, his chin high and set, but his gaze guarded and sad.

Aleida inhaled deeply. "Sebastiaan hid Theo's condition to protect his own pride. It hurt Theo and would have kept hurting him. Theo wouldn't have grown into a confident young man who could make his way in the world."

Hugh's mouth firmed. "I also hide my condition to protect myself. It's dishonest, and I'm not proud of it at all."

"There's a difference." Aleida pinned him with her gaze.

"Hiding your condition never hurt anyone else, and it gave you the confidence to make your way in the world."

"Regardless . . ." He crossed his arms and hunched his shoulders.

Aleida set her empty cup on the cabinet. "You underestimate your friends. You have all the advantages of wealth, position, intelligence, and temperament. Your friends think you had an easy road to success and resent you for it. They don't know what you've overcome. I think they'd respect you more if they knew. I do."

Muscles worked beneath his jaw, and he tucked in his lips.

A gray-and-white cat stepped into the study, rubbing his side along the doorjamb.

Aleida smiled and stretched out her hand. "You must be the famous Lennox. Hugh praised your cleverness, but he failed to mention how handsome you are."

"Do be careful," Hugh said.

Lennox lifted his nose and sniffed her fingers.

"So handsome," Aleida said. "Look at those green eyes."

"Flattery will get you nowhere. It takes him a long time to . . ."

Lennox lowered his backside, wiggled it, and leapt into Aleida's lap.

"Well, hello." She stroked his soft fur as he settled down.

"He . . ." Hugh's jaw dangled. "He never . . ."

"He's never sat in your lap?"

"No." Hugh gaped at her, and he rubbed the back of his neck. "He only recently let me pet him."

"Have you ever *made* a lap?" Aleida scratched behind velvety ears. "You sit with your knees apart, and you rarely sit still."

"Quite right." A grin cracked his face, then he leaned over and addressed the cat. "You may have won her heart now, but when the bombers come, she'll see what a coward you are."

"Poor Lennox." Aleida covered his ears. "I don't blame you for not wanting to sit on his lap if he maligns you like this."

"The bombers." Hugh straightened up and checked his wristwatch. "The Germans are running late. Rather rude of them."

"Do you think the weather's keeping them away?"

"We can hope."

Lennox twisted his head, and Aleida scratched under his chin. "What would you do tonight without a story to chase?"

"My days and nights are topsy-turvy. I suppose I could write my story about—" He patted his side and frowned. "Ah yes, it's in my jacket."

"Your notebook?"

"I interviewed men in a dozen government ministries. Would you like to see my notes? I organized them." Eagerness brightened his smile.

She laughed. He was adorable. "I'd like to see."

He darted out of the room. In a minute, he returned with a frown and tossed a notebook onto his desk. "It's Jouveau's notebook. I grabbed the wrong one when I left in such a hurry. Bother."

"Shall we go back?"

"He'll have left for his clandestine meeting. I'll give it to him tomorrow." Hugh leaned his hip against his desk and smiled at her. "Although my cat would like to detain you indefinitely, if the bombers don't come, you could get a full night's sleep. Shall I walk you home?"

Aleida buried her fingers in gray fluff. She didn't want the evening to end, but at least they'd have a long walk. "Yes, please."

After she planted a kiss on Lennox's soft head, she dislodged him from her lap and followed Hugh to the entry. He helped with her coat, and while she pinned on her hat, he put on his own hat and coat.

Outside, they raised umbrellas. Only the patter of raindrops broke the silence. No sirens, no bombers, no antiaircraft guns. "Dare we hope this lasts all night?"

"I dare." Hugh grinned at her, and they headed south through Mayfair.

On the way, Aleida asked what he liked to read, other than *The Secret Garden*. They chatted about books and shared childhood stories, some of which Hugh said he'd never told anyone before.

Simmons had said Hugh could use a genuine friend. He meant it.

All too soon, they turned onto Aleida's street.

Hugh stepped into the vestibule of her building. "What do you have on tomorrow's schedule?" His voice sounded funny again, not thin—but tight.

"I'm visiting two orphanages." Why was he asking? He'd seen her diary.

"Is that all? You should check."

He spoke with such certainty, she pulled out her diary. Hugh aimed his torch at the page. Someone had written in it. Hugh—and his handwriting was horrendous.

Her lips twitched. "I'd forgotten. I'm having lunch at the Savoy with Itush. At a quarter past noon, Itush and I will discuss a myriad of topics—it says so here. And at half past one, Itush is taking me to the London Zoo, where we'll laugh with great merriment at precisely 1:48."

"Itush?"

"Yes." She turned the diary to him. "An *I* and a *t*—see how the line crosses only the second line, not the first? Then a *u*, and this is hard to read, but it must be an *s*. It can't be a *g*—the loop isn't closed. And an *h*."

Standing close in the vestibule, Hugh tapped the page. "What if Itush fails to show?"

"He won't. It's written in the diary."

"But if he should fail to show and if I were to meet you—"

"He'll come."

Hugh chuckled. "If he didn't and I did, would you have lunch with me?"

Warmed by his nearness, her face lifted to him. "Only if you take me to the zoo afterward."

"I will." He swayed closer, and his gaze drifted to her mouth.

Did she want him to kiss her? Was she ready? Her heart shifted back and forth, yes and no, and the shifting lowered her chin a notch.

Hugh inhaled, stepped out of the vestibule, and raised his umbrella. "Good night, Aleida."

She gripped the doorknob for support. "Good night, Itush."

## 20

**TUESDAY, NOVEMBER 19, 1940**

I'm sorry," the secretary said in French. "We have not seen Monsieur Jouveau for a fortnight."

Hugh tapped his foot on the tiled floor of the office in Broadcasting House, and he gritted his teeth. "He isn't at his flat, and none of his neighbors or friends have seen him."

"Jouveau?" A thin-faced man stormed out of the office behind the secretary. "Have you seen him?"

He had to be Jouveau's editor, Pierre Chastain. Hugh extended his hand. "I'm Hugh Collingwood. I haven't seen Jouveau since the third of November, and I'm worried. No one—"

"Worried?" Color mottled Chastain's hollow cheeks. "I'm enraged. A fortnight! He didn't ring. He didn't send a message. Do you know how I've scrambled to fill his broadcast times?"

Hugh lowered his arm, his handshake ignored. "That must be a dreadful bother."

"Reporters! Irresponsible lot. When he returns, I might just murder him."

Sourness swelled and filled Hugh's mouth. Without replying, he left the office.

If Uncle Elliott hadn't been murdered two months earlier

with Jouveau involved in the intrigue, and if German bombers didn't continue to leave hundreds of victims in their wake, Hugh might have humored Chastain's remark.

Not when his friend had been missing a fortnight and no one seemed to notice or care. Had anyone filed a report with the police?

He strode down the curving hallway, past offices filled with a symphony of languages. The European Services' shortwave broadcasts beamed to every occupied nation on the continent, providing unbiased news to ears hungry for truth.

A woman laughed, then spoke in Dutch.

Since the night Aleida had followed him home, their friendship had grown closer than ever. Their day at the Savoy and the zoo had been jolly good fun.

But she'd ducked her chin that rainy evening when he'd leaned in to kiss her.

Hugh trotted down the stairs to the lobby. Was it too soon? Or would she ever be ready after what Sebastiaan had done to her?

He passed the guard at the door, put on his hat, and shivered in the cool mist. Might it have nothing to do with trust at all? She'd seen Hugh gasping for breath, tethered to his Pneumostat, tended like an invalid.

What a fine romantic hero he made.

Hugh marched south. He refused to feel sorry for himself. He had far more pressing matters, like finding Jouveau.

His new notebook poked in stiff corners inside his coat pocket, not supple like the notebook he'd left with Jouveau by mistake.

A notebook filled with information for the story he was scheduled to broadcast tomorrow. He'd delayed as long as possible, determined to check his quotes. He should have rung the ministers to check, but he hadn't. He was too distractible. Too foolhardy. Too hopeful in his conviction that Jouveau would breeze into the pub one evening.

Hugh could no longer delay his broadcast. The story was too important.

He passed the Hart and Swan. If only he'd been more careful when he'd left that evening. Now he'd have to trust his memory.

That was the last time he'd seen Jouveau. His friend had been so smug about his lead on Uncle Elliott's murder, and he'd promised to tell Hugh what had transpired.

It wasn't like Jouveau to break a promise.

Hugh walked faster, swinging his arms hard. Was Jouveau's disappearance connected to the murder? To that appointment with the odd initials?

JI-GB.

If only he could find Jouveau's notebook. It might contain clues to his whereabouts—appointments or excursions or names. Hugh had tossed Jouveau's notebook onto his desk whilst Aleida sat in his favorite armchair with Lennox in her lap.

Now he couldn't find it, despite diligent searching.

Hugh released a grunt into the chilly air. An irresponsible lot indeed.

In ten minutes, he entered the West End Central Police Station on Savile Row.

A constable in a blue uniform greeted him at the front desk.

Hugh introduced himself and showed his BBC identification card, which always opened doors. "A friend of mine has been missing a fortnight. I'm inquiring whether a report has been filed."

After the constable checked and found nothing about Jouveau, Hugh filed a report.

"I'm afraid it'll be some time until we can investigate," the constable said. "You can imagine how many people are missing."

"It must be quite a burden." What if Jouveau had been injured or killed during an air raid? A far likelier scenario than the one blackening Hugh's thoughts. And yet . . . "Might I speak to your detective inspector?"

Annoyance sparked in the man's broad face.

Hugh made a show of tucking his BBC card back into his breast pocket. "For a story?"

The spark transformed to a sparkle. "Of course. Right this way."

He led Hugh down a bustling hallway into an office. A middle-aged man in a brown suit sat behind a desk teeming with paperwork.

"DI Clyde?" the constable said. "This is Hugh Collingwood with the BBC. He'd like—"

"I don't have time for the press." DI Clyde flopped back in his chair and ran his hand into fair hair in need of a trim. "Make an appointment."

"I won't take but a moment." Hugh held his hat before his stomach in a penitent pose. "A friend of mine is missing, and it might be connected to the murder of Elliott Hastings."

"The MP?" The detective inspector sat forward.

"Mr. Collingwood filed a missing person's report." The constable presented it to the DI.

Clyde read it, then sighed. "François Jouveau. A Soho address."

"Yes, sir," Hugh said even as he tensed at the loss of interest. "He's a reporter for the BBC European Services. A few months ago, he broadcast an interview with Mr. Hastings, in which the MP inadvertently mentioned the departure date of a ship repatriating French troops. The ship was sunk. The police are convinced the murderer is French, but Jouveau disagreed. The last time I saw Jouveau, he had an appointment that evening, in which he expected to solve the murder."

The detective inspector rolled a pencil on the desk. "Who was he meeting?"

"I don't know. It was a scoop. We reporters can be rather secretive about such matters."

"That isn't much of a lead."

Hugh measured his next words. "I believe the case has to do with censorship."

"Censorship?" DI Clyde drew back his square chin.

"Both Mr. Hastings and Mr. Jouveau were known for speaking somewhat brashly and critically. They each had enemies in the Ministry of Information and the BBC."

"Censorship isn't much of a motive for murder." He slid the report aside on his desk. "The Hastings case is outside my constabulary, but I'll look into Jouveau's case. Good day, Mr. Collingwood."

Hugh swallowed his disappointment. "Thank you for your time, Inspector."

He followed the constable back to the front desk. Hugh had failed to convince the man, and the case of one missing refugee would be of little importance in a city reeling from air raids.

Outside, the haze had thickened into fog, blurring the damaged buildings into gray.

Perhaps he should have mentioned his suspicions, but they seemed circumstantial.

Albert Ridley had almost come to blows with Uncle Elliott and had been furious with Jouveau for professional indiscretion and for allegedly flirting with his wife. Except Ridley was in London the day of Uncle Elliott's murder.

Gil had been in the country that day, and he'd argued with Jouveau the night before the Frenchman disappeared.

What about Fletcher? Perhaps Hugh shouldn't have dismissed him as a suspect. The police had cause to question him, Uncle Elliott had pressed the BBC to fire him, and Ridley had unfairly criticized him for Jouveau's reporting. And hadn't Fletcher ordered Jouveau to drop the story?

Why would he do so?

Fog pressed around Hugh, cold and clammy.

Censorship was indeed motive for murder.

**21**

### Carmarthen, Wales
### Thursday, December 12, 1940

Thanks to Mrs. Owen's thorough local registry, Aleida's work in Carmarthen went quickly, leaving time to interview evacuees and foster parents. Miss Granville still encouraged her to visit the country to build the national registry of evacuees, but Aleida hadn't mentioned she continued her interviews.

Her initial goal for collecting the stories had been to persuade families to evacuate their children. Now she simply wanted to document conditions, good or ill. With hundreds of interviews, she would soon be ready to type her report.

After Aleida packed her notes and registry cards in her small suitcase, she smiled at the billeting officer seated across the desk from her. Mrs. Owen showed extraordinary care for evacuees and foster families. "Thank you for your help. The evacuees here are blessed."

"It's our blessing to help them." A slender woman around forty, Mrs. Owen wore her light brown hair in a simple pageboy cut. "Are you finished?"

Aleida rubbed the nubby brown leather of her suitcase. To ask about Theo on the twelfth day of the twelfth month—on

Theo's fourth birthday, nonetheless—felt like yielding to superstition.

Yet she'd be remiss not to ask in every town she visited. She gripped the suitcase handle to busy her hands. "Has anyone mentioned a boy of four, blond hair, blue eyes, possibly a Dutch accent? He's missing the fingers on his right hand."

Mrs. Owen pressed her fingertips to her round chin and frowned. "A few months ago we had a little boy with some sort of hand deformity. We had to send him to the hostel."

"The hostel?"

"For the children who are hard to place—persistent bedwetters, delinquents, those with delicate health—and we're required to send all refugees to hostels as well." Mrs. Owen raised a flimsy smile. "It isn't as medieval as it sounds. The children are cared for well, and they're better off than with foster families who can't manage their needs."

Aleida's face tingled as the blood drained away. Although stories of hard-to-place children peppered her interviews, no one had mentioned hostels. Theo was a refugee. Could he be in a hostel?

"The little boy is Dutch?" Mrs. Owen inclined her head. "You know him?"

"He's my son." Her voice cracked.

Mrs. Owen sprang up and flung her coat over her green WVS uniform. "My husband is a doctor, so we have petrol in the car. Shall we go?"

What if this little boy was Theo? Could it be? Would she see him today?

"Come." Mrs. Owen handed Aleida her dark blue coat.

With an intake of breath and hope, Aleida put on her coat and followed Mrs. Owen out of the guildhall and down to the road running alongside the ruins of Carmarthen Castle.

They climbed into a black car, and Mrs. Owen drove away, chatting about the history of the castle and of the new bridge that replaced a medieval structure a few years before. Dreadful, wasn't it, but necessary.

She was trying to distract Aleida, but it didn't work.

Theo.

Her heart fluttered. How much had he grown? Would he recognize her? If she'd known she might find him today, she would have brought Oli and the little wooden lorry she'd bought for his birthday.

Tap, tap. Aleida grimaced and shoved her hand under her thigh.

Still Mrs. Owen talked, now about the Welsh language and how evacuees struggled to understand some of the foster parents at first, and how the foster families struggled with Cockney accents and such.

Even though trapped, Aleida's fingers jiggled on the seat.

It seemed a month until they reached the hostel, a three-story brick home surrounded by gardens and lawns.

"I resist sending children here." Mrs. Owen parked the car. "I believe there's a home for every child, but sometimes we have no choice."

"I understand." Aleida's voice quivered.

Mrs. Owen rang the bell, and a woman admitted them and led them to the matron's office. Miss Lloyd, a heavyset woman in her sixties, greeted them.

After introductions were made, Mrs. Owen nodded to Aleida. "Mrs. Martens is searching for her son, a little boy of four with a hand deformity."

"Like Charlie?" Miss Lloyd's small eyes lit up. "The nursery class is playing outside. Come with me."

As she followed, Aleida's stomach tumbled, and she prayed incoherent pleas.

Mrs. Owen entered a sitting room with a bank of windows overlooking a grassy slope. "They're playing caterpillar. Charlie's at the end."

Small children in light blue play smocks held hands and snaked across the lawn. The boy at the end of the queue . . .

Aleida's heart plunged into her tumbling stomach. Charlie was missing far more than his fingers—his arm ended above the elbow. And he had sandy curls, not Theo's straight, white-blond hair. "He isn't Theo. He isn't my son."

If she ever needed confirmation that looking to numbers for signs and answers didn't work . . .

Of course, it didn't. It couldn't. Turning a knob twelve times didn't cause God to release the desires of one's heart. God wasn't an automaton to manipulate.

She'd always known that. But now she believed it.

Aleida slammed her eyes shut and prayed to the only one who knew where Theo was, the one who could lead her to him—or not—in his timing and his way.

"I'm sorry," Mrs. Owen said in a gentle voice.

A wave of sorrow broke inside her. It was Theo's birthday, and no one knew. No one would celebrate with him.

"Let's return to town." Mrs. Owen threaded her arm through Aleida's.

Aleida thanked her with a glance and went with her out to the car.

Verdant countryside rolled past on the drive back. She had two more days to visit towns in Wales, but all she wanted was to return to London and tell Hugh.

Those eyes of his—how soft they were when he hurt for her. Those arms of his—how he'd hold her and comfort her.

Was it fair to lean on him for comfort when she hesitated at any sign of romance?

He never pressed. He never touched her other than gentle-manly gestures. He took her to lunch and for walks in the park, more friendly than romantic. He was all kindness and humor and chivalry . . . and veiled longing.

She groaned and massaged her squirming belly. He de-

served a woman who could give generously, not one preoccupied with troubles.

Hugh had enough troubles of his own. François Jouveau
had been missing for over a month, and the police believed
him to be an air raid victim. Guy Gilbert had mentioned a
rumor that Jouveau had parachuted into France as a spy. Mac-
Leod remembered Jouveau talking about French refugees in
America—had he crossed the Atlantic for a story?

Hugh believed none of it. The connection to his uncle's
murder loomed in his thoughts. In vain, the poor man had
turned his study inside out searching for Jouveau's notebook,
for any clues it might contain.

Aleida sighed out another prayer. Only the Lord knew
where Theo and Jouveau and the notebook were. Only the
Lord knew who had killed Elliott Hastings. If only the Lord
would show them.

Back at the guildhall, Aleida asked Mrs. Owen to use the
telephone and she left money to cover the charge.

In a few minutes, the operator connected her to the Ministry of Health. Nilima Sharma transferred her to Miss Granville,
and Aleida told her about the hostel.

"Oh yes." No surprise colored Miss Granville's voice. "There
are fifty hostels and camps throughout the country."

"Fifty?" Aleida clapped her hand to her chest. Now she had
forty-nine new locations to search. "We can't find homes for
that many children?"

"Must you always sound outraged? We've removed these
children from squalor and given them proper food and clothing and a sanitary home. They ought to be grateful."

Aleida mashed her lips together. Yes, the children received
care. But they didn't receive love.

"Please, Mrs. Martens." Miss Granville's tone softened. "This
is for the best. I persuaded you to abandon your last crusade.
Please don't take up a new one. Now, I must—oh, do you—"

A voice murmured in the background. "Mrs. Martens, Miss Sharma would like to speak to you."

The phone clicked in transfer. "Mrs. Martens?" Nilima whispered into the phone.

"Yes?" Why was she whispering?

"I heard everything. Take up that crusade. Write your report. I'll help as best I can."

"Thank you." A light chuckle escaped. Her fellow foreigner, eager to upset the status quo. But if they spoke up, would anyone listen?

## 22

**LONDON**
**SUNDAY, DECEMBER 29, 1940**

Huddled in a cramped studio in the basement of Broadcasting House, Hugh listened to his recording with Tom Young and another engineer.

An exuberant Cockney voice rang out from the recording, but the only coherent words were cuss words.

Hugh and the engineers laughed. "Not him," Hugh said. Neither Fletcher nor Ridley would approve, nor would the listeners.

Young made notes, then played the next section, another Cockney man, but intelligible and not as colorful. "Excellent," Hugh said. "I like his enthusiasm."

After church, he'd stood outside Westminster Abbey with his microphone and the mobile recording van, asking passersby about their hopes for 1941.

An eager crowd had formed. Even though he needed only five minutes of material for his New Year's Eve broadcast, he'd recorded for an hour as the joy spread, infectious and bright.

"Excuse me." A young man slithered between Hugh's chair and the desk behind him.

The bomb Hugh and Aleida had witnessed hitting Broadcasting House on 15 October had killed seven and destroyed the news and music libraries. Then on 8 December, a parachute mine had floated down and exploded in Portland Place near the main entrance. Burst water pipes had turned the staircases into waterfalls and flooded entire floors.

After the second bombing, more departments, including the European Services, had evacuated to other locations. The news department remained but had descended into a warren of makeshift studios and offices in the basement. Many of the staff slept in a dormitory in what used to be the elegant concert hall.

The next voice on the recording was an elderly woman, quivering with emotion and wisdom.

Hugh jabbed his finger at the machine. "That's the one. We'll close with her."

The other engineer turned dials. "I'll cut the disc and add your introduction and closing."

"Good man. Thank you." Hugh took off his headphones, stood, and stretched. "Ready for our next excursion, Young?"

"I'll meet you at the van in fifteen minutes." A smile wiggled on Young's face. "Your favorite ARP post."

Hugh shrugged. He liked the narrative of following the same post over the course of several months. He also liked a certain lady who happened to be volunteering that evening.

Guy Gilbert stood inside the door, scowling at Hugh.

Hugh sent him a curious tilt of the head and joined him.

Gil stepped into the hall, and his nostrils flared. "You've caused trouble for me."

"Oh?" Hugh kept his voice low to encourage calmness. "In what way?"

"I was to interview James Morris in Home Security today, but he refused to see me."

"How odd. I interviewed him a few weeks ago, and he was most helpful."

Red spots formed on Gil's cheeks. "You misquoted him. He

never said what you claimed. And his words—you ascribed them to Herbert Little on the London City Council."

A pit opened in Hugh's stomach. Morris and Little hated each other. This was even worse than misquoting—this was a personal insult. "Oh no. I thought I remembered correctly."

"Remembered?" Gil's voice tightened. "Did you lose your notes?"

Hugh rubbed his temple, and his mind spun. "When I last saw Jouveau, I accidentally switched our notebooks."

"He must have taken your notebook to France—and your credibility with it." Gil made a scoffing sound. "How could you broadcast without notes?"

Hugh grimaced. "I was certain."

"You were wrong. You were sloppy and too lazy to ring Morris and Little to verify."

Hugh opened his mouth to defend himself, but he stopped and swallowed a vile mouthful of pride. "That is correct."

Triumph shone in Gil's blue eyes. "Tell Fletcher, or I will."

It was the right thing to do, and Hugh sighed. "Fletcher's in the country with his family for the holidays, but I'll tell him when he returns."

With a hard smile, Gil departed.

Hugh marched away. What on earth had he done? All reporters knew better than to trust their memories, especially when quoting people. How arrogant to think he could evade protocol.

On Christmas Day, his mother had told him once again to get serious about his life and find a more fitting position. If Fletcher fired him, her wish might come true.

After he used the loo, he washed his hands and studied his image in the mirror. What business did he have pining over a respectable woman like Aleida Martens? He was sloppy, arrogant, and soon he'd lose his job. Then he could add aimless to his fine list of credentials.

He slapped his image in the mirror and headed out to the recording van.

Tom Young and Gerald MacTavish joined him, and they drove slowly over darkened streets. The sun had set two hours earlier, and no moon would light the sky tonight.

Through November and December, the Luftwaffe had turned their attention to other British cities but had never abandoned London for long.

The van parked outside the ARP post, and Young and Mac-Tavish made ready.

Hugh mustered a smile and entered the post.

Across the room, Aleida stood by the lockers, donning her blue ARP coat. She spotted Hugh, and a smile bloomed on that loveliest of faces.

She already knew he was sloppy. She knew of his infirmity. And tonight he'd tell her of his arrogant mistake and what might result.

Still she beamed at him and hurried his way. If she should ever fall for him, she'd fall for the real man. He would never be so foolish as to turn away such a gift.

Hugh gripped her small warm hands in greeting. "How was Christmas with your aunt and uncle?"

"I'm afraid it was a bit sad." She squeezed his hands and released them. "We miss Theo and our family in the Netherlands, but we do have each other. How was your Christmas?"

Stiff. Unpleasant. Mourning the lost family members and criticizing the living. "We had a beautiful dusting of snow, and my parents invited you to Collingwood Manor next weekend. Some of their friends have billeted mothers and children in private arrangements. They thought you might like to visit them."

"I would. How kind of them." She stepped back and gestured to the other wardens. "We're ready for the recording. I'll take you on my rounds, then you'll join Mr. Peabody on the roof of this building at seven—he's a spotter. At eight you'll—"

The phone rang, and the room fell silent. "Yellow warning," the lady on the phone announced.

Everyone sprang into action. The warning came when the bombers' course was clear, about ten minutes before the air raid siren, allowing services to prepare.

Hugh took a stack of tin helmets from Aleida. "I'll meet you outside," he told her.

At the van, Hugh handed Young and MacTavish their helmets. "Yellow warning."

"The Hun is early tonight." Young leaned out of the van and gave Hugh his headphones and microphone. "It's only a few minutes past six."

Aleida and her messenger, Tommy, a boy of about sixteen, came out with helmets, gas masks, and torches.

The siren wailed.

Hugh strapped his helmet quite uncomfortably and precariously over his headphones, but the headphones were vital to hear Young's instructions from afar. "Ready?"

Young gave him a thumbs-up. "MacTavish will follow you with the van. Mind the cord."

Hugh spooled out cord and looped it over one arm. After he reached Aleida, he waited for Young's signal. "This is Hugh Collingwood reporting from an Air Raid Precautions post somewhere in London. As you can hear behind me, the siren is sounding. With me this evening is Aleida Martens, an ARP warden. Mrs. Martens, please tell us your first responsibility."

"First I guide passersby to the nearest shelter, but the street is empty."

"Quite right." Hugh gestured for her to continue with her rounds, and he walked beside her, with Tommy behind them. "Ah, there go the guns. Always a comfort to know our men are on duty at the antiaircraft batteries, making life difficult for the enemy. May your aim be true, my friends."

Hugh told Young to stop recording, and he lowered his

microphone. Later in the studio, Young would trim the extra or empty bits.

The van rumbled behind them, and the thumps of gunfire crept nearer. He and Aleida turned a corner. A handful of people exited Green Park Station, and Aleida urged them to return to the depths of the Tube.

As the siren died, the throb of bombers filled the void. The Germans rarely came in one massed attack anymore, but in dribs and drabs throughout the night, the better to disrupt sleep.

A sound like hail fell in the distance, and Hugh's mouth set in a stiff line. Incendiary bombs. Weighing only a few pounds, they did their diabolical work not with the blast of a high explosive bomb, but by burrowing through roofs and setting buildings alight.

Hugh squinted into the dark. To the east, pops of light and sound. Soon a reddish glow pulsed over the rooftops.

"It isn't far," Aleida whispered.

Distance was difficult to determine, but the fires seemed to be north of the Thames, perhaps in the City, the original square mile colonized two thousand years ago by the Romans, now filled with banks and offices and government buildings.

Whistles pierced Hugh's ears.

"Get down!" Aleida crouched then flattened herself to the pavement.

Hugh merely crouched, encumbered with microphone and cord.

A blast shook the ground.

Hugh stood. Dust rose one street over, and orange light built within the cloud.

On her feet again, Aleida stuffed her torch in her coat pocket. No need for it anymore.

Hugh raised his microphone and told Young to resume recording. "A high explosive bomb fell about one street away. Our intrepid warden is on her way to investigate." He trotted after her, making sure the cord never went slack or taut behind him.

They rounded the corner to the next street—nothing.

One more street. There it was.

"A house has been hit," Hugh said. "Flames of yellow and orange disregard the blackout, and are crackling, cackling."

What Hugh couldn't report was how the bomb had sliced off the front of the house. Floors jutted out like stage sets, with furniture intact. A bathtub dangled from the second floor, and a man pressed against the back wall, hurriedly wrapping a towel about him.

Aleida dashed closer. "Stay put, sir. Is anyone else in the building?"

"No, I'm alone. My wife's in the country." He gripped his towel about his waist.

Hugh stepped twenty feet away from Aleida and Tommy so his microphone wouldn't pick up the details Aleida would relay. "Upon reaching an incident, an air raid warden's first duty is to send a report back to her post, and that is in fact what Mrs. Martens is doing at this instant."

He whipped microphone cord out of Tommy's way. "Our young messenger mounts his bicycle to hasten to the post. There they will pass along the report, so the Control Center can dispatch any necessary services. Whilst our warden waits for these services, she can assist with first aid or firefighting. As I speak, she's slitting open a sandbag to smother the fire."

Amid the rubble on the ground floor, flames devoured. Aleida dragged the sandbag closer—too close to that dangling bathtub.

Hugh lowered the microphone. "Be careful, Aleida."

She glanced his way, shook her lowered head, and kept going. She hadn't seen it.

"Aleida! Watch out! It isn't safe." Hugh set down the microphone, scrambled to her—the bathtub directly overhead—and yanked her out of the way.

She yelled and turned on him, flailing her arm. "How dare you! Let go of me!"

He refused to let go until she was out of danger.

"Let go of me! Let go! How dare you?" Anger and grief shredded her voice.

That was how her husband had treated her, wasn't it?

With a crushing in his chest, a crushing of his hopes and dreams, he turned to her. That lovely face warped with betrayal and fury.

He pointed to the bathtub. "That was directly over your head. It could fall at any moment. I had no time for niceties."

She glanced behind her, and her jaw softened.

"Aleida." He waited for her to turn back to him. The fire in her eyes dimmed but didn't die. "Aleida, I am not Sebastiaan. I will never hurt you, but I refuse to pussyfoot around you either. I only wanted to protect you."

Liquid filled those lovely eyes and shimmered in the firelight. "Oh, Hugh. I'm sorry. You've always been—"

A crackle and a crash. The bathtub fell into the flames, sending up sparks and dust.

The man on the ledge cried out and sank to his knees. His ledge was much smaller now.

"Stay put, sir!" Aleida cried. "The rescue party will arrive soon."

Now that it was safer, Hugh dragged over a sandbag, ripped it open, and scattered the contents onto the fire.

But the flames had taken hold, licking up the wall, consuming the jumble of furniture.

Aleida scrambled to the street and flagged down a fire crew with a trailer pump.

Hugh's story! With the fire crew on the scene, he could return to work. He motioned for MacTavish to move the van out of the way of the pump, and he snatched up the microphone. "The fire crew has arrived. Ah yes, and a rescue party too. The rescue party is raising a ladder to aid a gentleman in a rather precarious situation. Now the hoses have been turned on, and streams of water leap toward the flames."

Not leaping. Trickling. Hugh's jaw and his microphone lowered.

One of the firemen cursed. "No water pressure."

"The Thames—it's at low ebb," his mate said. "I was afraid of this."

The flames cackled their evil laughter, rising, sending out whirls of black smoke. Filling Hugh's lungs.

Aircraft droned, guns pounded, and bombs screeched to earth.

Hugh dropped to his knees, and a blast of sound and light and heated air threw him flat onto his face, ripped the helmet off his head.

Aleida! There she was, on hands and knees in the street, staring at him wild-eyed. But safe, thank goodness.

A great grumble and crack of masonry and wood, and the back wall of the house collapsed in a cloud of dust and smoke.

Hugh cried out, yanked off his headphones, and plunged into the rubble, Aleida beside him. The man in the towel! The two men with the ladder! Hugh followed the ladder and the cries.

He and Aleida burrowed, tossed aside rubble, and the rest of the rescue party joined them. The two men who had held the ladder emerged, kicking off debris, bloodied and white with dust. Aleida guided them to the street.

Moans led to the other man, and they dug him out. "My . . . towel," he said.

Nakedness was the least of the man's worries. A twisted leg and a deep gash on his torso were more pressing matters.

Hugh's chest seized, and he coughed. No. Not now.

After he removed his notebook and pen from his pocket, he took off his coat, draped it over the man's shoulders, and arranged some privacy. The rescue party carried the man to the curb.

Soot smudged Aleida's cheek. "The stretcher party hasn't arrived."

"How far is the first aid post?" Hugh's voice crackled like the flames behind him, and he coughed.

"In the same building as the ARP post." Aleida frowned at him. "Do you need to go there too?"

A groan rose. "Not yet. But I can't record with my voice like this, and I need to get out of the smoke before I do indeed need a doctor."

A fierce red glow throbbed to the east, and embers danced in the air, taunting him. This felt like one of the biggest raids yet. How could he miss this story?

"Collie?" Young picked up the microphone and headphones from where Hugh had abandoned them. "We can transport the injured in the van."

"Excellent idea. I'll go with you." But he'd miss what might be the story of the year.

"Hugh?" Aleida touched his arm. "You want the story, yes?"

He grimaced. "I can't record."

"But you can write." She swung her gas mask container in front of her and pulled out the rubber contraption. "This will filter out smoke."

Like his Pneumostat, marking him as different, defective. "I refuse to walk around in that thing like a—"

"Hugh." Her voice came out insistent. "I am not your mother. I will never treat you like an invalid, but I won't pussyfoot around you either. I only want to protect you—and to help you write your story."

His own words came back to him in her beautiful voice, and he fell over the precipice into love, loving her strength and her weakness, her stubbornness and her bending.

Weak with it all, he bent. He took her gas mask and strapped it on.

Dark rubber fumes filled his nostrils, and the rush of his

own breath filled his ears. Unlike the Pneumostat, the gas mask covered his eyes too.

Through the clear screen, he could see the van drive away with the injured men, could see the firemen train dribbling hoses on the raging flames.

And he could see Aleida smiling at him. "Write your story. You're due to join Mr. Peabody on the roof."

He shook his head. "I'm not leaving you."

In the morning, the sun rose, obscured by whirling black clouds of smoke. But sunlight wasn't necessary in the glowing red sky.

London burned.

All Hugh wanted was to wipe the grime from Aleida's face and to soothe the concern under that grime. Then he wanted to sleep for days.

As he walked Aleida home, they left the worst of the devastation behind, even as ash and bits of burnt paper drifted down around them.

Throughout the night, Hugh and Aleida had fought fires. Dug men and women from ruins, some living, some not. Helped survivors to the rest center.

Throughout the night, words had billowed in Hugh's mind like that smoke. He'd captured many in his notebook, but the rest would have to wait.

They crossed the street leading to Aleida's flat. She stumbled on the curb, and he caught her arm. She lifted that grimy, exhausted, beautiful face to him, with a tiny smile like none he'd seen from her.

Throughout the night, something had shifted between them, and that was what he wanted to capture most of all.

## 23

BUNTINGFORD
SATURDAY, JANUARY 4, 1941

Servants cleared dishes in the breakfast room at Collingwood Manor. Across from Aleida, Hugh looked handsome in brown tweeds, the color bringing out the richness of his hair. As soon as he excused himself, they could go on their visits.

"Hugh," Mrs. Collingwood said. "Have you given further thought to your position?"

The muscles under his jaw went taut. "Not now, Mother."

Couldn't his parents see what good he did with the BBC? But Hugh said his parents listened to the wireless only when necessary. How could they have seen?

After everything Hugh had done for her, couldn't she do something for him?

Aleida turned a bright smile to her hostess. "Hugh's position at the BBC? You must be so proud of him."

All three Collingwoods gaped at her.

"His broadcasts are brilliant, yes?" Aleida released a sigh. "Insightful, intelligent, and moving. He's too humble to tell you, but he won fine praise for his report last week after the Second Great Fire of London."

"Is that so?" Mr. Collingwood's mouth bent in a pensive frown.

"Yes," Aleida said. "He interspersed recordings made during the air raid with commentary written afterward, after everyone saw St. Paul's Cathedral rising above the smoke. What was it you said, Hugh? 'Her buildings may have burnt, but London still stands.'"

A wide-eyed pause, then Hugh nodded slowly.

Aleida pressed her hand over her heart. "Then he closed with interviews he'd conducted with people on the street hours before the raid. Interviews he'd been tempted to scrap, he said. But he didn't. They reflected the determination and good cheer that have helped us through so far and will help us through whatever the new year brings."

Mrs. Collingwood stared at the table, her mouth tight.

Aleida folded her hands in her lap. "Radio correspondents like Hugh are one of the reasons England keeps carrying on. You must be very proud of him."

Mrs. Collingwood gave her a little smile, twitching with English propriety. One mustn't disagree with one's guest, after all.

Hugh cleared his throat and pushed back his chair. "Please excuse us."

"The car will be ready for you," Mr. Collingwood said. "We have petrol."

"Thank you." Hugh escorted Aleida out of the breakfast room and to the entrance, where he helped her on with her overcoat. "Thank you for what you said to my parents, but you won't change their minds."

Aleida faced him and buttoned her coat. "I didn't expect to, but I wanted them to hear that most people disagree with them. I wanted you to hear it too."

So many emotions flickered among the colors in Hugh's

eyes, and he reached for her hand. Then drew back, whirled around, and grabbed his coat and hat.

Her fingers flexed, eager for his. His affection for her was more than apparent, and he'd been patient while she hesitated.

Life had taught her that hasty decisions ended in disaster, but choosing Hugh wouldn't be hasty. She'd known him six months, cared for him, and trusted him. Genuinely trusted him.

In front of the house, the chauffeur had parked the car, black in a sea of snow. Hugh opened the door for her, then took the wheel and drove away.

Barren trees rose dark under a sky cobblestoned with clouds.

In a few miles, Hugh nodded to the right. "This is my Uncle Elliott's estate—my cousin William's estate now."

Aleida peered into the trees. "Still no arrests. Such a dreadful affair."

Hugh slowed at the driveway. "The house is a mile that way, over a rise."

"And the murder?" Aleida said in a hushed voice.

"Do you want to see the location?" Hugh's jaw firmed with a sad resolution. "We won't find anything the police missed, but . . ."

But he needed to see it. "Yes, let's. We're early anyway."

Hugh drove up a rise and down into a hollow, and he pulled over. He led the way through several inches of snow, and Aleida trod in his footprints to keep her feet dry.

"You can't see the house from here," Aleida said. "Or the road."

"No. The guests heard a shot and thought nothing of it. My mother said the police have dismissed the guests as suspects. All were down to breakfast."

"Someone came from outside."

In a partial clearing, Hugh pressed his hand to a tree trunk. "They found him here, under this tree."

The roughness of his voice rubbed her heart raw. "I'm sorry. I know how fond you were of him."

Hugh gave a jerky nod and traced an arc through the snow with his foot. "The leaves were shoved about, the earth dug up, indicating a struggle. They found two sets of footprints from wellies. One pair from my uncle, coming from the house. The other pair, about the same size, coming from the drive, the way we came."

Aleida crossed her arms against the chill. "You can see the drive from here. Do you think the murderer was driving toward the house when he saw your uncle and confronted him?"

"I do." Hugh puffed out a long, frosty breath. "Do you know what the detective inspector told my mother last week? They think Jouveau killed my uncle."

Aleida gasped. "Jouveau?"

Hugh sank his gloved hands in the pockets of a new charcoal gray overcoat. "They think he was angry that Uncle Elliott's slip of the tongue harmed his reputation as a reporter and led to the deaths of Frenchmen."

"He never said anything like that."

"No, he didn't." Hugh's chin edged out. "They say he fled because he's guilty. They think he returned to France somehow, as Gil insists."

Aleida gave her head a shake, trying to disengage the nonsense. "If he were guilty, wouldn't he have fled straightaway? Not after several weeks?"

"Over a month." A vein of cynicism flowed in his words. "Convenient, is it not? Now they can declare the Hastings murder solved and ignore the case of the missing French refugee. Meanwhile, the murderer goes free, Jouveau is still missing, and no one cares."

"You do."

He lifted a sad smile and gestured toward the car. "Shall we go? Mother gave me three addresses of homes nearby."

In the car, Aleida pulled out her notebook and wrote the addresses on a new page, numbered seventy-three. Not a good number. Perhaps she should have bundled them in a different way so it would be seventy-two—six times twelve.

She slapped her notebook shut. Or perhaps she should stop thinking such nonsense. Search, pray, and hope—that was all she could do.

Hugh pulled up a drive to a stately gray stone home. A servant led them into a sitting room hung with drapes of deep red. A couple in their forties greeted them, Mr. and Mrs. Thomas Warwick, and they all sat on two facing sofas by the hearth.

Mrs. Warwick handed Aleida a piece of paper. "Mary Collingwood told us you're collecting names for a registry with the Ministry of Health. Four mothers and six children are staying with us—all private arrangements. Here are their names, ages, and home addresses."

"Thank you." No four-year-old boys graced the list, and her heart sank a little, but not much. Disappointment had become routine.

She pressed on with her usual speech. "Have you heard of a four-year-old boy with blond hair and blue eyes, possibly a Dutch accent? He's missing the fingers on his right hand."

Mr. and Mrs. Warwick exchanged a frown, and Mrs. Warwick gave Aleida a curious look. "That sounds like Teddy Randolph."

"Teddy?" The paper crinkled in her grip.

"A nickname for Theodore." Hugh touched Aleida's arm. "Please tell us more."

Mr. Warwick's close-set eyes widened. "Do you know him?"

"I think so," Aleida said, her voice thin and warbling. "I hope so."

Hugh sat forward. "Tell us everything you know about him."

"Mrs. Randolph and Teddy stayed with us this summer," Mrs. Warwick said. "He was a sweet boy, but he spoke only a little English at first. He was shy around the other children, as if he'd never seen a child before."

Aleida pressed her hand to her stomach, the paper fluttered to the carpet, and she fixed her gaze on Hugh. "Sebastiaan never allowed Theo to play with other children."

"Theo?" Mr. Warwick said. "That's what Teddy called himself at first. Mr. and Mrs. Randolph thought the child would fare better with an English name."

A sob hopped into Aleida's mouth, and she covered it.

Hugh pressed his hand firmly over Aleida's arm. "How did the Randolphs find Theo?"

"Oh my." Mrs. Warwick set her fingers to her lips. "Such a sad story. They were in the Hague when the Nazis came. Mr. Randolph is in the Foreign Service. When they were fleeing, a man asked them to take his little boy. He said the child was sick, the mother was dead, and he didn't have a car."

Sick? Dead? Aleida's fingers dug into her cheeks.

Mr. Warwick's high forehead wrinkled. "Mrs. Randolph said the oddest thing—the child's father didn't want their name or address, as if he never intended to find them in London. And Teddy—he was perfectly healthy."

Aleida's hand flew from her mouth to Hugh's hand and clutched it hard. "That was Sebastiaan." He'd lied about her, about himself, and about Theo. "Theo's hand." Her voice choked off.

"Tell us precisely what his hand looks like," Hugh said.

Mr. Warwick made a fist. "Like this, but with tiny bumps where the fingers and thumb should be."

Aleida nodded over and over, joy bubbling away fear and anger and worry. "It's Theo."

"Where is he now?" Hugh said. "Do you have their address?"

Mrs. Warwick darted from her seat to a writing desk. "Mr. Randolph rented a home in the country for his wife and the boy. I don't know where, but I do have their London address."

"If you would, please." Hugh gave Aleida's arm a squeeze. "Theo is her son."

"Your son?" Mrs. Warwick whipped her gaze back to Aleida. "But the man said Teddy's mother was dead."

Hugh sniffed. "As you've already surmised, the child's father was a liar of the worst sort."

"Theo." His name poured out of Aleida's mouth. "My Theo. My Theo."

Hugh grinned. "That address, if you would, please."

"Yes, yes." Mrs. Warwick hurried back and handed Aleida a piece of stationery. "You've been searching . . ."

"Since May." Hugh took the paper and picked up the list of evacuees Aleida had dropped.

Aleida let out a laughing, sobbing sound.

Mrs. Warwick twisted her hands together. "You should know the Randolphs are the best sort of people. They love Teddy—Theo as their own. They've cared for him well."

"Thank you." A wet trickle raced down her left cheek. "I—I found him."

"Yes, you found him. You found him." Hugh helped her to standing. "Let's go back to the house, fetch our luggage, and visit Mr. Randolph in London."

Aleida's feet moved as if floating. "Theo. Today. I can see him today."

"Probably tomorrow. He's in the country." Hugh led her outside and down the steps. "See how well they've cared for him? They sound like lovely people."

They did, and Aleida sob-laughed. "I found him."

"You did." Grinning, Hugh pulled out a handkerchief and dabbed her cheeks. "It seems a shame to wipe away tears of joy, but people will think I made you cry."

Never, and she laughed and laughed. The dear, darling man.

"That is the most beautiful sound. Your laughter." His smile encompassed his whole face.

He was almost as happy as she, and she loved him for it.

She cupped his face in her gloved hands, pressed up on her toes, and kissed him on the lips.

She'd done it. She'd charged right through the sea, and she released him.

His expression—his eyes wide with longing and confusion and joy. Slowly building joy.

"Rechtdoorzee." She ran to the car. "Now take me to London."

# 24

Hugh couldn't stop watching Aleida, seated beside him in the train compartment on the Buntingford Branch Line. She'd never looked more beautiful. And she had kissed him.

Her eyes were bright, her cheeks pink, her lips curved in a smile.

They'd curved rather nicely around his lips too. If only she'd given him a few more seconds so he could have kissed her back properly.

She gazed out the window at the passing countryside. "London." Gave Hugh a dreamy smile. "Theo." Smiled around the compartment. "I found him."

Round and round she went, smiling at everything and everyone. "London . . . Theo . . . I found him."

She could think of nothing but her son—quite rightly.

Hugh could think of nothing but the kiss—quite selfishly.

Yet in an entire day devoted to elation over Theo, was it truly selfish to squeeze in some elation over the kiss? Perhaps squeeze in another few kisses?

He leaned closer. "Recht . . . door . . . zee."

Her smile tipped higher into mischief.

Excellent. She was open to flirting. "I admire that about you," he said in a low voice. "Especially today."

She swung her gaze to the window, and the pink of her cheeks darkened.

He nudged her with his shoulder. "I have one complaint."

Her gaze flew back to him. "A complaint?"

"Far be it from me to complain about a kiss from a beautiful woman." He spoke as low and as close as possible. "Much less a woman I care for deeply, but complain I must."

"Must you?" Her breath tickled his lips.

"It was too short. I didn't have time to respond."

Laughter frolicked in the sea-blue of her eyes. "Is it my fault you're slow?"

He chuckled. He did like her. "When dealing with a man of my limitations, you must make certain allowances. Next time, I ask for fair warning."

"You want . . . a warning?"

"Allow me time to prepare and kiss you properly, as you deserve."

Color rose even higher in her cheeks. How he wanted to kiss her right there, but the older woman facing them was trying most desperately not to watch.

Aleida sat back. "May I see your diary? And a pen, please?"

"My diary?" At her nod, he fished diary and pen from his pocket.

She flipped through, wrote something, and handed it back.

It read, "8:52 p.m.—Share a kiss with Aleida." Everything good and wonderful stirred in his chest.

Aleida tapped the top of the page, where it read, "Saturday, 11 January."

"The eleventh of January?" His voice rose high enough for the curious onlooker to hear. "That's a week away."

"Isn't this St. Margaret's Station? It's hard to tell with the signs removed." Aleida nodded out the window. The train had slowed and was pulling to the platform.

Yes, this was where the line ended and they transferred to London.

His mind scrambling, Hugh fetched both suitcases from the overhead rack. "May I suggest we move that forward to this evening?"

"A week." Aleida gave him a bland smile over her shoulder as she followed their fellow passenger out of the compartment. "Fair warning. I know your limitations."

He stepped out onto the platform behind her. "I don't need a week. I'm ready now."

She clucked her tongue. "I won't risk further complaints."

"I shall never complain again. You have my word." He trotted to catch up with her, passing through a cloud of steam from the locomotive.

"Then I have nothing to fear next Saturday." She took her suitcase from him.

He stepped in front of her, walked backward, and affected the pout that had never failed to get him his way as a child. "I don't want to wait a week."

"You need to learn to follow the schedule in your diary."

Pouting failed to move her? What did he have left? Would logic work? He slowed his pace, allowing the other travelers to pass them by. "I'm also supposed to be teaching you—to be less organized, to toss aside the schedule at times."

As he came to a stop, she did too.

"But the . . . schedule." She stood a foot away, and hesitation flickered in her lovely eyes.

For months, he'd backed away from that hesitation, but not today. He set his gloved hand on her waist and closed the maddening distance between them. "Whatever your reservations were about me—and I'm sure they were many—you've overcome them, yes?"

Her eyes enlarged even more, and her breath hopped in little white puffs between them.

"You kissed me," he said, "and you scheduled another kiss. You've already decided."

"I—I have." Her voice came out breathy, and she swayed a bit.

He pulled her closer and pressed his lips to her forehead beneath the narrow brim of her hat. "We're only debating the timing of that kiss. Next week?" He slid the kiss down the slope of her nose. "Tonight?" He met the pink of her cheek with another kiss.

"Oh, Hugh." Her arm worked around his back.

"Now it is." He met the pink of her lips, soft and supple and willing and blending into his. His suitcase fell, and he embraced her fully.

The months of waiting melted away into perfection, and he held her and kissed her, his own sweet Aleida. The woman he loved.

She pulled back a bit, her eyes bleary and her lips full. "I have a complaint."

"A complaint?"

She caressed the back of his neck and gave him a teasing lift of one eyebrow. "You're supposed to be taking me to my son."

Hugh chuckled, accepted the short kiss she gave him, and gave her another. "To London we go."

# 25

"Even if the bombers don't come tonight, I'll never sleep." Aleida laughed and hugged Hugh's arm as they rushed up the street in Hampstead toward the Randolph home.

Hugh grinned at her, seemingly enchanted by her rambling.

"I have so much to do." She ticked off tasks on his arm. "I need to make Theo's bed and bring Oli and the other toys into his room. And clothes! He'll have outgrown what I have. Do you suppose the Randolphs would send his wardrobe with him? I'll compensate them."

"I'm sure they would." Hugh guided her around a corner in the wealthy neighborhood.

How she loved his smile, his joy, him. Her chest expanded with the thrill of falling in love, not just with Hugh—but with *life*. "I can hold Theo again and kiss his face. How much do you think he grew?"

"He's certainly taller than you by now."

Aleida laughed and bumped Hugh with her shoulder. "I can put him to bed and make his meals and—oh! I'll need to quit my job. I have no one to watch Theo during the day."

Hugh's lips bent down slightly. "Will you go to the country?"

"I should. Tante Margriet will be happy to have us. She didn't want me to go to London anyway. She and Uncle James adore children."

"I'll miss you here, but I'll visit often." His smile became rueful, but deepened to genuine happiness.

Aleida faced him. "This is the best day of my life, and you—you're a part of why it's the best." She leaned closer.

He put one finger to her lips. "As much as I enjoy being the object of your affection, every time we kiss, you promptly order me to take you to the Randolph home."

She gave his finger a little kiss, whirled away, and pulled him down the street. "Come. I haven't seen Theo for 239 days." A delighted laugh spilled out. "Tomorrow will be 240 even—the day I'll see him. It's perfect."

"You counted?" Then he laughed. "Of course, you did."

All she could count now was houses. There—a stately red brick home with shining white trim.

Everything danced inside her, a jumble of excitement and nervousness and relief and gratitude. After a moment's hesitation, she rang the bell.

A servant answered the door and showed them to the sitting room, tastefully decorated in dark woods and muted greens.

Aleida couldn't sit, couldn't stand still, could barely think. What would she say? Should she have planned a speech?

A man in his forties entered the room, with dark hair and a mustache and a look of authority. "Good evening. I'm Julian Randolph."

"Thank you for seeing us." Aleida shook the man's hand. "I am Mrs. Sebastiaan Martens. Aleida is my given name."

No recognition sparked in Mr. Randolph's blue eyes, which turned to Hugh.

"How do you do, Mr. Randolph? I'm Hugh Collingwood." The man frowned. "From the BBC?"

Hugh chuckled. "I'm not here on business, only as a friend to Mrs. Martens."

Mr. Randolph gestured to two sofas flanking the fireplace. "May I ask what *is* your business, since you declined to state at the door?"

How could Aleida sit? "I suppose Sebastiaan didn't tell you his name."

Mr. Randolph's frown grew.

She sounded daft. "I'm looking for my son, Theodoor— Theo. You call him Teddy."

Those blue eyes narrowed. "Pardon?"

Aleida's hand fluttered in the air. "I've been searching for almost eight months, and today we met Mr. and Mrs. Warwick, and Theo matches their description of Teddy perfectly."

Hugh took a step forward. "We understand that when you fled the Netherlands, a man asked you to take his little boy. That man was her late husband, Sebastiaan Martens."

Mr. Randolph drew back his chin. "That is not the name the man gave us."

Aleida's hands went cold. Her heart. It had never occurred to her that she'd have to prove herself.

Hugh patted the sofa back and tipped his chin to Aleida, inviting her to sit, then gave Mr. Randolph a grim smile. "As you've already learned, that man was a liar. Theo wasn't sick as he claimed, and his mother, as you can see, is very much alive."

Aleida didn't sit. She gripped her hands together so tight the bones rubbed together. "I—I am."

"My dear madam," Mr. Randolph said in a cool voice. "Even if I were to believe you, why would I give a precious little boy to a woman who abandoned her child?"

Aleida's chest caved in, and a gasp flew out. "I was sleeping in the car with Theo in my arms. My husband took him, gave him away without my permission, without waking me. In the morning, Theo was gone. Gone. I love my son. I'd never—"

"Do you have any proof he's your son? Any papers?"

How could she breathe? "I have no papers for him. He's too young for a passport, and Sebastiaan didn't pack his birth certificate."

Mr. Randolph spread his hands wide. "Where is this Sebastiaan? I'd recognize the man I met on the road."

"He's dead," Hugh said. "Killed by a German fighter plane. But I assure you, Mrs. Martens is telling the truth."

Mr. Randolph acknowledged Hugh with a lift of his eyebrows, then returned his gaze to Aleida. "May I see a family photograph?"

A low moan built in Aleida's belly. She clamped her lips shut and stifled that moan. "I have none. My husband was ashamed of Theo's hand. He never allowed me to have Theo photographed."

Hugh rested his hand on her shoulder. "Please, Mr. Randolph. Sebastiaan Martens was a horrid man. Don't let his cruelty and his lies keep a mother from the child she loves."

Mr. Randolph moved toward the door, his gait stiff. "For eight months, my wife and I have raised Teddy, calmed his nightmares, taught him English, taught him to laugh again. I don't know what you want with him, but you've failed to provide a single shred of proof that he's your son, and the story you've told could easily have been pried from the Warwicks."

Hugh's eyes widened. "It wasn't like that, sir."

Panic hopped in Aleida's belly. How could this be happening? It couldn't be happening.

"I will not be fooled by a charlatan." Mr. Randolph gestured to the doorway. "As for you, Mr. Collingwood, don't let your love of a heart-wrenching story—and a pretty face—cloud your judgment."

Hugh's grip tightened on Aleida's shoulder. "Sir, you've misinterpreted everything. I assure you, Mrs. Martens is no charlatan."

Mr. Randolph nodded to them, his gaze as chilly as Aleida's heart. "I must ask you to leave. If you return, I shall ring the police."

No, no, no. Her breath came hard and fast. Theo . . . Theo . . .

"Come along, Aleida." Hugh guided her toward the door.

Somehow her feet moved across the floor, out the door, down the steps, out into the cool evening air. She wouldn't cry in front of Mr. Randolph. She would not.

With his arm around her shoulder, Hugh eased her around the corner, and then he folded her in his arms. He didn't say a word.

She gripped his lapels and buried her face in his shoulder. No. No. No.

She'd found Theo. Found him. And now she'd lost him forever.

# 26

Scaffolding supported the circular, colonnaded, spire-topped vestibule of All Soul's Church. The December parachute mine blast that had damaged Broadcasting House had rendered All Soul's uninhabitable.

Snow drifted around Hugh as he plodded up Portland Place. The same weather that had produced wonder and romance only two days before seemed bleak now.

Aleida was inconsolable.

Hugh jammed his gloved hands in his coat pockets. If he'd known Mr. Randolph would be skeptical, he would have helped Aleida prepare her story to unfold in a different manner.

At the side door to Broadcasting House, Hugh flashed his card to the guard and was admitted. Had his presence as a member of the press caused even more skepticism?

Hugh descended the stairs to the sub-basement. Yesterday, he'd taken Aleida to church, where she'd kept her head bowed through the service. Then she wanted to go home and sleep.

Her desire for solitude had allowed Hugh to take the train back to Hertfordshire to see the Warwicks. He didn't tell Aleida, didn't dare raise her hopes, but the Warwicks promised to write

Mr. Randolph to explain the situation and testify to Aleida's sincerity. Hugh had asked them to enclose Aleida's address in case Mr. Randolph had a change of heart.

He paused in the corridor outside the news offices, and a second strand of dread threaded through his soul. He had to confess to Fletcher.

Hugh had rehearsed, not to justify the unjustifiable, but to soften the blow.

Inhaling courage, Hugh opened the door to the tiny office Fletcher now shared with his secretary.

Norman Fletcher scowled, bolted from his desk chair, and jabbed Hugh in the chest. "What on earth were you thinking?"

Hugh sucked in a breath and drew back. What else had he done wrong? "Pardon?"

"I've been looking for you all morning, ever since Gil told me you misquoted Morris and Little—and how it happened."

A rumble of anger, and Hugh's jaw tensed. "That's why I came here now—to inform you. I told Gil I would do so."

Fletcher waved him off and marched back to his desk. "You lost your notes? Then you didn't check with your sources? Is this your customary mode?"

Hugh clutched the hat in his hands. Gil's accusations had fermented in Fletcher's mind into a potion even more noxious than the truth. "No, sir. This is the first—and last time."

Cocking his head to the side, Fletcher rested one hand on his desk. "What made this story so special?"

Time to edit his rehearsed speech. "François Jouveau and I accidentally switched notebooks. When I was due to broadcast my story, Jouveau still hadn't shown up, so I proceeded from memory. I was wrong to do so."

"You certainly were." Fletcher slapped at his phone, making it jingle. "I spent this morning apologizing to the men you misquoted."

Regret sank in a putrid pit in his stomach. "I do apologize. It won't—"

"And if one more person comes in here praising your New Year's Eve broadcast, I'll throttle him."

Hugh frowned. "Sir, I promise everything was on the square in that broadcast."

"Everyone praised it." Fletcher stepped closer, his gray eyes like icicles. "But I noticed what was missing."

"Pardon?" What had he missed?

Fletcher wagged his head back and forth. "You recorded on the scene when the alert sounded and when you spotted a fire. An excellent start. But your report on the rest of the raid was recorded in the studio, not by the mobile recording unit. Why?"

All the putridness swirled in his belly. "The stretcher party hadn't arrived, so we transported the injured men to the first aid post in the van."

"You didn't go with them, report from the post? Or have the van return?"

No. Because smoke had ravaged his voice. Because the gas mask muffled what voice remained.

Fletcher shook a fist. "Hugh Collingwood, one of the most vocal proponents for outside broadcasts, a man present at the worst air raid of the war, one of the biggest stories of the year, failed to record on the scene."

Hugh had no excuse other than his asthma, and admitting that would only worsen his predicament. He swallowed hard. "I did not."

"I should fire you."

Hugh's eyes fluttered shut. Through negligence and infirmity, he'd destroyed the career he loved.

Fletcher groaned, strode behind his desk, and pounded it with his fist. "If I fire you, one of your posh school chums will hire you, probably in the Ministry of Information. Then you'll have me ousted."

"Sir, I would never—"

"No . . . no . . ." He jammed his hand into his silvery hair. "I'm too short of staff. Everyone is joining up. I can't afford to fire you."

Some of the tension eased from Hugh's shoulders, but why? Fletcher would fire him as soon as the situation allowed.

"No, I can't fire you." Fletcher aimed one finger at Hugh like a spear. "But I can watch you like a falcon over a mouse. No more outside broadcasts. You'll record in the studio only. You'll run every script past me first, and you'll give me your notes as well. Then I'll check the recordings against the script before broadcast. You will be allowed no deviations."

How humiliating, but Hugh had forfeited any right to complain, so he nodded.

"As soon as I find someone to replace you . . ." Fletcher flung his hand toward the door. "Get out of my sight, you worthless toff."

Hugh winced and left the office, left the building, and his fine and expensive shoes pounded the pavement. A worthless toff indeed.

Snowflakes prickled his cheeks. Reporting was the only profession he loved, the only one he excelled at, and he'd tossed it away through carelessness.

Hugh marched south. Away. He had to get away.

He passed the Hart and Swan. He crossed Oxford Circus. He kept marching as snow flurried around him and dusted the ground in a deathly pallor.

Boyle Street. Hugh stopped. He hadn't checked with the West End Central Police Station about Jouveau for at least a week.

He charged down Boyle Street to Savile Row, where the modern concrete police station stood, blandly imposing.

The constable greeted him. "Mr. Collingwood—DI Clyde hoped you'd come by. He wants to speak with you."

"Good. Thank you." Hugh followed the constable to the detective inspector's office.

DI Clyde shook Hugh's hand. Although the inspector barely reached Hugh's shoulders, he carried an imposing force about him.

After the constable left and the men took their seats, DI Clyde folded his hands on his desk. His forehead furrowed. "I'm sorry to inform you that on Friday we found the body of François Jouveau."

All the air rushed out of Hugh's lungs, and he sagged back in the chair. "Oh no."

"He was shot, and his body was weighted down and dumped in the Long Water at Hyde Park near the Italian Gardens." DI Clyde stared at his folded hands, and his cheeks agitated. "He had no papers, no identity card, but we identified the body based on the location of the scar you described."

From when Jouveau was wounded at Dunkirk. Hugh gave a stiff nod. His friend. His bright, humorous, vigorous friend. Murdered. Dumped. Forgotten. No one deserved such a fate.

The inspector raised a folder. "Thanks to you, we're aware of the connection between Mr. Jouveau and Mr. Hastings, and we believe their murders are related. This allows us to refine our investigation."

"Thank goodness. I'm glad you realize censorship was the motive."

DI Clyde tipped his square head and frowned. "Revenge was the motive. A Frenchman killed them in reprisal for the soldiers who died on that repatriation ship."

Now Hugh tipped his head and frowned. "When I last saw Jouveau, he said he'd almost solved the murder of Elliott Hastings—and the culprit was definitely not French."

"Who was it?"

"He wouldn't tell me." Why couldn't Hugh find Jouveau's

notebook? It had to be in his study, but he'd searched every pile and drawer.

The inspector raised a smile bordering on condescending, and he stood, ending the meeting. "We appreciate all you've done for this investigation. We have solid leads and expect to make an arrest soon. Thank you for your assistance."

Hugh gave him a respectful nod and departed. Uncle Elliott and Jouveau deserved justice. But how could justice be served when it bent in the wrong direction?

## 27

In the back room of the Hart and Swan, surrounded by boisterous reporters, Aleida turned a page in her notebook. Smoothed it once, twice, thrice.

Why stop herself? Following rituals relaxed her. And what had she accomplished by sacrificing them? She'd found her son, only to have him ripped from her arms again.

Once. Twice. Thrice.

Aleida blinked hard at the blank page. In some ways, her renewed search would be simpler. She no longer had to search orphanages and hostels. She only had to search among private evacuations. Granted, a more difficult search than for government evacuations.

One hope remained. If—when—she found where Theo was staying with Mrs. Randolph, her son would recognize her, convincing the Randolphs she was telling the truth.

She'd considered bringing Oli to Mr. Randolph, but she doubted it would serve as proof, and he might have her arrested as promised. If she sent Oli by post, the man might dispose of the toy. Then she'd lose her closest connection to her son.

Her pen pecked the notebook frenetically, a telegraphist sending a message into the void.

Each day she and Theo were separated, the likelihood that he'd remember her dribbled away.

Laughter erupted around the table, centered around Leonard Kensley, a young reporter with the *Daily Express*, and Louisa nudged Aleida. Although Aleida hadn't heard the joke, she managed a smile.

Hugh entered the room to the usual refrain of "Collie," but in the gentled, lengthened tones used with someone in mourning.

And he mourned threefold—for her dilemma, for Jouveau's death, and for the embarrassing blow to his career.

Hugh raised a twitchy smile for his friends. Then his gaze landed on Aleida and softened, warmed, comforting and comforted all at once.

He sat beside her, squeezed her hand beneath the table, and murmured his greeting. Her heart strained to him. The early days of a romance ought to be sealed by laughter and kisses and overflowing joy. Not by grief.

"How were your interviews today?" she asked.

"Difficult." Hugh swept his gaze around the table. "I talked to a dozen of Jouveau's friends, colleagues, and neighbors. At first they didn't trust me. Since the police are convinced the killer is a Frenchman, they've been interrogating Jouveau's acquaintances."

Aleida stroked her thumb over the back of his hand. "If anyone could earn their trust, you could."

He ducked his head to the side. "I did convince them I only want the truth. Jouveau had a scoop about Uncle Elliott's murder. He said it sparked from a conversation we had the day we went to the Strand Palace Hotel. We were visiting Dutch refugees, looking for Aleida's son," he said to the others.

Aleida's recollection of the day's conversation centered on the refugees forgotten in the rubble of the Blitz.

Hugh's gaze sharpened. "Jouveau mentioned men in high positions who hated him for being outspoken. They wanted to censor him, as they wanted to censor my uncle. I believe someone killed both men to do so."

MacLeod let out a wry chuckle and crossed thick arms over his potbelly. "That's quite an accusation. It would have been a sensational scoop for Jouveau."

Hugh patted the table. "Jouveau left a clue about his meeting on the day he disappeared—a set of initials in his diary— JI-GB."

"Could it be the initials of the man he was meeting?" Aleida said. "Or the location?"

"Yes." Hugh hunched his shoulders. "It could be in English or in French or in code."

MacLeod frowned at the ceiling. "*J* for Jouveau? But why would he write his own name in his diary?"

"*I* for information, as in Ministry of Information?" Hugh said. "Perhaps he met a man whose last name starts with *J*."

Irwin swept in and set beers before Louisa and Kensley. "Ah, Collie. What can I get you?"

"Your hottest, strongest tea, please. And lots of it. That's a good chap."

Louisa raised her pint to the pub owner. "Thank you, *Jerome*."

The man gave her a quizzical look and left.

Aleida clucked her tongue at Louisa. "I know you Americans prize informality, but . . ."

Louisa raised a wicked grin. "Jerome Irwin."

Aleida gasped. "You don't think—"

"Not seriously, but where was he when Hastings was killed?" Louisa's green eyes glinted. "He wasn't here for several days, never called in. He claimed he was sick, that his phone was down. Flimsy alibi, if you ask me."

"Huh." Kensley narrowed his eyes at the doorway. "JI is an unusual set of initials."

"Circumstantial evidence," Hugh said. "Irwin had no love for Uncle Elliott or for Jouveau, but to murder? He's the dearest of old chaps."

Aleida gave him a fond wrinkle of her nose. "Too kindhearted to be a detective."

Guy Gilbert entered the room, spotted Hugh—and froze.

Aleida sucked in her breath. How would Hugh treat the man who had caused him so much difficulty?

"What nerve." MacLeod all but spat the words at Gil.

Kensley shoved back his chair and stormed over to Gil. "How dare you come here after what you did to Collie? You betrayed a fellow reporter."

Gil turned ashen and took a staggering step back.

"Now, now," Hugh said. "Let's not—"

"You ratted on Collie," Louisa said. "He told you he'd confess to Fletcher, but you couldn't wait. Nothing but a schoolyard tattletale."

"That's enough." Hugh stood, his voice low but commanding. "If you won't welcome Gil, don't welcome me either."

All eyes swung to Hugh, and Aleida pressed her hand to her chest. How would he treat Gil? With grace, and she loved him for it.

Hugh jabbed his finger at the table. "I was the one who violated our professional standards, not Gil. Don't blame the police for catching the thief—blame the thief."

MacLeod screwed up his face. "You're no thief."

"No?" Hugh jutted out his chin. "My carelessness stole my own credibility, as it should. But it also stole Gil's and Fletcher's, which isn't fair or right."

Louisa flung her hand toward Gil. "He ratted on you."

"He informed our editor of my infraction." Hugh grabbed a free chair and pulled it closer. "Gil, please have a seat."

Aleida's heart swelled with the goodness of Hugh's offer. "Yes, Gil. Please join us."

Still ashen, Gil gripped the doorjamb. "You—"

"I forgive you." Hugh patted the back of the chair. "And I beg *your* forgiveness."

Gil's gaze darted around the table. The other reporters glanced away, not forgiving, but no longer banishing.

With hesitant steps, Gil circled the table and took the offered chair.

Hugh returned to his seat and raised a mischievous grin. "The communists are having a convention in London next week. What do you think will happen?"

Chins rose, eyes lit up, and banter erupted.

Under the table, Aleida found Hugh's hand, warm and strong and dear. She gave him a smile full of admiration for his humility, grace, and contrition.

How, in these darkest of days, had love taken hold?

**Friday, January 31, 1941**

On her way to work, Aleida passed vacant lots cleared of rubble. In January, the Luftwaffe had bombed London only a few times, and the city had repaired and rebuilt.

She adjusted the heavy satchel over her shoulder. She almost missed the regularity of nightly raids. Now she never knew when the bombers would come, which seemed more disconcerting.

At a newsstand, headlines proclaimed Australian troops had taken the city of Derna in Libya as the Allies drove the Italians westward.

Poor Hugh. His latest broadcasts lacked his usual luster. Much of his charm came from interacting with others in interviews, and his worry about the murder case and his position at the BBC further dimmed his glow.

Aleida sighed and entered the Ministry of Health.

In the office, Nilima Sharma rushed over, her dark eyes shining at the satchel. "Do you have it?"

At the desk, Aleida opened the satchel and pulled out her report on the evacuees, which had taken several weeks to type.

"Oh my." Nilima gasped and thumbed the edges. "It must be a hundred pages."

One hundred twenty-four. "I summarized hundreds of interviews and organized them by the types of problems faced by the children, the foster families, and the billeting officers." She turned for Miss Granville's office.

"You're not giving it to Granny, are you?" Nilima asked in a fierce whisper.

"This is her responsibility." Aleida gave her colleague a reassuring smile. "I know she'll put this out for scrap, but I did make a carbon copy."

"Don't give it to her." Nilima grasped Aleida's forearm. "Take it to Armbruster."

"Mr. Armbruster?" Miss Granville's superior?

"He has a heart." Dark eyes gleamed like onyx. "He was working on a bill to aid the refugees, with that MP who was murdered."

"Elliott Hastings?" Aleida's voice came out thin.

"That's him. Armbruster cares about the children—the poor, the foreigners, the bedwetters—all of them. Granny cares only about the appearance of caring. Give the report to Armbruster. He'll force Granny to act on it."

The door beckoned, leading to the corridor, to Mr. Armbruster's office, to an appreciative audience for her report. Yet it felt like Gil "ratting" on Hugh. She'd compiled the report for Miss Granville, under her authority.

Aleida eased Nilima's hand off her arm with an understanding look. "I won't bypass her. It wouldn't be fair or proper."

Nilima whirled away. "Propriety!"

The door to the office stood ajar, and Miss Granville's voice rose through the gap. "You shut down those communist papers. Why can't you do something about this?" Her gaze snapped to Aleida, and she motioned her in.

A man's voice pleaded over the line.

"I'll ring you back," Miss Granville said, crisp and calm. "Good day."

Aleida offered a little smile. "Not fond of communists?"

Miss Granville blinked rapidly. "Last summer we locked up the fascists, and rightly so. But the communists are just as evil a threat. They claim the British establishment is a greater danger than Nazi Germany. They undermine our war effort at every turn. Communism is a beastly foreign idea. You aren't a communist, are you?"

"No, ma'am." Aleida set her report on the desk. "Here is my report on the conditions faced by the evacuees."

Red lips went taut. "I told you not to write that report."

"I finish what I start. We agreed I would interview evacuees and foster families and would compile the information. I've done so. I do confess I continued my interviews after you asked me to stop."

"Asked?" Miss Granville's brown eyes burned. "I ordered you to cease."

Aleida smoothed the top page. "It was incomplete. The stories need to be recorded. Most of the children are in good situations, but those who aren't—those are the stories that return to London and cause parents to keep their children in town, in danger."

"Exactly." Red spots bloomed on Miss Granville's cheeks. "Those complaints interfere with our work, which is precisely why I ordered you to cease."

Aleida pressed her fingers flat so they wouldn't coil in frustration. "We shouldn't be ignoring the complaints but addressing them. Our department is entrusted with the welfare of the evacuees. We need to help the children in bad situations. We should also seek ways to support foster families and billeting officers."

Stiff red lips bent upward. "Are you still compiling your registry of evacuees?"

"Yes, ma'am." Aleida clasped her hands behind her back. "We've collected thousands of names, all recorded on cards. The billeting officers have been most helpful, and they inform us when children arrive or leave."

Miss Granville slid Aleida's report to the edge of the desk. "Why are you still visiting the country for this project? It's a dreadfully inefficient process. Why not simply use the post? Send letters to any remaining towns. They can send the information by post."

Aleida's fingers went numb, and her cheeks tingled. If she didn't go to the country, how could she search for Theo? Could she . . . she'd have to go on her own. She could still meet with the billeting officers. Of course she could. She worked for the Ministry of Health, after all.

Miss Granville folded her hands on top of the desk. "From now on, you will conduct inquiries by post only. You will no longer visit billeting officers. I will not countenance any more reports from the country saying you've visited and meddled in their affairs. You will not defy me—again."

Aleida's breath lodged in her throat, throbbing. Miss Granville knew she was searching for Theo—she'd never hidden that.

But Aleida had crossed Miss Granville, so Miss Granville had crossed her back.

"That is all, Mrs. Martens."

Unable to inhale or exhale, Aleida gave what passed for a nod, and she fled.

Without visiting the country, how, how, how could she find Theo?

28

The hazy sky dimmed in the sunset as Hugh trudged to the Hart and Swan after recording yet another broadcast chained to the studio.

Frustrating. Humiliating. But he'd earned it.

"Be thankful you still have a job," he muttered, and he pushed open the pub door and the blackout curtain.

If Fletcher fired him, what then? He could return to the newspapers, a better fate than the one wished upon him by his parents. But his heart was in radio, his talents, and Britain had but one broadcasting company. If only he could earn his way back into Fletcher's good graces.

In the back room, his friends greeted him warmly—Lou, MacLeod, Barnaby Hillman, Leonard Kensley. And Gil.

Hugh might have publicly forgiven Gil, but he didn't always feel it.

He worked up a sunny "good evening," pulled up a chair, and plunged into the conversation. The Luftwaffe had rarely visited London since the New Year. Was this a temporary reprieve or permanent? Would the Nazis mount an invasion in the spring?

"The Germans may try, come spring," Hugh said. "But before they can invade, they must gain air superiority. If they failed to gain it last summer when we were at our weakest, they certainly shan't now. The RAF grows stronger every day."

Murmurs of agreement rounded the table. These men and women liked him and respected him, and Hugh's chest filled with the sweet air of approval.

His chest clenched. He needed to rest in God's approval alone. Hugh knew it. But did he believe it?

If only the Lord would sit down with him, look him in the eye, and say Hugh was a decent old chap and he was proud of him.

More sweet air entered the room in the form of Aleida Martens.

Hugh sprang to his feet, kissed her on the cheek, and helped with her coat.

She smiled up at him, glowing with warmth.

Words surged in his mouth, but he swallowed them. Telling her he loved her didn't seem proper when she was mourning the separation from her son and he was burdened by murders and career problems.

Hugh held out a chair for her and returned to his seat.

Irwin entered, brought Gil a fresh beer, and took Aleida's order for tea.

Gil pulled the pint closer. "Nothing stronger, Irwin?" His words slurred.

Hugh frowned. He'd never seen Gil drunk before.

"Nothing but beer today." Irwin gathered two empty pint glasses from Gil's place. "I serve what I get."

Kensley pulled a draft from his cigarette and let loose a gray stream of smoke. "If the Royal Navy sank more U-boats, more liquor could get through."

"Don't criticize our Navy." Irwin shoved past Kensley's chair, bumping him, making beer slosh. "You don't write that in your paper, do you?"

Kensley wiped beer off his chin. "I write the truth."

Hugh spread his hands and a smile wide. "Ah, Irwin. Kensley trumpets the Admiralty's successes, but he also mentions weaknesses."

Irwin glowered at Kensley. "The government ought to shut down your paper like they did the communist papers."

"Quite right." Gil raised his beer glass high—it was already half-empty. "Under—undermines the war effort."

With her hands folded in her lap, Aleida tapped on her knuckles.

Hugh winced. She needed a more peaceful conversation tonight, and a virulent shade of red flooded Gil's face. The last time Hugh had seen that shade of red, Gil had almost come to blows with Jouveau.

"Speaking of the war effort," Hugh said, "isn't it smashing how our troops are advancing in Libya? An entire Italian army surrendered to our boys."

"Indeed." MacLeod tipped his head toward Gil with a conspiratorial lift of his eyebrows.

The conversation spun in the new direction, Irwin left the room, and Hugh set his hand over Aleida's tapping fingers to still them.

With a mild smile aimed at the room, she freed one hand, slid Hugh's grip up to her forearm, and resumed the relentless tapping.

Hugh's heart plummeted into his stomach. She didn't even try to stop anymore.

The search for Theo had taken a toll on her the last month and a half, especially the past fortnight since Beatrice ordered her not to visit billeting officers in the country. No fruit had come from the Warwicks' letter to Julian Randolph either.

Although tempted to speak with Randolph himself, Hugh had no desire to spend a night in jail.

Out of the corner of his eye, Hugh studied the woman he

loved. Her face drawn. Her eyes too bright. Her hair pulled back tighter than usual.

There was an emptiness within her that he couldn't fill.

An ache throbbed inside, and he stroked her arm with his thumb.

What options remained for her? Even if she found Theo and he recognized her, would that be enough to convince the Randolphs without physical proof? After nine months apart, it seemed unlikely that little Theo would leap into her arms.

That was the only hope she had, and it grew thinner each day.

Bleak darkness swamped his heart. Would a time come when she would need to give up the search? *Should* she give up?

His chest tightened, but not merely from Aleida's dilemma.

Everyone was smoking except Hugh and Aleida, and a toxic haze filled the room.

He leaned close to Aleida to whisper in her ear. "The smoke's bothering me. I need to leave. Would you like to come with me or stay?"

She turned to him, and her gaze strengthened with an affectionate challenge. "What if they knew?"

Hugh held his breath. Indeed, what would happen if they knew? Aleida didn't think less of him for having asthma. Would his friends? Were they true friends if they thought less of him?

He'd kept his secret partly to protect his career, but Fletcher already wanted to fire him. How could the situation worsen?

If he believed God's approval sufficed, he should act accordingly.

Aleida's lips curved in a knowing smile, as if she followed his thoughts. Maybe she did.

He stood, as did Aleida, and he directed an apologetic smile around the table. "Excuse me, ladies and gentlemen, but I need to leave. I have asthma, and I'm afraid the smoke aggravates my lungs."

Aleida wove her fingers together with his.

Lou stared up at him. "You have asthma? For heaven's sake." She smashed her cigarette in the ashtray.

"I'm sorry, old chap." MacLeod snuffed out his cigarette too. "I wish I'd known."

Barn chuckled and pulled the ashtray toward him. "Here I thought I was doing you folks a favor with my gifts from across the pond."

Waving his hat, Kensley swatted the smoke toward the door.

Words and actions and expressions of concern. Not pity.

"Sit yourselves back down." Lou tugged on Aleida's sleeve.

"What do you want to do?" Aleida asked him in a low voice.

He could always leave later if necessary. He squeezed her hand, then held out her chair for her again.

Gil leaned across the corner of the table, his eyes bleary, and he blew smoke right in Hugh's face.

Hugh coughed and turned his head.

"Guy Gilbert!" Lou reached over the table, snatched the cigarette from Gil's fingers, and ground it into the ashtray. "Shame on you. Collie forgave you for ratting on him, and this is how you repay him?"

Gil's face crumpled, and he moaned. "I—I don't know. I shouldn't have told Fletcher. I shouldn't have—" He waved an unsteady hand toward the ashtray.

"Indeed not," MacLeod said.

Poor old Gil. Hugh patted his back. "That's quite all right."

Gil's gaze swam around and latched on Hugh. "Everyone likes you. No one likes me."

"That isn't true. We like you." Hugh gave a determined look to the others in the room.

They avoided his gaze, not ready to forgive.

"The wireless listeners." Gil massaged his forehead. "They're sending letters, clamoring for you, complaining about me. But I can talk as posh as you. I can."

"Yes, you can." Hugh patted the man's back. Gil had mastered the Oxford accent.

"But they know—they know I only pretend to be posh. They hate me for it." His voice cracked.

Hugh sighed. Gil's lack of popularity had nothing to do with his class and everything to do with his dry delivery.

Gil swigged beer, then slammed down his empty glass. "All we care about in England is class. Like Jouveau—no one cared that he was missing. Not until they connected his death to the death of an aristocrat. Now they care."

Hugh grimaced. "I'm afraid that's all too true."

"And they arrested the wrong man."

"What?" Hugh said. "Arrested?"

Kensley leaned his forearms on the table. "Didn't you hear? This afternoon they arrested Philippe Larue."

"Who's Philippe Larue?" Aleida asked.

"He's a leader amongst the French communists in London." Hugh frowned. "Why do they suspect Larue?"

"His handwriting matches the death threat sent to Hastings," Kensley said. "And as a communist, he hated how Jouveau supported de Gaulle and encouraged the French to resist the Germans—the Soviets' allies."

"Jouveau said the murderer wasn't French." Gil pounded his beer glass on the table. "It's one of Hastings's political enemies, I know it. Someone angry that Hastings couldn't keep his mouth shut. Sure made me angry."

Hugh exchanged a glance with Aleida. That anger had led him to toy with suspecting Gil.

"Remember?" Gil poked Hugh in the arm. "Remember the last time we saw Jouveau? He knew who the murderer was. I think the murderer knew that he knew. That's why he killed him."

Hugh stared into Gil's bleary but adamant eyes. Would Jouveau have said that in front of Gil if he'd thought Gil was the murderer? Of course not.

"I never cared for Hastings." Gil shook his head heavily. "I never cared for Jouveau. But I care for justice. They deserve justice."

If Gil were guilty, he'd be glad the police had arrested Larue and were distracted from him. And Gil was too drunk to lie effectively.

Hugh gave Gil's back one final pat. "Thank you, Gil. That means a lot to me."

"They do." Aleida's voice and her chin quivered. "They do deserve justice."

So did Aleida and Theo.

Yet justice eluded them all.

# 29

Outside the Foreign Office building facing St. James's Park, Aleida peeked around the base of a statue. With the veil on her hat shielding her eyes and a scarf around her neck concealing her hairstyle, Mr. Randolph wouldn't recognize her.

Since he'd threatened to ring the police if she came to his house again, he wouldn't hesitate to do so if he realized she was following him.

In twelves, she counted the men leaving the white Italianate building, the rhythm familiar and soothing. She'd never been in more control.

Miss Granville's order had been devastating, but only temporarily. Visiting towns, inquiring of billeting officers—that method of searching for her son depended on serendipity. Why continue an inefficient process when there was a man who knew Theo's precise location?

Mr. Randolph had refused to tell Aleida in words, but he could tell her in actions.

Surely he visited his wife in the country on occasion.

It wasn't prudent for Aleida to follow him, nor for Hugh, so she hadn't asked him to help. But Louisa had agreed.

One morning last week, Louisa had followed Mr. Randolph from his home to the Foreign Office, confirming that he did work there. Now to follow him to the country.

But today Louisa had been called away for a story. She'd tried to dissuade Aleida from going herself, but she couldn't let a Friday slip past. Every week, every day, her son drifted further from her.

Where was that man? One, two, three, four, five—

"Aleida?"

She spun around. "Hugh? What are you doing here?"

His fedora shadowed his eyes. "Louisa told me what you're doing."

He'd come to help? What was he thinking? She took his arm and pulled him to the far side of the statue, sacrificing her view of the door. "You shouldn't have come. He might recognize you, especially if we're together."

Hugh's lips rolled together. "Is this a wise plan?"

"I've thought through every contingency. I won't follow him all the way tonight, only to the Underground to see which line he takes. Next week we'll trace his route from London to the railway station in the country. Then from that station to the home. And this is the only time I'll follow him. Louisa will take over again next week."

"I'm afraid not. Louisa has decided not to help anymore."

"What?" Aleida gripped her hands together. Tapped. "Why not?"

Hugh wrapped his hand around her arm and rubbed his thumb along her sleeve. "We're concerned about you. I can't imagine how difficult this is for you, how frustrating it must be. But Mr. Randolph isn't a man to trifle with."

Aleida's arm squirmed beneath Hugh's touch. "I'm not trifling with him. Once I find where Theo is staying, I'll wait until Mr. Randolph returns to London. Then I'll appeal to his wife."

Hugh glanced away and sighed. "What if Mr. Randolph warned her? What if she's as intransigent as he is? If she's attached to the boy, she might not listen to reason."

Her chin firmed. She'd thought through that contingency as well. "Then I'll wait for the right opportunity, and I'll take Theo with me."

Hugh gasped. "Take him? You—you can't abduct him."

How dare he try to control her, try to tell her what to do? She jerked her arm free. "Taking my own son isn't abduction."

"What do you think would happen?" He leaned closer, his eyes urgent, almost frantic. "Where would you hide? The police would find you. You have no papers for Theo, no photographs. How could you prove to the police that he's your son? You—Aleida, you'd go to jail."

Cold, hard stone pressed against her back, chilling her blood, stiffening her spine. "You have no right to tell me what to do."

Hugh let out an annoyed grunt. "I'm not—I just—I don't think you're thinking straight."

Everything within her turned to stone.

Just like Sebastiaan. Whenever she showed any emotion. Whenever she dared disagree with him. "You think I'm hysterical, yes?"

His face scrunched up. "Hyster—no. I don't think that. But I think this ordeal has taken a toll on you. This deserves more thought. You may not be able to persuade the Randolphs, and you simply can't abduct Theo. At some point, you may want to consider . . ."

He stopped. His expression shifted to pity.

Into the void of silence, Aleida's heart tumbled. She'd trusted Hugh. Loved him. And now—he couldn't. He couldn't.

Hugh cleared his throat. "Sweetheart, Theo's safe. He's with people who care for him. At some point, you may want to consider letting him go."

"Let him *go*? He's my son! My *son*!"

"I know, but—"

"You don't know." She glared at him through the dark filter of the veil. "You don't care about the welfare of a little boy. You're just like Sebastiaan."

"Aleida . . ." Hugh groaned and closed his eyes, then opened them with a weary expression. "You might not have a choice but to let him go. Everything depends on the memory of a four-year-old child."

She snapped herself taller. "You think he's forgotten me."

"I didn't say that." His voice frayed around the edges. "Didn't I tell you he'll never forget your love?"

"But he'll forget me. Who wouldn't?"

"Sweet—"

"Don't call me that." Aleida edged along the base of the statue until she was free. "As far as I'm concerned, you can forget me too."

"Pardon?" The word plummeted to the ground.

"Forgetting me will be easy, because you'll never see me again." With a flip of her chin, Aleida spun around and marched away.

But her chin wobbled. Once again, she'd placed her trust in the wrong man.

30

W hat happened? Hugh's arms stretched before him, empty, as Aleida strode away at a crisp pace, out of his life.

His feet jerked forward to run after her. But he could still see her fury and terror when he'd grabbed her during the Second Great Fire of London in December.

It was over.

How could it be over?

He'd been direct, rechtdoorzee. Well, as direct as an Englishman could be. Why would she fault him for it? For speaking the truth?

Hugh's arms drifted down to hang limp at his sides. Over? It had barely started. Why, he'd never even told her he loved her.

Deep in that emptiness, a spark flared. How dare she compare him to Sebastiaan? And if she reacted that strongly to any sort of rational advice . . .

The spark fizzled and died. He swayed, and he braced himself against the statue. Beneath his coiling fingers, the stone felt as if it were crumbling away.

Aleida would never love him. His parents would never approve of him. His career lay in shambles.

He shoved away from the statue and walked. Walked somewhere. Away. His hands clenched and flexed, over and over.

What did he have in this world? An aristocratic name, an estate, and money. None of that mattered to him.

He had to get out, get away, do something vital. *Be* vital.

A trio of naval officers passed him in their smart blue uniforms.

He should try to enlist again. If he died for his country, he'd finally be good for something other than a laugh.

Hugh groaned, and his swinging hands slapped at the skirt of his overcoat. Every time he'd tried to enlist, he'd failed the medical exam. Even the Army and Navy didn't want him.

Great restlessness bulged inside him, punching fists in all directions, pushing him, driving him. He had to get away. Had to.

Fletcher—he always worked late. It was only a quarter past five. He'd still be at Broadcasting House.

Hugh broke into a run toward Westminster Station. He paid his fare, boarded the District Line, transferred to the Bakerloo Line, and traveled to Oxford Circus.

In the dying light, he ran up Regent Street to Broadcasting House, as passersby stared. He didn't care. He had to get away.

He burst into Fletcher's office, panting, bordering on wheezing. "I can't do this anymore."

"Collie?" Fletcher rose from his desk, concern etched on his forehead.

Hugh gestured toward the studios and gulped a lungful of air. "I can't do this—these vapid, meaningless stories. I must get out of London. Can you transfer me out of domestic news? You'll be glad to be rid of me. I'll go anywhere. I'll go overseas. I'll go to the jungle or the desert or the bottom of the sea. I don't care. I only—"

"Would you go to Scotland?" A strange light infused Fletcher's eyes.

Hugh tried to catch his breath. "Scotland?"

"Our regional reporter in Scotland joined the RAF, and they called him up earlier than expected. We need a replacement immediately. It's rather a desperate situation. He'd arranged a story—an excellent story. But it's dangerous. It would—"

"I'll do it."

"I haven't told you—"

"I'll do it."

Fletcher took a step back and rubbed his hand over his mouth. Then he sighed. "You'd report on the scene again, but honestly it's what you do best. No live broadcasts, mind you. You'd send your recordings and ring me with your notes. I will not have another Morris-Little affair."

Hugh raised both hands, splayed wide. "I'll never do that again, sir."

With his mouth set hard, Fletcher stared him down. "I'm still looking for a new man."

"I know." Hugh shoved out the words.

Fletcher darted behind his desk and flipped through papers. "In the meantime, we need to send you to Scapa Flow tonight."

"The naval base? Tonight?"

"Go home." Fletcher jerked his head to the side. "Pack a bag with your warmest clothes—that's all I can tell you—then go to Croydon Airfield. I'll arrange your flight. Then I'll ring our office in Aberdeen. They've already sent a light mobile recording unit to Scapa Flow for this—this event. You'll find out the details when you land. Now, go."

"Yes, sir. Thank you." Hugh bolted out the door and down the corridor.

He had a chance to breathe life into his career, and he'd grab it.

## Svolvær, Lofoten Islands, Norway
## Tuesday, March 4, 1941

Freezing Arctic air invigorated Hugh as the landing craft plowed through calm waters toward shore.

Norway! What a thrill to report on the first large-scale Allied commando raid. Hugh tightened the scarf around his neck, thankful he'd packed his thickest jumper and his wellies.

His landing craft, the last to shore, carried Hugh, a photographer and crew from the Crown Film Unit, and two BBC engineers with the components of the light mobile recording unit.

The craft streamed past fishing boats, and the Norwegian fishermen cheered. Hugh waved back. Nazi Germany had occupied Norway for almost a year, but this morning five hundred British commandos and fifty-two Norwegian soldiers were raiding the Lofoten Islands, home of fish oil factories vital to the German war industry as a source of glycerin for explosives.

Hugh had barely arrived in time to participate. His military plane had flown from Croydon Airfield to RAF Grimsetter in the Orkney Islands, a car had sped him to the naval base at Scapa Flow, and a motor launch had shuttled him to the transport HMS *Queen Emma* only minutes before the midnight departure of the fleet.

The next few days at sea, Hugh had been briefed on the raid—and what he was allowed and not allowed to broadcast. He'd taken careful note.

Under clear and sunny skies, the Lofoten Islands jutted from the sea, craggy black rock draped thick with snow. Seagulls swooped overhead as if rejoicing to see the Allies tweak their noses at Herr Hitler.

The only gunfire Hugh had heard came from British vessels sinking German cargo ships. Apparently no German troops had opposed the commandos.

The landing craft scraped up onto the rocky shore. Sailors lowered the bow ramp, which splashed in a few inches of water.

Hugh helped the BBC engineers carry the recording machine, amplifier, power supply unit, batteries, microphone, and cables ashore and to a level spot on the wooden wharf.

Then he turned to Lieutenant Andrews, the Army officer assigned to him. "Whilst they set up the equipment, would you care to chaperone me around town?"

Thank goodness Andrews had a sense of humor, and the lieutenant swept his arm in a grand gesture toward the fishing village. "After you."

Hugh tramped down a snowy street between wood-frame buildings of red, white, and green. British commandos in helmets and earth-brown battledress strolled past grinning civilians. Soldiers with Tommy guns guarded a larger building, and other soldiers escorted out two scowling men in long black leather SS coats.

Hugh would interview neither prisoners nor civilians. After the commandos left, German troops would return, and any Norwegians heard on the BBC would be in grave danger.

His foot slipped in the snow, and he caught himself against a bright red wall.

Around the corner, a road led back down to the harbor. At the end of the road, an explosion ripped out, and a factory shattered into a flurry of matchsticks and dust.

Commandos cheered, and Hugh smiled. After so many British defeats and setbacks, how good to see a victory.

On a loudspeaker, a man made an announcement in Norwegian. Lieutenant Andrews tipped his freckled face toward the sound. "We're inviting Norwegians to come to Britain with us and fight for the Allied cause."

"I hope our transports are large enough." Hugh resumed walking, selecting images and impressions that would best convey the raid to his listeners.

At a large official-looking building, civilians cheered as men hauled down the Nazi swastika flag and hoisted the red Norwegian flag with its blue-and-white cross.

More frowning men were escorted out at gunpoint, four well-dressed, middle-aged civilians. The men at the flagpole spat at the prisoners, shouting, "Quisling!"

Quislings—Norwegian traitors who collaborated with the Germans. Hugh edged out of their way, not even honoring them with a glance.

"Have you seen enough, Mr. Collingwood?" Andrews asked.

"I have. The engineers should be ready now."

They turned back for the wharf. Ahead of them rose three giant oil tanks.

With three mighty booms, the tanks exploded. Whorls of black smoke and orange flame billowed from the tops of the tanks, then flowed in a roaring river of fire down atop the ocean.

Hugh's breath snagged on memories of the Blitz, of Aleida handing him her gas mask, her green-blue eyes glittering in the firelight, as she protected his life and saved his story.

He grunted and charged forward. She wanted him to forget her, and he'd do his best to obey her wish.

A few dozen commandos rolled barrels of fish oil down the wharf, hacked them open with axes, and shoved them into the sea.

Off to the side, the BBC engineers beckoned. "We're ready."

"Thank you." Hugh took his microphone. When the engineers gave him the thumbs-up, he launched into his introduction.

"This is Hugh Collingwood reporting from high above the Arctic Circle in the Lofoten Islands of Norway. Behind me, you may hear the crackle and roar of flames—flames consuming thousands of gallons of fish oil, never to be used by Hitler's war machine."

As he described the details of the raid, the commandos stopped dumping barrels and gathered around Hugh. After Andrews agreed, Hugh interviewed the men. Their excitement and pride would make for an engaging broadcast.

The engineers signaled Hugh. The four-minute recording disc was full, and they needed to start a new one. Whilst they changed discs, Hugh chatted with the commandos.

"Wait till me wife hears me talking to Hugh Collingwood." A strapping young commando elbowed his mate.

If only Hugh could bottle the bubbling praise and carry it around with him, drink it when his parents badgered and Fletcher ranted and Aleida turned her back on him.

Hugh's mouth dried out with thirst. He could never drink enough. It would satisfy only briefly. Then the thirst for approval would return, drying out his soul.

"*Drink from the Living Water.*" Hugh could almost hear his tutor George Baldwin's voice in his head. Drink. And he'd never thirst again.

Hugh gave his head a light shake. He had only to learn how to do so.

These men's grinning faces would turn to the next amusement the BBC offered, whether *It's That Man Again* or *Hi, Gang!* His parents would approve only if he acted as they wanted. And Aleida's affection had evaporated the instant he'd questioned her plan.

Such praise, such approval was ephemeral, and he mustn't live for it.

Lieutenant Andrews shepherded the commandos back to their work.

From the town, a stream of men and women approached, smiling and talking and carrying bags. Norwegian patriots, leaving their homeland to fight abroad.

Hugh's heart swelled as sailors helped them crowd into a landing craft.

Escaping from under the German jackboot to freedom.

His breath froze in the icy air. As much as he and his friends complained about restrictions, they were at least free to complain. Those restrictions existed to protect the public, not to enslave them.

But someone in England wanted greater restriction, greater censorship. Someone willing to kill twice to do so.

In that man's eyes, Jouveau and Uncle Elliott had committed a capital offense, because careless words killed.

Careless words had killed Uncle Elliott. Killed Jouveau. Wrecked Hugh's career.

Hurt Aleida.

He winced. He hadn't meant to imply that Theo would forget her, but that was what she'd heard.

He'd been careless, he'd hurt her, and he couldn't help her.

"Collie?" The engineer nudged him. "We're ready with a new disc."

Hugh pulled himself together and reported on those brave, freedom-loving Norwegian men and women.

Not for the approval of Fletcher or his listeners or his parents, but because good broadcasting informed the public and aided the war effort. Because God had given him a good voice and the talent to be a correspondent.

And using those talents for a good purpose made a far more satisfying beverage.

# 31

MONDAY, MARCH 10, 1941

At her desk at the Ministry of Health, Aleida smoothed a letter from a billeting officer in Northamptonshire. No mention of a Teddy Randolph or a Theodore Randolph or a Theodoor Martens, which was his real name.

She was no closer to finding him. Thanks to Hugh's interference, she'd missed Mr. Randolph that Friday. The next Friday, she'd followed him to Trafalgar Square Station, where he'd taken the Bakerloo Line, which revealed nothing. He could take the line to Paddington Station and to the country—or to the Northern Line, which went to his home.

How many more weeks before she found Theo? Mr. Randolph might not visit the country every weekend.

The letter wouldn't lie flat, and she smoothed it over and over. Until it lay flat, she couldn't work with it, couldn't record the information from the billeting officer onto registry cards.

What about the billeting officer's plea to transfer some French children from a hostel to private homes? The officer said the WVS ladies accompanying the children to her village insisted the Ministry of Health reserved home billets for

British children. If it was indeed policy, it was unjust, and the billeting officer wished to lodge a protest.

After Aleida added to her registry, she'd pass the letter to Miss Granville for clarification.

Behind her, Miss Fuller clucked her tongue. "You've fussed with that letter for a quarter of an hour. With Miss Sharma absent, we don't have time for such nonsense."

Aleida's hand pressed hard on the letter, and she glanced up to Miss Fuller. "I wonder where Miss Sharma is."

Standing by a filing cabinet, Miss Granville flipped through a folder. "I tried to ring, but her family doesn't have a telephone. I'm sure she's simply ill."

Something didn't feel right, twisting in Aleida's belly. "This isn't like Miss Sharma at all. Last month when she was ill, she had her sister ring from her office first thing in the morning."

Miss Granville stopped flipping, stood still, then whirled around with a stiff smile. "Very well, Mrs. Martens. It's time for lunch. If you're so concerned, why don't you pay a call to her home?"

And skip lunch, of course. "Yes, ma'am."

After Aleida wrote Nilima's address on a slip of paper, she put on her spring coat in a muted dark pink.

She stepped outside to a gray sky, but at least the morning drizzle had dissipated.

Louisa Jones approached, wearing a plum-colored coat and hat.

Aleida's step hitched. She hadn't visited the Hart and Swan or seen any of Hugh's friends since the argument.

Louisa waved. "I came to take you to lunch."

"Thank you." Aleida watched her step on the damp pavement. "I'm afraid I won't be having lunch. One of the ladies didn't come to work this morning, and she doesn't have a telephone. I'm concerned about her."

"Want some company?"

"You don't want to miss your lunch."

"I'm a reporter. I eat whenever I have time. Come, child. Where are we going?"

Aleida frowned at the slip of paper. "It's in Willesden, on the Bakerloo Line."

"Off we go." Louisa strode up Whitehall toward Trafalgar Square. "I've missed you at the Hart and Swan. You can still come when Collie's not there, you know."

Aleida cringed. Louisa didn't know they were no longer together.

"Would you look at that bomb damage?" Louisa gawked at rubble outside a government building. "That was a whopper of an air raid on Saturday."

"It was." How could she tell Louisa she'd never return to the pub? How she missed the distraction and the company? How horrendous the last ten evenings had been?

Her empty flat, maddeningly quiet and lonesome. She couldn't even turn on the wireless, for fear of hearing Hugh's voice. All she could do was read, counting pages. Counting and counting and not reading. The counting that usually relaxed her made her more anxious. And the more anxious she grew, the more she counted.

She couldn't break free. If she'd never been more in control, why did she feel as if she were spiraling into chaos?

Louisa stepped around two workmen clearing rubble. "How long will Collie be in Scotland?"

"Scotland?"

Louisa's eyebrows lifted. "He's been in Scotland almost two weeks. Well, Norway for some of it."

Aleida gasped. "Norway? But it's occupied by the Germans."

"Didn't you hear his report on the Lofoten Islands Raid?"

She'd read about the raid in the *Times*. Although not a single Allied soldier had been hurt, it was dangerous. What was Hugh doing there?

"You didn't know he's in Scotland?" Louisa stopped in her tracks. "What's going on?"

"We had an argument." Aleida kept walking. "I told him I no longer care to see him."

"Was it because you're playing Nancy Drew?"

"Pardon?"

Louisa grunted. "American books about a girl detective. Was it about you following Randolph? If so, you ought to be angry at me too."

Aleida's chin tightened. "You didn't order me to give up my son. Hugh did."

"He did?" Louisa's voice rose.

With a roll of her shoulders, Aleida adjusted her words. "He said at some point, I might want to consider letting him go. He said I have no proof, that everything depends on Theo's memory."

"Sounds more like a suggestion than an order."

Aleida allowed a quick nod. "How could he even suggest such a thing? Theo's my son. He's my very heart."

"Hmm," Louisa said. "So, you dumped Collie for making a suggestion?"

All the frustration of that day roiled inside her. "He doesn't care about Theo. He's just like Sebastiaan."

Before them, Nelson's Column ascended to the cloudy sky, and the ladies descended into the Tube. Although disapproval radiated from Louisa, she stayed by Aleida's side.

When they reached the platform for the Bakerloo Line, Louisa turned that probing gaze to her. "You said Collie doesn't care about Theo. Is that true? Hasn't he helped you search?"

Aleida's mouth contorted. He had indeed helped. She could still see his look of joy when they'd left the Warwick home, the look that had compelled her to kiss him. All that joy for a boy he'd never even met.

A ripping inside, and her face crumpled. "He did help."

Louisa released a long sigh. "That explains why Collie took the assignment. Typical heartbroken man flinging himself into danger."

"What? You think—"

"I do." Louisa gave her a cool, hard look.

Aleida hugged her purse to her stomach and gazed down the dark tunnel, searching for their train. "You think I'm insensitive, unreasonable—"

"Insensitive? If anything, you're too sensitive."

Aleida glared at Louisa. Sebastiaan always accused her of being insensitive to his needs, then in the next breath would say she was too sensitive. How could she be both?

Louisa's eyes softened. "I think you're sensitive because you're wounded. Cruel men do that to us. They mess with our minds, then blame us for the mess. That doesn't go away overnight. Poor Collie got caught in the middle."

He'd looked devastated. Anguished. Not furious like Sebastiaan looked when she crossed him. Now Hugh was wounded too.

She'd done that. Had she made a horrible mistake?

Louisa nudged her with an elbow. "I'm still your friend. You can't get rid of me that easily. We'll just meet for lunch until you and Collie kiss and make up."

Aleida offered a feeble smile, but they wouldn't make up. She might have made a mistake, she might be wounded, but he'd poured acid in her wounds.

The train pulled into the station, and Aleida and Louisa found seats on board. Before long, they arrived at the Willesden Junction Station. A few streets over, they found the address, a two-story row house of golden brick with white trim.

Aleida rang the bell. In a moment, a woman in her twenties opened the door, a woman who shared Nilima Sharma's eyes—her sister, perhaps. A pungent scent of incense poured out the door. And a heaviness, a gloom.

A house in mourning? That would explain Nilima's absence. Aleida gave the woman a slight smile. "My name is Mrs. Martens, and I work with Miss Nilima Sharma. We were concerned by her absence this—"

The woman's face puckered.

From deeper inside the house, another woman wailed. "Nilima! My beautiful Nilima."

Oh no. What had happened to Nilima? Aleida exchanged a worried glance with Louisa.

The woman at the door composed herself. "Please come through. My name is Indira. I'm Nilima's sister. This is my mother, Manjula."

The weeping woman sat on a sofa. She wore her silver-streaked black hair in a long braid, and she looked up at Aleida with dismay.

Dread churned in Aleida's stomach, but she gave the woman a respectful nod. "Good day, Mrs. Sharma. I'm Mrs. Martens, and this is my friend Miss Jones."

"Please have a seat." Indira motioned to two empty chairs. "I'm afraid Nilima was killed during the air raid on Saturday night."

Killed? Her mind reeling, Aleida sat and gripped her purse. "Oh no. I'm so sorry."

"I offer my condolences," Louisa said.

Fire burned in Mrs. Sharma's dark eyes. "German bombs didn't kill her. An Englishman did."

"Pardon?" Aleida said. "What happened?"

Indira sat and took both her mother's hands in her own. "It looks like an air raid death. She was found—found buried in a collapsed trench in Green Park."

"But she was strangled." Mrs. Sharma's voice shook. "With the strap from her helmet. I saw her body. I saw the marks on her neck."

"She was on duty that night," Aleida whispered. Then she

shook her head. "I volunteer at the same post, though I wasn't there on Saturday. But why was she in Green Park? It's adjacent to our sector, but she would have been patrolling the streets."

"That's what we told the police." Indira squeezed her mother's hands. "She wouldn't have been in Green Park, wouldn't have been in a shelter. No one else was in the trench, so she wasn't escorting people there."

"And strangled." Mrs. Sharma rocked back and forth. "My Nilima. My beautiful Nilima."

Aleida's throat swelled for the vivacious woman she'd longed to befriend, for the family grieving a beloved daughter and sister. "The police—what do they—"

"Police." Mrs. Sharma spat out the word.

Indira winced. "The police say Nilima's helmet must have caught on something when the trench collapsed. I don't think it would have caused—" Her face buckled.

"Someone killed her." Mrs. Sharma pounded her fists in her lap. "I know it."

Louisa harrumphed. "I hope they find the monster that did this."

"I do too," Aleida said. "Nilima was always kind and friendly, and she was very good at her job. I will miss her dearly. I am so sorry for your loss."

"Thank you." Indira gave her a shaky nod.

Aleida and Louisa said goodbye, and Indira walked them out. Heading back to Willesden Junction Station, Aleida twisted her purse strap. "Another murder. Do you think it's connected?"

"Connected?" Louisa frowned at her. "To the murders of Hastings and Jouveau? Why do you ask?"

Aleida chewed on her lower lip. "It just seems . . ."

Louisa cocked her head. "Did Nilima know either man? Have a connection to the BBC French Service or to Hastings's work or to the French community?"

"I didn't know her that well. One day she did mention El-liott Hastings and his bill to help refugees, but come to think of it, she didn't remember his name."

"It's the biggest city in the world." Louisa swept her hand. "Eight million people in Greater London. I don't know how many murders are committed here every year."

"I know." So why couldn't Aleida shake off the sensation? The sensation that they were related.

## 32

### RAF Sullom Voe, Shetland Islands
### Monday, March 31, 1941

Microphone in hand, Hugh peered out a round window. "This is Hugh Collingwood reporting from inside a Short Sunderland flying boat of the RAF Coastal Command. That roar you hear is the Sunderland's four mighty engines as our aircraft plows through the icy waters of this inlet and releases—ah, do you hear it!—releases from the water into the sky."

Since seeing a Sunderland patrolling on the Lofoten Raid, Hugh had angled for this story. He'd spent the past week at the airfield of RAF Sullom Voe in the Shetland Islands, and he'd sent a series of recordings to London about the men of No. 201 Squadron. Now he could capture their work in the air.

"We are soaring above our airmen's remote base in a land of stark beauty, a land iced in the sugar of snow, in blatant defiance of the Ministry of Food's prohibition on iced cakes."

Above him on a scaffold platform, the two beam hatch gunners snickered at Hugh's joke.

"Now that we are airborne, shall we tour this fine aircraft, my dear listeners?" Hugh pushed to his feet and braced himself against the plane's metal hull, more unsteady than he cared for.

"You'll be happy to know the Sunderland offers a great deal of comfort for our boys on their long patrols. I am not a short man, but I have ample room to stretch. The aircraft contains bunks, a galley for preparing meals or a pot of tea, and a lavatory—my apologies to my more delicate listeners."

Hugh worked his way aft, spooling out cord as he walked. "Of course, our airmen are not here for comfort. They're here to fight. And fight they will. The aircraft bristles with machine guns, should any German fighter pilot test his chances. And a full load of bombs awaits any Nazi U-boat that might meander beneath us."

He peeked out another window. He would not mention that for every German ship sunk, about ten Coastal Command aircraft were lost. "Now we are flying over open seas. Hours will pass until we reach our destination, but our crew of eleven will remain ever vigilant."

He faced his BBC engineer, Robert Ferguson, and gave him a signal.

Rob nodded and stopped the recording machine.

Hugh leaned against the riveted beams forming the internal framework of the plane. Blue-gray seas rippled below, and the Shetland Islands diminished behind him.

He'd taken the assignment in Scotland to escape and to revive his career. At least he'd achieved the latter. His report from the Lofoten Raid had been widely praised, and also his reports from the devastating Luftwaffe air raids in Glasgow and Clydebank during the Clydeside Blitz earlier in March. In between, he'd found intriguing stories at the naval base at Scapa Flow and with Scottish farmers and shipbuilders.

Despite the busyness, he couldn't escape. With each recording, he had to ring Fletcher with his notes, like an errant schoolboy—which, in fact, he was. To report to Fletcher, Hugh had to keep his notes organized.

He could still hear Aleida's sweet, lightly accented voice. *"Open to a fresh page. Date it at the top. Don't change pages until you fill the first one."*

Hugh's gut wrenched, and he rolled up cord and brought it back to Rob. Escape? How could one escape memories? The past month's activity could only blur the memories, not erase them. Couldn't erase the regret.

He'd lost her, and loneliness gnawed at his insides.

Although he'd spoken without care, was it wrong to lay the suggestion before her? Her appropriate determination to find her son had become an obsession so dangerous she considered abducting the boy. What could abduction accomplish? She'd be found, imprisoned, and separated from Theo again—but in worse straits. Without proof, she had no recourse.

Hugh sat on a bunk and reviewed his notes. He planned to record three four-minute discs on this flight, and he wanted to use the time well.

If he could learn to take orderly notes, perhaps he could learn the orderly ways of a solicitor or a government minister. A safe job to protect the Collingwood heir. Far safer than patrolling the North Sea.

A job that might earn his first sliver of respect from his parents.

Hugh groaned. If he took such a job, he could end up like his father. Nigel Collingwood would have been a brilliant professor of some esoteric subject. But he'd obeyed his father and taken a commission in the Army. During the First World War, the Army had given him mundane posts in London where he could do no harm, where he'd performed in a thoroughly lackluster manner. After too many years, the Army had retired him with more pomp than he deserved. He was a failure, and he knew it.

That would be Hugh's fate if he chose the law or the government. In his head, Uncle Elliott's voice roared. *"Stuffing a vibrant young man like Hugh in a stodgy desk job would kill him."*

Uncle Elliott. Pain crushed Hugh's chest, and he folded his notebook shut. The newspapers insinuated that Philippe Larue would be charged for writing the threatening letter but not charged with murder. The police simply hadn't enough evidence.

Why couldn't they see the murderer had to be a man like Bert Ridley who prized security over freedom, a man who'd almost come to blows with Uncle Elliott and who despised Jouveau? Hugh frowned. But a man with an alibi.

Or someone with a temper, a career at stake, and no alibi, like Norman Fletcher. Or someone with the initials of G.B. or J.I., like Jerome Irwin, another man who disliked both victims.

"Is that a periscope?" one of the gunners called from high on his perch.

Hugh sprang to standing and caught Rob's eye.

"I'm ready when you are." Rob fiddled with dials.

Hugh climbed the ladder to the gunners' platform, not an easy task in a bumping aircraft with a microphone in hand.

The two gunners sat back-to-back, wearing padded jackets and hoods with implanted headphones.

On the left, an affable gunner called Blackie grinned at Hugh. "I can't believe I'm going to be on the BBC."

Hugh gave Rob the thumbs-up. "Here we are, not even an hour into our mission, and one of our alert gunners has observed something." Hugh gave Blackie raised eyebrows to proceed.

"Down there." Blackie pointed his machine gun to the waters. "I saw a periscope."

"Or a whale," his mate said with a laugh.

"Or a whale," Blackie said with a resigned sigh. "But we can't be too careful."

Hugh nodded. "The pilots are circling lower. What comes next?"

"We keep watching." Blackie's dark gaze fixed on Hugh, his voice low and portentous. "If we think it's something, we drop bombs."

His mate let out a scoffing noise. "So keep watching, Blackie."

"I'll leave you to your duties. Now I'd like our listeners to hear what this crew's engineer has in store for any U-boat lurking beneath these waves."

After he gave Rob the signal to stop recording, Hugh descended the ladder, made sure his headphones were in place so he could hear Rob, and headed forward, his knees bent, his feet wide, and his free hand gripping anything stationary.

Toward the front, the plane had two decks, the lower deck with the comforts Hugh had described earlier and the upper deck for pilots and navigator and engineer and bomb-aimer and radio operator.

Trailing cord behind him, Hugh climbed a ladder to the upper deck. In the first compartment, the engineer checked bombs on a rack overhead.

"Ready, Rob?" Hugh spoke into his microphone.

"Ready, Collie." Rob's voice spoke in his headphones.

Hugh lifted a smile. "I'm now standing in the center of the plane between the two massive wings that hold us aloft, with the crew's engineer. Whilst you work, would you please tell our listeners what you're doing?"

"Yes, sir." The engineer, a lanky young man with a Welsh accent, kept to his duty without glancing at Hugh. He turned a crank, and gears clanked. "I'm winching out our bombs."

"Quite clever, I say." Hugh studied the contraption as icy air swirled through the open window. "Like a conveyor belt at a factory, moving hundreds of pounds of bombs from inside the plane into position under the wings. Let's go forward, shall we?"

Hugh worked his way through a narrow door. "I'm passing the stations for our navigator and our radio operator with banks of modern equipment at their fingertips."

As he passed the radio operator, Hugh covered his microphone to avoid picking up coordinates or call signs. He looped out more cord and entered the cockpit, occupied by two pilots.

Hugh wouldn't interview them, only observe. "Here in the cockpit, our pilots conduct the crew's activities like an orchestra. Each man in our crew knows his instrument and plays it well, but the pilots ensure they play together."

The captain of the aircraft called for bomb release on the bomb-aimer's signal.

Peering over the pilots' heads, Hugh saw only the nose of the plane and sky.

The aircraft suddenly lifted. "The bombs have released, and the plane rises from the loss of weight."

"Hold tight, Mr. Collingwood," the captain called.

Hugh leaned against the side of the fuselage and grabbed a support beam, and the Sunderland tipped in a tight circle.

Hugh glanced down through a window. "Our bombs have hit the water. White plumes erupt in the sky, with white circles rippling away from the point of impact. How any submarine could survive such an explosion, I can't imagine."

After the plane leveled, Hugh talked his way back to the gunners' platform, gathering cord as he went. Then he climbed the ladder to the platform. "So, chaps, did we sink a U-boat?"

"It was nothing." Blackie's voice twisted with disgust.

"No U-boat this time," Hugh said into the microphone, "but this crew's vigilance, their diligence, are sure to bear fruit. Their very presence, their ever-watching eyes, force German submarines to stay beneath the waves, where they are slower and less dangerous. No, my friends, those bombs were not wasted. And this patrol has just begun. More bombs and bullets remain, and the Germans would be foolish to stand up to this Sunderland and her exemplary crew."

Hugh signaled to Rob and pulled off his headphones.

A flush colored Blackie's thin cheeks. "Ah, you make us sound more heroic than we are."

"Not at all." Hugh wound up the mass of cord. "I report only what I observe. I admire what you do."

Blackie and his mate exchanged a sheepish smile.

Hugh's parents insisted his job was nothing but a lark, that his work was meaningless.

Was it? Was it meaningless to show the nation what these quietly heroic men did in service to the crown? Was it meaningless to build up the confidence of those men, to show appreciation by shining the light of attention on them?

"No," Hugh muttered. Not meaningless at all.

# 33

HADDENHAM
SATURDAY, APRIL 12, 1941

Grayness swirled in the clouds, radiated from the stone walls of Bentley Hall, and permeated Aleida's spirit.

Her heels clicked along the flagstone path leading to the house.

Tante Margriet stood in the garden to the left of Bentley Hall and waved. "Aleida! You're here."

Aleida mustered a smile, joined her aunt, and set down her suitcase.

"I'm so happy to see—" Tante Margriet's face fell. "Are you all right, Schatje?"

No amount of rouge or lipstick could bring color to her face. "I'm fine, Tante. I'm glad I could visit for Easter. How are you?"

"We're well." Tante Margriet gestured to a table on the lawn. "I have tea. We saved our ration for your visit. We can watch the ducklings on the pond."

"Thank you." Aleida took a seat and smoothed the skirt of her dove-gray suit. The lawn sloped in emerald tones toward the deep green pond, ringed by trees bearing the grassy green leaves of spring.

Tante Margriet wore a tweed suit and matching hat and a look of concern. "Any progress finding Theo?"

Aleida couldn't speak. Every Friday, her attempts to follow Mr. Randolph from Trafalgar Square Station had been foiled. Once she'd had ARP duty, once she'd needed to work late, and twice Mr. Randolph hadn't come—or she'd missed him.

Yesterday, though, she'd found him on the platform for the Bakerloo Line. As the train approached, she'd moved into position to board the car behind his. But then he'd turned. He'd spotted her. Had he recognized her? Even with the veil and scarf? Or did the veil and scarf only make her look suspicious?

With her heart pummeling her rib cage, she'd slipped behind a pillar—and fled.

Aleida's face crumpled. "I don't know what to do."

"You dear girl." Tante Margriet gripped Aleida's clenched hands, then gasped and stared. "What happened to your hand?"

The knuckles on her left hand flamed red. From frenzied tapping. She could no longer stop herself. And the pain of tapping raw flesh felt right somehow.

"Did it happen on ARP duty?" Tante Margriet frowned and inspected her hand. "Such dangerous and rough work. I thought you'd had fewer air raids recently. Oh dear. I'll have Mrs. Swinton bring some salve."

"Thank you." Aleida tugged her hands free and wrapped them around a teacup.

Her aunt's blue eyes swam with worry. "Any news on that young lady you worked with? I haven't read anything in the papers."

A month had passed with no answers, adding to the heaviness of the gray. "I talked to the police. They were very kind and very concerned about the marks on Nilima's neck. They did investigate, but she had no enemies, not a single suspect. She hadn't been robbed or—or violated. They simply can't imagine why someone would kill her."

Tante Margriet clucked her tongue. "How odd. And how dreadful."

"It is." Aleida had returned to the Sharma home and told Mrs. Sharma what the police had said. Mrs. Sharma already knew, and she discounted the whole investigation. She knew her daughter had been murdered, and she believed she'd been killed due to the color of her skin.

Suspicion lurked around the edges of Aleida's mind. Nilima was a foreigner. Jouveau was a foreigner who spoke up for his fellow refugees. Elliott Hastings had been devoted to improving the lot of refugees. Was that enough to connect the murders? Louisa doubted it, and Aleida hadn't voiced her flimsy theory to the police.

"Aleida?" Tante Margriet laid a hand on Aleida's forearm. "I'm worried about you. I've never seen you so—"

"I'm fine. I'll *be* fine." She took a nourishing sip of hot tea. "Staying at Bentley Hall will be good for me. So many happy memories."

Tante Margriet nodded toward the pond, dotted with white ducks and brown ducklings. "I can still see you and Gerrit and Cilla building a dam in that pond."

The two cousins closest to Aleida in age, and a genuine smile bent Aleida's mouth for the first time in weeks. "That would have been Gerrit's idea."

"Already a civil engineer, that boy, with you and Cilla his ready accomplices." Her aunt chuckled.

"I worry about them, living under the Nazis. I can't even imagine what they're enduring."

"Hush." Tante Margriet topped off her tea. "Every day I pray for my parents, my three brothers, and my nieces and nephews over there. However, this weekend I mean to cheer you up. So, no more of that. Only happy talk."

"I'm always happy here." Aleida forced her face to relax.

"Not always," Tante Margriet said with a chuckle.

Aleida shrugged. "We cousins did have our squabbles, as children do. My squabbles were mostly with my sisters."

Tante Margriet's forehead furrowed. "I do wish those two—"

"It doesn't matter. They're so close to each other, they never had room for their little sister." She gave her head a shake. "But I had Gerrit and Cilla, and we had such fun. As I said, I was always happy here."

Tante Margriet's eyes twinkled above the rim of her teacup. "Have you forgotten your first summer here without your parents?"

"I remember it well." At eight, she'd finally joined the cousins for a month at Bentley Hall. "It was the most delightful adventure."

"Ah, you have forgotten. Your first week, at least."

Aleida frowned. "I was so excited to come. I felt grown up."

"Until bedtime. Then you cried for your mother. I couldn't console you. After a few days, I wanted to take you home, but James believed you'd adjust. In a week or so, you did. When the time came to leave, you cried once again. You wanted to stay here forever, you said."

Aleida did remember the sadness, repeated at the end of each summer. But her initial homesickness had faded from memory, faded in the brightness of her aunt and uncle's love, the adventures with her cousins, and the beautiful countryside.

Tante Margriet smiled, and the skin around her eyes folded in amused lines. "How quickly children adapt."

Like a slug to her chest.

Theo.

Had he adapted? The Randolphs cared for him well, the Warwicks had insisted. Mr. Randolph said that Theo's nightmares had passed, that he was learning English, learning to laugh again.

Theo was happy.

If Aleida found him, would he miss the Randolphs and

cry for them? Would he want to return to them? Would he be happy going away with a mother who had faded from his memory?

"Lunch is served." Mrs. Swinton peeked out the side door.

"Thank you." Tante Margriet patted Aleida's arm. "Come eat, Schatje. You look like you need a solid meal."

This time Aleida couldn't find a smile, but she followed her aunt into the sitting room. In the corner, the wireless played.

"The German plane is coming on another run." Hugh's voice spoke on the wireless, bright as ever, and strident. "But our merchant vessel is no sitting duck. Hear our guns? Oh! That was closer than I like. Those Nazi bombs missed though, thanks to our boys and their antiaircraft guns. All that German steel lost at sea, where it can never—"

"Oh dear." Tante Margriet marched to the wireless set. "Your Uncle James forgot to turn it off again. He's very concerned about the German invasion of Greece and Yugoslavia."

"No!" The volume of Aleida's voice surprised her. "Don't turn it off. I—I'll catch up with you."

"All right." Tante Margriet frowned but left Aleida alone.

Alone with Hugh's voice. Hugh at sea somewhere, under attack.

Aleida pressed her hand to her chest and drew near to the wireless set.

"A thin gray plume twists away from one of the bomber's four engines. Excellent shooting, chaps." Elated masculine laughter rang out in the background. "Yes, even if they didn't shoot down that Fw 200, they sent it home. That bomber won't harass any more British ships today."

Aleida rubbed the polished wood of the cabinet, savoring Hugh's voice.

How she missed him.

Over the past six weeks, her anger had waned. Hugh hadn't ordered her to abandon her son. He hadn't stripped Theo from her arms. He'd merely suggested she consider giving up the search.

For that, she'd thrust him out of her life. She'd lost a good man.

"On this Easter weekend," Hugh said, his voice low and serious, "as we commemorate the selfless sacrifice of our Savior, take a moment to remember the selflessness and sacrifice of the courageous men of our merchant navy."

Aleida's legs almost gave way, and she planted both hands on the cabinet for support.

The Father had sacrificed his beloved Son. The Son had laid down his life for the world he loved.

Could Aleida lay down her rights? Lay down her very heart?

34

Three minutes early for the meeting, Hugh entered the conference room at Broadcasting House to see Norman Fletcher, Albert Ridley, and Robert Clark, Chief News Editor and Fletcher's superior.

A pit formed in Hugh's stomach. When Fletcher summoned him from Scotland, Hugh knew it didn't bode well, but the presence of the two other men confirmed it.

Regardless, he'd climb the career gallows with dignity, so he smiled and shook all three men's hands.

Clark, a light-haired man in his fifties with a mustache and a trace of a Scottish brogue, motioned for the men to sit around the table. "Thank you for coming from Scotland, Mr. Collingwood. I wanted to compliment you on your fine work. Your reports have been very well received."

Ridley glowered. "Not by the Ministry of Information."

Fletcher looked as if he were sucking on a lemon. "Mr. Collingwood—Mr. Ridley came to my office to discuss your latest reports. When he heard you were coming today, he insisted on attending this meeting."

Hugh nodded at his brother Cecil's friend. "It's always good to see you, Mr. Ridley."

Ridley's mouth pulled taut. "If your brother were alive, Hugh, he would be ashamed. You push the limits."

Hugh forced his face to an impassive expression and clenched his hands over his knees beneath the table. How dare he use Cecil's memory as a weapon? How dare he treat Hugh as a child by using his given name in a professional meeting?

With his hand flat as a cleaver, Fletcher gestured toward Hugh. "All of his reports were vetted by military censors. His recordings were reviewed before broadcast—without a single problem. He hasn't broken any guidelines."

A weight eased off Hugh's shoulders. "Thank you, Mr. Fletcher. I've been most careful."

"Careful?" Ridley wrinkled his rather large nose. "You broadcast about our aircraft being shot down and our ships being sunk."

"I mentioned no numbers, no names, no locations, no dates," Hugh said in a measured tone. "I complied with the guidelines."

Ridley jutted out his jaw. "You shouldn't mention any losses. It's bad for morale."

Clark removed the cigarette from his mouth and blew out a slow puff of smoke. "The only way to strengthen the morale of the people is to tell them the truth, and nothing but the truth, even if the truth is horrible."

Clark had a reputation for fighting for his boys, a stance for which he'd almost lost his position in 1938.

That sense of fight burned in Hugh's veins. "The people of this nation already know we're losing aircraft and ships. When we ignore that truth, they lose faith in us."

"Quite right." Fletcher's gray eyes went hard as steel. "If they lose faith in us, how will they trust us when necessary?"

Ridley's cheeks darkened. "But Hugh pushes the limits."

"With all respect, Mr. Ridley," Hugh said, "even limits have limits."

"Aye." Clark made little glowing circles in the air with his cigarette. "I will remind you, Mr. Ridley, that we work closely and amiably with the ministry. We listen to your concerns and honor them when possible. But the BBC is independent of the government, and your ministry serves as advisor—not controller. We do thank you for your time and your advice."

Then Clark stood and ushered a flustered Ridley to the door.

After the door shut and Clark returned to his seat, Fletcher muttered, "Pompous twerp."

Hugh didn't disagree, but he allowed only the slightest smile.

Fletcher leaned back in his chair and nodded at Hugh. "I called you back to London to stay. I'm sending Butler to be the new regional reporter in Scotland."

The bottom fell out from Hugh's stomach. He knew the assignment was temporary, knew his days at the BBC were numbered, but the tone of the discussion had allowed hope to fluff up. He licked dry lips. "Yes, sir."

Clark chuckled. "I see you're reluctant to leave. Found a bonny Scottish lass?"

Teasing a man when he was being fired didn't seem sporting, and Hugh frowned. "No, sir."

"Reluctant to leave your work, then. Excellent." Clark's deep-set eyes glinted. "We want you to do that same sort of work here in London."

He wasn't being fired? "Pardon?"

"You're one of our most popular correspondents," Clark said. "The letters from the listeners! You have it all—the patrician voice that lends authority to your reports, the common touch that connects with all classes, the reporter's eagerness to get the tough stories, and the emotion appropriate for each situation."

Hugh blinked over and over. He *wasn't* being fired. "Why, thank you, sir."

Clark shook his head. "Sadly, many of those qualities are lacking in Mr. Gilbert."

Fletcher winced, then nodded.

Hugh winced too—Fletcher considered Gil his protégé. "Mr. Gilbert tries very hard." Too hard, and the strain of it stole all sincerity from his voice.

Clark tapped his cigarette into an ashtray. "We want you to do what you do best—talk to people. Talk to airmen and sailors and munitions workers. We've added more light mobile recording units, and we want you to use them."

Precisely what Hugh wanted most—and what Fletcher wanted least. Hugh cut his gaze to his editor.

Fletcher's mouth set in grim lines. "You know what's necessary."

He didn't mention the Morris-Little affair, and more weight lifted from Hugh's shoulders and his heart. "I do."

"You start Monday," Fletcher said. "Take the train back to Aberdeen tomorrow. Meet with Butler on Friday and show him the ropes."

Clark stood to end the meeting. "I'm looking forward to your broadcasts, Mr. Collingwood."

"Thank you, sir." Hugh stood to leave, but Fletcher motioned for him to remain.

After Clark departed, Fletcher stacked papers. "I'm sure you'll be glad to be closer to your family again."

Not necessarily, but Hugh smiled as expected.

"Your family has had a rough run lately. What do they think about the police dropping the murder charges against Philippe Larue?"

Was it wise to discuss the case with a man Hugh hadn't dismissed as a suspect? Or was this an opportunity? Hugh gathered raincoat and hat. "I'm afraid I haven't spoken to them for a fortnight. What do you think?"

Fletcher grumbled. "They arrested the wrong man. I know

Larue wrote the death threat to Hastings, but every reporter's instinct tells me Hastings's murder has nothing to do with the French community."

Hugh sorted his words with care as he donned his raincoat. "That's what Jouveau believed as well."

"Yet he insisted on pursuing the story." Fletcher huffed. "I told him to drop it. I told him it was dangerous. He was badgering MPs and other prominent people and inquiring into their personal business."

Hugh's fingers coiled around the belt of his raincoat, and his heart seized. "Did he mention names? Give you any details?"

"No. He cared more about protecting his scoop than protecting his life. If he'd told me, his killer would be in prison by now." Regret flickered in Fletcher's eyes. "If only I'd insisted. If only I'd promised he could broadcast on the Home Service in exchange for the details."

"You couldn't have known, sir."

"He was your friend." Fletcher's voice went husky, and he coughed. "He—he might have caused problems for me with Ridley, but I admired his work, his tenacity, his zeal. I argued his case with Ridley. The broadcasts of the European Services are a powerful weapon in the Allied arsenal. The MoI shouldn't interfere."

Hugh's throat swelled. He forced out a thank-you and a goodbye, and he departed.

After dinner, Hugh sat in the armchair in his study with Lennox squeezed beside him, his front portion on Hugh's thigh.

Hugh stroked Lennox's fur as he recorded his conversation with Fletcher in a notebook. Fletcher had shed new light on Jouveau's last day—and raised frustrating new questions as well.

Fletcher said Jouveau had questioned prominent people

about personal business. Jouveau stated his lead developed on the day they'd visited the Strand Palace Hotel, a day they'd discussed his feuds with Fletcher and Ridley. It all revolved around Uncle Elliott.

Hugh rolled his pen over the pages. "How, Lennox? What did Jouveau uncover? And where on earth is his notebook?" He'd emptied every drawer in his desk, sifted through every pile of papers.

He itched to go to the Hart and Swan and discuss the case. The company of others stimulated his thoughts, especially the company of his reporter friends.

His chest ached. How could he return to the Hart and Swan? What if Aleida was there? He couldn't face her. And if she'd stopped visiting the pub, he'd face questions and accusations.

Lou, for one, would want him drawn and quartered, his head on a pike.

He scratched behind Lennox's ears. "At least you're happy to see me."

Lennox leaned into the scratch, and his green eyes drooped from the pleasure of it. A rumble emanated from his throat.

Hugh's chest turned soft and warm. How had this bit of gray-and-white fur clawed his way into his heart?

Outside, the air raid siren keened.

Twenty tiny knives pierced Hugh's thigh, and a gray-and-white streak flashed across the room and out the door.

Hugh groaned and pressed his hand to the wounds. Lennox would take his customary station under Hugh's bed.

Perhaps Hugh should go out in search of a story. London hadn't been bombed in an entire month. But he wasn't on duty in town until Monday.

He gathered important notebooks and a book to read, put on his overcoat, and checked that his identity card was in his pocket. In the garden he descended a few steps to the corrugated tin arch of the Anderson shelter, buried beneath a "Dig for Victory" garden of peas and cabbage.

Simmons joined him. While the butler lay down to sleep, Hugh read by the single dangling light bulb.

Tin and earth did little to blunt the sound of bombers and antiaircraft guns. It sounded like a big raid. Perhaps Hugh should seek a story after all. But he wouldn't have the recording unit. Next week, he could use one whenever he wanted.

For the first time, the joy of it welled inside, the satisfaction of redemption, and he breathed out a prayer of gratitude.

The ground shook, harder and harder.

Simmons sat up, his eyes wide, and Hugh lowered his book. A stick of bombs, falling closer and closer.

Noise rent the air, shoved Hugh back against the tin wall, drove the air from his lungs. The light bulb went out.

"That—that was close," Simmons said.

Hugh pressed his hand to his chest, coughed to start breathing again. That strong of a blast meant a close call indeed.

The house?

He scrambled to his feet.

"Mr. Collingwood, sir!" Simmons cried. "It isn't safe."

Hugh paused with his hand flat on the door. His ears rang, and he strained to listen over the ringing. The thud of explosions had ceased, the stick of bombs spent.

He opened the door.

In the pale silver moonlight, in the orange glow of fires in the distance, the silhouette of his house rose dark.

And jagged.

"Oh no." His house was hit.

A smoking crater defaced the garden near the back corner of the house—which was sheared off. Directly through Hugh's study on the ground floor and his bedroom above it on the first floor.

His bedroom. Where Lennox hid.

"No, no, no, no, no." Hugh flung open the back door, wrenched his torch from his coat pocket, and tore up the stairs and into his bedroom.

Plaster dust filled his lungs, glimmered in the torchlight, and he coughed and swatted away the haze. "Lennox! Lennox!"

Cold air swirled around him in the darkness. A quarter of his room had disappeared. His bureau, his armchair.

His bed teetered on the edge, one leg in the void.

"Lennox!" Hugh dropped to his knees and shined the torch beneath the bed.

Nothing but dust.

"Oh no. No. No." Hugh crawled to the edge and peered down. In the garden, the crater smoldered like a witch's cauldron. In the remains of his study lay a jumble of broken furniture and clothing and papers. But no little gray body.

"Please, please, please. Let him be all right." Hugh dashed downstairs, outside.

Simmons stood by the crater and dumped the contents of a sandbag into the cauldron.

With his heart thumping, filling his chest and his throat, Hugh sifted through the rubble in his study. "Lennox? Lennox?"

He tossed aside clothing, lifted shattered lumber. No Lennox.

Thank goodness.

And yet.

"Lennox?" he called. "Where are you? Here, kitty, kitty."

In his terror, the cat must have run away.

His terror became Hugh's, and he climbed out of the crater. "Lennox! Lennox!"

He had to find him. Had to. He aimed his torch under every bush, inside every flowerpot.

How could he find him? Where could he look? What would he do without him?

Hugh's chest heaved with the pain of it, of losing his friend, yet another friend.

"I won't give up, Lennox!" he yelled into the night. "I won't give up until I find you."

Everything inside him seized.

This terror, this panic, this determination—it was only a fraction of what Aleida had to be feeling.

And he'd told her to give up the search.

Hugh sank to his knees and wrapped his hands over the top of his head. "Forgive me, Aleida. Forgive me."

35

Cream and burgundy tiles lined the walls as Aleida climbed the final flight of stairs from Hampstead Station, the deepest station in the London Underground. Her breath came hard, and her legs burned.

An elderly man in a brown overcoat passed her and gave her an odd look, the same odd look she'd received the entire journey. How many women rode the Underground carrying a stuffed elephant?

The night before, Aleida had hunkered in the Anderson shelter, sobbing, as bombs pounded the earth and pounded conviction into her soul.

Now as she emerged into the hazy sunshine of early evening, her steps felt strangely light. She should be trudging, wailing, beating her breast, but peace permeated her being.

Her breath calmed as she made her way up the street, and when she reached the house, she paused and stroked Oli's trunk—one, two, three, four, five, six, seven, eight, nine, ten, eleven—and she stopped.

She didn't have to force herself to stop. Her decision made, she had no more compulsion to count.

Without veil, without scarf, wearing the same midnight-blue hat and coat she'd worn on her previous visit, she rang the bell of the Randolph home.

The housekeeper answered the door.

"Good evening," Aleida said. "Is Mr. Randolph home? Might I speak with him?"

"Yes, ma'am," the housekeeper said. "Come on through."

"No, thank you. Please have him meet me at the door."

The housekeeper gave her a look of utter astonishment. It simply wasn't done. But Aleida didn't move and kept smiling.

"Very well, ma'am." The housekeeper disappeared inside.

In a few minutes, Julian Randolph came to the door in a dark gray suit.

"Good evening, Mr. Randolph. I'm Aleida Martens, Theo's mother."

His face went hard. "I warned you—"

"No fear." Aleida raised a soft smile. "I didn't come to plead my case. On the contrary, I've come to tell you I'm giving up my son."

Confusion dampened the anger in his blue eyes. "Pardon?"

"I confess that since we met in January, I've continued searching for him. I hoped that if I found him and he recognized me, I might convince you I really am his mother."

Mr. Randolph clenched the doorknob. "Do I need to ring the police?"

"No, sir. I will no longer search. I give you my word. The past few days, I realized I was no longer searching for his sake, but for mine alone."

His jaw worked back and forth, as if he were formulating words, deciding whether to turn to his telephone.

Aleida drew a long breath. "When my husband ripped my son from my arms and thrust him into your car, he did so with no regard for Theo. He cared nothing about him. But the Lord did. The Lord loves Theo far more than I do or you do or your wife does—far more than all of us ever could."

A smile arose from that paradoxical place of peace. "For almost a year, I've fretted over Theo. Where was he? Was he safe? Was he even alive? But God knew. The Lord put Theo in *your* hands. He provided for my little boy through you, and I will always be grateful for how you've cared for him. I know you'll love him and provide for him and raise him well. Most importantly, I know the Lord will always hold Theo in his hands. That knowledge has given me the peace—and the conviction—to let him go."

Mr. Randolph's eyes softened, but his mouth remained stern. "Mrs. Martens, I—"

"I will not bother you again. I refuse to rip my son out of the arms of people who love him, people he loves. I will not rip him from the only family he now knows or force him to go with a woman he surely can't remember. You have my blessing."

Dozens of emotions raced across Mr. Randolph's face.

Aleida hugged the familiar stuffed elephant. "This is Theo's best friend. His name is Oli, short for *olifant*, the Dutch word for *elephant*. Theo loves him dearly. He used to hold him like this . . ."

She pressed Oli's soft form to her right cheek, wrapped his trunk under her chin and pressed the tip to her left cheek. Her eyes slipped shut, and she breathed deeply, inhaling the slightest remaining scent of her son.

Her throat thickened, but she refused to sully the moment with tears. She opened her eyes, gave her head a little shake, and held out the elephant.

Mr. Randolph only stared at Oli.

"Please," Aleida said. "Oli doesn't belong to me. He belongs to Theo—to Teddy. To Teddy Randolph. Teddy should have him."

Slowly, Mr. Randolph stretched out his hand and took the gift.

He would never know how much it had cost her. "Goodbye, Mr. Randolph, and God bless."

She descended the steps and walked down the street toward Hampstead Station until she heard the door close.

Then Aleida removed her hat. She plucked a hairpin from the coil of hair at the nape of her neck. She plucked out another and another and another until her hair spilled down her back.

Tomorrow, she'd cut it.

## 36

**LONDON**
**SUNDAY, APRIL 20, 1941**

With his suitcase between his feet, Hugh stood in the crowded corridor of the overnight train from Aberdeen. All night he'd jostled against the shoulders of his fellow passengers, dozing off and on.

After a delay outside London as they waited for the all clear from yet another air raid, the train pulled into King's Cross Station.

Hugh stifled a yawn and followed the herd out to the platform.

Glass and steel arched high above, and he made his way through the railway station to the Underground station of King's Cross St. Pancras.

Soon he'd be home. Would Lennox be there to greet him? Hugh had searched for his cat all Wednesday night, but since returning to Scotland, he hadn't been able to ring Simmons for news. What if Lennox had been hurt and was hiding somewhere, wounded, dying? What if he'd fled instinctively to his previous home, where the owner wanted him tossed into the Thames?

Hugh's step quickened.

He passed a newsstand, black with headlines about recent British setbacks in North Africa and the return of the Luft-waffe to London.

Two major raids in the past few days—were the Germans preparing to invade Britain? How could they with so many Nazi troops in the Balkans? Yugoslavia had fallen and Greece couldn't endure much longer, but transferring forces west again would take time.

Hugh bought his ticket for the Piccadilly Line and found his platform.

"Hugh Collingwood?" a man said in an American accent.

To his right, a dark-haired man in his thirties waved and grinned.

"Tony Da Costa!" Hugh grinned back and shook his friend's hand. He'd met Tony in Belgium, whilst the American reporter followed the exodus of refugees south and Hugh followed the British forces north. "What have you been doing this past year?"

"I was in Japan for a while." Tony pointed his thumb to the side and frowned. "Things are brewing over there. Mark my words, we're going to have trouble."

Hugh sighed. Didn't the world have trouble enough already? "How long have you been in London?"

"Two weeks." Teeth shone white in his broad smile. "Ed Murrow offered me a job."

"Congratulations. You're a 'Murrow Boy' now."

"I am. He's got fellows posted all over the world. He's decid-ing where to send me."

"Sounds smashing."

Tony clapped Hugh on the shoulder. "Speaking of smash-ing, I heard one of your reports from Scotland. What brings you to London?"

Hugh gazed into the dark tunnel. "The BBC transferred me back."

Tony laughed. "You sound disappointed."

"Not at all. It's rather exciting. I'll have full use of a mobile recording unit, and I can tell the stories I've been longing to tell."

"And yet . . ." Tony's coffee-dark eyes narrowed. The man had a reporter's inquisitiveness and tenacity, combined with American nosiness.

Everything English inside him told him to deflect the attention. Yet Hugh always thought more clearly when talking to others, and he hadn't told a soul what happened with Aleida. "It's a woman, if you must know."

"I must. She broke your heart?"

That would be far easier to bear. "I broke hers."

Tony whistled. "What'd you do?" Compassion bent down the corners of his mouth.

In their short acquaintance, Hugh had found Tony to be a man of integrity. No one stood within ten feet of them. And Hugh's exhaustion drained away the last of his reserve.

He lowered his voice. "She's Dutch. When she was fleeing the Netherlands, her husband gave her little boy to a British couple bound for London."

Tony groaned. "I saw a woman do that during the exodus. Almost tossed her kid through a car window. I wonder if she ever found him."

"Precisely. Aleida's husband was a dreadful man. He refused to give her the name or address of the British couple—then he was killed the next day. She came here looking for her son."

"No name? No address? Talk about looking for a needle in a haystack."

"Indeed." A wind built from the tunnel as a train approached. "The only thing in her favor is that her son has a distinguishing feature, a hand deformity."

Tony's mouth dropped open. "A hand deformity?"

"Poor little chap is missing all the fingers on his right hand."

How many times had he heard Aleida describe Theo in her lilting accent?

"Missing . . . all . . ."

The red Underground train entered the station with a flurry of air.

Hugh raised his voice above the noise. "It did help her find him." Then he groaned. "Rather, she found the couple. However, she has no papers to prove he's her child, not even a photograph. The husband didn't believe her and refused to give up the child. That's when I made my error."

The train doors opened. Tony stood with his mouth hanging open.

"Come along." Hugh nudged his friend on board. He needed to finish the story, although relating the embarrassing details in the confines of a train made him cringe. "I made the error of—"

"A Dutch boy, you said?" Tony grabbed a pole for support, and his gaze pierced. "How old?"

"He's four now. He was three at the time."

"Blond? His mother's blond?"

"Well, yes." Many Dutch were.

"Missing all his fingers like this?" He raised a fist, and the light in his eyes brightened.

"Yes." Why was Tony acting so strangely?

"Collie!" Tony bumped Hugh's arm with that fist. "I took their picture during the exodus."

"Pardon?"

"It had to be them. I saw a woman and her son sitting under a tree. The contrast—the love and devotion between them—and in the background, the refugees traipsing by. I took a dozen shots, some of my best ever."

The doors shut, the train pulled away, and Hugh wobbled, his brain spinning. He gripped the pole above Tony's hand. It couldn't be.

"Would have won me the Pulitzer if I could have published them."

"You lost the film?"

"No, the woman's husband was a raving lunatic. Threatened to destroy my career if I printed them."

Hugh's fingers went as cold as Sebastiaan Martens's heart.

Tony snorted. "I wasn't worried about my career, but I was very worried about what he'd do to his wife. He was furious with her for letting her picture be taken. Ever heard of such nonsense?"

"It must be Aleida." Hugh's voice came out in a wisp. "Her husband forbade her to have her son photographed. He was ashamed of the boy's hand."

"That's him, all right. Crazy. He's dead, you say? Good riddance."

Hugh's hands tightened around his suitcase handle and the pole. "If only she had that photograph, she could prove Theo was her son."

Tony spread his hands wide. "I have the prints in my room at the Savoy."

Everything froze inside him, not daring to hope. "You do?"

"Sure. I may be a reporter, but I'm also a photographer, and a photographer always takes his portfolio with him." Tony slapped Hugh's arm. "We're going to the Savoy."

When they reached Leicester Square Station, Hugh had to restrain himself from running the half mile to the hotel.

Up in his room, Tony thumbed through a portfolio. "Here you go. Is it her?"

It was. Hugh sank into an armchair with the stack of photographs.

Aleida's exquisite face, lit up in absolute love, and a little boy. Theo.

Hugh's heart lurched. What a beautiful child he was, laughing, with his clublike hand raised high. Hugh flipped through the photographs, and Aleida and Theo came to life, speaking with each other, smiling, Theo touching Aleida's cheek, her mouth, Aleida kissing his hand.

She saw no deformity. She saw her beloved son.

Hugh had never loved her more.

Seeing that child's face, seeing the love between them—now he knew why Aleida couldn't give up the search.

Tony sat on the bed. "Is it her?"

"Most definitely." The photographs proved not only her maternity but also that she was neither negligent nor abusive.

Tony waved his hand at the portfolio. "Give them to her."

"But they're—"

"I've got the negatives back in New York. I can make more prints." His wide mouth curled into a mischievous smile. "If they'll help you get back your girl . . ."

"They won't." He'd hurt her too deeply, and he wouldn't insult her by trying to win her back. "But they will help Aleida get back her son."

"Then what are you waiting for? Leave your suitcase here." He jerked his head to the door. "Go on, now. Scram."

A smile built, nearly as wide as Tony's. "Right-o."

Aleida folded Theo's jacket into the suitcase, set his cap on top, and shut the lid. In her heart, she'd always be a mother, but not in her everyday life.

A bit light-headed, she slid the suitcase under her bed. Was this how mothers felt when their children died?

Only in part. At least Aleida knew her son lived and thrived.

But he lived and thrived apart from her, and it threatened to drown her. Never again would she see him. Never would she read his handwriting or hear his voice change or watch him become a father himself. Never would she know how he did in school or on the playing field or on the job. Never would she meet his friends or his wife or her own grandchildren.

Aleida knelt by the bed until the pain subsided to a bearable level. It would never entirely go away, and yet the peace remained. She'd done the right thing for her son.

Her doorbell rang, and she rose to her feet and straightened the skirt of her dress. The lady upstairs had borrowed a bit of butter the other day and promised to pay Aleida back when she received her next ration.

Aleida opened the door.

Hugh stood in the hallway in a khaki raincoat and a fedora, both sprinkled by raindrops.

Her chest squeezed hard. She thought she'd never see him again.

"Good afternoon." He removed his hat and smoothed his wavy hair. "I do apologize for visiting against your wishes, but—"

"I thought you were in Scotland." Her words tumbled out. "That—that's what Louisa said."

"I was." He frowned and blinked a few times. "I was transferred back to London. You—you cut your hair."

Aleida fingered the pageboy cut, the ends flipped under a few inches below her chin. "I did."

"It's very pretty. Very becoming." He closed his eyes and shook his head. "I didn't come today—I promise, I didn't come to try to win you back."

Of course, he didn't want to win her back after how she'd treated him, and she fought back a wince.

"No," he said. "I came because of Theo."

Her mind careened in another direction. "Theo?"

"May I come in?" He gestured to the door, and his frown cut deep. "I do believe you should sit down for the news. For happy reasons."

"Yes. Of course." She stepped back and reached for the English cure for every awkward situation. "Would you like some tea?"

"No, thank you." He entered the flat and hung his hat and raincoat on the coatrack.

Aleida sat on a sofa and gripped her hands in her lap. What news could Hugh have about Theo? And what sort of happy news would require her to sit?

"I returned from Scotland an hour ago and ran into my friend Tony Da Costa at the Tube station. Tony's an American reporter." Hugh cocked his head at the coatrack, on which

Theo's little coat and hat no longer hung—then he whipped his gaze to her, to her hair—and his eyebrows sprang high.

From those clues, he'd realized something had changed—because he knew her so well.

Grief washed through her. She'd lost such a good man, such a wonderful romance.

But she hefted her chin high. "An American reporter, you say?"

"Yes." Clamping a black portfolio under one arm, Hugh tugged down the sleeves of his gray suit jacket. "Tony and I met in Belgium last May. He followed the refugees during the exodus. One day he took photographs of a Dutch woman and her son sitting under a tree by the road."

All at once she could see the golden barley waving in the sun, feel the solid weight of her boy in her lap, and taste his sweet hand against her lips. "The photos . . . Theo and me."

"Yes." Hugh's smile grew, crinkling the skin around his hazel eyes.

Aleida gasped and pressed her fingers to her mouth. "I warned him—the reporter. Sebastiaan was furious."

"He threatened to destroy Tony's career."

"Sebastiaan—that night—that's when he gave Theo away."

Hugh huffed. "Thanks to Tony, we can undo some of the damage your husband did. Tony never published those photographs, as he promised. But he did print them." He sat in an armchair at the end of the coffee table.

Aleida's gaze locked on the portfolio in his lap. Could it be . . . ?

"Are you ready?" That caramel voice melted in gentleness.

She could only nod. After Hugh slipped the portfolio onto her lap, Aleida forced wooden fingers to open it.

There was her boy, smiling up at her—at the image of her. Sitting on her lap, his head tipped back in laughter, his hair catching the sunlight, pointing up at the tree.

A tiny sob hopped in her throat. "Theo . . ."

With a trembling hand, she reached to touch him. Stopped herself, lest her fingerprints mar the image.

"He really is a beautiful child," Hugh said.

"He is." The round cheeks, the perfect mouth, the gleaming eyes. "I—I can hear his voice so clearly. We were playing a game. He was naming colors. Here he's saying, 'Green,' and pointing to the leaves."

"There are more photographs. About a dozen."

Holding the edge of the print, she flipped to the next one, to "Blue," where he'd almost poked her in the eye, to "Red," where he tugged down her lower lip. Then she kissed his sweet hand.

Each image was blurrier than the one before. "If only they weren't so blurry."

Hugh chuckled and handed her a handkerchief.

It blurred before her too. She took it and wiped her eyes, her damp cheeks. Another sob hiccupped out. "I thought I'd never see him again."

Hugh rocked forward in his seat, his eyes alight. "Now you can. Now you have proof. Your face is clear and recognizable, and so is Theo's. And the last photograph—the man must be your husband."

Aleida flipped to it, then slammed her eyes shut against the face she'd wanted never to see again. "That's him. That's Sebastiaan."

"At the edge of the picture, I can see you and Theo. You both look scared."

"We were terrified." She turned the photograph of Sebastiaan upside down.

Hugh tapped one finger on the portfolio. "All three of you in one image. That will convince Mr. Randolph, most assuredly."

Aleida gasped. "Mr. Randolph?"

Hugh's face went grim. "If it doesn't, you can take him to court. Tony Da Costa will serve as witness, I'm certain."

She could get her son back.

Instead of joyful relief, something nasty and gripping dug claws into her heart. Had she acted hastily in surrendering Theo? What if she'd waited only a few more days? She could have waved these photos in Mr. Randolph's face, proven herself, snatched back her son.

And those nasty, gripping claws shredded her peace.

Because snatching back her son wasn't best for him.

"No," Aleida said. "I won't do that."

"Won't do . . . what?" He gaped at her.

"You were right. A time came to give him up."

"No." His gaze bored deep, a bit wild. "I should never have said that. I had no way of knowing what you were feeling. Then Lennox went missing during an air raid, and—"

"Lennox? Is he all right?"

Hugh's lips mashed together. "He hasn't returned. I've been rather distraught. And if I felt that way about my cat, what must you feel for your son? Now I've seen how you love each other. I've seen why you couldn't—why you must never give up. Please forgive me."

"Forgive? You did nothing wrong. You only made a suggestion, asked me to consider giving up the search." Her thumb stroked the smooth edge of the portfolio.

"I should never—"

"I disagree. You were concerned for my well-being. You didn't order me to give up my son. You didn't make the decision for me. I shouldn't have said you were like Sebastiaan. You aren't. Not in the slightest."

Hugh sighed and gave a sharp nod. "Thank you. But I shouldn't have suggested you give up—"

"Yet that is exactly what I've done." Peace lifted a sad smile.

"On Thursday I told Mr. Randolph I would no longer search for Theo. I gave the Randolphs my blessing to raise him."

Hugh's eyes rounded and rounded, and his mouth drifted open. "Pardon?"

"I surrendered my son. For his own good." Her smile lifted higher, light and free. "Theo is happy with the Randolphs. They are the only family he knows. If I were to rip him away from them, force him to go with a woman he hasn't seen for almost a year, a woman he surely doesn't remember—how would that be kind or loving? How would that be good for him?"

"Aleida . . ." Hugh's face swam with emotion.

"I gave Mr. Randolph Theo's toy elephant to give to him, and I packed away his clothes."

"That's why you"—he fingered his own neck—"why you cut your hair."

A wet little laugh erupted. "I won't pretend surrendering him doesn't hurt. It hurts dreadfully to know I'll never see him again in person. But I did the right thing. I haven't felt this much peace for ages."

His eyebrows drew together. "You aren't tapping your fingers."

"Oh, I still do, but not as much."

Hugh searched her face in the most intimate and caring way. "I see it. I see the peace."

"Now I have his photographs." Then she sucked in a breath. "May I?"

"Yes. Tony wants you to have them. He can make new prints."

Aleida closed the portfolio and hugged it to her chest. "This means so much to me. I'll frame them, all of them—except the last one. I can see him. I can see my son every day for the rest of my life. This is such a gift."

Hugh's mouth curved in a smile, mournful but full of admiration.

How she loved him. But how she'd mistreated him. As much

as she missed the romance, more than anything, she simply missed *him*.

Aleida swallowed and wet her dry mouth. "Hugh, do you suppose, if you could ever forgive me for being so cruel to you—"

"Cruel?" He jerked his chin back.

"I compared you to Sebastiaan, when you've never been anything but kind to me. If you could forgive me, could we— could we be friends?"

Hugh dipped his chin and lowered his gaze. "I would be honored." His voice sounded gravelly.

"I would too."

Silence settled thick and awkward.

Then Hugh lifted a bright smile. "Tomorrow at the Hart and Swan?"

"Yes," she said, and her peace deepened. "Tomorrow."

38

A light wind outside buffeted the tarpaulin protecting the remains of Hugh's study. He picked through the broken bits of his desk—the right half blown to pieces and the left half collapsed in on itself. "What a beastly mess."

Simmons gathered Hugh's discarded papers into a bin for salvage. "I fail to detect any difference from its previous state."

"Ah, Simmons. Your wisdom is surpassed only by your wit." From a shattered drawer, Hugh sorted papers and notebooks, most of which he no longer needed. Why ever did he keep them?

He scrambled over the rubble and dumped more papers into the scrap bin, then returned to his desk and lifted the bottom drawer.

Underneath rested items that had fallen behind the drawers, particularly from his overstuffed top drawer—crumpled papers and—

And a small black notebook.

His breath caught. Could it be?

He picked it up, opened it, and saw writing in French. "It's Jouveau's!"

"Jouveau's?" Dirt streaked Simmons's face.

"My reporter friend who was murdered." Hugh flipped through frantically. "I've looked everywhere for this. It slipped behind the drawers."

The thrill of discovery raced through his fingers, followed by a rush of grief for his friend, then by pangs of annoyance at himself. If he'd been neater, if he'd taken more care with the notebook, he would have found it—and any clues it contained—back in November.

He had to take it to the police, but first he wanted to study it. He wanted to discuss the contents with someone.

With Aleida?

He frowned. Should he?

In the past week and a half, she'd come to the Hart and Swan five times. He'd been careful to be as open and friendly with her as before, but also careful not to sit beside her. She'd requested friendship, which was more than he'd hoped for, but he did pine for what had been.

He'd told her he wouldn't try to win her back, and out of respect for her, he'd stay true to his word.

But right now, her friendship was precisely what he wanted.

"That's all for today, Simmons," Hugh said. "I'll sort more tomorrow after church."

"Very well, sir."

Out in the sitting room, he rang Aleida's flat. Thank goodness she owned a telephone and thank goodness she was at home.

"Good news," he said to her. "I found Jouveau's notebook."

"You did? I thought you'd looked everywhere."

"Everywhere except underneath the desk drawers. It must have fallen behind." He clutched the notebook. "Would you like to see it?"

"Oh yes."

"I'll come over in about an hour. I'm rather grubby from sorting through rubble." He frowned at his ancient gray jumper and his rumpled corduroy trousers.

"May I come to your house? I'd rather not wait."

He chuckled at her enthusiasm. "Excellent. Then I can take it to the police."

"The police? Of course, you must. But what a shame for you to lose those clues."

A shame indeed. "Whilst I wait for you, I'll copy every word."

"Yes, do. Be precise, Hugh. Copy everything you read, with dates and times."

He tipped up a salute she couldn't see. "Yes, ma'am."

After he hung up, he sat down with Jouveau's notebook and one of his own, and he took careful transcription.

His nerves jangled. So much to analyze, so much to ponder. Soon another mystery asserted itself—Jouveau had met twice with Hugh's cousin, William Hastings. But why?

Hugh rang William's townhouse, and William offered to come over to discuss the matter.

As Hugh sat down to resume copying, the doorbell rang.

Aleida stood on his doorstep, pretty in a pinkish coat, and she directed a smile down to her side, where only rusty holes remained on the steps after the iron railings had been donated for scrap. "I'm so glad Lennox returned."

"Lennox!" Hugh leaned out the door. Could it be? After ten days' absence?

His gray-and-white cat sashayed inside, rubbing against Hugh's ankle as he passed.

"Lennox!" Hugh scooped him into his arms, and his heart brimmed to overflowing. "Where have you been?"

"He just returned now?" Aleida came inside and shut the door behind her.

"Yes. Where have you been, Lennox?" Hugh inspected for injuries. Although dirty and a bit thinner, Lennox seemed intact. "I should have known you'd wait for Aleida. You always preferred her to me, not that I blame you."

As feisty as ever, Lennox hissed and squirmed out of Hugh's arms.

"Simmons!" Hugh called. "The prodigal puss has returned. I imagine he's rather hungry. Bring out the fatted calf."

Simmons stepped out of the study with the scrap bin, his eyebrows high. "Lennox, where on earth have you been?"

A single meow in reply, which Hugh couldn't translate, and the cat trotted after Simmons down to the kitchen.

"You must be relieved," Aleida said.

"You can't imagine how awful it's—" He winced and shot her an apologetic glance. "Yes, you can imagine, and even more so."

Sadness darkened her lovely eyes, but a soft smile and smooth forehead spoke of the peace she claimed.

"Come," he said. "Allow me to help with your coat. Please pardon my attire."

Aleida shrugged her coat off her shoulders and into Hugh's hands. "I'd hardly expect you to sift through rubble in a Savile Row suit."

He led her into the sitting room, and they sat on the sofa side by side. "Here is Jouveau's notebook."

She took it in hand and stroked the cover with reverence. Her hair slipped forward, the clipped ends curving beneath her chin in a charming way.

If only he could stroke her hair, caress her cheek, kiss her lips.

Never again, and he took a bracing deep breath.

Aleida lifted her gaze, and the light through the window brought out the green-blue of her eyes. "Would you like me to read the entire thing?"

"Why don't I show you the most pertinent information?"

He took the notebook, and his fingers brushed hers. Another bracing breath, and he flipped to the correct page. "The third of November. The notation JI-GB, as I remember."

"Did anything you read reveal what it means?"

"Not that I can determine. In the weeks following our visit to the Strand Palace Hotel, Jouveau had appointments with a dozen Members of Parliament, all of whom opposed my uncle. Do you remember when Jouveau said Fletcher ordered him to drop the story? Fletcher recently told me this is why he did so—because Jouveau was asking MPs about personal matters."

"Oh my. Do you think one of them is the murderer?"

"Possibly, but not one has the initials JI or GB." Hugh turned a page. "Look at this notation on 29 October—'*Vérifier les rendez-vous du 20 Septembre.*'"

"Verify the meetings on 20 September?"

"The twentieth of September is the day my uncle was murdered." Hugh jabbed his finger at the entry. "And on 31 October—'Hastings, William'—Uncle Elliott's son and heir. Jouveau met with him, and for the second time."

"What about?"

"I don't know, but I rang William, and he'll be here shortly." Hugh thumbed through the notebook. "Jouveau used this as a diary to record appointments. He must have had a separate book for his notes, as I do. Since Jouveau—since his body was found without papers, the murderer must have taken that notebook or destroyed it."

Aleida worried her lower lip. "You don't suspect William, do you?"

"Not at all. He got on famously with his father, and he was at sea when Uncle Elliott was killed."

The doorbell rang. "That must be the man himself."

It was. His cousin entered, tall and smart in his naval officer's uniform, and he hung up his coat and hat.

There stood Hugh, rejected by the Forces, and in dusty work clothes at that. But he smiled, joked about his attire, led William to the sitting room, and made proper introductions.

William settled into an armchair.

Hugh returned to his place beside Aleida. "As I mentioned on the telephone, François Jouveau and I accidentally switched notebooks before he disappeared, and today I found his notebook at last."

William lifted his pugnacious Hastings chin and a grim smile. "The Luftwaffe is doing a rather spectacular job of unearthing bits of London's history. Shall we thank them?"

"I think we should return the favor and unearth bits of Berlin's history."

"Quite right."

Hugh brushed dust off his jumper sleeve. "I see Jouveau met with you on 12 October and 31 October. May I inquire as to the purpose?"

"He was investigating Father's murder." William's mouth turned down. "In our first meeting, he inquired about my father's refugee bill."

Aleida nudged Hugh. "We discussed the bill on the way to the Strand Palace Hotel. Jouveau said that conversation led him to the murderer."

"He did," Hugh breathed out. "What did you tell Jouveau?"

William shrugged broad shoulders. "We discussed the opposition to the bill, but it's all public record, Father's usual political opponents. The police have investigated them thoroughly."

Hugh's left leg jiggled. "Yet somehow, something in your conversation led him to the man he was convinced killed your father, a man who quite probably killed Jouveau as well."

A frown creased William's face. "Well, there was that other matter . . ."

Hugh's leg stilled. "What other matter?"

"I mentioned it as an aside during my first meeting with Jouveau," William said. "He showed no interest. But in our second meeting he all but interrogated me about it."

"What was this matter?" Aleida asked.

William gripped his hands together. "My father discovered an illicit affair. He told me how useful the information might be. I'm afraid he was not above using underhanded tactics."

Hugh sighed. "What more did he say? Or do I want to know?"

"Father didn't divulge much." William raised a wry smile. "For a man known for his own illicit affairs and a man not above underhanded tactics, he could also be discreet. He only mentioned that the man involved had opposed him at every turn—and was married. And the woman—Father seemed quite giddy. He wouldn't tell me why, but I imagine the man would do anything to conceal the identity of his mistress. Do you think . . . ?"

Hugh glanced at Aleida, at her wide-eyed alarm. "It's quite possible."

Aleida nodded. "If the man came to your estate to confront Mr. Hastings, to beg him not to reveal the affair . . ."

They tussled. The gun went off.

Jouveau had stumbled upon the truth. For that, he had to be silenced.

Hugh gave himself a little shake. "No names? No other details?"

"I'm afraid not," William said. "Jouveau was rather giddy himself during our second meeting. He was convinced he knew the couple's identity and said everything made sense."

Hugh gripped the notebook hard. "Did he explain? Give names?"

"If only he had." William blew out a loud breath. "Do be careful, Hugh. The murderer has already killed twice."

"I know," Hugh said. "Have you told the police about this?"

"I did, but they said without names, the information was useless."

Hugh opened the notebook to the perplexing clue and handed it to William. "JI-GB. Does that give you any insight? Perhaps the initials of the man and the woman?"

As William studied the page, his mouth worked side to side. Then he shook his head. "I'm afraid not, but I'll think on it."

"Please do." Hugh took back the notebook. "I'll take this to the police now. I do hope they find something of use in here."

"As do I." William's voice lowered to a grumble.

After appropriate inquiries into family and health, Hugh saw William and Aleida to the door.

Aleida lingered after William departed, and creases divided her once-smooth brow. "Might I walk with you to the station? I've finished my chores and have nothing to do at home."

She didn't have a Simmons or a Lennox to keep her company. An offer to fill her leisure time welled in his throat, but he swallowed. He'd gladly settle for an hour. "I'd be honored. Please have a seat while I make myself presentable."

Hugh dashed up to the guest room, where he now slept, and exchanged corduroys and jumper for a suit.

Back in the sitting room, he found Aleida studying the notebook. She rose and handed it to him. "If the man caught in the affair is our suspect, that means the murderer is married."

"Which officially eliminates Guy Gilbert." Hugh led Aleida to the door. "Which officially pleases me."

Aleida smiled and accepted Hugh's help with her coat. "What about the others on your list? Is Mr. Fletcher married? Irwin?"

"Both are." Hugh slipped on his own coat and put on a fedora. "Fletcher certainly opposed my uncle at every turn, but Irwin? Although he disliked my uncle, I wouldn't call him an opponent."

"Hmm." After Hugh opened the door, Aleida stepped outside. "Yet you never seem to consider Mr. Fletcher a serious suspect."

"No, I don't." Hugh trotted down the front steps. "Perhaps because I respect him as an editor and as a man. Perhaps because Jouveau wouldn't have told his prime suspect he was about to solve the murder. Perhaps it's my naïve refusal to think Fletcher capable of such crimes."

"Or . . . ?"

A brisk breeze threatened to steal his hat, and he pulled it lower. "Or because my mind persists in picturing Bert Ridley as the murderer. He is, by the way, married. But he has an alibi. Why can't I write him off as a suspect? I've known him longer than I've known Fletcher. He was my brother's best friend. Surely I should give him as much grace as I do my editor."

Aleida frowned at the sky, streaked with high clouds. "If none of those men fit, perhaps the murderer is someone outside your acquaintance."

"That would explain all." He rubbed his coat pocket containing Jouveau's notebook. "I have to trust the police to do their work. I certainly don't do it well."

"That's all right." Aleida gave him a sweet smile. "You're already one of the most beloved and respected correspondents on the BBC. You can't do everything, Hugh Collingwood."

He chuckled. "That wouldn't be quite fair, would it?"

They strolled through Grosvenor Square past buildings under repair. The Mayfair area had been heavily damaged in the air raid on 16 April, the one Londoners simply called "The Wednesday."

"Hugh?" Aleida's mouth curled in a pensive way. "When you were in Scotland, a woman I worked with at the Ministry of Health was killed during an air raid."

"I'm so sorry."

"Her name was Nilima Sharma. We volunteered together at the ARP."

"Miss Sharma?" With tens of thousands of deaths since the Blitz began, why did each one feel like a horse kicking him in the chest? "I remember her. How dreadful."

Aleida turned a stricken gaze to him. "She was murdered."

"Murdered?"

"Strangled with the strap on her warden's helmet. She was found in Green Park, in a collapsed trench. It was supposed to look as if she'd been killed by a bomb blast."

His arm itched to encircle Aleida's slight shoulders, which had already borne more than they should. "Perfectly dreadful. Do the police have any leads?"

"None. Nilima had no enemies at work or in her neighborhood or at our post. She hadn't been robbed or—or violated. The police dropped the investigation."

Did Aleida think . . . ? He dipped his voice low in respect. "Are you wondering if she was having an affair with a married man?"

"I doubt it. But . . ." She tucked her lips between her teeth, then released them. "Nilima was a foreigner. Jouveau was a foreigner who spoke up for refugees. Your uncle was working on a bill to aid refugees. I can't help but wonder."

"All right." He turned south on Bond Street. "Let's give this some thought. Was Nilima acquainted with my uncle or Jouveau or any of our current suspects?"

Aleida let out a long sigh. "Not that I know. One day she did mention the refugee bill, but she couldn't remember the name of the MP behind it. It isn't much, I know."

It wasn't, and he lifted one shoulder.

Her hair twirled in the wind, and she clapped her hand to the dancing strands. "All along, you've thought the case was about censorship. But what if the murderer wasn't concerned about the *fact* that the victims spoke up, but about whom the victims spoke up *for*?"

"Refugees."

"Yes."

"It's worthy of consideration." But darkness twisted inside. "However, in the case of your friend, we have to remember there are monsters in this world who kill for the sheer sport of it."

Aleida shuddered, and she leaned closer until her arm brushed his.

Briefly.

Hugh firmed his chin. How could he bear being only a friend when she needed more than a friend's comfort? When he longed to give her that comfort?

He breathed out a prayer for help. This was far more difficult than he'd imagined.

# 39

Aleida flipped through the filing cabinet. "The cards are filed by county alphabetically. Within each county, by town alphabetically. Within each town, by the child's last name."

"I see." Miss Winthrop, who had taken Nilima's position, pursed pink lips in her porcelain face as she studied a card in her hand. "Child's name, date of birth, names and addresses of the parents and of the foster family."

"We make notes on the back if necessary." Aleida took the card from Miss Winthrop and pointed to an address crossed through. "If the billeting officer tells us of a change in address, we note it here. And if the child returns to London or another evacuation area—"

"We throw the card away."

"Never." Aleida opened another drawer. "We move the card to this file. See—Liverpool, London . . ."

"Ah yes. We don't want to lose a child."

"No." Pain crushed her chest, but each day the pain crushed a bit less.

Even though she'd lost Theo, at least she had his image. She'd framed his photographs and hung them in her bedroom.

288

The photograph of Sebastiaan, however, she'd burned without ceremony.

How kind of Hugh to bring her the pictures. If only . . .

He'd insisted he didn't want to win her back, and he seemed satisfied with half of what they'd had before. He acted comfortable and friendly with her, with none of the longing looks he'd given her before they'd first kissed.

Aleida, however, had to restrain herself from taking his hand, his arm, from leaning against him.

After she returned the card to the filing cabinet, she and Miss Winthrop sat down at the desk with a stack of letters from billeting officers.

Aleida slit open the first envelope and opened it. "From Bedford. Three children have returned to London."

Miss Winthrop went to the filing cabinet. "Bedfordshire . . . Bedford . . . child's name?"

"Good afternoon, Mrs. Martens." Mr. Armbruster stood in front of her desk in a black suit that rounded over his portly form.

Aleida stood and greeted the head of their division. "Shall I fetch Miss Granville?"

"You're the young lady I came to see." Dark eyes twinkled from deep in his full face. "How is your talk coming along?"

"Talk?"

"Yes. We're all very interested in hearing more about the status of the refugee children."

Aleida tilted her head as if doing so might sift missing knowledge into place. "I'm afraid I don't understand."

"You did receive my invitation, did you not?"

"Invitation? No, sir."

Mr. Armbruster frowned over Aleida's shoulder. "Miss Granville?"

"I'll fetch her, sir." Miss Winthrop scurried off to Miss Granville's office.

Mr. Armbruster returned his gaze to Aleida. "I sit on the board for the Refugee Aid Society. We're holding a charity banquet, and I want you to talk about the refugee children. I'm sure—ah, Miss Granville. It appears you forgot to pass on the banquet invitation to Mrs. Martens."

Color rose in Miss Granville's cheeks. "As the head of this department, I shall speak about the matter. I am more informed about the situation than Mrs. Martens. And—I do apologize, Mrs. Martens—but I don't believe a foreigner would be accepted by this stratum of society. She does have an accent."

Aleida tensed. How did Miss Granville manage to look prim and contrite while saying such things?

Mr. Armbruster chuckled. "Her accent is charming. And I specifically invited her to speak because her status as a refugee will lend poignancy and authenticity to her talk."

Miss Granville folded in her lips. "It isn't proper."

"Proper?" Mr. Armbruster's voice dropped a forbidding octave. "Who better to speak about the refugee children than the very woman who wrote that excellent and thorough report?"

"Report?" Aleida could think of only one report that fit— but how had Mr. Armbruster received it? Hadn't Miss Granville dumped it in the scrap bin?

No joviality remained in Mr. Armbruster's expression. "The invitation, Miss Granville."

"Very well." She turned on her heel and marched back to her office.

"A ten-minute talk," Mr. Armbruster said to Aleida. "Please summarize the information about the refugee children from your report. Would you like to borrow it so you can prepare?"

"No. I—I made a carbon copy." Her words came out breathy. She couldn't believe Miss Granville had passed on the report she despised.

After Miss Granville returned and handed Aleida a creamy envelope, Mr. Armbruster departed.

Aleida followed Miss Granville back to her office. "I didn't realize you gave my report to Mr. Armbruster."

At the office door, Miss Granville turned to her with a contorted smile. "Of course, I did. Why wouldn't I?"

Aleida could think of many reasons. The same reasons Miss Granville didn't want Aleida speaking at the banquet.

"Do be careful to do this department proud." Miss Granville's mouth formed a compassionate little moue. "I didn't want to embarrass you in front of Mr. Armbruster, but you're so quiet. I was afraid you'd faint in front of an audience, especially an audience of this caliber—some of the finest families in London. I wanted to protect you."

"How kind of you." With effort, Aleida strained the sarcasm from her tone. "But I've always enjoyed public speaking."

Without waiting for a response, Aleida returned to her desk and her letters.

Insufferable woman. But because of her actions, Aleida would have an opportunity to address an issue close to her heart.

**Sunday, May 4, 1941**

With long sleeves and a high neck, the pale gray evening gown was elegant but unassuming, appropriate attire for speaking as a representative of the Ministry of Health.

Aleida shimmied out of the silk chiffon and back into her Sunday dress, and she folded the gown into the suitcase she'd brought to Hugh's London house.

How thoughtful of him to ask his mother if Aleida could borrow a gown for the event, and how sweet of Mrs. Collingwood to agree. Fleeing from the Netherlands, Aleida had brought no evening wear. London shops now had little in the way of luxury items, and Aleida had no time for alterations.

Downstairs, Hugh waited for her with Lennox sitting on the back of the armchair behind him. "Did you find something suitable?"

"I did, thank you. I'm shorter than your mother, but with high heels it'll be fine."

Hugh stood and smoothed the front of his dark gray suit. "How is your talk coming along?"

"I'm finished. The difficult part was making it fit in ten minutes. I'm excited to speak about this."

Hugh cocked his head and grinned. "How would you like to speak about it on the BBC?"

"Pardon?"

"I talked Fletcher into it." His grin threatened to crack his face in half. "The BBC often features charitable causes. My theme will be that even in times of war, a civilized society continues to care for 'the stranger, and the fatherless, and the widow' amongst us, as the Bible says."

Her chest warmed with hope. "Splendid. Maybe listeners will be moved to bring refugee children out of the hostels and into their homes."

"You're the woman to persuade them." His smile held friendly affection but nothing more.

"Thank you." She dropped her gaze to her suitcase. "Please thank your mother for loaning me her gown. I'll have it cleaned before I return it."

Hugh gestured to the suitcase. "Would you like me to carry that to your flat? I could use a Sunday stroll, and it's a glorious day."

"That would be lovely." She spoke too quickly and eagerly, and she resisted the urge to take his arm as they stepped outside into the cool air.

Clear blue skies arched above as they strolled along Brook Street.

Hugh aimed a smile at the approaching greenery. "I've always loved Hyde Park on a Sunday. Well, not as a child, of course, banished to the country as I was, and trapped indoors. But now I love it."

She smiled at his relaxed profile. She loved how he openly discussed his asthma, not only with her, but with his friends at the Hart and Swan.

At Park Lane, they waited for a bus to pass, crossed the street, and entered the park through Brook Gate. Although with the iron railings removed for scrap, it little resembled a gate.

Shouting voices rose before them.

Hugh's face lit up, and he led her to Speakers' Corner. Dozens of people stood about, speaking on all manner of subjects as passersby shouted objections.

"This," he said. "This is why Britain must survive."

A man called out a pacifist slogan, and several onlookers laughed him down.

Aleida smiled. So much disagreement, so much passion, so loud. Yet it all sounded good-natured.

Hugh shifted the suitcase from one hand to the other. "On the BBC, we mustn't broadcast anything that might give information or comfort to the enemy. The newspapers have more latitude but mustn't directly oppose the war effort. But here in the very heart of London, people are free to say the most outrageous and ridiculous and incendiary things."

A small man in his sixties approached, with a bright red scarf tied about his neck, and he handed Hugh a pamphlet. "End this capitalist war," he said in a thick Eastern European accent.

Hugh smiled at him, put his hand to the small of Aleida's back, and led her away. "If he wants to end this war, he should talk to Hitler."

Aleida peered at the pamphlet, titled, "A People's Peace," which claimed that suing for peace would save Britain, but that her greedy imperialist leaders preferred to let the nation burn.

She clucked her tongue. "If your government followed this advice, Hitler could sail across the Channel without firing a shot."

Hugh flipped over the pamphlet to where the man's name was printed with the date and location of his group's next meeting. "Ironically, if Hitler came, our friend Mr. Filip Zielinski would no longer be free to print pamphlets or publicly proclaim his opinion."

Aleida brushed aside a pebble with the toe of her shoe. "In a way, Speakers' Corner reminds me of Beatrice Granville."

"End this capitalist war?" Hugh raised his eyebrows in a playful way.

She laughed. "Definitely not. But even though she opposed my report, even though it might lead Mr. Armbruster to make changes she doesn't want, she passed it on. She respected my right to speak even though she disagreed. That shows integrity, and I admire her."

The shouting intensified behind them.

A large man in a fine suit grabbed Mr. Zielinski by the collar. "How dare you? You came to our country. You benefited from our generosity and hospitality. You benefitted from our liberties. And for what?"

"Albert Ridley?" Hugh's eyes stretched wide.

"Your friend from the Ministry of Information?" Why did he look familiar?

Hugh's mouth twitched. "My brother's friend. Not mine."

Mr. Ridley shook the smaller man. "For what? You want to destroy the very liberties you enjoy. You want to destroy the nation that sheltered you."

Mr. Zielinski struggled to break free. "I want to destroy the capitalist system that enslaves—"

Mr. Ridley cried out in inarticulate rage.

"Bert!" A petite blonde tugged on his sleeve. "Stop at once. You're making a scene, and in front of the children."

Two young girls cowered behind Mrs. Ridley.

Aleida exchanged an alarmed glance with Hugh.

Mr. Ridley shrugged off his wife's grip and shook Mr. Zielinski, causing pamphlets to cascade to the ground. "Those who oppose the war effort deserve the severest punishment."

"You *do* take pleasure in embarrassing me." Mrs. Ridley raised her reddening face high. "I'm going home. Come along, children."

"See? You're undermining the English way of life." Mr. Ridley shoved Mr. Zielinski.

The older man fell on his backside.

Mr. Ridley stood over him and pointed a finger at him. "High treason—that's what this is." He kicked at the pamphlets and marched after his wife.

Hugh rushed forward and helped Mr. Zielinski to his feet, and Aleida and other onlookers gathered the scattered pamphlets.

"Are you all right, sir?" Hugh asked.

"Yes, yes. Thank you." The man straightened his red scarf and uttered what could only be curse words.

After Aleida returned his pamphlets to him, she and Hugh resumed walking.

Hugh drew a dramatic intake of air. "Ah! Nothing like a peaceful spring day in the park."

Aleida chuckled, then glanced behind her. "I remember where I've seen Mr. Ridley. He visited the office a few months ago."

"Ridley? What business would he have with the Ministry of Health?"

"I don't know." Aleida turned down a path shaded by graceful trees. "I remember because it was unusual. He walked on through to Beatrice's office as if he worked there, but Nilima said he didn't have an appointment and she hadn't seen him before. She said Beatrice was annoyed with him. He hasn't returned."

"How curious." Hugh shrugged. "But Beatrice and Bert and William and Cecil were the best of friends, and the best of friends do have rows."

"With his temper, Mr. Ridley must cause many of those rows." She shuddered. "I can see why you keep considering him a murder suspect, even though he has an alibi."

"Yet you persist in saying I see only the good in people." Hugh bumped her with his elbow, and dappled sunlight danced in his eyes.

Love and affection for him welled inside her. "I'm glad to learn you aren't completely angelic but have failings like the rest of us mortals."

Even though he laughed, regret twitched in his cheeks.

Did he feel he'd failed her? He hadn't.

Hugh folded the pamphlet in half and stuck it in his jacket pocket. "Oh yes. This is for you." He drew something from his pocket.

A small, flat elephant of gray wool felt, held together with large and uneven stitches, with a single button eye. "My sister Caroline made this for me."

"Oh, Hugh. I couldn't take it."

"I'd forgotten about it." He nudged his hand closer to her. "I found it in the debris and thought of you straightaway. It was good of you to give Theo his stuffed elephant, but now you have nothing to remember him by."

"I have the photographs."

Hugh ducked his head to the side. "You do. But I'd like you to have this. It won't—it can't—replace Oli or your son. But I hope it can help you remember."

"Elephants never forget," she whispered. She took the gift and held it to her heart. "Thank you, Hugh. I'll treasure it always."

"You're welcome," he said in a gruff voice, and he gestured down the path with suitcase in hand. "Shall we?"

Everything in her wanted to take his face in her hands and kiss him, to be rechtdoorzee and declare her love.

But everything in her also knew he wouldn't welcome it.

Aleida moved her feet forward and raised a cheery smile.

With each day, with each act of kindness, she loved him more. Never before in her life had friendship seemed insufficient.

# 40

A full moon cast golden light on Hugh's patent leather shoes as he strode up Regent Street in full evening dress.

Tonight would be crucial.

Most importantly, he'd help Aleida give voice to a cause she held dear. Through her nationwide appeal, perhaps good changes would come for the refugee children.

Hugh also intended to use the evening for romantic reconnaissance. Would Aleida be impressed with his finely tailored black tails and trousers, his crisp white tie and waistcoat? Would she let him twirl her around the dance floor? Would she melt in his embrace as she once had done?

He could no longer continue as mere friends. But if he told her of his love, he might destroy a friendship that meant a great deal to both of them.

Ahead of him, the door to the Hart and Swan swung open, and two men exited—Gil and MacLeod.

"Good evening, gentlemen," Hugh said.

Gil shined his torch at Hugh. "White tie? Where are you going?"

Hugh made a show of twirling his cane, doffing his top hat,

and dipping a bow. "To the Dorchester Hotel to record a broadcast at a charity banquet."

MacLeod choked back a laugh. "Another thrilling BBC broadcast."

"It will be when Aleida Martens makes a touching appeal on behalf of refugee children."

Gil buttoned his overcoat, his chin down. "I thought you and Aleida weren't . . ."

Hugh swallowed hard. "We aren't, but her story needs to be told. Fletcher agreed."

"You should return to the papers," MacLeod said. "That's where the excitement is. Today I covered a murder."

"Oh?" Hugh had rather lost his taste for murders.

"A communist agitator." MacLeod pointed to the side with his thumb. "Strangled with his own scarf in a trench in Hyde Park near Speakers' Corner."

Hugh could still see the impassioned face, the red scarf . . . "Speakers' Corner, you say? What was the man's name?"

"Filip Zielinski."

Hugh's chest caved in. "Oh no. When was he murdered?"

"Last night. They found him this morning. Why? Do you know him?"

Hugh rubbed his hand over his mouth. "I saw him on Sunday. Albert Ridley attacked him."

"Ridley?" Gil said with a gasp. "He attacked him?"

Hugh's stomach and thoughts churned, and he clamped his hand to the back of his neck. "Ridley shook him, shoved him down, accused him of taking advantage of English liberty. He said Zielinski was guilty of high treason."

"High treason?" MacLeod whipped out his notebook. "Gil, shine your torch this way."

Gil complied. "The punishment for high treason—it's death."

"Do you think Ridley's capable of murder?" MacLeod said.

"I don't know." Hugh's fingers dug into the back of his neck.

"I must admit, I suspected him in my uncle's murder. He had rather public altercations with my uncle—with Jouveau too. But he was in London the day my uncle was murdered."

"London?" The torchlight gave Gil's frown a ghostly glow. "Hastings was killed that Friday morning, right?"

"Yes," Hugh said. "Why?"

Gil shrugged. "Ridley might have been in London later that day, but in the morning he was in Hertfordshire, only a few miles from your uncle's estate. Do you remember how Fletcher and I went to visit his family?"

"Of course."

A smirk turned up one corner of Gil's mouth. "We arrived on Thursday evening. When we got off the train at Braughing, we noticed Ridley disembarking from another carriage. A redhead greeted him with a passionate kiss. She's not Ridley's wife, according to Fletcher."

"No." A sick feeling twisted in Hugh's stomach. Ridley's wife was blond.

"They didn't see us—they had eyes only for each other—but they went to an inn. And I saw them stroll past the cottage on Friday around noon. Ridley was most assuredly in Hertfordshire on Friday morning."

Uncle Elliott had uncovered an affair. Was it Ridley's affair? "Ridley doesn't have an alibi after all. Gil, did you or Fletcher tell the police about this?"

"The police? No. I never saw him as a suspect."

MacLeod scribbled fast. "If this is what Jouveau uncovered, I can see why he thought it a scoop—a man of Ridley's prominence."

JI-GB. Albert Ridley. It didn't match, but everything else did. Ridley had ample reason to kill Jouveau. "Three murders?"

"Sensational," MacLeod said. "Simply sensational."

"I'm a witness." Hugh blew out a hard breath. "I saw him attack Zielinski. I need to tell the police straightaway."

He headed back south along Regent Street, then stopped in his tracks. "The charity banquet!"

The story he'd persuaded Fletcher to let him broadcast. How could he let Fletcher down? He'd tarnish the reputation he'd worked so hard to polish. Irresponsible worthless toff in his top hat and tails.

And Aleida? How could he simply not go? She'd think he'd forgotten her.

He turned back to Gil and MacLeod. Perhaps he could send Gil to the police. Except Hugh had witnessed the attack, heard the threatening words, knew about Uncle Elliott and the affair, and pieced together the case against Ridley for all three murders.

Telling the police took priority over his career, over his romance, over the approval of man.

A sour taste filled his mouth. "Gil, are you free tonight? Do you own white tie?"

"Yes." Gil's voice rose in excitement. "Would you like me to cover the story? With Aleida?"

"Yes, please." Hugh pulled out his notebook and tore out the relevant pages. "Here are my notes. The banquet is at the Dorchester Hotel, in the ballroom. Tom Young is waiting at Broadcasting House with a light mobile recording unit. Go there first, tell him you need to change into evening dress. You'll be late to the banquet, but it can't be helped."

"Yes. I'll do that." An eager smile lit up Gil's face.

Would Gil cross Hugh with Fletcher as he'd done before? Would he cross him with Aleida as he twirled her around the dance floor?

Hugh clamped off a groan. "Please tell Aleida about Zielinski, about Ridley's lack of alibi. She'll want to know."

"I will."

"And please tell her how much I wanted to be there for her." He turned away from all his lovely plans and ran down Regent Street toward the police station.

❧

Aleida politely turned down a request to dance. Mrs. Collingwood's dress hung half an inch too long, even with Aleida's high-heeled shoes, and she had to hold herself tall and walk with care.

Perhaps she'd take a chance and dance when Hugh came. If he came.

She frowned and continued her stroll around the ballroom of the Dorchester Hotel. Although Hugh often ran late, he'd improved lately, especially when he cared.

Maybe he no longer cared, now that the romance was over. Maybe he'd forgotten her.

She huffed. If he was late, he had good reason. She trusted him.

Brilliant crystal chandeliers illuminated couples dancing in white tie or in elegant gowns. On the walls, crystal sconces hung on mirrors framed by blue-veined marble, while drapes flowed down the walls between the mirrors.

She knew no one in the room other than Beatrice Granville and Mr. Armbruster. Today, of all days, she could use a friend.

Aleida gripped her evening bag, and her grandmother's sapphire ring glimmered.

A year ago today, the Nazis had invaded the Netherlands. A year ago today, she'd last seen Theo.

Three hundred sixty-five days.

With dizzying pain, her heart crumpled. She treasured Theo's photographs, the images of how he'd looked a year before. How did he look now? Did his voice sound different?

A wail built inside, threatening to erupt, but she shoved it down. She'd made the right choice. Theo—Teddy—was happy. He'd be all right. In time, she would be too.

"Mrs. Martens." Beatrice Granville approached in a long emerald gown, her hair swept up with diamond-encrusted combs. "How charming you look."

"Thank you, Miss Granville. You look lovely."

Beatrice dipped her chin, then rounded her eyes. "I want to apologize. I dismissed your report without due consideration. Upon reading it again, I see the welfare of the children transcends merely evacuating them from danger. We must address their deeper needs, and we must care for all the children, even those who aren't English."

"Thank you. I'm pleased to hear that." Had the woman had a change of heart? Or was she maneuvering for favor, knowing Mr. Armbruster would address the problems Aleida had exposed?

Regardless, Aleida raised a sincere smile.

Beatrice tapped Aleida's arm. "How did you arrive this evening? By taxi?"

"Well, yes."

"That won't do." Beatrice clucked her tongue. "I have a car and a driver. I simply insist you ride with me."

If only Hugh could accompany her home. She scanned the ballroom in vain. "Thank you," she said. "I'll keep that in mind."

A bright smile, and Beatrice sashayed away.

At the entrance to the ballroom, Mr. and Mrs. Armbruster welcomed some familiar faces—Guy Gilbert, Tom Young, and Gerald MacTavish.

Why was Gil here with the recording crew? Where was Hugh?

Mr. Armbruster peered around the dance floor and pointed Aleida out to Gil and the others. Gil smiled and waved.

Aleida did her best to return the gesture, and she met Gil halfway around the ballroom.

He bowed, sweeping back the tails of his coat. "Good evening, Aleida. You're a vision of beauty."

"Thank you." She dropped a curtsy, but disappointment colored her words. "Is Hugh with you?"

"No." His gaze darted to the side, and chandelier light shined on his slicked-back blond hair. "He asked me to come in his place."

"Oh." Hugh had sounded delighted with the story. Why would he give it to Gil? She worked up a smile. "I'm glad the story will still be broadcast. How good of you to come."

Gil wrinkled his nose and sighed. "Collie does have good reason. A man was murdered last night—Filip Zielinski."

"Oh no." Aleida's mouth fell open. "We saw him on Sunday at Speakers' Corner."

"His body was found nearby." Gil lowered his voice. "In a trench in the park, strangled with his scarf."

Strangled? In a trench? That was how Nilima died, and a chill raced up Aleida's spine.

Gil leaned closer. "Collie went to the police station to report an altercation he witnessed between Mr. Zielinski and Albert Ridley."

"We saw—"

"Yes. Collie is certain Ridley killed Zielinski, and he thinks Ridley also killed Hastings and Jouveau."

"But Ridley has an alibi."

Gil leaned still closer, his light blue eyes earnest. "No, he does not. Mr. Fletcher and I saw Ridley near the Hastings estate on the day of the murder. He was with a redhead—who was not his wife."

An affair. Was that the affair Hastings threatened to expose? With a redhead?

Aleida's gaze swept the ballroom and found Beatrice Granville. A redhead. A friend of Albert Ridley's. Ridley had visited the office, which had annoyed Beatrice. A visit from an old friend wouldn't be cause for annoyance, but a visit from a married lover . . . ?

"Gil?" Aleida murmured. "Be very discreet. There's a tall woman with red hair about twenty feet to your left."

With a bored expression, Gil glanced around the ballroom and back to Aleida. His eyebrows rose. "In the green dress? That's her. I saw her with Ridley."

Aleida's mind spun pieces into place. "Her name is Beatrice Granville. The police need to know. Go to the police station straightaway and tell them, tell Hugh. He'll understand."

"But the story, your speech."

As much as she wanted this story on the BBC, she wanted the murderer caught far more. "Hugh is an eyewitness in the Zielinski case, but his theory about Hastings and Jouveau is speculation. You—you're the witness who can verify Ridley's lack of alibi. And Miss Granville—her father is an MP. It's crucial to Ridley's motive in the Hastings murder. Hugh will understand. You must tell him. You must tell the police."

Gil blinked in a dazed way. "Yes. Yes, I'll go straightaway."

Aleida reached out and squeezed Gil's hand. "Thank you."

Gil glanced down at her hand, then raised eyes full of regret. "Collie—he also said to tell you how very much he wanted to be here tonight for you."

Everything melted inside. She'd been more than satisfied with the excuse that he'd gone to the police to solve three murders. But Hugh had taken the time to send a message to her. And how thoughtful of Gil to relay the message, especially since he had a crush on her.

She squeezed the man's hand once more. "You're a good friend, Gil. Please tell Hugh I'm fine and I'm proud of him."

"I will." Gil took his leave, stopping to send Tom and Gerald home.

Once again, Aleida stood alone in a crowd, but now elation danced in time to the music. Tonight justice would be served.

And Hugh cared.

# 41

Slightly out of breath, Hugh followed the constable to the detective inspector's office. Thank goodness DI Clyde was working late.

The inspector raised fatigued eyes and smirked. "Good evening, Mr. Collingwood. I'm afraid the gentlemen's club is on the next street."

Hugh smiled at the joke, and he hung his top hat, overcoat, and white scarf on the coatrack. "I have information on the murder of Filip Zielinski, and I believe we can connect it to the murders of Elliott Hastings and François Jouveau."

DI Clyde closed his eyes and rubbed his temples. "Not every murder in London is related to the death of your uncle."

"I regret that you must suffer yet more foolishness from this amateur sleuth." Hugh took a seat in front of the inspector's desk. "However, on Sunday last I witnessed an attack on Mr. Zielinski at Speakers' Corner. The man who attacked him was Albert Ridley of the Ministry of Information. His family and mine are long acquainted."

Slowly, DI Clyde's light eyes opened. "An attack, you say?" He grabbed a pencil and a notepad.

In detail, Hugh described what he'd seen and what Ridley had said.

"'Those who oppose the war effort deserve the severest punishment'—he said that?" Clyde puffed his cheeks with air. "That makes him a person of interest. We'll question him, but we'll need to be careful with a man of his prominence."

Hugh rocked forward in his chair. "Please humor me a moment as I make my case."

Clyde circled one hand in the air, as if flourishing a top hat, mocking Hugh's highbrow attire. Nevertheless, he'd granted permission to proceed.

Hugh folded his hands on top of the desk. "Ridley and my uncle were political opponents. They almost came to blows in July."

"Hastings had many political opponents."

"Quite right, but he had information on Ridley and planned to use it against him. My cousin, William Hastings, said my uncle had discovered a man was having an affair."

The inspector set down his pencil. "I read about the affair in William Hastings's statement, but he didn't mention Ridley."

"No, but I believe Ridley was the man. This evening, I talked to my colleague Guy Gilbert. On the evening of 19 September, Gilbert saw Ridley in Braughing, kissing a woman who was not his wife. Gilbert also saw the couple around noon on 20 September, only a few hours after my uncle was murdered—and only a few miles from the Hastings estate."

Clyde's gaze locked on Hugh and flickered in thought. "Ridley was in the area at the time, with motive to kill Hastings—not only for political reasons, but to conceal his affair."

Clyde sprang from his desk and leaned out the door. "Constable Bright—fetch me the evidence for the Hastings-Jouveau case. At once."

Hugh waited until Clyde returned to his desk. "Mr. Gilbert can testify as to what he saw, as can his companion, Norman

Fletcher. Mr. Fletcher was questioned earlier in the investigation."

"Fletcher, yes." Clyde scribbled notes. "He didn't mention seeing Ridley."

"I doubt he suspected him." Hugh's mouth went tight. "But I believe Jouveau did. In his diary he noted, 'Verify the meetings on 20 September.' Jouveau was with me when Ridley claimed he'd had meetings in London on that date. I think Jouveau checked Ridley's alibi."

Clyde's chin and eyebrows elevated, and he resumed scribbling. "Quite possibly."

"Ridley had ample motive in Jouveau's case. They often argued about Jouveau's broadcasts to France. And when Jouveau interviewed my cousin, William told Jouveau his father had uncovered an affair."

Tapping his pencil to his square chin, Clyde frowned. "What were those initials in Jouveau's diary again?"

"JI-GB." Hugh shrugged. "No, it doesn't help."

Clyde cursed under his breath, then shook his head. "Regardless, we have reason to bring Ridley in for questioning."

Hugh relaxed back in his seat. A good start.

After Clyde rushed to the door again, he beckoned to a sergeant. "Bring in Mr. Albert Ridley for questioning about the murder of that refugee in Hyde Park—Filip Zielinski."

Then he turned back to Hugh. "If you wouldn't mind, please stay. I'll help Bright fetch the evidence."

"Yes, sir."

Clyde marched away.

Hugh's left leg bounced. Zielinski was a refugee.

Aleida thought the refugee cause linked the murders. She also thought . . .

Miss Sharma.

Hugh sucked in a breath. Strangled in a park in a trench. The same modus operandi.

Was Miss Sharma's death connected to the others? But how? Did she know Ridley?

He stood and paced. If only he could talk to Aleida. He missed the second half of his brain.

The second half of his heart.

"It's time for your speech." Mr. Armbruster escorted Aleida to a platform at the rear of the ballroom. "I do apologize for running late."

Standing by the platform, Mrs. Armbruster kissed Aleida's cheek. "You'll be marvelous, my dear."

"Thank you again for this opportunity," Aleida said.

Mrs. Armbruster's plump cheeks dimpled with suppressed laughter. "I'm afraid my darling husband has ulterior motives. He has great hopes to resurrect Elliott Hastings's bill to aid refugees. Some of the key supporters—and opponents—are in this room."

Mr. Armbruster smoothed his gray-streaked brown hair. "I hope that by calling attention to the plight of refugee children, you'll awaken compassion for all refugees."

"Thank you, sir. I would like to help."

"That was clear in your report," he said.

A warm smile rose. "I'm glad Miss Granville gave it to you."

Mr. and Mrs. Armbruster glanced at each other and chuckled.

"Miss Granville?" Mr. Armbruster smirked. "She didn't give me the report."

"She didn't?"

"No, that Indian girl brought it to me, with a brave speech about defying Miss Granville and rescuing the report from the scrap bin for the sake of the children."

A sick feeling descended into Aleida's belly. Beatrice had lied about giving Mr. Armbruster the report. But why? "Miss Sharma? Nilima Sharma did this?"

"Delightful young lady. I was sorry to hear she'd passed away."

"Yes." Aleida forced out the word.

The police said Nilima had no enemies. They were wrong. Beatrice wouldn't stand for being defied by a foreigner, for being humiliated in front of her boss—over an issue she opposed. But was it enough of a motive to commit murder?

Mr. Armbruster leaned closer with a conspiratorial gleam in his eye. "Miss Granville was livid when I confronted her about the matter. I'm surprised she didn't fire Miss Sharma on the spot."

"Hush, Howard." Mrs. Armbruster gave her head a decided tilt.

Aleida followed the tilt.

Beatrice Granville stood behind her, not three feet away, where she could have heard every word.

Chilled furor radiated from Beatrice's brown eyes.

She had indeed heard.

Could she have killed Nilima?

Beatrice hadn't been on ARP duty the night Nilima died. But what if she'd shown up in uniform? What if she'd told Nilima of some incident in Green Park? Led her to the trench?

Aleida's gaze froze in that chilled furor.

Why had Beatrice lied about the report? To deflect attention from her anger at Nilima. From her motive.

Once before, Aleida had noted that Beatrice wasn't a woman to be crossed.

Aleida sucked in a breath.

Something snapped in Beatrice's gaze.

She knew.

She knew that Aleida knew.

With every ounce of effort, Aleida composed herself and turned back to her host. She needed to ring the police at once. "Excuse me. I need to use a telephone."

"Of course. I'll help you find one after your speech."

"No, now," Aleida said in her lowest voice. "It's quite urgent."

"We're already running late, and you'll be finished in ten minutes." Mr. Armbruster strode to the podium and clapped his hands.

Aleida gripped her notes so hard they crinkled. It couldn't wait. She'd already incurred Beatrice's wrath. But to speak out for refugee children would double that wrath.

Mr. Armbruster thanked his glittering guests at their glittering tables. Thanked them for attending, for their generosity, for their compassion.

At the table directly in front of Aleida, Beatrice sat with rigid posture and a rigid smile, with her evening bag in her lap.

Aleida's insides squirmed in familiar terror, a terror she'd known too often living with Sebastiaan. Speak her mind and take a beating. Or be silent and protect herself.

Her finger tapped her notes, and the words swam before her. Why had she even come tonight?

Mr. Armbruster read Aleida's introduction and lifted an arm to her, an invitation.

Aleida dragged her feet toward the podium. Her toe caught in the hem of the too-long dress, and she gasped, braced herself on the podium, and dropped her notes.

Dozens of expectant faces stared back at her.

"Why am I here?" The words tumbled out.

Silence trembled in the opulent space.

Mrs. Armbruster gathered Aleida's notes and held them out to her.

Aleida ignored the offer. "I'll tell you why I'm here. A year ago today, I fled the Netherlands. Due to my husband's cruelty, I was separated from my young son. After my husband's death, I came to London to find my child. I searched in orphanages and hospitals, and I took a position at the Ministry of Health so I could search for him amongst the evacuees."

She directed her gaze past Beatrice, seeking souls who cared, finding them. "I saw the plight of the children, and I recorded their stories, the idyllic stories of children thriving in loving homes and fresh country air, and the horrific stories—far less common but not to be overlooked—the children neglected or mistreated."

Men gave grim nods. Ladies pulled handkerchiefs from evening bags.

"One day," Aleida said, "a billeting officer took me to a hostel, one of fifty hostels and camps established for children who are difficult to place in homes. Some of the children need medical care. Some have delinquency problems. Some have emotional problems. And some are refugees. The hostels are clean and comfortable and safe. The staff care for the children well. But a hostel is a poor substitute for a home."

A woman at a table to Aleida's left grumbled and nodded.

Aleida rubbed the polished wood podium. She'd been asked to discuss the needs of the refugee children, but another topic bubbled to the top of her mind. How disorganized to veer from her plan. How spontaneous. How like Hugh.

And how right. "Something curious arose. A billeting officer informed me—and others confirmed—that when the ladies of the Women's Voluntary Service escorted children to the country, they often told the billeting officers to take the refugee children straight to a hostel. The billeting officers were perplexed—many foster families are willing to take children from foreign lands. The WVS ladies were just as perplexed and bothered, but said they'd been informed it was Ministry of Health policy."

Sitting to Aleida's side on the platform, Mr. Armbruster gasped.

Those conversations had occurred after Aleida wrote her report. "The WVS ladies had been told foster homes were reserved for English children." She glanced to Mr. Armbruster.

His mouth hung open, and he shook his head.

Certainty and decisiveness coursed through her veins. "It was not—it *is* not—Ministry of Health policy. Rather it is the opinion of one person, passed along as policy."

That one person's eyes burned with vitriol. Murderous vitriol?

Aleida wrenched her gaze from Beatrice to the MPs and officials who made policy. "For the children of Britain's allies to be treated negligently is beneath the honorable character of this great nation, a nation known throughout the world for her courage, tenacity, and compassion."

A year ago, a coiled spring had burst inside her in the face of cruelty, leading her to break away from Sebastiaan and to freedom.

Now came that same crack and release and sense of rightness. "But there are those who fight against such virtues, those who are willing to neglect refugee children to prevent more refugees from coming. Perhaps even willing to kill."

Gasps circled the ballroom.

Aleida locked her gaze with Beatrice. She'd do it. She'd name Beatrice Granville as the person who had strangled Nilima Sharma in a trench.

The same way Filip Zielinski had been killed. Could she have murdered him too? He was a foreigner, a refugee, a communist, a man who had crossed her lover.

A love affair Elliott Hastings had been willing to expose.

An affair François Jouveau had discovered.

All four? Had Beatrice Granville killed four people?

Sickness churned in her stomach, green as Beatrice's dress, vile and hateful as her glare.

Tonight it would end. Aleida opened her mouth.

A wail rose—but not Aleida's.

She frowned.

All around, people sighed, rose, gathered evening bags.

The air raid siren.

Mr. Armbruster edged Aleida to the side. "Ladies and gentlemen, as you are aware, the Dorchester Hotel is one of the safest structures in all of London. Please proceed to the shelter in the basement."

No. No. Beatrice hadn't yet been accused, detained, arrested. That murderous vitriol latched on Aleida.

"Sir," Aleida said. "I need to use the telephone at once."

Mr. Armbruster took his wife's arm and helped her off the platform. "Proceed to the shelter, Mrs. Martens."

No. She had to ring the police.

The room was emptying, the Armbrusters merging into the crowd, Beatrice surging forward. "I'll help Mrs. Martens find a telephone."

The crowd was far safer. Aleida stepped off the platform, tripped—on her dress?

As the ground rushed up, a green-clad leg filled her vision. Beatrice—she'd tripped her.

Aleida cried out and hit the floor.

42

With papers from the evidence box laid out on his desk, Detective Inspector Clyde read aloud a transcription from Uncle Elliott's journal. "'How ironic that I, a man known for dalliances, should hold a dalliance against a man and a woman. In this case, I have no qualms, even though both parties are of long acquaintance.'"

"Both parties?" Hugh rapped his fingers on his knees. "The woman is in my family's circle too?"

Clyde adjusted his reading glasses. "'Since the young man has the nerve to call me "quite indiscreet," has publicly treated me like an errant child in his quest to silence me, and—'"

"Ridley! He called my uncle 'quite indiscreet.'" Hugh slapped the desk. "Uncle Elliott also said Ridley treated him like an errant child."

The inspector took notes then lifted the transcription. "'As for the young woman, her father opposes my bill in Parliament in the most underhanded manner, turning friends against me. This fool puts his daughter on the highest of pedestals, and he would do anything to keep her haughty nose out of the mud.' That's the end of that journal entry."

"No names." Hugh clamped his lips together. "But I have no doubt the man is Ridley."

"And the woman?"

"Does it matter?" Yet the information sifted through his mind. A redhead. Of Uncle Elliott's acquaintance. A daughter of an opponent in Parliament.

For some reason, Beatrice Granville's face swam into focus. Hadn't Aleida mentioned Ridley visiting her office?

To name her felt slanderous.

"Excuse me, Inspector." Constable Bright stood in the doorway—with Guy Gilbert in evening dress.

Clyde leaned back in his chair. "Apparently I'm underdressed for the evening's festivities."

"Gil?" Hugh sprang to standing. "Why are you not at the banquet?"

"Aleida sent me."

Clyde cleared his throat loudly.

Hugh turned to the inspector. "Detective Inspector Clyde, may I introduce Mr. Guy Gilbert, the man I mentioned earlier."

"Ah yes." Clyde leaned forward again. "Mr. Collingwood told me what you witnessed. I'll need to take your statement."

"I have further information." Gil gripped his top hat in hand, and his gaze darted between Hugh and Clyde. "The woman I saw kissing Mr. Ridley was at the banquet. I recognized her. Aleida said her name is Beatrice Granville."

It *was* her. Hugh felt no sense of victory, only displeasure and disappointment.

"Have a seat, Mr. Gilbert," Clyde said.

After Hugh and Gil sat, Clyde took Gil's statement.

As Gil was finishing, a sergeant entered the office, the sergeant who had been sent to bring in Ridley. "Excuse me, Inspector. Mr. Ridley isn't at home. The butler said the family has been in Scotland since Wednesday. Mrs. Ridley's grandmother passed away, and they went for the funeral."

"Wednesday," Hugh whispered. Zielinski had been murdered on Friday night.

"We need to verify that alibi," Clyde said.

The sergeant set a folded newspaper on the desk and pointed to an article. "The funeral was Friday morning. Mr. Ridley is mentioned in the paper."

Clyde released a long sigh. "Find out where he's staying in Scotland and—"

"I already rang. I spoke to the host and to Ridley. He was there all day Friday and all day today."

Another muttered curse from the inspector. "Ridley couldn't have killed Zielinski."

Hugh grabbed the paper and scanned the article. How could it be? "I was so certain."

Clyde shrugged. "When Ridley returns from Scotland, I'll still question him about the Hastings case."

"If it isn't Ridley, who is it?" Hugh slumped back in the chair.

Jouveau's notebook peeked from halfway through the pile. Hugh pointed to it. "May I?"

At the inspector's nod, Hugh flipped through Jouveau's list of appointments with MPs, ending 25 October with "Granville, Geoffrey." Then his notation on 29 October about verifying meetings. Then 31 October—"Hastings, William," 3 November—"Fletcher, Norman" and "JI-GB."

Everything turned backward in his mind. "Jouveau recorded last name first. 'JI' might be 'IJ,' and 'GB' could be 'BG.'"

Oh no. Everything turned to ice inside.

Beatrice Granville?

"What is it?" DI Clyde asked.

"GB—could it be Granville, Beatrice?" He shook the notebook. "What if Uncle Elliott threatened to expose her affair with Ridley? Her father—Sir Geoffrey is a proud and stubborn man—he'd never agree to support the refugee bill. Beatrice knew that. What if she went to talk to my uncle? She knew of the party. She'd been invited. She told me so at the funeral."

"I'm sorry," Clyde said. "But we know Hastings's murderer was a man from the size of the boot prints."

"Beatrice is as tall as I, and she's of sturdy build, a sportswoman."

"All right, then." Clyde's eyes narrowed, and he made notes. "We know she was near the Hastings estate—with motive."

Hugh riffled through the diary to discern the trail his friend had followed. "After Jouveau met with Sir Geoffrey, he didn't interview other MPs. Why not? What if his investigation swerved in a new direction? What if Sir Geoffrey had a photograph of Beatrice in his office? Jouveau would have recognized her. He told me he'd seen Ridley flirting with the daughter of an MP at a reception. What if he then recalled William's mention of the affair?"

Gil's eyes went wide. "Then he would have suspected Ridley. He'd want to check his alibi."

"Yes, yes. Verify the meetings." Clyde's pencil flew over the paper. "Not two days after he did so, he told William Hastings he knew the identity of the couple."

Hugh jabbed at the initials in Jouveau's writing. "GB—if he made an appointment with Beatrice to find more information about her lover, maybe trap her into revealing something incriminating, not suspecting her . . ."

Clyde scribbled rapidly. "This time it would be premeditated murder."

"What about Zielinski?" Gil asked.

"Not so solid a case," Clyde said, his pencil in motion. "Zielinski might have angered her lover, but this murder is different. To strangle a stranger in cold blood? It's a huge leap from the previous murders, not to mention a different modus operandi."

But the same modus operandi as Miss Sharma's murder.

Hugh's stomach clenched. "What if . . ." His mouth felt sticky, and he swallowed. "What if there was an intermediate step? Another murder by strangulation—but of someone Beatrice knew? Nilima Sharma."

Clyde's nostrils flared, and he pulled in his chin. "The girl murdered in Green Park? What's the relation?"

"I don't know what the motive might be, but Miss Sharma worked in Beatrice's department and they volunteered at the same ARP post."

"I'd wondered if those murders were linked." Clyde's voice lowered. "Both foreigners, same method. But in the Sharma case, the murderer tried to make it look as if the victim died in an air raid. In the Zielinski case, the murderer didn't even bother."

"Sloppier," Gil said. "Bolder."

Overhead, the air raid siren screamed, and Hugh almost jumped from his chair.

"The siren's mounted on the roof of the station." Clyde stood and went to the door. "Don't worry about the case. We work through air raids. Sergeant? Bring in Miss Beatrice Granville for questioning—"

"She isn't at home." Hugh's stomach squeezed hard enough to threaten his last meal.

Gil stared at Hugh. "No, she's at the Dorchester Hotel."

With Aleida.

Aleida couldn't breathe. A knee pressed her shoulder blades hard to the floor.

"Oh dear, Mrs. Martens. Let me help you up." Beatrice fiddled with Aleida's arm as if helping, but her knee ground hard.

Aleida fought to haul air into her lungs, to scream. Swishing skirts and black trouser legs receded before her and disappeared between tablecloths and chair legs. Soon no one would remain to help.

She squirmed, flailed her arms, kicked, hunched her shoulders, pulled in a breath.

The scent of fine perfume drew near, an emerald satin evening bag entered her vision to her right, and something hard pressed to her temple. "Not one sound," Beatrice said in a low, fierce voice. "Or I'll shoot you. I have a gun in my evening bag."

Shallow breaths puffed in Aleida's constricted lungs. Why would Beatrice bring a gun to a charity banquet? For the same reason she'd offered to give Aleida a ride home—because she'd already planned to kill her tonight.

Aleida grimaced. She had to get up, had to break free. But how?

"Everyone's left now." Beatrice eased the pressure with her knee. "You may stand up, but don't make a sound."

Aleida worked her hands and knees beneath her and pushed up to kneeling.

Beatrice gripped Aleida's right arm with one hand. With her other hand, she pressed her evening bag into Aleida's ribs—a drawstring pouch of green satin. The strings were drawn around Beatrice's wrist, and inside, she held something hard.

Aleida caught her breath. "Is that the same gun you used to kill François Jouveau?"

Beatrice gasped. "How dare you! The impertinence." She stood and yanked Aleida to her feet.

Not one soul remained in the ballroom. Screaming wouldn't help and would only get her shot. Oh, why hadn't Hugh come? He wouldn't have left her alone.

"This way." Beatrice tugged her arm and shoved her toward the back of the room, toward a service door. "Open the door."

With shaky hands, Aleida fumbled with the handle. She had to think. Most likely, Beatrice would want to take her to a park, to a trench. The Dorchester Hotel overlooked Hyde Park.

Aleida had to stall her, fight her, distract her, find someone—anyone.

"Open the door." Beatrice spat out the words.

The doorknob turned, and Beatrice pushed Aleida out into the cold night air. Searchlights sliced the sky, bombers droned in the distance, and antiaircraft guns boomed.

Beatrice all but dragged Aleida to a street that ran at a diagonal behind the hotel to Park Lane. Hyde Park lay on the far side of Park Lane.

The street was deserted. With each step, Aleida kicked her skirt out with her toes to avoid tripping.

On the other hand, tripping would create a diversion.

Aleida slumped lower, letting the skirt touch the ground. Her toe snagged, and down she went, catching herself on outstretched hands, breaking Beatrice's grip.

"What on earth?" That iron hand clamped Aleida's arm again and jerked her to standing. Satin-encased steel rammed into her ribs. "Don't you dare try that again. If you escape, I'll shoot. I'm an excellent shot."

Aleida stumbled forward, careful with her step again. Her heart rate skittered, and her fingers coiled, tapping on the heels of her hands. If she saw someone on the street, tripping might create the distraction she needed.

Aircraft engines rumbled louder, and to the east, bombs thudded to earth.

Ahead of them, toward the curved façade of the hotel's main entrance, several shapes shifted in the light of the full moon. Men in warden's helmets.

Holding her breath, Aleida marched forward. When close enough, she could scream and trip. Beatrice wouldn't shoot her in front of witnesses.

"Oh no." Beatrice ground to a stop and whirled Aleida around. "This way."

Aleida winced. But a detour would lengthen their route and increase her chances of seeing someone. Perhaps she could reason with the woman. Aleida cleared her dry throat. "If you kill me, you'll be the prime suspect, since you were the last person seen with me."

Beatrice let out a sharp laugh. "No one will even notice you're missing. You're just a foreigner."

"Like Miss Sharma?" Aleida's voice hushed.

A loud huff. "Why can't you people keep your noses out of our business? Miss Sharma had no right to interfere with the English way of life."

Everything inside her recoiled. That wasn't the England she knew. "If you kill me in the same manner you killed Nilima, the police will suspect you. We both worked with you at the Ministry and at the ARP. Mr. Armbruster knows my report angered you. He knows Nilima angered you. And tonight, you and I are the only guests who didn't go to the shelter. It's all over."

"Poppycock. No one cares. The police barely investigated Miss Sharma's death, and they won't investigate yours. You're just a dirty foreigner." Beatrice turned north along a street running parallel to Park Lane.

Aleida scanned the street, looking for a place to slip away. Perhaps she could use the same move she'd used to break Sebastiaan's grip on the road in Belgium, spinning backward and slamming into Beatrice's arm from behind.

Except Sebastiaan hadn't held a gun.

A rushing sound, the tinkling of hundreds of tiny incendiary bombs hitting roofs nearby. A dozen bounced harmlessly in the street before them.

Aleida clapped her free hand over her head for protection.

"You shouldn't even be here." Beatrice blew out a harsh breath. "Why couldn't you stay on the continent where you belong? You and your wars and your communism and your greedy refugees—eating our rations and sleeping in our homes and wearing our clothes. Always demanding more. You foreigners disgust me."

Keeping the woman talking would also distract her. With bombs falling along this street, ARP wardens would soon arrive, people who could help her.

Aleida sniffed. "Elliott Hastings wasn't a foreigner."

Beatrice gasped and dug her fingers into Aleida's arm. "That was an accident! I didn't mean to kill him."

Her confession sank like a stone in Aleida's stomach. "I understand. You only wanted to reason with him, ask him to drop his refugee bill, beg him not to expose your affair with Albert Ridley."

"What?" Beatrice stopped in her tracks. "How did you know?"

Aleida didn't want to add more names to the woman's murder list. "You didn't plan to kill Mr. Hastings, but he wouldn't listen to reason. You pushed each other, and you snatched his gun from his hands."

"It was propped against a tree." Her voice shook, frantic and furious. "I only threatened him with it. I only wanted him to know I was serious and he shouldn't cross me."

"And the gun went off."

"He rushed me, startled me. It was an accident."

They crossed a street, and Aleida walked straight rather than turning left toward the park. "François Jouveau had the misfortune to figure it out."

"Hardly. The filthy Frenchman. He suspected my Bert."

Aleida tried to follow Jouveau's train of thought. "Jouveau must have known about the affair. He wanted to interview you, so you arranged a meeting in . . . ?"

"In Hyde Park at the Italian Gardens." An element of pride entered her voice. "Late at night, so the air raid would ensure privacy. Instead, a rainstorm did so."

Italian Gardens . . . in French, *jardins italiens*. JI?

"And you shot him." The thought of it soured Aleida's stomach.

"I had no choice. He knew Bert had no alibi. The police would have arrested him. They might have arrested me too."

Jouveau's smile, his laugh, his passion for refugees swam in Aleida's mind. How could Beatrice be so callous? "And you dumped poor Jouveau into the Long Water."

Beatrice lifted a cold smile. "I shot him so he fell over the railing into the water. I brought my wellies and a rope, and I waded in and tied his body to a rock. For weeks, no one found him. No one cared. They won't care about you either."

Flames erupted from a roof across the street, and Aleida slowed her pace as if watching the conflagration. Now she had even more reason to live—she'd heard Beatrice confess to three murders. Should she try for four?

"It became easy, didn't it?" Aleida said. "An easy way to eliminate those who crossed you, like Miss Sharma. Like Filip Zielinski."

"Oh!" Beatrice yanked Aleida's arm so hard, she stumbled to the side. "How dare you!"

Aleida faced her and glared at her. "Why did you kill him? Because he was a foreigner? A communist? Because he argued with your lover? Because Ridley made a fool of himself in public over him?"

"He had no right, the disgusting little man." Beatrice's voice shook, and firelight flickered in her eyes. "And you have no right. No right to accuse me of such things. I am Beatrice Granville, daughter of Sir Geoffrey Granville. And you—you're nobody. Nothing. All alone in this world, and no one—no one will care when you're gone."

Was this how Jouveau had felt in his final minutes? Nilima? Because Aleida had never felt more alone.

43

etective Inspector Clyde turned back to his sergeant. "Take officers to the Dorchester Hotel and bring in Beatrice Granville for questioning in regard to the death of Elliott Hastings."

"What about the other three murders?" Hugh asked.

Still facing the sergeant, Clyde held up one hand to silence Hugh. "This is of utmost urgency, even higher priority than the air raid."

"Yes, Inspector." The sergeant left and called out orders to his men.

The inspector returned to stand by his desk. "We have ample reason to question her in the Hastings case. Once we have her in custody, we can build evidence for the other cases."

"My friend—Aleida Martens. She's at the banquet. Is she in danger?"

Clyde crossed his arms and shrugged. "At a large gathering, I doubt it. Does Miss Granville have any reason to harm her?"

Hugh turned to Gil. "Could anything have aroused her suspicion?"

Gil's eyebrows knit together. "Miss Granville wasn't looking our way when I identified her to Aleida."

The sense of unease in Hugh's stomach only intensified. "Aleida was to speak at the banquet about the problems faced by refugee children. Beatrice didn't want her to speak. In fact, she tried to prevent Aleida from attending."

Gil grumbled. "I don't like it."

Hugh bolted to standing. "Sir, may I please ride with your officers to the Dorchester?"

Clyde shook his head. "They will have left by now. Besides, you have no need for concern. My officers will have Miss Granville in custody within minutes."

Hugh's left heel bounced. The woman he loved was at a banquet, probably in an air raid shelter, with a murderer—a murderer she didn't even suspect. "May I ring the hotel, warn my friend?"

"We must keep the telephone lines open during raids."

"What if the officers are delayed? I need to go. I need to warn her, protect her."

Gil stood. "I'll go with you."

Hugh set his hand on the shoulder of his colleague—no, his friend. "Thank you."

Leaving behind his top hat, cane, overcoat, and scarf, Hugh rushed out of the station with Gil beside him.

Then he took off running, faster than was wise with his asthma. But time was of the essence—he felt it in his bones.

Bombers rumbled overhead, answered by solid thumps of antiaircraft guns. The full moon and crisscrossing searchlight beams illuminated Hugh's path. His shoes pounded the pavement, and he took even breaths.

"Collie, my leg," Gil called from behind. "I'll catch up. Don't wait for me."

Hugh sent his limping friend an acknowledging nod and resumed his pace. His path jogged to the left, then the right.

Each breath felt more constricted, and he groaned. He

wasn't used to running so fast for so long. If he didn't slow down, the exertion would lead to an asthmatic attack.

"Not now," he muttered through gritted teeth. He had to reach Aleida.

She thought the murderer was motivated by opposition to aiding refugees, and she'd suspected Miss Sharma's death was connected to the others. If Hugh had taken her theory more seriously, they might have solved the case earlier, might even have prevented Zielinski's death.

No, he couldn't think such things. Neither of them had suspected Beatrice, and suspecting her had been the key that unlocked the murders.

His breath whistled in his throat, but the hotel's façade soon rose before him. A man in an ARP helmet patrolled in front.

"The police," Hugh said to the warden. "They came a few minutes ago. Which way did they go?"

"Down to the shelter, sir." The warden pointed to the main doors.

"Thank you." Hugh barged inside and followed the signs to the shelter. He took the stairs two at a time, jolting his knees.

A belt of pain cinched his chest, but he'd arrived.

A trio of police officers, including the sergeant, stood talking to a portly guest with graying dark hair.

Where was Beatrice? Why didn't they have her in custody?

"Excuse me, Sergeant." A wheeze betrayed his condition. "Have you arrested Miss Granville?"

"She isn't in the shelter," the man in evening dress said. "I last saw her in the ballroom after the siren sounded, helping a lady who had tripped. No one has seen her since. It's very curious."

The pain in Hugh's chest no longer mattered. He scanned the crowd for the lovely blonde. "Do you know Aleida Martens? Have you seen her?"

"Yes, I know her." The man's round cheeks lowered as he frowned. "She was the lady who tripped."

Hugh gasped. The lady Beatrice was helping? "Where is she?"

"She hasn't come to the shelter either."

He felt as if someone had kicked him in the stomach. All the air rushed from his shrinking lungs. "Oh no."

"Collie? What's wrong?" Gil stood by his side, panting.

"Sergeant." Hugh locked his gaze on the man and tried to catch his breath. "DI Clyde suspects Miss Granville—not only for Hastings's murder but for the murders of two people found strangled in parks."

"I say!" the portly gentleman said.

Hugh had no time for niceties, not even for avoiding potential slander. "Miss Granville might have Mrs. Martens with her. If she follows her previous pattern, she'll lure her to a park."

Concern raced through the sergeant's eyes. "Hyde Park is right here, but . . ."

But the park was huge. And how much time had passed since the ladies left the hotel? If Aleida didn't suspect Beatrice, she'd be in significant danger.

"All right, men," the sergeant said to the other two officers, "we'll organize a search. Wilkins, ring the station, tell them to send more men. Bright, come with me."

"I'll come too." But Hugh's voice sounded fragile.

"As will I," Gil said.

Doubt twitched in the sergeant's lips, but he blinked. "We can use the help." He assigned the men to sections of the park, starting at Park Lane and working west, with Hugh assigned to the northernmost section, near Speakers' Corner.

The men hurried out of the hotel and fanned out to search.

As Hugh ran north up Park Lane, orange firelight brightened the sky, and screaming bombs crashed into buildings ahead of him.

His chest seized from the burst of cold air and the resumption of exertion. "No, Lord." He couldn't have an attack. He had to save Aleida.

"Aleida!" His call disappeared into the noise of explosions and crackling flames.

He coughed from the effort of raising his voice, and his pace slowed.

"No." Hugh forged ahead, crossed a street, ran harder. Speakers' Corner lay only a half dozen streets away.

Black smoke roiled from the building straight ahead. To detour around it would add delay, and every second counted.

Hugh whipped out his handkerchief and pressed it to his nose and mouth. He charged forward, veering into the street to avoid the worst of the smoke.

His eyes burned and watered. Despite the handkerchief, he could feel particles depositing in his lungs, clogging them.

He gasped for breath, pushed through to clear air on the other side, and lowered the handkerchief.

He wheezed, coughed, struggled for air. Each breath ached on the way in, whistled on the way out. Stars formed in his vision.

Hugh's pace lagged. He stumbled down off a curb, scrambled to get his feet beneath him, staggered forward.

What if Beatrice took Aleida to Hugh's sector? If Hugh didn't arrive, no one would.

Now his old enemy, his asthma, his weakness, was endangering the woman he loved.

Hugh stepped up onto a curb, but his foot disobeyed him, and he fell flat on the pavement, slamming out the whisper of air remaining in his lungs.

Battling for breath, he dragged his knees beneath him, planted one foot, pushed up. His leg shook, and he collapsed against the wall of a building.

"Aleida." Her name evaporated in his mouth.

The scream of a bomb, a rush of wind.

Hugh hunkered low, flung his arms over his head, flung up a prayer for Aleida. Hugh wouldn't be able to help her. He'd never see her again.

The pavement leaped beneath him. Sound exploded in his ears. Debris pummeled his back.

And the stars in his vision winked out.

44

Beatrice marched Aleida up the paved walkway in Hyde Park with her grip tight around Aleida's right arm.

Soon that grip would be tight around Aleida's throat. She gagged from the imagined sensation.

Trees loomed over the pathway, but enough moonlight and firelight shined through so she couldn't pretend to stumble in the dark. She couldn't even trip on the hem of her dress anymore. The last time she'd done so, Beatrice had ordered her to hold her skirts high.

What other hope did she have? None.

Sebastiaan's revenge was complete. In payment for her defiance, he'd stolen what she most treasured, her son. Now she'd die alone and forgotten.

Gray chiffon crumpled in her shivering grip. Gray as Oli.

Elephants never forget. *"Olifanten vergeten nooit,"* she murmured.

"What was that?" Beatrice said in a loud whisper.

Aleida shook her head. Even if her little boy no longer remembered her, even if the police ignored her death, God— God would never forget her.

"I told you." Beatrice dug long fingernails into Aleida's arm. "Not one sound."

Aleida winced from the pain, but God remembered her. Even now. Even in the dark. Even with her footsteps drowned by the sounds of an air raid. Even as a foreigner in a foreign land.

He saw her. He remembered her. He loved her.

Just as the Lord held Theo in loving hands, he held her in his hands too.

He was with her. Live or die, she wasn't alone.

Warm peace filled her, strengthened her. Live or die, yes—but she'd rather live.

Hugh—he wouldn't forget her. If she died, he'd mourn the loss of another friend. Would he hold himself responsible for not coming to the banquet? Berate himself for not suspecting Beatrice earlier?

Would anyone even realize Beatrice was the killer? If Aleida lived, she could testify. She'd heard confessions to four murders. She had the duty to report them.

Somehow she had to break free.

Perhaps she could spin backward and break Beatrice's grip. The woman would shoot, but if Aleida slipped through the trees, she might spoil her aim.

If only she could get the gun away from her.

Beatrice yanked Aleida between the trees and out into open lawn.

Toward the trenches.

Aleida's heel sank into the grass, and she lurched to the side. "Stop it." Beatrice wrenched her closer.

Her heels . . . the grass . . . a delay . . . a diversion?

She'd have only one chance, and she tossed up a prayer.

Her heel sank into the grass again, and she let it, made a show of it. "My heels. The soil is too soft."

"Take them off."

Aleida's mind whirred. She wanted both shoes off so she could run. And she wanted time to plan.

With her right arm in Beatrice's grasp, Aleida leaned over, lifted her left foot, fumbled under her skirts, and removed her shoe.

Taller than Aleida, Beatrice had to lean over to keep the gun pressed to Aleida's ribs, to maintain her grip on Aleida's right arm.

Her heart hammering, Aleida planted her stockinged left foot in the damp, cold grass, and she lifted her right knee.

Ducking her chin to her chest, she could see the evening bag. The drawstrings had loosened, and the satin draped over Beatrice's hand and gun.

Aleida worked off her shoe and took a slow breath.

With her knee still raised, she slid her left hand up between her knee and her stomach.

Now!

Aleida grabbed the gun, jerked it forward as hard as she could. Her hand slipped off the sleek fabric, and she plunged to a crouching position.

Beatrice cried out, tumbled forward, and braced her fall with both hands. Steel thumped on the ground.

Aleida scrambled to her feet, ran through the trees, back onto the pathway.

Fingernails tore at her arm, and Beatrice clamped her hand on Aleida's wrist.

So hard, Aleida screamed.

"How dare you?" Beatrice yanked Aleida's arm, spun her around. "Filthy little foreigner."

One hand circled Aleida's throat, then another.

Aleida gagged, gasped, tried to work her fingers in to Beatrice's grip.

The woman bore down.

Aleida—she couldn't breathe.

She stomped on Beatrice's foot, pitiful, powerless.

Beatrice hovered over her, tall, strong, cruel, fury burning in her dark eyes in the dark night.

Embers of that fire danced in Aleida's sight.

Her lungs swelled, her mind spun, woozy and woozier.

No! She couldn't fall unconscious.

Her hands—her hands were free! She jammed them into Beatrice's hair, pulled and tugged and scraped diamond-encrusted combs along Beatrice's scalp.

Beatrice grunted in protest, loosened her grip, bore down again.

Aleida had been a younger sister, a younger cousin. She knew how to be annoying.

She gripped Beatrice's cheek, dug her fingernails in hard, pulled out her lip, poked her nails deep into moist tissue, jammed a finger up her nose. The eyes! She clawed upward, aimed one fingernail—

Beatrice writhed, cried out, tried to break free.

Forgot about strangulation. Released her grip.

Aleida planted her hands on the woman's chest and shoved with all her might.

Beatrice screamed and fell back. A thud as her head hit the path.

Aleida dropped to her knees beside her, scraping her palms on the pavement.

Gasping for breath, she scrabbled up to her feet, swayed.

Beatrice lay still. Was she dead? Injured? Or only momentarily dazed?

Aleida wouldn't wait to find out. She turned to run, stopped herself.

The gun!

Not only did she need to keep it out of murderous hands, but it was evidence.

In the grass, steel glinted in the moonlight. Using her skirt to pick up the weapon, Aleida thrust the gun into Beatrice's evening bag.

Her throat aching, her skirts held high, she ran across the path, out of the park, onto Park Lane. "Police!" she yelled, but her voice croaked, her windpipe throbbed.

Black smoke and orange flames erupted from buildings.

Despite the destruction, her heart soared. Civil defense workers would be out. They could help her.

Her stockinged feet slipped, and rough pavement pierced her soles.

She ran down Park Lane toward a bomb site. Firemen aimed arcs of glistening water at the flames, and a rescue party picked through the rubble, looking for survivors.

The incident officer—she had to find him—he could send a messenger to fetch the police.

Her breath came hard and her throat burned, but tears of relief dampened her eyes. Even if Beatrice came, she could no longer harm her.

"Thank you, Lord." Her stinging feet ground to a stop by a fireman. "Excuse me. Where's the incident officer?"

The man shrugged as he wrestled the snaking hose. "That way, I think." He tilted his head to the right.

After Aleida checked behind her—no sign of Beatrice—she headed down the street, skirting workers and equipment and scanning for a police officer or ARP warden.

At the end of the building, Aleida stepped back onto the curb.

Around the corner, masonry lay in a shallow heap.

One hand and a man's head peeked out from the rubble.

"Oh no!" Aleida turned back to Park Lane and waved her arms. "Rescue party! Stretcher party. One injured man around the corner, partly buried."

"Yes, ma'am." A rescuer nodded to her as he helped a man out from the debris.

Aleida needed to find the police, but the injured man's life came first. Besides, now that she could name Beatrice Granville as the murderer, the police would eventually arrest her.

Around the corner she dropped to her knees. The injured man lay on his stomach toward the edge of the heap, only partly buried. He might stand a chance.

"I'm from the ARP, sir, and I'm here to help." She rolled the largest chunk of masonry from the man's back.

He groaned and turned his head to the side. "A . . . lei . . ."

She gasped and brushed dust and plaster from the man's head, from wavy hair. It couldn't be. "Hugh?"

Eyes opened, familiar and beloved and wracked with pain. "You're . . . safe?"

"Yes. Yes." She swept bits of stone from his shoulders. "What happened?"

"Came . . . fr'you." His voice crackled, and he wheezed.

"Oh no. You're having an asthmatic attack."

One nod.

"Help! Stretcher party! At once!" Aleida yelled, scratching her throat. "Hugh, tell me where it hurts."

A raspy moan. Surely he hurt everywhere.

She lifted masonry from his left hand, which lay with fingers twisted. "Oh no," she whispered, and she cleared his back, his hips. "We'll get you free, get you to the hospital."

"Beatrice . . . murder."

He'd figured it out too. "I know. She—she tried to kill me."

"What? How dare . . ."

She stroked his hair. "I'm all right. I need to find the police, but first we need to help you."

"P'lice . . . looking fr'her . . . fr'you."

Aleida paused with her hand cupping the back of his head, his dusty hair. He'd come for her. He'd sent the police to find her. He hadn't forgotten her for one moment.

She loved him so much, and she pressed a kiss to his temple, aching for him. Dare she tell him she loved him?

Two men rounded the corner with a stretcher, and Aleida eased out of the way. "His name is Hugh Collingwood. His left hand may be broken—be careful. He has asthma and he's having a severe attack. He'll need care immediately."

Hugh groaned and nodded. Yes, the attack was severe. If he didn't receive treatment soon, he'd die. Aleida pressed her hand to her churning stomach.

The stretcher party removed the last of the rubble and rolled Hugh onto the stretcher.

Encased in black tailcoat and white waistcoat, Hugh's chest rose and fell visibly. With anguished eyes, he stretched one hand to her. "A . . . lei—"

The stretcher party hustled away with him.

Aleida picked up Beatrice's evening bag and followed. The first aid post would have a telephone or a messenger, some means to summon the police.

One street away, the party entered a building and found a doctor. Aleida stood nearby to make sure the doctor was informed of the asthma.

The doctor pressed a stethoscope to Hugh's chest. "Sister—epinephrine," he said to a nursing sister, then craned his head toward a young lady sitting by a telephone. "Send for an ambulance."

"Already here." She pointed to the door.

"Thank goodness." Aleida stepped aside.

First aid workers cut off the sleeves of Hugh's evening jacket and his shirt.

The doctor took a syringe from the nurse, and he plunged the needle into Hugh's vein. "All right, send him to the hospital."

If only Aleida could ride with him. But the ambulance would be full, and they wouldn't allow it.

"Hugh." She stroked his arm as he passed, grasped for his good hand, missed. And he was gone.

## 45

**Sunday, May 11, 1941**

The hospital ward teemed with men in far worse shape than Hugh. He bore a cast on his left hand, bandages on various cuts, and a rattle in his chest from the worst asthmatic attack of his life.

But he lived. As did Aleida.

If only he could get out of bed, find a telephone, and ring her, find out how she was doing, ring the police station, learn whether they'd arrested Beatrice.

Under the blankets, his legs jiggled. The physician had restricted him to bed.

An invalid.

Hugh grimaced. At least Simmons had visited earlier in the morning and had brought Hugh's pajamas and dressing gown, as well as some books.

He didn't want books, though. He wanted news. Simmons and the nursing sisters said last night's raid had been the worst they could remember. Rumors on the ward spoke of damage to Houses of Parliament, Westminster Abbey, and more.

What of Beatrice? He'd heard not a word. Surely the arrest of a society woman on four counts of murder—and an attempted murder—would be on every tongue.

The air shifted, and a woman entered the ward. "Aleida!"

He swung his legs to the side to stand to greet her.

She rushed forward. "No, no. The nursing sister said you're not to get out of bed."

All he wanted was to touch her, to hold her hand, to embrace her. But he couldn't. "I'm glad to see you."

"You look much better." Wearing a suit of medium blue, she settled into a chair. "How do you feel?"

"Much better, thank you. I should go home in a few days." Heat rose in his cheeks. The last time she'd seen him, he'd been gasping like a fish out of water. Weak. Helpless. But . . . "I'm glad you found me."

"I was so worried." The proof of it etched her forehead. "I wanted to follow you to the hospital, but I had to go to the police station and give my statement."

His pulse quickened. "Beatrice—have they caught her?"

"The police found her in the park. You sent the police to search for me?"

"Yes. I went to search for you myself, but . . ." But he'd failed.

"Thank you." Her voice broke, and her eyes shimmered.

"Think nothing of it." His own voice sounded ragged. "They arrested her? She's in jail?"

"Yes." She let out a scoffing sound. "They brought her to the first aid post soon after you departed. She had the nerve to accuse *me* of attacking *her*."

"I beg your pardon!"

"I do take responsibility for the bump on her head and the scratches on her face, but I do not apologize for them. Thank goodness the police didn't believe her. They had orders to arrest her, and I had her evening bag with her identity card and her gun with—"

"Gun! She had a gun?" Hugh's hands fisted around the thin blanket.

Aleida dropped her gaze to her lap. "She had already planned to—to kill me."

Woman or not, Beatrice Granville could be thankful she wasn't standing in Hugh's presence. He'd put a fist in that haughty, scheming mouth of hers.

Aleida gave her head a little shake and raised her chin. "The gun will have her fingerprints on it. And I presented other proof." A quivering hand rose to her throat.

Once again, Hugh could barely breathe. "Proof?"

Her eyes went dark, and she pulled down the collar of her blouse, revealing angry purple bruises.

"Aleida!"

"It's all over. Beatrice will never hurt anyone again." She patted her collar back in place. "She confessed all four murders to me, and the police have my statement."

Four murders and an attempted murder. Beatrice would hang for it.

"I'm afraid your mother's dress is ruined," Aleida said. "I'll pay her—"

"Nonsense. I know she won't take a shilling from you."

Aleida fell silent.

It was time to be honest about his love, even if he lost her friendship. Yet today wasn't the day for such a speech, not from a hospital bed, not wearing pajamas, not with two dozen witnesses on the ward.

She raised a wobbly smile, and she tapped her knuckles in the familiar pattern. "Please don't worry about me. I can see you worrying, but I'm fine."

"Are you?" He flicked up half a smile. "Your mouth says you're fine, but your fingers say otherwise."

"Oh dear." She slapped her hand as if it were naughty. "It

isn't about last night. I really am all right. The Lord was with me, and you came, and so did the police. It isn't that."

"What is it, then?" It was serious, yet he couldn't help but joke. He stroked the satin collar of his dressing gown. "Is it the dismay of seeing me in my nightclothes? How can you ever respect me again?"

A smile flitted over her lips, then flitted away. "I have something to say. I keep debating, but I need to say it."

A pit carved into his stomach. Had she decided she no longer wanted to be friends? Or had he offended her in some way?

A commotion arose from the doorway, and Louisa Jones marched in, Guy Gilbert, Norman Fletcher.

Aleida's face fell, and she bit her lip.

As much as Hugh wanted to see his friends and colleagues, even more he wanted to hear what Aleida had to say. Even if it was dreadful.

"Collie!" Lou planted a fist on her rounded hip as Hugh's friends gathered around his bed. "Don't you know you're supposed to report the news, not make it?"

"Oh, I didn't—"

"Balderdash," Gil said. "I was there when you solved the case, and so was Inspector Clyde."

The inspector stood to Gil's side.

"Good day, Inspector," Hugh said.

"Mr. Collingwood." He nodded to Hugh, then to Aleida with a warm smile. "And dear Mrs. Martens."

Fletcher held a fedora before his stomach. "Gil rang me early this morning about last night's events. François Jouveau was correct—this is a big story, worthy of broadcast. I want you to broadcast it, Collie—live."

"Live?"

DI Clyde crossed his arms. "The police have not yet issued a statement to the press about the case. Mr. Fletcher and I agreed you had more than earned the scoop."

"This was Gil's idea," Fletcher said. "He insisted you had to report the story. I agree."

Gil lowered his chin, and his cheeks colored. "It's only fair."

"Thank you." Hugh blinked over and over. "But when? The news of the arrest can't be delayed much longer."

"On the one o'clock news," Fletcher said.

"Today?" The clock on the wall read 12:45. "How on earth?"

"That's why we brought the detective inspector," Gil said. "So you can interview him. And look—Aleida's here too."

"Can you?" Hugh swung his gaze to her. "Would you?"

"Gladly." She was quite at ease on the air.

"But I'm in hospital." Hugh patted the bed in case they'd forgotten.

Fletcher gestured toward the ward door. "We have permission. Young and MacTavish are hooking into the telephone line. They'll bring in the equipment shortly. You have fifteen minutes to prepare your story. You'll have five minutes on the air."

Lou gave him a notepad and a pencil.

"I have only five minutes to prepare." Hugh found a blank page. "Five for the equipment, and five for you to review my notes, Mr. Fletcher."

"Not necessary." His editor waved his hand.

He had ten minutes, then. He puffed out a hard breath, which hurt only a little.

After he conferred with DI Clyde about what he should and should not broadcast, he scribbled an outline.

Tom Young entered the ward, spooling out cord.

Hugh shoved his feet out of bed, stood, and caught the gaze of the nursing sister. "I do apologize, but I need to stand. Ten minutes, and I shall return to bed, docile as a kitten."

"Very well, sir." She gave him a stern look. "Ten minutes."

After the nursing sister turned away, Aleida lifted a playful smile. "Docile as Lennox?"

"Shh." Hugh put a finger to his lips. "She need never know."

The sparkle in Aleida's eyes lit an idea in his mind. A foolish idea, most certainly. Yet it took hold.

After he put on his headphones, Hugh gestured to his dressing gown. "I'm afraid I'm not properly attired."

"Here." Gil slapped his fedora on Hugh's head, but it slipped off his headphones and tumbled to the floor.

Everyone laughed, and a sense of awed contentment flooded his soul. His hard work was being recognized. But his contentment ran deeper, because such recognition was no longer what made his heart beat.

"One o'clock." Young clasped one hand to his headphones.

Hugh would go live at five minutes past, after the news reader at Broadcasting House announced the major stories.

Fletcher and Gil circled the ward, urging quiet from patients and visitors. Excited whispers rose, then a hush fell.

Hugh showed Clyde and Aleida where to stand, and he read his notes one last time.

Young held up his hand and ticked off the final five seconds as Hugh heard the announcer read his introduction back at Broadcasting House.

Hugh raised his microphone. "This is Hugh Collingwood reporting live from a hospital somewhere in London, where I am a patient. Last night a murder mystery unfolded, even as bombs fell on our fair city. Standing here with me is Detective Inspector Richard Clyde of the West End Central Police Station. Inspector, please tell us about this rather surprising arrest."

DI Clyde nodded as if the listeners could see him. "Last night we arrested Miss Beatrice Granville on suspicion of four murders—of Mr. Elliott Hastings, Mr. François Jouveau, Miss Nilima Sharma, and Mr. Filip Zielinski."

"Truly shocking," Hugh said. "I must say, for many months I've taken a personal interest in this case, as Mr. Hastings was my uncle and Mr. Jouveau was my friend and colleague, formerly of the BBC French Service. I'm afraid I rather made a pest of myself with the good detective inspector with my amateur sleuthing. Am I correct, Inspector Clyde?"

He cracked a smile. "You are correct. Until yesterday, when your sleuthing helped solve the case. Your presentation of a new clue connected Mr. Zielinski's murder—and then Miss Sharma's—to the previous cases."

"In the process, Miss Granville's name arose and it all came together." Hugh turned toward Aleida. "As I was giving my statement to the inspector, Miss Granville was attending a charity banquet. Also attending that banquet was a young lady whose name will be familiar to my faithful listeners, our intrepid air raid warden, Aleida Martens. Mrs. Martens, how did you come to suspect Miss Granville of these sordid crimes?"

"Miss Sharma and I worked with Miss Granville at the Ministry of Health. At the banquet, I learned Miss Sharma had embarrassed Miss Granville, crossed her, in fact. Soon I realized she must have been the murderer. But Miss Granville—she—she realized I suspected her." Her voice trembled, and her gaze flickered.

Hugh drew back the microphone. "I will not ask you to recount your ordeal. I am afraid Miss Granville used the cover of the air raid to attempt to murder Mrs. Martens as well."

His voice caught, and he swallowed hard, staring into Aleida's sea-blue eyes. "This fair damsel was in distress. I intended to be the gallant knight galloping to her rescue. But this knight has asthma, and between the exertion and the smoke from the fires, I collapsed from an asthmatic attack and became half-buried when a building collapsed."

"Oh, Hugh," Aleida mouthed, her eyes liquid, full of pride in him for confessing his affliction on the air.

Hugh sank in that liquid gaze, wanting never to surface

again. "Fear not, dear listeners, for our fair damsel rescued herself and proceeded to rescue this tarnished knight as well."

Aleida's mouth bent so softly.

Hugh spun away to DI Clyde. "Inspector, please tell us about the climax to this mystery."

"Our officers apprehended Miss Granville in a park, where she'd sustained minor injuries during Mrs. Martens's escape. We have Miss Granville in custody and have filed charges. She pleads innocent, but she made a full confession to Mrs. Martens for all four murders."

"Congratulations to Detective Inspector Clyde and to the brave men of the West End Central Police Station. On behalf of the family of Elliott Hastings, I thank you. On behalf of the friends of François Jouveau, many of whom are present with me today, I thank you. I'm sure the families and friends of Miss Sharma and Mr. Zielinski are grateful as well."

Tom Young shook his head vigorously, pointed at his watch, mouthed, "Two minutes," and made a stretching motion with his hands.

Perfect. Hugh had confessed his asthma to the nation. Now he had another confession to make.

He turned to Aleida. "Those of you sitting around your wireless this Sunday afternoon may be whispering amongst yourselves wondering why Hugh Collingwood spends so much time interviewing this Aleida Martens."

She cocked her head and gave him a questioning look.

"I shall tell you," he said. "I met this lovely young widow almost a year ago when she was training as a warden. We became friends."

Aleida's eyes widened. Did she suspect what he was about to say? Would she welcome it or toss him out of her life forever?

He plunged through the sea, rechtdoorzee. "Bombs have destroyed parts of our cities, leveling what was once good and beautiful. But that is not the end. We shall rebuild. We shall reclaim what was good from the past and build our nation better and stronger than it was before."

Hugh started to reach for Aleida's hand—but he had a cast on his left hand, a microphone in the right. "Aleida, I hurt you."

She gasped and covered her mouth.

"You have forgiven me, but I long for more." His voice roughened, but it couldn't be helped. "I long to build on the foundation of our friendship, reclaim the beauty of the romance I damaged, and build higher and stronger and better."

Her eyes shimmered, but the fingers covering her mouth concealed whether they were tears of grief or of joy.

"I love you, Aleida." The words poured out. "I am irrevocably in love with you. Now I have declared my love for you to the entire United Kingdom. Whether or not you choose to accept me, I hope this proves once and for all how truly unforgettable you are."

"Oh, Hugh." She swayed forward.

He reached to steady her, his stiff cast about her waist.

She collapsed against his chest and lifted her face, her eyes glimmering between blue and green. "Oh, Hugh. I love you too. I love you so much."

Someone plucked the microphone from Hugh's hand and wrenched off his headphones. "This is Guy Gilbert, taking over for Hugh Collingwood, who is otherwise occupied."

He was. The joyful exclamations around him, Gil's finish to the broadcast, the ward full of watching people—all of it fell away.

All that remained was Aleida—in love with him.

He lowered his forehead to hers and drank in her warmth, drank in the beauty of forgiveness and restoration and her precious love.

Drank in the sweetness of her kiss.

Her arms circled his waist, and he pulled her close, dissolving into her.

Someone tapped his shoulder. "We hate to intrude, Collie," Lou said.

He glared at the American. "Do you? Do you truly hate to intrude?"

Lou and Gil and Fletcher and Clyde and Young all grinned at them.

"The broadcast is over," Fletcher said. "Excellent work, even with the . . . unconventional ending."

Gil laughed. "You'll be the talk of England."

"We'll leave you now, children," Lou said. "Just invite us to the wedding."

With a final burst of laughter, they departed.

"Oh my goodness," Aleida murmured, her face pressed to his chest.

He tipped up her chin. "Did I embarrass you?"

"Quite. But in a very good way." Her gleaming smile confirmed it.

Something surged in his chest. "Shall we invite them all to the wedding? Even Lou?"

"Especially Lou." Then her eyes widened, as if she realized what he'd asked and what she'd blithely accepted.

He couldn't look at her, could barely speak. He pressed his lips to her forehead. "Will you come? Will you come to the wedding?"

Aleida's breath pulsed against his exposed throat, his exposed heart. "Nothing—nothing would make me happier."

Hugh pulled back to study her face, to ensure he'd heard properly. Peace and joy and trust and absolute love radiated from her.

Only one response was possible. He kissed her.

# 46

**SUNDAY, MAY 18, 1941**

Hugh's arm felt good in Aleida's hand—strong and capable—even when suspended by a sling with a cast on his poor hand.

Spring sunshine and humor danced in his hazel eyes as they walked back to her flat after church. "How does it feel to be a celebrity?"

"Goodness." Aleida laughed and leaned her head on his shoulder. Not only had Hugh's hospital broadcast made her a household name, but in the past week she'd been interviewed by many of the papers about the Granville case. "I'm glad the radio waves carry only voices, not faces."

"Wait until after the war when the BBC can bring television back."

"Will you be on television? Everyone knows your name and voice, and sometimes your photograph is in *Radio Times*, but for everyone to recognize your face like a film star . . ."

Hugh rubbed his chin. "You would deprive the nation of my distinguished jawline?"

She laughed and nudged him. "You might become insufferable."

"Then I shall stay with radio so you can continue to suffer me. For life."

Aleida's chest swelled with the magnitude of her decision. All week she'd asked herself if she'd acted hastily, if she could trust her own judgment. But this was Hugh, her beloved Hugh, and he'd offered as lengthy of an engagement as she desired.

She squeezed his arm. "For life."

Across the street, three boys played amongst the trees in the square. Although German air raids now came infrequently, they had grown in severity, with the raid of 10 May the worst ever.

She sighed. "Despite our best efforts, too many children remain in the cities."

"The situation is bound to improve with the changes coming to your department."

"In time." Aleida turned the corner of the square to her street. "Mr. Armbruster is excited that Mr. Farnsworth will take Beatrice's position. Mr. Farnsworth is eager to help the evacuees and to support foster families and billeting officers. It's good to—"

A man stood by the door to her building. He looked like . . . "Mr. Randolph?"

"Pardon?" Hugh said.

The man met her gaze. Yes, Mr. Randolph.

Terror snaked in her belly. She dropped Hugh's arm and ran forward. "Theo? Is Theo—Teddy—is he all right?"

Mr. Randolph jerked back his chin. "Yes. Yes, he's fine. I didn't mean to alarm you."

Hugh came up beside her. "May I ask what brings you here?" He sounded stern and protective.

Mr. Randolph's mouth twisted and shifted.

Across the street, the boys halted their game to watch.

Whatever he had to say, it shouldn't be in front of the neighborhood. With trembling hands, Aleida unlocked the door. "Would you care to come in?"

"Yes, thank you. How kind of you." His face relaxed, but his cheek twitched. Perhaps he remembered his own lack of hospitality to her.

Regardless, this man was raising her son, and she would treat him well. She climbed the stairs to her flat and led the men to the sitting room. "Would you care for tea?"

"Allow me, darling," Hugh said.

"But your hand."

"I'll make do." He gave her a quick smile, gave Mr. Randolph a quick scowl, then hastened to the kitchen.

Aleida sat on a sofa and clamped her hands in her lap.

On the sofa across from her, Mr. Randolph smoothed his dark blue trousers. "This is rather difficult. Last weekend I visited my wife in the country. And Teddy."

Aleida's heart jolted. What she wouldn't give to see his sweet face once more, even from a distance.

Mr. Randolph's dark mustache contorted. "On Sunday afternoon, we listened to the news on the wireless whilst Teddy played nearby. Mr. Collingwood reported on that ghastly murder case, and you came on the air."

Fingers started tapping, and she clenched harder.

"Teddy." Mr. Randolph put his hand to his ear. "He turned to the radio. My wife said he'd done so another time you were on the wireless. She—she thought it was sweet that he responded to the lilt of a Dutch accent."

"Aleida." Hugh stood in the doorway to the kitchen, his face stark. "He recognizes your voice."

Her breath tumbled down steps in her throat. Could it be?

Hugh came to the sofa and put his arm around her shoulders.

Mr. Randolph lowered his chin. "I never told my wife of your visits or of your claim to be Teddy's mother or of Thomas Warwick's letter—which I'd skimmed, ignored, and stashed away. But at that moment, my conscience assaulted me, and I told my wife everything."

Aleida's face tingled. "What did she say?"

His blue-eyed gaze stretched to her. "You must understand, over the past year she's come to love the boy as her own, as have I. She was heartbroken at the prospect of losing him—as was I."

"I—I understand." Their love was one of the reasons she'd given them her son.

Mr. Randolph folded his hands on his trim stomach. "However, Mrs. Randolph was quite upset that I'd concealed the matter from her. She believes you deserved a fair hearing. If you were indeed his mother, to prolong your heartbreak was a great evil."

Aleida's breath spilled out in broken pieces. "Please don't. I understand. You love Teddy, and you're protecting him."

"You acted to protect him too, my wife said. You remind her of the mother who stood before King Solomon in the Bible. A woman who would rather have her child raised by another than to have him divided, if you will."

Aleida's head shook slightly. She hadn't meant for her decision to influence them—only to provide a good life for Theo.

Red mottling marred Mr. Randolph's cheeks. "I claimed you had no proof Teddy was your son. Yet you did offer proof, if unwittingly."

"Proof?" She glanced at Hugh. Had he taken one of the photographs to Mr. Randolph? But Hugh looked as bewildered as she.

"The toy elephant," Mr. Randolph said in a raspy voice. "On Friday I returned to the country and brought the toy. We said nothing about it, only placed it on the sofa. Teddy was drawn to it, as I suppose any small boy would be. But he held him—he held him precisely as you described. And he said, 'Oli.'"

Aleida covered her mouth and swayed.

"He remembers," Hugh said. "He remembers."

Nothing felt real. She'd surrendered. She'd made her decision and felt incredible peace about it. Now everything shifted inside her, furniture scraping the floor of her soul.

Mr. Randolph lifted his chin, and his mouth set. "Mrs. Randolph and I have decided to do what you did earlier—surrender a beloved boy. It is the only right and honorable course of action. And I beg your forgiveness. If I had believed you in January, if I'd at least given you a chance, you would have been reunited four months ago."

"Oh, darling." Hugh hugged her shoulder and kissed her temple.

Her dream, her obsession, her decision, her love, her hard-earned peace—all careened in her head, upending all she knew and wanted and hoped and feared.

A whistle pierced her ears. The teakettle.

Aleida dashed to the kitchen.

"Aleida," Hugh said. "Allow me."

She could barely see, but she pulled the kettle off the stove and poured boiling water into the teapot.

"Darling." Hugh set his hand on her shoulder. "This is wonderful. Shouldn't you—"

"I need to think." She flipped up a hand to silence him. But how could she make sense of the cacophony of thoughts rioting in her mind?

She pulled a tray from the cupboard, three saucers, three cups.

"Your hands are shaking. Use the tea cart." Hugh wheeled it over. "I'd carry the tray myself, but . . ." He raised his cast.

Her hands shook horribly. With Hugh's help, she assembled the tea things on the cart and took it to the sitting room.

Since the tea needed to steep, Aleida and Hugh took their seats.

"This must come as a shock to you," Mr. Randolph said with a compassionate frown. "With your permission, I'll return tomorrow evening to make arrangements."

Aleida closed her eyes and breathed deeply. Only one choice calmed the cacophony. "I thank you for your kind offer, but my decision stands."

"Aleida!" Hugh said. "What do you—"

"But Mrs. Martens—"

"Don't you see?" Hugh said. "You can have your son back."

She wiggled a hand at him. "I will not uproot him again and cause more upheaval in his life."

Mr. Randolph gave his head a firm shake. "Teddy asks why he has no mother, only an aunt and uncle—that's what he calls us. He wants a mother. He wants *his* mother."

Aleida scrunched her eyes shut. That couldn't be. He couldn't possibly . . .

"Look at me, darling." Hugh gripped her forearm.

She dragged her gaze to his face, his gleaming, earnest face.

"You have so much to offer him," Hugh said in a husky voice. "So much love to give him. Don't deprive him of his mother's love."

Her heart and her face crumpled, and she leaned against Hugh's side.

"May I make a suggestion?" Mr. Randolph said. "Come to our country home this weekend. We'll see how Teddy responds."

Aleida clamped her hand over her quivering mouth, and a sob bubbled up. "I could see him again. I could see him."

Hugh pressed her head to his shoulder and caressed her hair. "Yes, you can. And soon."

"We thought a gradual reintroduction would be best," Mr. Randolph said. "It may take a while, but when Teddy—when Theo is ready . . ."

As Hugh stroked her hair, a new peace filled her heart, not the sad peace of before, but a peace that soared.

She opened her eyes, prying apart damp eyelashes, and she sent Mr. Randolph a soft smile. "If he chooses to come with me someday, I want—I insist that you and your wife continue to serve as his uncle and aunt."

He blinked, and his cheeks agitated. "We—I don't deserve—"

"Yes, you do. And Teddy—that's the name he knows—Teddy deserves to have you in his life. A child can never have too many people who love him, yes?"

Mr. Randolph mashed his lips together and nodded.

Aleida patted Hugh's leg, raised her head, and went to the tea cart. "And now, Mr. Randolph, please call me Aleida, for we shall be lifelong friends. Milk? Sugar?"

A smile twitched on his lips. "Milk, please. And call me Julian."

After Aleida served the tea, she took her seat. A wide and genuine smile unfurled across her face. "Please tell me all about Teddy."

Julian took a sip. "May I say that he is simply the brightest and sweetest-natured child to ever walk this earth?"

"Yes," Aleida said. "You may."

## 47

**BUNTINGFORD**
**FRIDAY, MAY 23, 1941**

After the servants cleared the dinner dishes at Colling-wood Manor, Mother stood. "Shall we adjourn to the sitting room?"

Hugh rose and offered his uninjured hand to Aleida.

She stood and gave his parents an apologetic smile. "If you don't mind, I'd like to retire early. I had ARP duty last night, I worked today, and tomorrow . . ."

Hugh squeezed her hand. Tomorrow she'd see her son for the first time in a year.

"Please do, my dear. Your room is prepared for you." Mother kissed Aleida on the cheek and gripped her shoulders. "I can't tell you how pleased we are that you and Hugh will marry."

"I'm rather pleased too." Aleida gave Hugh a playful smile.

He walked her to the stairs, with his parents behind him. "Good night, darling." He kissed his fiancée's cheek, only proper, but hardly satisfactory.

"Good night, my love."

He watched her climb the stairs. At the top, she blew a kiss, and he caught it. Not satisfactory at all, not when he knew the delights of the real thing.

In the sitting room, he and his parents sat by the fireplace, with a crackling fire battling the day's rain and chill.

Neither of his parents picked up a book and they disdained the wireless, but Hugh had gathered topics of conversation for such an emergency.

Now that the Nazis had conquered Greece and invaded Crete, everyone whispered about a summer invasion of Britain. Would the air raids intensify again? But this spring, RAF night fighters had roamed the skies with some secret means of seeing in the dark, and the Luftwaffe bombers paid a high price.

Hugh's instincts told him Hitler had lost the will to attack Britain.

"We do like Aleida," Mother said with a warm smile. "Such a lovely young woman, and so bright and sensible."

Hugh much preferred discussing his fiancée to the war. "She is indeed, and so much more."

"Have you given any thought to a wedding date?" she asked.

"It depends on when her son is ready to move in with her. We want to marry before that, so he'll have to make only one adjustment." Hugh suppressed a smile. He hoped little Theo—Teddy—wanted to live with his mother immediately.

"As I said," Mother said with a firm nod, "very sensible. We're eager to welcome her into the family."

Hugh draped his arm in its cast along the sofa back. Of course they were eager to welcome an upper-class woman capable of producing an heir to the Collingwood estate. That was the last reason Hugh wanted to marry her, but a baby would make his parents happy. They did love children.

Father adjusted the collar of his tweed jacket. "She is more than welcome to stay here whilst getting reacquainted with her son."

"Yes, we don't live far from the Randolph home," Mother said.

"Thank you," Hugh said. "Aleida plans to ask her new director if she can work for the ministry here in Hertfordshire in some way. Since she's labored to convince families to evacuate their children, it wouldn't be right—or safe—to bring Teddy to the city. We'll rent a cottage nearby—"

Mother clucked her tongue. "You'll stay here at your own home, dearest. The east wing shall be all yours."

Hugh held his breath. He worked in London and would visit only on the weekends. "I'll discuss it with Aleida." If she felt even slightly uncomfortable living with his parents, he'd rent that cottage.

And would his parents welcome Lennox? Hugh and Aleida planned to bring the cat to the country. But tonight, Hugh didn't want to discuss cats or the inevitable concerns about his asthma.

Not on a peaceful evening before a lovely fire whilst raindrops frolicked on the windowpanes.

Mother cleared her throat, glanced at Father, and then across at Hugh. "Now that you're to be married, it's time for you to find a more fitting position."

Peaceful evening shattered.

Mother pressed a hand to her chest. "After that dreadful Granville affair, surely you see the dangers of your work."

Hugh drew a long, even breath, determined to keep his voice gentle. "I had hoped that after that dreadful Granville affair, in which I helped apprehend Uncle Elliott's murderer, that you'd see the merits of my work."

Mother sucked in a breath, and her eyebrows shot up.

Even though Hugh no longer sought their approval, he wanted to honor his parents. He set his cast in his lap and rubbed the rough plaster. "Broadcasting may not be a traditional position for an aristocrat, but it suits me. More importantly, my reports inform and educate and elevate morale. I see no disgrace in such work. In fact, I see it as high and honorable. Whilst I respect your opinion, I will not change my profession unless the Lord indicates otherwise."

"But, Hugh . . ." Mother twisted her hands together, twisted her lips. "You have all the advantages, the best of education, the—"

"And I'm using all that for good."

"It's so unseemly, parading the Collingwood name beside those of common music hall—"

"Mary, that is enough," Father said with his face lowered and unreadable.

Hugh stared at his father. Never in his life had he heard the man contradict his wife.

"Pardon?" Mother said.

Father rose and walked to his desk, piled with ancient tomes. "My years at Oxford were some of the happiest of my life. How I loved learning and writing and the thrill of brilliant minds in conversation."

Hugh murmured. Father often waxed poetic about those days.

With a sniff, Father faced Hugh. "I wanted to continue my studies and become a professor, but my father wouldn't hear of it. The Collingwood name, you know. As a dutiful son, I obeyed."

"I know." Hugh kept his tone calm but strong. "I admire your decision, but I will not do likewise."

A strange light shone in Father's eyes. "Good on you."

"Pardon?" Hugh said, echoed by his mother.

Father's gaze lifted to the wall, where his Army portrait hung. "I joined the Army as my father wanted, and I despised every moment of it. By serving as a most dreadful example of an officer, I disgraced the Collingwood name far more than I would have in academia."

Hugh gaped at him. Never had he heard his father speak in such a manner.

"Nigel . . ." Mother's voice warbled.

Father took two steps closer to Hugh, one finger raised, the light in his eyes building. "You, my boy, are brilliant on the wireless. Brilliant. I've listened to your reports lately."

He had? Hugh's chest caved in.

"You . . . you have?" Mother said.

"You should too, Mary." Father stood taller than Hugh had ever seen him. "I will hear no more talk about Hugh resigning from the BBC."

Mother's mouth and eyes stretched wide. Had Father ever stood up to her in all their years of marriage? She wobbled in her seat, then drew herself up straight. "Very well, Nigel."

Hugh wobbled too, as if the very foundations of the Collingwood family had shifted, which perhaps they had.

"Hugh." Father fidgeted with his hands as if he wanted to reach out to his son but didn't know how. "I am—I am very proud of you. I always have been."

As a man who made his living by talking, why could Hugh find no words? His mouth opened, empty. But his heart opened, full.

# 48

STEVENAGE, HERTFORDSHIRE
SATURDAY, MAY 24, 1941

Hunkered under an umbrella, Aleida and Hugh scurried to the house Mr. Randolph rented in Stevenage, about ten miles from Collingwood Manor.

On the porch, Hugh lowered the umbrella and shook it out.

Aleida's stomach jolted side to side, up and down, and she gathered back her hair on one side. "I wish I hadn't cut my hair."

Hugh took her hand, and her hair swished down around her chin. "If he remembers you, he'll remember your voice, your smile, your lovely eyes."

"And if he doesn't remember . . ." Her breath snagged.

"Shh." He pressed his lips to her forehead.

She inhaled Hugh's love and God's peace. "If he doesn't remember, we'll make new memories, the three of us."

"Right you are." Hugh kissed her nose. "Are you ready?"

For a year and a fortnight—379 days—she'd dreamed of this moment, labored for it, agonized over it, even surrendered it. Now it had arrived. And now, every word and thought and action had to be only for Teddy, not for herself.

At her nod, Hugh rang the bell.

Mr. and Mrs. Randolph opened the door and let Aleida and Hugh inside.

Dora Randolph wore her fawn-brown hair rolled around her face, and she had large eyes of the gentlest brown. Aleida liked her at once.

"Welcome. It's so good of you to come." Dora pressed her fingertips to her lips. "Oh, Julian. Her eyes—so like Teddy's. How could you have doubted her?"

Julian stammered and flushed.

"Please don't." Aleida took Dora's hand and smiled at Julian. "I am thankful for how you protected a vulnerable child, for how you've cared for him."

Dora's mouth twitched beneath her fingers. "We do apologize for keeping you away—"

"For keeping Teddy safe? Please don't apologize." Aleida squeezed the woman's hand. "God placed him in your arms, and you have cherished him. When I think of all the horrible things that could have happened—they didn't happen because of you."

Hugh rubbed the small of her back.

"Where are my manners?" Aleida said. "Dora, this is my fiancé, Hugh Collingwood."

Dora shook his hand. "I feel as if I know you already from the BBC."

Hugh dipped his chin. "My deepest apologies."

Everyone chuckled, and Aleida gave him a warm smile.

With his hand in the cast, he awkwardly helped with her coat, removed his, and hung them up in the entry.

"Now that we are all acquainted, we have tea in the sitting room." Dora gestured to a room to the left. "Teddy is playing in there. He is . . . a shy child."

Aleida nodded. She would not swoop him up with tears and kisses. "I'm ready," she said, but the words came out wispy.

Her ankles and knees threatened to fail, but she made her way forward, and Hugh kept his hand at the small of her back.

She stepped through the doorway.

In the back corner by a window sat a little boy on his knees, playing with blocks. His legs in their short pants were no longer chubby, his hair had darkened to a light blond, and his cheeks had lost some of their roundness. But even with his face in profile, Aleida would have recognized him anywhere.

A splendid ache built around her heart, the same ache she'd once felt every night as she peeked into his nursery, and she pressed her hand to that precious pain.

"Teddy," Julian said. "Our guests have arrived."

Teddy pushed to standing and came over, so much taller and more grown up.

"Mr. Collingwood, this is Teddy."

Hugh squatted in front of the little boy and extended his hand. "How do you do, Teddy? You may call me Uncle Hugh if you like."

Teddy slipped his left hand in Hugh's and shook—with his right arm tucked behind his back. "How do you do?"

The sound of his voice—the same, yet different. Aleida's fingers dug into her chest.

"And this woman," Dora said. "This is—"

Aleida held up her hand to stop her. "Good morning, Teddy. Would you show me what you're building with your blocks?"

His green-blue gaze rose to hers, met hers for the first time in over a year, and her heart seized with the pain and joy of it.

She managed a smile.

Teddy blinked hard, jerked his head to the side, and scampered to the blocks.

"I'll take your purse, Aleida." Hugh took it from her hand.

"I'll pour the tea," Dora said. "Take your time."

Aleida shoved her feet forward, past the sofas and the fire-

362

place, to her son at play. He'd stacked wooden blocks in columns with Oli standing in the center.

She knelt a few feet away. "Is Oli in the zoo?"

Teddy shook his head and added another block to a column, using his left hand. "He's in the jungle. These are trees. Oli ate the tops off of them."

A chuckle escaped. He spoke so clearly, in perfect English, without a hint of an accent. "How clever."

Teddy ignored her and built another tree, block by block.

Aleida gripped her hands in her lap. "I doubt you remember me, but we used to know each other well. You used to call me Moeder."

Teddy paused with a block midair. Another jerk of his chin, he rolled one shoulder, and he set the block in place.

"I am so glad to see you again, Teddy." Now she'd leave him be and let him think.

She joined Hugh on a sofa facing the Randolphs, a spot where she could see her son.

"I understand you were with the Foreign Service in the Hague, Julian. What are you doing now?" Hugh gave the man the same intense, interested look that made everyone open up to him, even as he gathered Aleida's hand in his in a comforting way.

As Julian talked about his work, Teddy's building project slowed and he frowned at his blocks.

In the past year, he'd changed so much. She'd missed so much.

Teddy picked up Oli, curled up next to the wall, and held Oli to his cheek, curving the trunk under his chin. Soothing himself.

Aleida's chest collapsed, splintering the pain into sharp needles. Her arrival had caused him distress. She'd worried he wouldn't remember her, but what if he *did* remember—but only the bad?

What if his only memories of his early years involved the tension of living in that house, the dread of his father's anger? What if he remembered his father's derision and neglect? What if he remembered the chaos of the exodus? The terror of being thrust into a car with total strangers?

"Aleida?" Hugh patted her hand. "Why don't you tell Julian and Dora about your work with the Ministry of Health? It's exceptional." Those hazel eyes of his glowed.

He'd probably sensed her growing anxiety and meant to distract her. Also, he'd told her it was important for Teddy to hear her talk, since he'd responded to her voice on the wireless.

Her breath hitched on the way in, but she spoke, her voice shaky and flimsy. She described the registry for evacuees and the collection of the children's stories, careful to avoid certain details with young ears in the room.

Hugh, being Hugh, took over when she flagged, and he soon had the Randolphs chatting about rambles in the country.

The sofa cushion beside her dipped, and Teddy climbed up with Oli.

Aleida's breath stopped.

Teddy didn't look at her. He clasped both arms around Oli, his right hand on top, no longer as round, no longer dimpled, but as precious to Aleida as ever.

A hush fell over the room.

An ocean of time and experience separated her from her child. The moment shimmered in the hush, a chance to transcend time. Aleida had only to plunge into the ocean, stride through, *rechtdoorzee*.

And Oli—Oli seemed the key.

Aleida breathed a prayer. "Is Oli your friend?"

Teddy gathered the elephant closer. "He's my best friend."

Whether the child considered the friendship brand-new or rekindled, Aleida cared not. She put a smile in her voice. "Long ago, in a faraway land where you and I once lived, I used to say to you, 'Olifanten vergeten nooit.' In English, 'Elephants never forget.' Do you think that's true, Teddy?"

Teddy rubbed his little chin against Oli's gray head. "Oli didn't forget me. He found me."

The truth of it slammed into her chest with poignant, piercing pain, and she stifled a gasp. "He—he did. He did find you. May I see him?" She held out her hands.

A long moment pulsed in the hush. At last, Teddy passed Oli to her, and she thanked him.

Aleida addressed the elephant. "Oli, do you remember the game we used to play with Teddy? Teddy would hide, and you'd look for him. *'Waar is Theo?'* I'd say." Aleida swung the stuffed gray trunk in a circle and pointed it at Teddy. "You always found him, Oli. There he is. There's Teddy."

Teddy's perfect pink mouth puckered at the edges, a semblance of a smile.

"Oli never stopped looking for you, Teddy." She waved the trunk from side to side. "Oli took a boat to England to look for you. He looked for you in London. He looked in hotels and hospitals and tall government buildings. He looked for you in the country. He looked in big houses and little houses and behind every bush. And then he found you. He never, ever forgot you. And—and neither did I."

Teddy reached for his friend, and Aleida returned him.

Then Teddy tucked his feet under him and leaned against Aleida's side.

Warmth coursed through her. Slowly, respectfully, watchfully, Aleida circled her arm around her son, her very own little boy.

Across from her, Dora dabbed at her eyes with a handkerchief, while Julian's face mottled red. Both raised quivery smiles.

On her other side, Hugh twined his fingers with Aleida's and pressed a kiss to her temple.

A moment Aleida would never forget.

## 49

## BUNTINGFORD
## SATURDAY, AUGUST 2, 1941

Thi is Hugh Collingwood reporting from outside a church in a village somewhere in England. If it weren't for the war, you would hear bells pealing for this is no ordinary day. For on this day, this BBC correspondent married his intrepid air raid warden."

Hugh smiled down at the lovely new Mrs. Collingwood, who stood with her arm around his waist and her face gleaming. Since clothes rationing had begun in June, she'd chosen to buy a suit of pale blue rather than a wedding dress, an outfit that would serve her longer. She could have worn the dowdiest of tweeds, and he wouldn't have minded.

Tom Young slashed a hand through the air to get Hugh's attention.

"My apologies. This correspondent is dazzled by the radiance of his bride." Hugh grinned at Young. "Weddings are not only a time to celebrate romantic love, but to gather with family. Here as witnesses today are my parents and the bride's aunt and uncle." Hugh nodded to Father and Mother, to Tante Margriet and Uncle James, all beaming with joy.

"Somewhere in this churchyard, if one searched diligently,

one might find my wife's darling son, the child who brought Mrs. Collingwood into my acquaintance."

Giggles arose across the churchyard as Teddy chased Hugh's cousin William's three boys under a clear blue sky. Over two months had passed since Aleida had reunited with her son. Each time they met, they grew closer, and they hoped to move the child to Collingwood Manor in a month or so.

"At weddings, we also gather with those as dear as family." Hugh nodded to Simmons and to Julian and Dora, who would indeed be lifelong friends—then to his fellow reporters. "And we gather with those whom we barely like but must indeed tolerate."

Louisa and Gil and Fletcher and MacLeod and Tony Da Costa broke into laughter. Gil's eyes twinkled especially. The shift from competition to friendship had changed his demeanor on air and brought out a relaxed sincerity that elevated his reporting.

Hugh dropped the timbre of his voice. "However, weddings are also a time when we sense the passing of generations, when we remember those who are no longer with us." His throat clamped shut. His brother, Cecil, and his sister, Caroline, should have been at his wedding. Uncle Elliott. François Jouveau.

The murder case worked its way through the courts, the scandal and sensation capturing the nation, distracting them from the war. Beatrice Granville would indeed hang for her crimes, and Albert Ridley was all but ruined.

Aleida hugged Hugh's waist. "Sweetheart," she whispered.

Hugh cleared his throat. "We also remember those who ought to be here and can't, like my wife's loved ones, who remain in the Netherlands under Nazi oppression."

Aleida murmured and leaned against his side.

He kissed the top of her head. When the Germans invaded the Soviet Union in June, Britain had sighed in relief that Hitler had turned his eyes from her shores, but a sigh tinged with grief for another people to be afflicted.

How long until Germany could be overthrown and the Netherlands and the other occupied nations could be freed?

Hugh hefted up a smile. "Why do we celebrate weddings in wartime? Because weddings prove that love defeats hatred, that light conquers darkness, and that life triumphs over death. Love glows in the midst of the flames, and new life—new life stirs amongst the embers."

A pretty pink blush colored Aleida's cheeks.

"I must now say goodbye and good day to you all. Because, my dearest listeners, I must find some privacy so I can kiss my bride."

After Young signaled that he'd ended the recording, Hugh handed him the microphone, took his bride by the hand, and led her around the side of the church.

There he leaned against ancient stone, stretching back through the generations, and he gathered Aleida close, fresh and beautiful, and hope stretched forward into generations yet to come.

"So many pretty words, Hugh Collingwood." Aleida wound her arms around his neck and wove her fingers into his hair.

"Why, thank you, Aleida van der Zee Collingwood. Pretty words are my specialty, and I have an endless supply, particularly in regard to you."

"So many pretty words and so much staring into my eyes as if you can see eternity."

"Ah, but I can." He swam in the green-blue sea, exhilarating in the warmth. "I can see the next Collingwood heir and the next and the next."

A laugh bubbled in her throat. "You've never cared for such things."

Not the estate, but he wanted their love to flow far into the future. "I care for you."

Aleida stroked his hair. "So many pretty words in that caramel voice, and yet you don't keep your word. You promised to kiss me."

Hugh mustered as much caramel into his voice as possible. "That, my love, can be remedied."

And he kissed her, as rich and as sweet and as golden as the years before them.

# Author's Note

Dear reader,

Thank you for coming along on the journey with Hugh and Aleida. My initial inspiration for this novel came when reading about the exodus in France and the Low Countries during the German invasion in 1940. Desperate parents were known to thrust their children into the cars of strangers believing they stood a better chance. Later, the classified sections of newspapers in the occupied countries carried pleas for news on these lost children. This broke my heart! And it made me wonder what a mother might do if separated from her child.

Starting on September 1, 1939, 1.9 million mothers and children were evacuated from London. Over the next few months, when German bombers failed to come to Britain, many returned to their homes. Throughout the war, the government tried to persuade further evacuations with varying success. Although most children fared well in the country—and many thrived—some had difficult experiences, as explored in the story.

Hostels and camps did exist for hard-to-place children, and

refugees were often hard to place due to language and cultural barriers. In the story, the "opinion of one person, passed along as policy" requiring refugee children to be sent to hostels was literary license on my part and not official policy in Britain.

In many ways, London served as an international capital during the war. Governments-in-exile of the Nazi-occupied nations were based in London, and thousands of refugees filled the city. As depicted in the novel, many welcomed the exiles with open arms but some resented them—not unexpected in a land suffering from shortages of food and housing. But for most Londoners, the various peoples added vibrancy and excitement to the drabness of war.

The story of the BBC during World War II fascinated me, and the pages of this novel didn't permit me to do justice to the BBC's exceptional work. During the war, the BBC made enormous strides in news reporting and recording engineering, and the shortwave broadcasts by the European Services were a lifeline of truth and hope for the oppressed peoples on the continent. Despite struggles with the Ministry of Information and the armed forces, especially in the early years of the war, the BBC maintained its independence and only required self-censorship. The two bombings of Broadcasting House were historical events.

London also served as headquarters for journalists from around the world, including Edward R. Murrow of CBS. The broadcasts of the "Murrow Boys" did have a significant effect in swaying opinion in the United States toward supporting the British war effort.

In the novel's depiction of the *London after Dark* roundup, Hugh "replaced" the BBC's Raymond Glendenning, who recorded live from an antiaircraft battery as bombers flew overhead. If you'd like to hear recordings of this program and of Murrow's first live, rooftop broadcast on September 20, 1940, please visit the "History Behind the Story" for *Embers in the*

*London Sky* on my website. Likewise, there is a link to the Crown Film Unit newsreel of the Lofoten Islands Raid on March 4, 1941.

Real people mentioned in the story include Minister of Information Duff Cooper, BBC organist Sandy MacPherson, and journalists Charles Gardner, Edward R. Murrow, Robert Bowman, Eric Sevareid, and Larry LeSueur. Robert T. Clark served as Chief News Editor at the BBC, and his quote about truth and morale in chapter 34 is from the historical record.

Writing this novel gave me greater appreciation and a more nuanced understanding of the challenges faced by the British in World War II, and I hope you enjoyed this peek into how these exceptional people endured a great trial.

Turn the page for a sneak peek
at another atmospheric historical
fiction novel from Sarah Sundin!

COMING SPRING 2025

W hen Cilla van der Zee volunteered to aid the resistance by infiltrating the Dutch Nazis, she never
imagined she'd be swept up in a mob set on attacking her friends.

Her adventure no longer seemed grand.

Black-uniformed thugs of the Dutch *Weerbaarheidsafdel-
ing* jostled Cilla as they prowled the open-air market of Amsterdam's Waterloo Square. WA men slapped at the colorful
awnings over the booths, stole fruit from baskets, and searched
for their human prey.

Cilla fumbled for her sister's elbow. "Hilde, stay back."

Hilde snatched an apple from a stall. "You're not my mother.
I'm staying with Arno."

Arno Bakker, Hilde's good-for-nothing boyfriend, shook
his fist and jeered at the men marching toward them—a small
group of Jews and their friends.

Friends like Dirk de Vos. Tall and vivacious and good for
anything and everything.

He'd come today because Cilla informed the resistance about
the WA's plans.

Cilla's stomach went as hard as the red bricks underfoot.

Through the mass of black-capped men, Dirk met Cilla's
gaze—sharp, short, and shattering. If Cilla showed any mercy,
she'd lose her standing with the Dutch Nazis and cut off Dirk's
source of information for his underground newspaper.

A jerk of her chin sufficed as a reply.

Nine months had passed since the Germans had conquered the Netherlands. Nine months of relative quiet, but a quiet pregnant with the swelling expectation of unrest. Of darkness.

Recently pangs had started. The Germans had dismissed Jewish civil servants, including teachers and professors, and then required all Jews to register. Men of the WA, the paramilitary branch of the Dutch Nazi Party, had begun attacking Jews, who had formed bands for self-protection, aided by good men like Dirk.

All around Cilla in the freezing fog rose shouts and cries of labor pains.

Dirk jutted a finger toward the mob, but the cacophony swallowed up his words.

Someone bumped Cilla from behind, and she edged aside. She had to get Hilde away. Women couldn't join the WA, but Hilde had insisted on coming with Arno.

Arno shoved a dark-haired young man.

Hilde laughed, big and sloppy, and she threw her apple at Dirk. She missed. She stank of beer, and lines etched her face as if she were ten years older than Cilla rather than two years younger.

Everyone else in the family had given up on Hilde. Rather, Hilde had driven them away with wild ways and cruel words, but Cilla refused to give up on her sister, on her responsibility.

And Hilde's embrace of the NSB, the *Nationaal-Socialistische Beweging*—the Dutch Nazis—had eased Cilla's infiltration of the group.

A lanky, long-faced man threw a punch at Arno, and Arno rained blows down on the smaller man.

Dirk lunged at Arno.

"Watch—" Cilla clamped her lips shut to silence her warning.

Shouts rang out. Black uniforms mixed with gray and

brown suits, and fists thudded on flesh. The WA outnumbered their foes.

Cilla grabbed Hilde's elbow and yanked her away from the melee.

This time Hilde didn't protest.

Dirk lurched to the side, his suit jacket hanging off one shoulder, and he yelled out insults to the manhood of everyone in black.

As one, the Nazis roared and charged him.

What was he doing? He was going to get hurt. Cilla's hand flew to her mouth.

Dirk ran, tossing taunts over his shoulder and making a shooing motion with one arm.

His friends—they helped their fallen comrades to their feet and scattered.

"Dirk, no," Cilla whispered into her gloved fingers. He was drawing off the mob so his friends could escape. Noble. Dangerous.

A black circle enveloped Dirk, punching and kicking, crouching lower and lower.

"No, no, no," Cilla muttered. A scream writhed inside her, and she wrestled it down.

The WA men straightened up, fell back, grinned.

Dirk lay on the ground, his head . . . misshapen. His mouth lax. His eyes wide. A scarlet puddle spread, flowing in the cracks between the bricks.

A guttural cry rent its way up Cilla's throat, tore past her fingers.

While Hilde cheered and laughed.

"How could you?" Cilla wheeled on her sister. "A man—a man just died."

Hilde's eyes narrowed to greenish-blue slits. "I thought you were on our side."

Cilla's breath bounced around, out of control. If she didn't pull herself together, she could die too. But how could she stay silent? "Not this. Not beating men to death."

With a roll of her shoulder, Hilde pulled free from Cilla's grip. "You still haven't become a member of the NSB. Arno is losing patience with you."

Arno sauntered closer, wearing a disgusting smirk. He met Cilla's gaze, and the smirk lowered to a scowl. "What's wrong with you?"

A pit formed in Cilla's stomach, as dark and vile as Arno's uniform, and she gripped the green wool of her coat. "I—I've never seen a man die before."

A laugh shot out. "You still haven't. That's a rat, not a man."

Cilla slammed her eyes shut against the sight of Dirk's body. Of Arno mocking his death.

"Look." Arno jammed a finger into Cilla's shoulder. "Open your eyes and look what those rats did to Hendrik Koot."

Cilla pried open her eyes and followed the line of Arno's arm to where a man in black lay on the bricked pavement. Bleeding. But alive.

"Next time." Arno jammed his finger into Cilla's shoulder so hard, she stumbled back a step. "Next time, I'd better see you cheering with your sister."

He marched away to aid the injured man.

Next time? Next time Cilla might say too much. Next time they might turn on her, might even turn on Hilde simply for being Cilla's sister.

Next time must never come to pass.

"I need to go home," Cilla said to her sister, and she hurried away without waiting for a reply.

At the far end of Waterloo Square, she hopped on a tram and found a seat.

Dirk. Only yesterday she'd seen him at her cousin Gerrit van der Zee's flat. She'd flirted with Dirk. He'd flirted back. Now he was dead.

A sob filled her throat, choked her.

Cilla struggled to regain composure. She had to break free, had to escape, had to protect Hilde.

When the tram reached her destination, she rushed to Gerrit's flat, where a dozen of his friends had gathered. Delighted calls of "Cilla!" greeted her.

But Liese Pender's brow warped. "What's wrong?"

"They—the WA—they killed Dirk."

"Oh no." Liese stood and wrapped Cilla in a fierce hug. "Oh no."

Cilla had no time for sympathy. She pulled away and found Gerrit's devastated face. "I need to talk to you alone. Now."

Gerrit ran a hand back into his blond hair and led her to his room. He sat on his bed, planted his elbows on his knees, and buried his head in his hands.

Cilla sat in a straight-backed chair, and her legs jiggled. Gerrit and Dirk had been close friends. He needed time to grieve. But Cilla couldn't wait. She needed his help.

"How did it happen?" Gerrit's voice came out ragged.

"Dirk drew off the WA to save his friends. The WA beat him to death." Her chin wobbled.

"You saw?" Gerrit's green-blue van der Zee eyes peeked at her from between his fingers.

Cilla could only nod.

"I'm sorry," he said.

"I need to get out."

"Out?"

"Of the NSB."

Gerrit lowered his hands, revealing his reddened face. "You can't. We need your reports for the paper. We need to know the NSB's plans."

Cilla squirmed in her seat, against the confines. "I can't do it anymore."

Gerrit wiped a hand over his mouth. "Last month your report helped us move our headquarters before a raid."

"And today my report got Dirk killed." Her voice broke. She waved her hands before her chest, shaking off the chains. "I can't do this anymore. They want me to do things I can't do. Things I won't do. It's only a matter of time. Someday I'll speak my mind and get arrested. I might lead them to you."

Gerrit stared at her, as maddeningly calm and steady as always. But hadn't she come for that very calmness and steadiness?

"Cilla," he said in a soft voice. "If you suddenly leave the NSB, they'll get suspicious. You'll get arrested."

Her chest caved in. "And lead them to you."

He nodded once.

Cilla's breath accelerated, raced. "I'm trapped. I need to escape. I'll go to England, to Tante Margriet." Their beloved aunt was married to an Englishman.

"How?" Still calm, still steady. "How would you get all the false papers you'd need to travel to Belgium, to occupied France, to Vichy France, to Spain, to Portugal? Hundreds of miles. Very few have done it."

"I'll take a boat then." Cilla waved toward the sea. "I have money. I'll pay a fisherman. People have escaped that way."

"In the early days, yes. But the Germans watch the coast. They're banning civilians and outsiders from much of the coastline. You know this."

She did. She groaned and cast her gaze to the ceiling. "Then I'll become an *onderduiker*."

"An under-diver? You?" A thin note of humor lifted Gerrit's voice. "Cilla van der Zee, always surrounded by a crowd of admiring friends, will go into hiding in a basement in the country? You'd never survive."

No, she wouldn't. Her breath built up inside and puffed out in short bursts. "I'm trapped. I need to be free."

Gerrit leveled his gaze at her, unspeaking, in that way of his, taking eons to compose his thoughts.

Cilla didn't have eons. She bolted to her feet, and her fists churned in little circles before her stomach.

Gerrit drew a long breath. "You want to escape the trap so you can find freedom."

"Of course." She couldn't keep the exasperation out of her voice. *That* was the thought it took eons to compose?

"Sometimes you have to find freedom inside the trap."

Cilla gaped at her cousin. "For a brilliant man, sometimes you make no sense."

Gerrit stood and set a firm hand on her shoulder. "You must stay in the trap. You have no choice. Attend the NSB meetings but keep to the fringes. And don't join any more mobs, no matter what nonsense Hilde gets involved with."

Her shoulder chafed under the pressure of his grip, and she shrugged him off.

One corner of Gerrit's mouth puckered. "You can do it. You're a good actress. Do it for Dirk."

Cilla managed a nod and spun away, out of the room, out of the flat.

Do it for Dirk? Dirk was dead, and if she stayed in the NSB, she'd be dead too.

## TUESDAY, FEBRUARY 25, 1941

How much longer could Cilla keep acting?

She sat beside Hilde in the NSB assembly hall as men and women muttered to each other before the meeting started.

In the two weeks since Dirk's death, so much had happened. Hendrik Koot had died from his injuries, and the Germans had cordoned off the Jewish neighborhood in Amsterdam. Over the past weekend, the Germans had rounded up over four hundred Jewish men and sent them to a concentration camp.

On Tuesday morning the Dutch people had risen up in protest. Tram workers walked off the job, and a general strike swept Amsterdam.

Cilla had never been so proud to be Dutch.

That sentiment wasn't echoed in the NSB, and tonight's meeting would overflow with vitriol. How could Cilla hold her tongue?

She sandwiched that tongue between her molars. The NSB was the only political party now allowed in the Netherlands, but it remained small and despised. She knew the names of each person in the room.

Except the middle-aged man standing to the side, one of the few not wearing the black WA uniform or the black armband of the NSB. Trim and neatly groomed, he scanned the seats with an analytical look.

If Cilla didn't know better, she'd think he was spying on the group, as she was. But who would spy so blatantly?

Cilla nudged her sister. "Do you know who that man is?"

Hilde let out a beer-scented chuckle. "He's too old for you."

Arno leaned around Hilde. "That's Dr. Schultz with the German Abwehr. He's recruiting spies."

"He tried to recruit Arno." Hilde's bleary eyes lit up.

"To be a spy?" Cilla fought to keep her voice low and to suppress a laugh.

"In England," Hilde said. "He refused. He can't bear to leave me."

"That's right." Arno clamped a hand over Hilde's knee.

All of Cilla's acting ability went into not smacking that possessive hand. And into raising an innocent smile. "I didn't realize you spoke English."

"I don't."

"But he's smart and ruthless." A spark of pride burnt in Hilde's voice.

Ruthless, yes. Cilla had seen for herself. But smart? The man would have been arrested five seconds after landing on British soil. What good was a spy so indiscreet that he told his girlfriend and her sister about his recruitment—and identified his recruiter?

Dr. Schultz's gaze landed on Cilla and slid away, uninterested.

The first speaker came to the podium, greeted by raucous applause. How could Cilla pay attention when an idea careened in her mind, new and reckless and liberating?

Dr. Schultz pushed away from the wall and strolled out of the hall.

That idea careened down to her feet, and she stood. She leaned down and whispered in her sister's ear. "I'm going to powder my nose."

"Now? The meeting's just started."

"I'll be back." She dashed out of the hall, driven by the pulsing rhythm of recklessness.

In the moonless night in the blacked-out city, Cilla strained to make out Dr. Schultz's figure.

There! A flicker of motion, a shuffle of footsteps on damp pavement.

Cilla trotted up behind him and then in front of him, and she extended her hand. "Good evening. My name is Cilla van der Zee. Arno Bakker told me you're recruiting spies to go to England."

Dr. Schultz grunted. "What! He shouldn't have—"

"One of the many reasons he is the wrong person." Cilla lifted a smile and wiggled her outstretched hand. "I, however, am the perfect person."

Dr. Schultz stepped to the side to pass her. "If you'll excuse me, miss."

"Miss van der Zee." Cilla blocked his path and extended her hand and smile again. "I speak fluent English. My aunt married an Englishman. I visited each summer, and I was educated in a prestigious British boarding school. I know England and have friends in high places. I am the perfect candidate."

Dr. Schultz paused, then shook her hand. "You certainly don't lack confidence."

"I don't." Her smile grew. "By the way, when I was in school, one of my boyfriends was a wireless enthusiast. Rather a bore, but he taught me Morse code and how to operate a wireless."

"Indeed?" Interest stretched out his voice.

Cilla had found her freedom. The Germans themselves would transport her to England, where she could disappear from their sight and start a new life.

To escape the Nazis, she would become a Nazi spy.

# Acknowledgments

This novel was written during a time of transition as my husband and I moved from Northern to Southern California—a time that filled me with gratitude. Gratitude for our friends in our former community, who have held us up in friendship and prayer. Gratitude for those we've met in our new community, who have welcomed and included us. And gratitude for my writing community, a constant in my life.

As always, I'm indebted to my outstanding critique partners, Marcy Weydemuller, Sherry Kyle, Lisa Bogart, and Judy Gann—Judy also lent her insight into living with a chronic illness.

A while back, my writer friend Debb Hackett, who is British, offered to read for me if I needed help with "Britishness." Why yes, I did. As it turns out, Debb is also a former BBC broadcast journalist! Not only did I learn that the British don't use the terms *block* or *intersection* regarding streets, but I received excellent input on the reporter's mentality. Thank you, Debb! Any remaining errors in "Britishness" are mine alone.

Thank you to my wonderful agent, Rachel Kent, my new editor, Rachel McRae—yes, I have two Rachels—and to the rest of the team at Revell, including Kristin Kornoelje, Brianne Dekker, and Karen Steele.

Thank you, my dear readers, for picking up my books. Please visit me at www.sarahsundin.com to leave a message, sign up for my email newsletter, and read about the history behind the story.

# Discussion Questions

1. Life on the British home front was difficult with rationing, shortages, and the blackout. And it was dangerous. What aspects of this stood out to you in the story? How do you think you would have made do in England during the war?

2. Aleida suffers a nightmare for any parent—being separated from her child and not knowing where to find him. What do you think of the various decisions she made regarding Theo? Also, would you have evacuated your children to the country?

3. Hugh struggles to balance his family's expectations and his personal dreams and talents. What factors come into play as he makes his choices? Have you ever had a similar conflict?

4. Aleida finds comfort in counting, routines, lists, and tapping—a condition we'd now call obsessive-compulsive disorder. When are such routines all right, and when do they become a problem?

5. Sebastiaan hid Theo's hand. Hugh hides his asthma. How are these similar? How are they different? Hugh

believes that if "he let his condition determine his life, he'd never go anywhere." What do you think of that? And how did he learn to be open about his condition?

6. What did you think of the various murder suspects? Who was highest on your list?

7. Hugh and his reporter friends debate freedom of speech and censorship, the right to criticize the government and the importance of morale. At one point, Hugh tells Ridley, "Even limits have limits." Discuss.

8. Louisa tells Aleida, "The human race is bound and determined to sort ourselves into categories and exclude people outside our own category." How do you see this in the story? How do you see this today? How can we counteract this?

9. As an abuse survivor, Aleida struggles to trust men—and to trust her own judgment. How does this affect her decisions? How does she grow? How does Louisa help her?

10. Hugh longs for approval. In what ways is this fine, and when is it a problem? How does he learn to change? Do you find that you care too much about the opinions of others—or too little?

11. "Elephants never forget"—why is this so important to Aleida? How does the fear of being forgotten drive her? How does she overcome this?

12. Hugh has troubles with organization. When is it simply an endearing trait, and when does it interfere with his life? Are you naturally neat or messy? If you're a "messy," have you learned to be organized? What helps you?

13. Much of the story revolves around the conditions and attitudes faced by refugees. Just as in World War II,

today we struggle with how to treat "the strangers, the fatherless, and the widows" among us. Did the events in the story give you any insight?

14. Hugh tells Aleida, "What we know and what we believe can be two separate matters. We know what we know, but we don't always know what we believe." What do you think of this?

15. Just for fun—Lennox! How does Lennox add to Hugh's life? Have you ever had pets? How have they added joy, amusement, or chaos to your life?

**Sarah Sundin** is the bestselling and Christy Award–winning author of *The Sound of Light*, *Until Leaves Fall in Paris*, and *When Twilight Breaks*, as well as several series, including Sunrise at Normandy. Her novel *Until Leaves Fall in Paris* won the 2022 Christy Award, *When Twilight Breaks* and *The Land Beneath Us* were finalists for the Christy Award, and *The Sky Above Us* received the 2020 Carol Award.

During WWII, one of her grandfathers served as a pharmacist's mate (medic) in the US Navy, and her great-uncle flew with the US Eighth Air Force. Her other grandfather, a professor of German, helped train American soldiers in the German language through the US Army Specialized Training Program.

Sarah and her husband live in Southern California and have three adult children and one adorable grandson. Their two rescue dogs make sure she gets plenty of walks and fresh air. Sarah enjoys teaching Sunday school and women's Bible studies and speaking for church, community, and writers' groups. She also serves as co-director of the West Coast Christian Writers Conference. Visit www.sarahsundin.com for more information.

"Sundin grounds this suspenseful tale in rich historical detail, weaving throughout probing questions of faith as characters struggle to behave in moral, godly ways, especially when it entails risking one's life for a stranger."

—*Publishers Weekly*

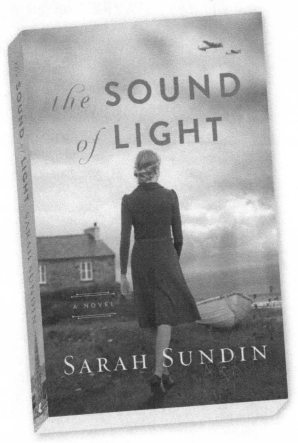

In WWII Denmark, Baron Henrik Ahlefeldt assumes the identity of a common shipyard worker, rowing messages to Sweden for the Resistance. His life depends on keeping his secret hidden—a task that proves challenging when he meets Else Jensen, an American physicist who seems to see right through him.

**Я Revell**
a division of Baker Publishing Group
www.RevellBooks.com

Available wherever books and ebooks are sold.

"Sundin is a master at her craft, and avid readers will devour this in one sitting. With meticulous historical research and an eye for both mystery and romance, Sundin rises to the top of World War II fiction in this latest novel with crossover appeal."

—*Library Journal*, STARRED review ★

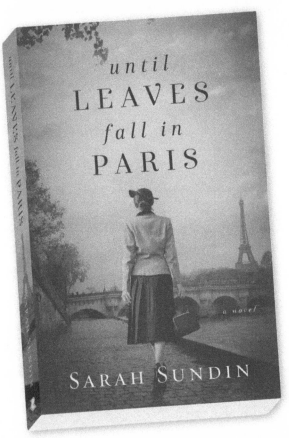

When the Nazis march into Paris, an American woman uses her bookstore to aid the resistance, while a businessman chooses to sell his products to Germany—and send vital information home to the US. Can they work together for the higher good, or will it cost them everything they love?

Ⱥ Revell
a division of Baker Publishing Group
www.RevellBooks.com

Available wherever books and ebooks are sold.

"Sundin's novels set the gold standard for historical war romance, and *When Twilight Breaks* is arguably her most brilliant and important work to date."

—*Booklist*, STARRED review ★

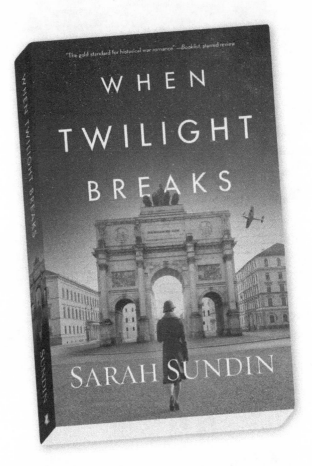

Two Americans meet in 1938 in the heart of Nazi Germany. Their efforts to expose oppression attract unwanted attention, pulling them deeper into danger as the world marches toward war.

GET TO KNOW

# SARAH
# SUNDIN

★ ★ ★

To Learn More about Sarah,
Read Her Blog, or See
the Inspiration behind the Stories,
Visit

## SARAHSUNDIN.COM

Printed in the USA
CPSIA information can be obtained
at www.ICGtesting.com
LVHW042109080224
771342LV00002B/135